LOVERS AT LAST

She giggled as he playfully nipped her ear, then turned her face to meet his. Hungrily, she parted her lips, inhaling his mouth, his breath, the love that he had finally confessed. She felt him shudder with pleasure . . . Burying her fingers in his golden hair, she leaned back, as all the desire she had denied for months released itself, rocking her body with delicious tremors.

"Oh Tasha!" he sighed, his breath warming and tickling her ear, "you are hardly more than a child, and yet you are more woman than any other."

"I am your woman, Jared," she responded simply. "Take me. Take me now and let me show you how completely I am yours."

This time she knew it was no dream. He was there, bringing her ecstasy beyond all dreams.

Bantam Books by Lynn Lowery

LOVESWEPT
SWEET RUSH OF PASSION

Love-swept

Lynn Lowery

BANTAM BOOKS · TORONTO · NEW YORK · LONDON

LOVESWEPT
A Bantam Book / December 1978

ISBN 0-553-12271-1

Published simultaneously in the United States and Canada

For Linda Price,
who made it all happen, and for
Stuart Applebaum, Esther Margolis,
and all who work behind the
scenes at Bantam Books.

1847-1848

Zelenograd, Russia

I

Mikhail Lisovsky had drunk far too much vodka. The innkeeper signalled the lateness of the hour by impatiently clinking glassware, waiting for this last guest to retire. But Mikhail was not ready to exchange the warm comfort of the tavern for a cold, lonely bedchamber. He rapped his glass sharply on the table. With a weary sigh, the old man shuffled over to the table and poured the last drops from a bottle into Mikhail's glass.

Staring moodily into the glass, Mikhail mused about the coming days. By tomorrow he would be in Moscow and within a month, crossing over the Ural Mountains into the vast, untamed steppes of Siberia. With good fortune, he should reach the Amur River bordering China within five months. There he planned to join one of the expeditions sent out by the Russian-American Company to colonize the region.

Then, at the nethermost reaches of the Russian Empire, he would begin building a new life, unbound by the rigid social systems of St. Petersburg and Moscow, which considered a merchant's son far inferior to the members of the nobility.

Another swallow of vodka turned his thoughts in a different direction. Until that very afternoon, he had been eager to move on toward the Amur, exhilarated at the prospect of starting anew. Then he had seen her—the young woman whose image had been haunting him all evening.

As he was leaving his room to go downstairs for supper, he caught sight of her entering a doorway quite near his own. Her raven tresses fell alluringly over a maroon-colored cloak. As she turned to address the older woman accompanying her, their glances met, and Mikhail was captivated. He was sure her dark eyes rested on him for a long moment, seeming to appraise his muscular young body, before they moved back to the old woman.

With a saucy smile, she quipped, "Let us hope the prince is worth all our trouble. The journey has made me positively weary!"

"Hush, Natasha," the old woman hissed, clucking her tongue disapprovingly. "Your father knows what is best for you. And you'll have plenty of time to rest after we reach Moscow tomorrow."

At that, the young lady tossed her head petulantly. "And tomorrow will be soon enough to judge if, indeed, my father knows what is best." Upon this remark, the older woman hastily shooed her young charge into the room, closing the door behind them.

After several moments, Mikhail had gone down to supper, hoping he might catch another glimpse of her later that evening in the tavern, which doubled as the inn's dining room. The hours passed, but she did not appear. No doubt, he reflected, the innkeeper's wife had taken a tray to her room. A genteel young lady would certainly find the tavern too rowdy a place. Most of the women who crowded around the tables were boisterous and rather bawdy. Several of them had approached his table during the evening, and had tried to engage him in conversation, but he remained curiously immune to their brazen suggestions.

Mikhail brought his glass down hard on the table, as if hoping to dispel the image of the dark-haired young woman. "You are behaving like some ridiculous schoolboy," he muttered to himself. "There will be plenty of women along the Amur to amuse you. Exot-

2

ic women whose bodies will smell of Oriental flowers and spices. They will make that girl upstairs look like a common scrubwoman."

He tried to envision an Oriental woman, dressed in delicately embroidered silks. But the face of the woman in his image had a flawless, pink and cream complexion, and as she opened her eyes, they were the taunting eyes of the woman called Natasha. Shaking his head, he gulped down the last drops of vodka and scraped his chair back from the heavy oak table.

In the humble inn's most elegant room upstairs, Natalya Ivanovna Nelidova tossed restlessly in the huge, carved cedar bed. Through the open door of the adjoining room, she could hear the regular breathing of old Olga, once her childhood nurse, now her personal maid. She wished she could sleep as peacefully as Olga, as she was very tired. But myriad uncertainties about the next day kept her wide awake, as they had every night since she and Olga left St. Petersburg. If only the railway between St. Petersburg and Moscow were completed, they could have traveled more quickly, and this dreadful wondering would be over. But, though six years had passed since construction had begun, the line was far from completion and Natalya and Olga had been obliged to travel by carriage.

Natalya slid from beneath the bed's festively embroidered quilt and tiptoed over to the window. As a cloud passed, the moonlight shone into the room. Standing in its aura, she wondered about the unknown man her father had chosen to be her husband. At eighteen, she was in no haste to marry, but for the last year—since suitors had begun to call—her father, Count Ivan Nelidov, had been preoccupied with finding a suitable husband for her. Natalya supposed that he was anxious for his responsibility as a father to come to an end. Since he had had only Olga's help after her mother died twelve years ago, the last years couldn't have been easy for him.

His note from Moscow revealed very little, stating

3

simply that a certain Prince Igor Petrovich Demidov had agreed to marry her, and would she and Olga please come at once to Moscow. Not a single word about the age of the prince, his past life, or how he had been enticed to marry her.

Olga, awed by the idea of joining a prince's household, seemed to think the arrangement wonderful. But Natalya was not at all pleased about being pledged to a man she had never met. Besides, she hated to leave her beloved city of St. Petersburg, where she had grown up.

Though she tried to be optimistic, Natalya kept imagining the prince as a miserly, overbearing old man who would watch her every move. The idea of life with such a man made her shiver. And the thought of sharing his bed was absolutely frightening. Well—tomorrow would reveal exactly what kind of man this Prince Demidov was.

Perhaps she would be lucky and her fears would prove unfounded. Perhaps he would be like the man she had seen in the hallway earlier in the evening as she and Olga were entering their rooms. Now *that* was a man she could call "husband"—tall and muscular, with straw-blond hair. Something in his manner, and the way his flashing blue eyes stared so openly at her, made Natalya think he had the spirit to match her own.

Well, if Prince Demidov was not to her liking, she could, like other noblewomen she had heard about, take a lover—a young, virile one like the man in the hallway. Closing her eyes, she tried to imagine the bliss of sharing her bed with the strong, handsome man. Embarrassed by her own thoughts, she felt herself blushing.

Enough of this, Natalya thought, when, ready to go back to bed, she heard the hallway door open. Still facing the window, she froze. Could Olga—usually so conscientious and protective—have forgotten to bolt the door? Might it not be another traveler stumbling into the wrong room? Her heart pounding wildly,

4

she waited for the intruder to discover his mistake and go away.

Mikhail Lisovsky hesitated in the doorway, captivated by the body silhouetted in the moonlight. A light flannel nightdress clung to her body, accentuating the graceful curve of her hips and hinting at long, shapely legs. Taking a deep breath, Mikhail entered the room and closed the door softly behind him. He covered the space between them in four long strides and clapped a hand over her mouth before she could turn to look at him. His other hand ran lightly down her body and slid around her narrow waist.

Feeling her trembling beneath his touch, he bent to whisper in her ear. "Please do not be frightened, Natasha. I've no intention of harming you."

The man's voice jolted Natalya from her shock. It was gentle and soft, not at all the kind of voice she would expect from a brute and ruffian. Who was he, she wondered, that he not only knew her name, but dared to use its familiar form? Squirming in his arms, she tried to twist her head to see him.

Instead, he spun her around to face him, crushing her body against his. He bent over her, bringing his face close to hers. And as she started to utter a cry of recognition, he slid his hand away from her face and covered her lips with his own.

She squirmed in his arms, but he simply strengthened his hold. One hand was at the back of her head, the fingers entwined in her flowing hair. His other hand slid downward from her waist and started to knead the soft flesh of her buttocks and press her even closer to his warm body.

His mouth moved slowly over hers, forcing her lips apart. His tongue explored the recesses of her mouth. Natalya could smell the alcohol on his breath, and she told herself that was the reason her head was beginning to reel. Overcome by faintness, she placed her arms around his neck and clung to him to keep from falling. His mouth continued to work over

5

hers, searching, licking, sucking, as if he wished to consume her.

Now, as he kissed her, both hands moved over her body, exploring her youthful curves through the thin fabric of her gown. As one hand caught an unfettered breast, a moan of desire escaped him. Conquering her faintness, Natalya tried to free herself. Quickly picking her up as if she was no heavier than an empty samovar, he carried her to the bed.

In a moment he was lying over her, trying to pull her nightdress off. As he rose slightly to loosen his own clothing, Natalya knew that she should cry out to Olga, who was asleep in the next room. But the sound seemed to die in her throat.

Now they were both naked, and he covered her warm body fully with his own. His fingers moved gently over her flesh, coaxing her to relax. She was amazed at the tenderness of his touch, and even more so at her own inability to resist. Tentatively, she let her fingers brush across his body, feeling the hard, firm muscles in his shoulders and back.

He was surprisingly patient with her. Slowly rolling onto his side, he held her close and guided her hand down to his pulsating maleness. She froze as her hand closed around it and he groaned with delight.

Gently he pressed her onto her back and rolled on top of her. His hand tickled her velvety flesh until she sighed and, in spite of herself, uncontrollably parted her thighs. His hard shaft of desire explored between her legs until it touched upon a moist spot and slowly began to work its way into her. Natalya moaned.

His mouth covered hers just before she felt a painful tearing inside her body. Her sobs were swallowed in his throat. He remained motionless for a few moments, kissing her tenderly the while, waiting for the pain to pass. He began to move gently within her.

For several moments Natalya lay rigid, unwilling to give in any further to her newly unleashed desire.

6

But she found she could not ignore the warmth creeping through her flesh. Though her mind was determined to fight it, her body wanted to respond. She dug her nails into his buttocks, holding him close as he moved over her. When he started to move forcefully, she began to writhe and arch upward, letting her body ride into the unexpected burst of ecstasy that followed, her half-cries, half-gasps echoing his moans.

Later, when the man lay motionless and spent beside her, Natalya felt every fiber of her body glowing, and a feeling of peace overcame her.

He raised himself on an elbow and traced a finger over her features, softly illuminated in the moonlight. "You are the most beautiful woman I have ever known," he whispered. "And the most desirable." Natalya smiled self-consciously.

When he sat up and swung his feet to the floor, she grasped his arm tightly. "Must you go?" she whispered.

Smiling ruefully, Mikhail nodded. He leaned over her and brushed his lips first across her forehead, then over the tip of her nose. "Yes, my dear, I must go. You've worn me out enough for one night. Besides, it would never do for your maid to awaken and find us."

She marveled at his magnificent body as he pulled on his loose trousers and simple, open-necked white shirt. Without turning to look at her again, he picked up his knee-high black boots and walked to the door.

Blanketed in contentment, Natalya slept.

II

Once back in his own room, Mikhail began to pace nervously. He was now thoroughly sober and began to realize the seriousness of his actions. In his twenty-six years of life, no other woman had captivated him so swiftly or completely. He had never desired a woman who had not offered herself to him—and afterward, he had never felt any sense of obligation. But the women in his past had been different; for one thing, none of them had been virgins.

Thinking back over the events of the evening, he was still not sure how everything had happened. He had come upstairs from the tavern, resolving to go to bed and forget the young woman. But as he passed her door, something impelled him to try it. When he found it open, he told himself he would only look at her for a moment, just long enough to convince himself there was really nothing extraordinary about her. How could he have guessed she would be standing in the moonlight, tempting him beyond the limits of his self-control?

It was her fault, he thought, sitting angrily on the bed. She could have screamed; she could have struggled more. She should have seen to it that her door was secured in the first place. Then the warm memories of their lovemaking floated back over him and his anger drained away, to be replaced by a feeling of helplessness.

Mikhail had made up his mind not to marry before he had made his fortune. But this Natalya was too beautiful, too deliciously responsive, to leave behind. If their first union had been so perfect, how much more bliss could they find on the long trek through Siberia! Besides, he could not deny that he owed her something for the way he had stolen her virginity. Still, the situation was impossible—she would never consent.

Mikhail Lisovsky resumed pacing.

Natalya Nelidova awoke before the sun began to lighten the sky. In those first drowsy moments, she felt luxuriously radiant. But as she stretched lazily, she felt an uncomfortable stickiness between her legs. Her nightgown lay on the floor beside the bed, a sudden reminder of all that had happened the night before. The sight of it shocked her into reality, and she was filled with dismay.

Rising, she crept softly to the door separating her room from Olga's. The old woman was still sleeping soundly. Carefully, Natalya closed the door between their rooms and hurried back to examine the bed. There was a bright spot of blood on the bed linen. Quickly, she drew up the quilt, smoothing out the covers so Olga would have no reason to fuss with them.

She picked up her nightgown, grimacing when she saw that it was ripped—Olga would be sure to notice it. She stuffed it into her valise, hoping to delay Olga's discovery and give herself time to think of some plausible explanation. Then she went to the pine nightstand beside the bed, and poured some water from the pitcher into the basin. She carefully washed away the sticky substance from between her legs.

As she dressed in the emerald green gown Olga had chosen for her arrival in Moscow, Natalya raged inwardly at the man who had dared to invade her room—and her body—during the night. Brushing aside her own feelings of guilt, she told herself that he was a scoundrel, a ruffian who had forced her to submit to his passion. If she had struggled more, after all, there was no telling what harm he might have done her. Oh dear! What could she tell the prince on their wedding night, when he was sure to question the state of her virginity?

By the time Olga arose, Natalya was fully dressed and sitting before the small mirror in her room, vigorously brushing her hair. Olga eyed her mistress and the neatly made bed with surprise.

"You seem anxious to be under way today, Natasha."

"Yes. I suppose I am anxious to meet my intended husband at last."

Olga looked even more perplexed. "How strange

9

—last night I had the impression you were in no hurry to meet the prince."

"Then apparently a night's sleep has changed my mind," Natalya answered with a tinge of irritation. "Now, if you will kindly prepare yourself, Olga, we can be on our way."

The old woman shrugged and shuffled back into her own room. Grumbling all the while, she nevertheless dressed and packed within twenty minutes and they were ready to begin the last day of their journey.

As Natalya entered the hallway, she heard another door, several rooms away, open also. Confusion overtook her and she quickly turned to run down the hall, but a mellow voice forced her to stop. It was he.

"Natasha, could I have a word with you? In private?"

She stared at the floor and forced her tone to sound icy. "I don't believe there is anything for us to discuss, sir."

"I believe there is a great deal," he countered, walking rapidly until he stood directly in front of her. "Please, I'll only detain you a moment."

Hearing her mistress conversing with someone, Olga rushed to the door. She surveyed the young man with alarm. His face was ashen from his sleepless night, his clothes were wrinkled, and it was obvious he had not bothered to shave. "I heard the young lady say she did not wish to speak with you," Olga said firmly. "I suggest you let us pass or I will be forced to call the innkeeper."

"Don't," Natalya said without thinking, as she lay a restraining hand on the old woman's arm. "It's all right, Olga. You go ahead to the stable and tell Georgi to prepare the horses and carriage. I will join you in a few moments."

Shaking her head, the old woman went downstairs. Mikhail took Natalya's hand and drew her back toward his room.

When she stopped at the door, he smiled tenderly and said, "Please come in. I won't hurt you."

10

"I've heard that before," she replied coolly, but she entered his room.

"I must explain. I—" He stopped a moment, his clear blue eyes pleading. "I will begin by telling you my name."

"It is a bit late for introductions," she murmured.

Ignoring her resistance, he continued. "I am Mikhail Pavlovich Lisovsky. My father is a well-respected furrier in St. Petersburg, and I am on my way to Siberia to join in the settlements sponsored by the Russian-American Company."

"Your business hardly concerns me, sir," Natalya said sharply and turned to leave the room. His next words stopped her in the doorway.

"I've only told you this because I would like you to come with me as my wife."

She whirled to face him, her dark eyes flashing. "Do you really imagine I would consent to marry a rapist?"

"Please try to understand. What happened last night was—" he paused, searching for words, "—most unusual. There was something about your beauty that made me completely lose control of myself. Never before have I forced myself upon an innocent virgin."

"But you seemed very practiced indeed."

Now it was Mikhail's eyes that flashed, and his own voice took on some of her acid tone. "If you'll forgive me, mademoiselle, your own response seemed hardly that of a novice in such matters."

The color drained from Natalya's face as she recalled her total surrender to his touch. Sensing her shame, Mikhail placed his hands gently on her shoulders.

"I think," he said softly, "that you are no more insensitive to romance than I am. Can't you admit it? Think about last night. And then think of what the future can hold for us."

Trembling under his touch, Natalya recalled all too vividly the rush of emotion he had awakened in her last night. Helplessly, she stepped closer to him, longing for the feel of his lips on her own. But a return of the sense of outrage she had felt earlier that morning quickly quelled her vulnerability. Who was he to think he could steal into her room, rob her of her virtue, and then expect her to follow him into the wilds of Siberia? His brashness appalled her.

Shaking off his hands, she turned again to the door. "You are mistaken in all of your assumptions, sir. And you can count yourself blessed that I have decided not to report your behavior to the authorities."

"Dearest Natasha, if nothing else, think of your honor. I know I have tainted it. But I am willing to make amends. I want to. I can give you a good life—"

"In Siberia!" She laughed scornfully. "Siberia is a land for criminals and foolish adventurers. And I would be a fool, too, if I agreed to your proposal. For your information, Monsieur Lisovsky, I am traveling to Moscow to wed Prince Demidov. I am sure he can give me a far better life than anything you might offer."

Without waiting for a reply, she fled into the hallway. Watching her proud back disappear down the stairs, Mikhail could not see how she trembled.

Only after she was inside the carriage, on her way to Moscow, did Natasha allow a tear to slide down her cheek. She turned away from Olga and brushed it away, wondering if she had, in refusing Mikhail for the prince, made the right choice. She secretly vowed that no one would ever learn what had transpired between her and Mikhail Pavlovich Lisovsky.

III

Natalya's first impression of Prince Igor Petrovich Demidov was more pleasant than she had dared to expect. He was undeniably handsome—tall, with gleaming dark hair, a thin black moustache, and brown eyes that seemed to dance in constant amusement. When she alighted from her carriage before his family's impressive stone mansion, he kissed her hand with all the practiced graciousness of a Moscow nobleman. Her eyes widened as they took in the splendor of the velvet-festooned ballroom. Natalya's father, Count Ivan Nelidov, following closely behind them, congratulated himself—such a handsome couple!

Princess Demidova, Igor's widowed mother, had planned a ball in honor of Natalya's engagement to her only child, the prince. When Natalya entered the ballroom on Igor's arm, an army of servants was busy making last-minute preparations for that evening's event.

"In a few hours this room will be massed with people eager to have a look at my intended," Igor informed her. Then his eyes traveled over her body and he added, with a courtly bow, "I am sure they will not be disappointed in what they see."

Natalya blushed and looked away just as Igor's mother bustled into the room. A petite woman with brightly rouged cheeks, she hurried to embrace Natalya.

"My dear, I am so pleased to have you here at last," she exclaimed. "Igor has been pacing for weeks, anticipating your arrival."

Igor grimaced at her remark, but did not protest.

"Now, Igor," the princess continued excitedly, "no doubt you're anxious to have your little Natasha to yourself, but we must allow her time to recover from her long journey."

"I am a bit weary," Natalya admitted.

"Of course you are. You must let me take you to your suite." Princess Demidova slipped her arm through Natalya's. "You will enjoy a hot bath and a long rest before it's time to prepare for our little party. You can spend the evening on Igor's arm, and after that you'll have the rest of your lives to become better acquainted."

13

As Natalya followed the chattering princess to her quarters, she felt she would be exquisitely happy in the Demidov household.

That evening, Natalya dressed carefully for the ball. She chose a cream-colored brocade gown that presented a striking contrast to her dark hair. The dress draped low enough in front to be intriguing without appearing indiscreet, and the short sleeves were puffed up in a girlish fashion. Around her neck she wore a simple emerald pendant, and matching earrings dangled from her delicate ears.

Olga fussed with Natalya's hair for an hour, smoothing it back from her face and creating a cascade of curls on the crown of her head. She wove a beaded satin ribbon through the curls, then stepped back to admire her accomplishment.

"Natasha," Olga exclaimed, "you look lovely enough to be married this very evening! What a beautiful dress you have picked—it is almost fit to be married in."

Yes, Natalya thought bitterly. The dress was an ivoried shade, not quite a virginal white. How appropriate, indeed.

Natasha's reception at the ball reaffirmed Olga's judgment. Igor seemed proud to have her on his arm, and the guests appeared totally enthralled by the striking young lady from St. Petersburg. Every nobleman at the ball signed up to dance with her. When the orchestra recessed and Igor led her to the buffet for a glass of iced champagne, Natalya feared she would collapse from exhaustion.

She and Igor had just seated themselves on a green and white damask sofa when a woman, who appeared to be only a few years older than Natalya, approached. She wore a well-fitted, light blue satin gown, her ample breasts swaying under the beribboned bodice. Delicate blond ringlets fringed her face. She gave the prince a flirtatious smile.

"Dearest Igor, you've been avoiding me all evening. And I have so wanted to meet your enchanting fiancée." The woman arched her brows at Natalya, surveying her as if she were a child.

The prince cleared his throat irritably. "Natalya Nelidova, may I present the Countess Maria Osipova, one of Moscow's most noted citizens." He placed a strange emphasis on the last words, but the countess continued to smile brightly.

"My, aren't we formal tonight?" She turned to Natalya. "Igor is an old and very close friend. I suppose you know, my dear, that you are robbing Moscow of its most eligible bachelor. Half the women here tonight would happily strangle you for winning him. My only concern is how an innocent young girl can possibly keep this gadabout in check!" The countess winked at Igor, and his eyes gleamed in response.

Natalya studied her champagne, trying not to attend to the countess's brazen remarks. Her fiancé appeared to be quite amused by them. When the music resumed, she was besieged with requests to dance, and in the flurry of meeting new people she forgot the Countess Osipova.

The wedding was to be held four weeks after Natalya's arrival in Moscow. There was scarcely enough time for the princess's dressmaker to work on Natalya's wedding gown and trousseau. But the date had to be met, as Ivan Nelidov was anxious to return to St. Petersburg before the heavy snows of winter blocked the roads.

The princess confided that Natalya's father had wanted the wedding to be held in St. Petersburg. "But I managed to convince him that an experienced woman like myself was needed to oversee the planning. There is so much to do! Besides, it seemed such a bother to close up the house and go trekking off to St. Petersburg when we have everything we need right here. Without a daughter of my own, I couldn't bear not to have a major hand in planning your wedding. I hope you don't mind—I've already begun to think of you as a daughter." She hugged

15

Natalya affectionately, and Natalya squeezed her in return.

Natalya was having great fun planning a new wardrobe, attending teas and soirées, and basking in Princess Demidova's indulgence. Except for old Olga, who was stern and not at all indulgent, Natalya had not felt close to another woman since her mother died. Later, she supposed, she might consider the princess meddlesome, but for the moment she was enjoying her advice and attention.

Only one thing disturbed Natalya as the weeks went by. Prince Igor, though always very polite, became more and more distant, as if the idea of marrying bored him. Some days she scarcely saw him. She confessed her anxieties to her future mother-in-law, who simply laughed and patted her hand reassuringly.

"Oh, my dear, you mustn't worry about Igor. All men hate the bustle of preparing for weddings. Why, even your own father, who was most anxious to arrange this match, prefers to leave everything to the women. Wait and see, when you and Igor are honeymooning at our country estate near Kolomna, he'll never leave your side. I think he's quite mad about you!"

Natalya was not so sure, but she supposed that the prince did find all the preparations a bit irritating. Anyway, the exhausting round of parties and fittings on her schedule left her little time to brood about the problem.

In truth, Igor was more than merely bored. He was not at all opposed to the prospect of bedding Natalya —he suspected she would provide a lively tumble, once she gained a bit of experience. But the permanence of marriage conflicted sharply with his style of living. He regarded women as amusing playthings, to be fleetingly enjoyed. The idea of love was foreign to him, and he had never met a woman he respected enough to want to share the rest of his life with. At thirty, Igor enjoyed the unbridled attention of a number of beautiful Muscovites, married as well as unmarried, but he had no intention of giving up his freedom for any of them. He had just as strong a determination not to give up any of them in deference to an innocent little wife.

He had agreed to marry Natalya Nelidova to please his mother, who had nagged him for almost five years about his duty to produce an heir. Since none of the Moscow women suited him enough for marriage, he had reluctantly agreed to marry the Nelidov girl from St. Petersburg. As Natasha was the daughter of a nobleman, the arrangement seemed to please his mother. Whether or not it would suit him for long remained to be seen.

IV

Not until late in the afternoon of her wedding day, while Olga was carefully dressing her for the ceremony, did Natalya begin to worry. What explanation could she give the prince when he discovered, as he must, that she was not a virgin? She could pretend pain, but if there was no blood, he would surely know and demand an explanation.

There was the added problem of the letter that had arrived that afternoon from Kazan. One of the house servants had brought it to her, and Natalya had opened it with nervous curiosity. She barely had time to determine it was from Mikhail when she heard Olga outside the door. She was about to toss the note into the fireplace when curiosity made her slip it into her valise instead. She would have to remember to read—and destroy—the letter later, for she was sure it contained some incriminating reference to that night at the inn.

17

Natalya was so preoccupied with her thoughts that she hardly noticed when Olga finished dressing her and pushed her proudly toward the mirror.

"There, Natasha, just look at yourself! If only your mother could see you. I'll wager your prince will be stomping with impatience to get the celebration over with and carry you away to your private quarters."

Natalya forced a smile as she studied her reflection in the mirror. Indeed, the dress was breathtakingly lovely—pure white satin, fitted tightly at the bodice, its long sleeves elaborately puffed above the elbow and fitted at the wrists. The skirt fell loosely from just below her bosom, and the sweeping train would cover almost a quarter the length of the cathedral aisle. Tiny pearls stitched into the bodice accentuated her firm young breasts. Larger pearls sewn into the train traced the design of the Demidov family crest.

Studying the bride, Olga exclaimed, "You're so pale, girl! You look as if you're going to a funeral. Here," she patted a bit of rouge on each of Natalya's cheeks, "this will perk you up a bit. There's no need to be nervous, my darling—this is the happiest day of your life."

Natalya obediently tried to radiate some sign of happiness, but she could not shake off a feeling of impending doom. She scarcely noticed anything as her carriage rolled toward the heart of Moscow. From cobblestoned Krasnaya Square, through the massive red brick gateway of Spasskaya Tower, into the Kremlin, past the gilded dome of Arkhangelsky Cathedral — which had taken her breath away the first time she viewed it—none of the sights made an impression on her during the ride.

At the wedding ceremony, she felt as if in a trance, murmuring the correct responses, and dimly hearing Igor's own clear-voiced responses. She scarcely noticed the weight of the heavy nuptial crown when the priest placed it on her head during the bridal coronation. She managed not to choke when the chalice of wine passed between her and the prince the traditional three times. And she managed not to stumble as she followed the priest around the gospel lectern the required three times.

Afterwards, in the Demidov ballroom, she danced with her new husband and smiled shyly at the repeated toasts to their happiness. Surrounded by well-wishers at the feasting table, Natalya tried to act carefree and gay, but she could hardly swallow. The braised veal with caviar sauce, cold suckling pig with horseradish sauce, roast woodcock, and countless other sumptuous dishes prepared especially for the wedding feast went untasted by her. As the guests began to drift away, casting knowing glances at the newlyweds, she felt herself begin to tremble.

Finally, only Natalya's father remained with them in the grand ballroom. He embraced her quickly, then stared at the polished parquet floor, shifting his weight from foot to foot nervously.

"Well, little one," Ivan Nelidov murmured, "today you have become a woman. Watching you in the cathedral this evening, my pride knew no bounds. But I suspect that I will not see you tomorrow, since I intend to depart for St. Petersburg very early in the morning, when I'm sure you will still be enjoying some private moments with your new husband. Who knows, the next time we see each other you may have the beginnings of a flock of children." He hugged her again, and his voice cracked. "Be happy, Natasha. That is what I wish for you."

Clearing his throat, he turned to the prince. "Igor, you cannot imagine how deeply I appreciate the hospitality you and your mother have shown me. And now, by wedding my darling Natasha, you have made me the happiest of fathers. I know I need not beg you to be good to her, so I will only wish both of you the happiness I found in my own marriage. I am sure you will never regret your decision to marry my daughter."

In a surge of emotion, the count quickly embraced

his new son-in-law, then, with teary eyes, he stumbled from the ballroom.

Natalya stared after her father, overcome by her own flood of emotions. Despite his anxiety to marry her off, he now seemed almost reluctant to let her go. Surely, if she ran after him, he would agree to take her home to St. Petersburg. The marriage could be annulled and she could spend the rest of her life in the security of her father's house.

The prince's touch on her shoulder dispelled any thoughts of escape. The pressure of his hand reminded her of that night with Mikhail Lisovsky and made her wonder if she could, after all, be content to go back to her father's house. Having sampled the delicious taste of passion, could she accept a life of abstinence?

Igor brushed her ear with his lips. His moustache tickled her skin. Gently squeezing her shoulders, he whispered, "Come, you have not yet seen our wedding suite. It is time now for the private joys of marriage to begin. I think I shall enjoy teaching you."

Wrapping an arm around her shoulders, he led Natalya from the now-empty ballroom, through a spacious hall, up the graceful marble staircase, through another long corridor, and then flung open a door to reveal a sitting room cascading with flower arrangements.

Natalya gasped in surprise, and Igor smiled as he drew her into the room. When she stopped in front of an array of roses, lilies and chrysanthemums, he pulled her gently toward another doorway. "Tomorrow will be soon enough to enjoy the flowers. For the moment we have more important things—" What they were, he left unsaid.

At the bedroom door, Natalya shrank back and froze, once again wishing for escape.

Igor laughed softly, his lips curling in amusement. "You look like a frightened little mouse! I suppose your old Olga has filled your head with all kinds of nonsense about the wedding night—as if an old maid could know." He tugged more insistently on her hand. "Come now, I'm not going to hurt you."

Again, his words reminded her of her night with Mikhail Lisovsky and she shuddered involuntarily. But she obediently followed her husband into the bedroom and stood motionless while he closed the door behind them. A welcoming fire crackled in a large, marble fireplace and a cloud of pure white roses decorated the dark pine chest of drawers. The matching pine bed was enveloped by a canopy and curtains brocaded in gold, but the curtains were drawn back on one side to reveal a pure white quilt covering the bed.

Glancing in the gilded full-length mirror on the wall opposite her, Natalya saw Igor coming toward her. He had already removed his jacket and vest, and was loosening his ruffled white shirt. Natalya stiffened as she felt his fingers on the tiny pearl buttons at the back of her neck.

"I have dismissed the servants. We will not be disturbed," he whispered. "I will be at your service for the entire night." His lips were at her neck as he slowly unbuttoned her gown. Natalya shivered.

Seating himself on the edge of the bed, he drew her between his legs to finish loosening the gown. He guided the sleeves down her arms and let the garment drop. Seeing her only in her undergarments, his movements became more hurried. He quickly stripped away her petticoats, her chemise, her pantelettes, and her thin silk stockings, until she stood naked before him. He lay back lazily on the bed, pulling her naked body down with him.

"Your father was right," he murmured, "I do not regret our marriage. You have the most exquisite body I've seen. And," he added, rolling away from her to finish removing his own clothes, "I have seen more women naked than I could ever recount."

Noticing her flinch at his words, he flashed another amused smile. "Surely that does not surprise you. I'm thirty years old and I could hardly be expected to

21

have lived a celibate life. After all, a man has certain urges that need to be satisfied from time to time."

"I know," she gave a strangled reply.

"Good." He dropped onto the bed beside her. "Perhaps after tonight you, too, will discover certain needs that you never before realized—many women have told me I make them crave my touch."

Natalya stiffened as he rolled onto her. His mouth pressed hers fiercely while his hands explored her body. As he pushed his way into her, she tried to feign the agony she had experienced a month earlier when Mikhail's body covered hers. Nothing in Igor's movements indicated any surprise or disappointment at her response, and she pretended her sigh of relief was one of contentment.

True to his boast, Igor Demidov was indeed an accomplished lover. Overcoming her uncertainty, Natalya surrendered herself to him completely. Guided by a passionate instinct, she responded to each of his thrusts as he carried her to the pinnacle of ecstasy. When at last he rolled away from her, sighing with satisfaction, Natalya quickly fell asleep, finally free from the fears that had plagued her all day.

Beside her, Igor lay awake, reflecting upon his unexpected discovery. So, he thought, Natalya Nelidova was not quite so virginal as she would have him believe. How many other men had known her? One? Two? A dozen? It hardly mattered. Someone had saved him the trouble of breaking her in, and he was not the least bit disappointed. He doubted that he would have had the patience to deal with a sniveling, timid wife. As it was, she had proved a superb lover, and he looked forward to their next union. And when he tired of her, and returned to Maria Osipova, or any other willing mistress, this bride of his would have little ground for complaint.

But for the moment he would not even hint to Natalya that he knew her secret. When the necessity arose, as it surely would, his knowledge would give him the kind of control over her which he might need.

V

Two days after their wedding, Natalya and Igor departed for Birchwood, the Demidovs' country estate near Kolomna. They traveled by boat down the Oka River and disembarked in the early evening. The family carriage met them for the short drive through a lovely birch forest to their honeymoon destination.

The house in the country was much less elegant than the Demidov mansion in Moscow. But it was large and charming, and from the moment the carriage drove through the gates, and she glimpsed the house through the trees, Natalya loved the sprawling, white building, with its steeply sloping roof and shadowy eaves. Across the crest of the roof and at the third-floor balcony, green wedding-cake trim decorated the house, giving it a fairytale look.

As he helped her from the carriage, Igor smiled ruefully. "I'm afraid it is no match for the splendor of Moscow, but it is quiet, and we shall have all the privacy we wish—the servants have separate quarters in the small houses behind the main house."

Natalya's eyes swept over the house and the group of tall birch and fir trees encircling it. "It is enchanting," she breathed. "In fact, I think I should be perfectly content never to return to Moscow. With you beside me, I have all the splendor I need."

Igor smiled again and kissed her brow lightly. How innocent she appeared, wrapped in her sable-trimmed cloak, gazing up at him with affectionate eyes. For the time being, he was quite happy to share his life with this sweet, new plaything.

For two weeks they shared an idyllic existence, sleeping late in the mornings, breakfasting in bed, enjoying long walks under the birch trees on the crisp October days. In the evenings, after large, savory meals prepared by Tanya, the cook, they lounged before the fireplace in the pine-paneled study and Natalya would read aloud some poetry of Aleksandr Pushkin while Igor contentedly sipped cognac. At odd times, Natalya thought her husband's eyes were filled with unexplained amusement. But he was so gentle with her by day, and passionate by night, that she believed there was little else she could ask for in the marriage.

Igor, too, felt strangely happy with his young wife. She was more beautiful than any women he had known in Moscow. She was utterly delightful in bed. A good education had given her a quick mind and a forceful way of expressing her thoughts. Instead of boring him with talk of balls, the latest fashions, and court gossip, she was eager to discuss Czar Nikolai's latest acquisitions in the Crimea, the political problems affecting the construction of the Nikolaievski railway line between Moscow and St. Petersburg, and the probable outcome of the Russian explorations along the Amur River.

On exactly the seventeenth day after their wedding, Natalya awoke early in the morning with an unsettled feeling in her stomach. Trying to ignore it, she turned and snuggled closer to her sleeping husband. But, several hours later, when Tanya knocked at the door with a breakfast tray, her queasiness had still not disappeared. Natalya consumed less than half the serving of blinis when, her stomach churning, she began retching.

Igor observed his wife with concern. "My God, Natalya, what is wrong?" he cried. "I'll send my man-servant, Semyon, for a doctor at once."

"Please don't." She turned her pale face and dark, frightened eyes toward him. "I'm sure it's only a touch of indigestion. Perhaps the cream was a bit sour."

Igor pursed his lips. "It tasted quite all right to

24

me. But if you prefer, I'll have Tanya dispose of it. Still, I wish you would consent to see a doctor."

She smiled weakly. "I would hate to disturb a busy doctor over something so silly. If you'll allow me, dear Igor, I think I will simply stay in bed this morning. If I do not improve later, I promise to consult a doctor."

"Very well, I'll leave you for now, and will look in on you in a bit."

By the time Igor returned from a ride around the grounds, Natalya was dressed and sitting in the main parlor, looking rosy-cheeked and in perfect health. For the rest of the day she had no further problems —she ate abundantly at dinner and supper, and romped with Igor in the winter's first sparkling snow.

On each of the next two mornings, the same scene was repeated in their bedroom, and Igor became insistent that a doctor be consulted. Each day, Natalya argued more vehemently that a doctor was unnecessary.

Returning early from his ride on the third morning, Igor strode down the hall to the bedroom he shared with Natalya. He was becoming concerned about her condition. As he hesitated outside, his hand on the doorknob, Olga's words drifted out to him through the door.

"Your condition these mornings has me at a loss, child. If you had been married a bit longer, I'd swear you were with child. But, as it is, it's too early for you to be having these symptoms. There must be something else that's not right with you."

The old woman stopped speaking as Igor abruptly opened the door and entered the room. Natalya, sitting up in bed, smiled sweetly at him.

"You're home early, darling. I was just about to get up and come downstairs to greet you."

"Yes, Prince Demidov, I'll have your wife dressed in less time than it takes you to enjoy a glass of cognac." Olga moved toward the large mahogany armoire to select a dress for her mistress.

"There's no need for you to trouble yourself," the prince said quietly. "I, myself, will help Natalya dress." When the old woman continued to stand by the armoire, his voice became firm. "You may go now, Olga. I wish to speak to my wife privately."

At these words, Olga scurried from the room, pulling the door closed behind her. Huddled beneath the cozy comforter, Natalya watched her husband slowly approach the bed. Outwardly, he appeared calm, but his eyes revealed a flicker of something she had never seen before. He sat down beside her on the bed and rested his hands on her shoulders.

His eyes held hers, and the corners of his mouth turned up in a thin smile as he said, "Is there something you wish to tell me, dear wife?"

She shook her head quickly. "No. I don't know what you mean."

"Something relating to the spells of illness you are having," he prodded.

Again, she shook her head from side to side silently.

With sudden fury, he wrested the comforter off her body and gripped the top of her nightdress. With a swift motion, he ripped the gown down the middle, baring her flesh. She trembled under his gaze. Another man might not have noticed, but to his practiced eye her stomach appeared just a touch less flat and firm than a brand new bride's should be. He placed a hand firmly on her middle and stared directly into her terrified eyes.

"Perhaps now you can guess what I am referring to, madame." His voice shook with barely-controlled anger, and Natalya stared back at him silently. "No? Then let me enlighten you—you are with child, are you not?"

"I—I don't know," she stammered weakly. "We've been married only a few weeks, Igor. I suppose I may be with child, but it is really too soon to be sure."

"But it is not too soon if the child was conceived before we were wed."

"I do not understand you."

26

"I think you understand precisely. Let me inform you, Natalya, that I know you came to me less than chaste. You have been a very fine little actress, but I have known this from the very first night."

She drew in her breath as the full import of his words hit her. "I didn't—" she began excitedly, but he cut her off before she could frame an explanation.

"It's too late now for denials or explanations. On our wedding night, I decided to accept your lack of virginity. Of itself, it made little difference to me. But I never dreamed you might have been so bold as to have relations with another man in the last weeks before our marriage—that you would bear a bastard under my roof and try to pass it off as mine."

He was pacing furiously now, his eyes dark and stormy. Natalya knew it would be futile to deny his accusations. Gathering the comforter around her, she struggled to speak calmly. "What do you intend to do?"

He whirled to face her, narrowing his eyes as he spat out the words. "I intend to go back to Moscow and resume relations with the ladies of pleasure who satisfied me before I entered into this mockery of a marriage. At least they have the honesty to admit what they are. They don't play these deceitful little games with me."

"And what do you propose that I do?" Natalya asked with forced coolness, though her heart was pounding in her breast.

"You, madame, will bear your child here, away from the wagging tongues of Moscow. I don't intend to allow society to think me a fool."

"If you wish, you could divorce me. Years ago, the Czar's own brother divorced his wife."

"That would be too easy for you," he scoffed. "Besides, I'd only have to suffer the annoyance of another marriage, since my mother will never rest until I have produced an heir."

"But you have already expressed displeasure at accepting my child as an heir."

"So I have, but that question can be settled later. At any rate, I do not intend to officially disown the child. It would be a pity to punish an innocent child just because his mother happens to be a disreputable woman." He strode to the bed and tore the comforter from her, flinging it far across the room.

His eyes traveled over her body appraisingly. Kneeling on the bed, he swung a booted leg over her and straddled her waist. His supple fingers massaged her nipples until they were erect, begging for more complete fulfillment. He slipped one hand between her legs, where he stroked and caressed her until he felt the silky wetness that signalled her desire for him. Unable to restrain herself, Natalya whimpered and moaned. Still his fingers moved over her, in her, stroking her, until she almost wept with the craving to have his maleness plunged into her quivering body.

He watched her passion rising through icily narrowed eyes, his lips pressed together tightly. Natalya's moans were becoming seductive, and when he felt his own desire begin to build, he abruptly pulled back from her and stood up. He leaned over her and laughed contemptuously. "You once said you could stay here forever, if I were with you. Now we shall see how much you will love Birchwood without me. Don't worry, I shall visit you from time to time. I intend to collect my due as your husband, though in future, I shall treat you like the harlot you are. For this moment, I have no further use for you."

Igor stomped out of the room, slamming the door behind him. Within an hour, Natalya could hear the clatter of a horse leaving the courtyard. She heard the wind whirling in gusts outside the window. In the past weeks, she had realized that even though it was winter, it was possible to feel it was spring in her heart. Now, all had changed. As twilight descended, Natalya thought to herself that the winter nights ahead would be awfully cold without someone to hold and to love.

Seven months later, in early June, Natalya Demidova gave birth to a healthy, dark-haired daughter. Prince Igor was not present at the time. In fact, he had not once returned to Birchwood since his stormy departure.

At Olga's insistence, a messenger was dispatched to Moscow with news of the birth, but the prince did not bother to visit until the child was nearly two months old. One afternoon, he arrived unannounced and burst into the chamber where mother and child were napping.

Casting a bored glance at the soundly sleeping infant, he prodded Natalya awake and demanded gruffly, "Have you named the brat?"

Natalya wiped the sleep from her eyes and nodded timidly. "I had hoped to consult with you about names, but Olga and the priest badgered me for weeks to have her properly baptized. She should have received her name in church eight days after birth, and been baptized on the fortieth day. I finally became so distraught over the fate of her soul that I could no longer delay it. She was baptized Natalya Igorovna Demidova only last Sunday in the Birchwood chapel."

"Perhaps you should have considered the fate of the child's soul before you surrendered your virtue," the prince said curtly. "Anyway, she is your daughter, so I suppose it is appropriate that she bears your name, though the use of my name for her patronymic is certainly not appropriate. Of course," he added grimly, "I wonder if you even know the identity of her real father; no doubt there are several possibilities." He wandered toward the window and looked down at the courtyard. "I suppose you call her Natasha?"

Natalya shook her head. "Not yet. She is so tiny—Natalya seems too formal, and even Natasha too long. Olga and I have taken to calling her 'Tasha.'" She hesitated, then asked, "Do you approve?"

"You may call her whatever you wish. As I said, she is your bas—" He did not finish his thought.

"But you are her father—in name at least," Natalya responded bitterly. Then, forcing a note of brightness, she said, "Would you like to hold her?"

"No, thank you, I would not. I'll spend the night in one of the guest rooms, then," his voice took on a taunting tone, "I'll return to Moscow in the morning to give my mother the glad tidings that she has a grandchild. Thank God, she is too ill to want to travel here. By the time she is fully recovered, it will be too late for her to appraise the child's size and count off the months on her fingers."

Natalya thought of the petite, cheery princess. "Your mother is ill? I hope it is nothing serious."

"You needn't concern yourself," Igor replied gruffly as he moved toward the door. "Good day to you, dear wife."

After the door closed, baby Tasha slept on, unaware of her first visit from the man who controlled her future.

PART ONE
1861-1863

Chapter One
1861

Tasha was thirteen years old when her mother died. Although the servants at Birchwood watchfully kept her away from her mother's sickroom on that last sorrowful day, for months afterward the girl was haunted by Natalya's agonized screams. Late that night, after the house had grown silent, old Olga came to Tasha's room and tearfully informed her that her mother and the child she had carried for more than eight months were both dead.

Prince Igor Demidov, the gruff, handsome man Tasha knew as her father, was not at his wife's deathbed. Business matters kept him in Moscow until long after Natalya and the son she would have borne him were laid to rest in the tiny family cemetery at Birchwood.

Watching the priest swing the smoking censer rhythmically over the caskets of her mother and tiny brother, Tasha could not help thinking, with a touch of bitterness, that her mother would not have wanted Prince Igor at her graveside. He had shared very little of her brief life, so he had no place among those mourning her death. Tasha suspected that he had somehow been instrumental in her mother's death—though she did not know how.

Neither Olga nor the other servants ever mentioned the estrangement between her parents in Tasha's presence. But from the time she was a very small child, Tasha had sensed the change that came over Birchwood on the rare occasions when the prince chose to visit. . . . Her gay, beautiful mother would turn somber and withdrawn, and a pall seemed to descend over the usually cheery estate. Her parents had treated each other politely, but displayed none of the natural affection shown by Yuri and Irina, Birchwood's married houseservants.

On several occasions, Tasha had been awakened late at night by the prince leaving her mother's bedroom, uttering curses as he slammed the door behind him. The morning after, her mother would announce, "Papa has returned to Moscow to attend to business." And within a few days, Birchwood would regain its cheerful air.

Even when Natalya told the prince she was carrying his child, his manner toward her had not softened. From Moscow he sent a terse message, which Tasha accidentally saw on her mother's dressing table. For months afterward, she puzzled over the strangely worded statement, "Let us hope this one is truly mine!"

Even if the prince had treated her mother more kindly, Tasha doubted she could feel more than a flicker of affection for him. Though the young child had tried hard to win his affection, he seemed barely able to tolerate her. As she grew older, he ignored her completely, except for a formal interview during each visit, when he would quiz her unmercifully about her lessons.

In the weeks that followed, as the pain of losing her beloved mother eased, Tasha began to hope that she would never have to see her father again. Surely he had no desire to visit with her, and Birchwood, with its staff of loyal servants, could almost run itself.

Tasha loved the spacious green and white house, the fragrance of the pines surrounding it, and, in the autumn, the sound of birch leaves rustling like old parchment when she walked through the forest. Reflecting on the unhappiness her parents had brought one another, she firmly resolved that she would never marry. She could imagine nothing more pleasant than spending the rest of her life at Birchwood in the company of Olga and Tanya, and all the other servants who made it so obvious they adored her.

Just as the girl had begun to overcome her sorrow, the prince came to visit. It was November, and more than a month had passed since Natalya's death. Snow had been falling steadily for two weeks and the roads were becoming impassable. The river shone with a thin layer of ice. Being so isolated, the group at Birchwood did not expect to see the master again until the spring.

Tasha was going over a geography lesson with her tutor, Monsieur Novotny, when she heard a flurry of activity in the hall. Hearing the cry, "The prince has come!" she dropped her books and fled the study. She had almost reached the sanctity of her room when a cold voice from below stopped her in mid-flight.

"Well, daughter, won't you even honor your father with a civil greeting?"

Looking over the balustrade, she saw Prince Igor just inside the door, shaking the powdery snow from his cloak. "Good afternoon, father," she whispered in a strained voice.

He nodded curtly. "Now, perhaps you will tell me where you were going in such a hurry?" His eyes darted down the hall to the doorway of the study, where Monsieur Novotny stood uncertainly. "If I am not mistaken, your tutor was not finished with you. Surely, your mother taught you better manners than to run off in the middle of a lesson."

Tasha flushed in sudden anger. "How can you mention mother to me when you hadn't even the decency to attend her funeral!"

The servants surrounding the prince were taken aback at the girl's outburst, but the prince simply raised an eyebrow in amusement. "So, your mother taught you to be impudent toward your father, too? We shall have to remedy your cheekiness."

33

He ran up the stairs two at a time, catching the girl before she could retreat. His open hand met her cheek in a resounding slap as the servants scattered in the hall below.

"Now, go to your room," he growled, "and think about a more suitable way to address your father. Remember, little Tasha, I own you, as I owned your mother when she was alive. You would do well to treat me with more respect." Turning to look at the tutor, still cowering in the study doorway, he barked, "You may go, Monsieur Novotny. My daughter appears too indisposed to appreciate any further lessons today."

Hours later, Olga came to Tasha's room. "Your father wishes to see you, dear," she said quietly.

"Well, I don't wish to see him," Tasha cried, her dark eyes glinting with a combination of anger and pain.

"Tasha," the old woman said kindly, "you must respect his wishes, no matter how you feel inside."

"Why? I can never respect him after the beastly way he treated my mother."

The old woman's eyes softened and she took the girl's smooth, young hands into her gnarled old ones. "I know how you feel, child, and I can't say that I blame you. But you mustn't be too hard on the prince. He has his own reasons for the things he does."

Tasha studied Olga curiously, but the old woman pressed her lips together, and wouldn't say more. Resignedly, the girl followed her out of the bedroom and downstairs to the small office where her father was waiting.

The prince sat in a winged, grey-upholstered chair beside the rosewood secretary where Tasha's mother had conducted her limited correspondence and kept her household accounts. He motioned the girl into a wooden, straight-backed chair and gazed at her a long time before speaking.

"How old are you now, Tasha?"

"Thirteen, sir."

"Only thirteen," he muttered, still studying her closely. "You know, you look so like your mother. Same eyes, same abundant hair. Even your body is beginning to develop the same delicate curves."

From anyone else, Tasha would have considered such observations to be complimentary, but he made them sound insulting. She glared at him without saying a word.

"And you have the same temper as your mother, I see."

"I don't recall that my mother was temperamental," Tasha said, controlling her voice.

"I suppose not. To you, at least, she must have been terribly indulgent—it is obvious you've been quite spoiled. But take my word for it, your mother was a wretched—"

"How can you speak of her so cruelly when she died bearing your son?"

The prince's voice was heavy with distaste as he responded. "No doubt, she did even that to spite me. Knowing I longed for a son, she obviously chose to die rather than to permit me the satisfaction an heir would have given me."

Tasha stiffened at his statement and looked away.

"It seems to me," he continued softly, "fortunate that she departed when she did. Since you are only thirteen, I have perhaps three or four years to undo the damage she has done, though it is barely sufficient time to mold you into an acceptable wife for a proper gentleman."

"You needn't waste your effort, sir," she replied. "You see, I have no intention of ever marrying."

The prince threw back his head and burst into laughter. "Surely you don't expect me to continue supporting you, here at Birchwood, for your entire life?"

She shrugged. "The estate is here and the servants live here anyway. I hardly think that I am much of an additional expense."

"True, but you do tax my mind—"

35

"Then I am happy to free you of that burden. I shall enter a convent forthwith."

He shook his head and bared his glistening teeth in a mirthless smile. "I see your instruction in Russian law is incomplete. Has Monsieur Novotny not yet informed you that a woman may not enter a convent before her fortieth birthday? Besides, no daughter of mine will take the veil. The convent is nothing more than a hideaway for women too homely to catch a husband." He paused and let his eyes roam over her body again. "And you, my dear Tasha, are far from homely. It would be a pity to rob the world of the beauty I see budding beneath your somewhat unfinished exterior."

In spite of the cold fury building within her, Tasha felt herself blushing. She wondered how her own father could make her feel so naked and embarrassed. For several moments she studied the intricate design of the fine Oriental rug, unable to lift her eyes to meet his.

Finally, she spoke, surprised at her own timidity. "Then what would you have me do? Though you are my father, I've no desire to continue living on your grudging charity."

"Good. Let's say, for the time being, you may remain here at Birchwood. Early in the New Year, I will arrange for you to be educated in a manner more suitable for the daughter of a prince."

"Oh, but I have been receiving a suitable education," Tasha protested, recovering her spirit. "Monsieur Novotny says my French is impeccable enough to stand up to anyone's in Moscow or St. Petersburg society. And he's been teaching me English. Last month we read a book of poetry by a Lord Byron. I know science and ciphering as well, and—"

The prince cut her entreaty short with a wave of his hand. "That's all very well, child, but I'm more concerned with your study of the social graces. You'll never get a husband if you just prattle on about all you know. You must learn to move properly in so-

36

ciety, and how to treat your superiors, particularly gentlemen, with the required courtesy. Really, from what I've seen today, you know very little of that. Of course, living here—so isolated—with only a group of servants and a sniveling tutor to talk with, I'm hardly surprised at your poor development."

Tasha's eyes filled with tears. "You mean you intend to take me away from Birchwood?"

He nodded, surprised at her reaction. "I should think you would be pleased. What young lady wouldn't love to travel—to broaden her horizons?"

"But Birchwood is my home," she ventured. "The servants are my dearest friends and Monsieur Novotny is good and kind."

"Monsieur Novotny is a doddering fool, who will probably be dead in a few years anyway," the prince persisted. "As for the rest of your complaint, a woman's home is wherever her father—or husband—chooses. At any rate, you'll forget all your unhappiness once you're part of Parisian society."

"Paris!" she shrieked. "You mean you will not only send me away from home, but from my homeland as well? What have I done to deserve such exile?"

The prince bolted from his chair and shook her roughly. "Enough of this nonsense," he growled. "I've already told you what I intend for your future. The upper-class young ladies of Moscow are educated in Paris and you shall be, too. I'll make the arrangements upon my return to Moscow."

"I won't go," she cried. She fought to control her tears. "You can't make me go."

He grabbed her chin, squeezing it between his thumb and forefinger as he held her face up toward his. "You will do as I say, Tasha. When I summon you to Moscow, you will come. Do not disobey me, for I warrant you would not like the consequences."

Their dark eyes met for a moment, one challenging the other. Then he sighed disgustedly and dropped his hand. Motioning her out of the room, he turned back to the rosewood desk.

Inwardly, Igor Demidov cursed himself for ever letting it be known in Moscow that he had a daughter living at Birchwood. Now that she was thirteen years old, it would be impossible to admit the girl was a bastard. It would be like admitting his wife had deceived him and he had been too foolish to know. As his friends saw it now, it had been the other way around—he living the free-spirited life in Moscow while Natalya pined for his company and his caresses at his country estate. He did not wish to dispel that image. But oh, how he wished he could be rid of his responsibility for Tasha.

Of course, the girl was right. Sending her to Paris was a form of exile. She would be far enough away not to cause him any inconvenience for the next few years—an important aspect since he planned to install one of his favorite mistresses at Birchwood. By the time Tasha returned from Paris, she would, hopefully, have learned enough to win a husband of the right class, and he would then be absolved of any further obligation toward her.

Irritably, he scraped the chair back from the desk, intending to go over the accounts before retiring with a glass of cognac. The jarring motion banged the chair against a concealed lever, causing a secret compartment in the desk to fly open. Curious, the prince pushed the lamp near the compartment. He saw a bit of yellowing paper at the bottom and plunging his hand in, withdrew it. It proved to be a letter addressed to Natalya Nelidova. Its edges were tattered, as though it had been handled much. Without the slightest qualm, he opened the letter and read:

My dearest Natasha,
I fear you will think me impertinent to write you and to address you so intimately while you are preparing to wed another. Nevertheless, recalling the sweet intimacy we shared that one night at Zelenograd, I feel constrained to beg

you once more to consider my proposal of marriage.

Not knowing your surname, I was obliged to use trickery to learn it from the innkeeper. Now, unsure of where you are staying in Moscow, I am forced to send this message to the Demidov household. I pray that it reaches you safely. I would gladly have carried it myself, but I would not risk embarrassing you with my presence if you are truly set on marrying this Prince Demidov.

Now, to the point, my darling. Please think again of the sincerity of my proposal, and of the magic I know you felt, as I did, in those fleeting moments we shared. If you will only think without fear, I know you will admit that the heartfelt love I offer is worth more than all the splendor of Moscow.

I traveled as far as Kazan before my longing for you overcame my desire to reach my destination. I will tarry here a while longer, beloved, hoping each new day will bring your reply. I would be most ecstatic if you came to me yourself, but if you will only send word, I shall rush to Moscow to take care of whatever impediments stand in the way of our mutual happiness.

If you choose not to respond to my plea, rest assured that I shall never again infringe on your privacy. My position with the Russian-American Company will no doubt keep me far from Moscow society and any chance meetings. Perhaps I shall be sent all the way to the American colony.

At least I shall have—locked in my heart for eternity—the exquisite memory of your unforgettable response to my love. Think, too, of that memory, beloved Natasha, before you make your decision.

> Your loving, obedient servant,
> Mikhail Pavlovich Lisovsky

Igor Demidov sat down at his wife's desk and read the letter twice again. Then he refolded it, slipped it into his pocket, and strode into the center hall.

"Olga," he shouted gruffly. "Olga, come at once."

The old woman hurried from the upstairs room, where she had been comforting Tasha. Behind her, Tasha stood in the shadows at the top of the stairs, listening to her father's conversation with the old woman.

"What is it, sir?" Olga asked breathlessly when she reached the foot of the stairs.

"Rouse Dmitri and tell him to saddle my horse at once. And tell Tanya to pack a hamper of food. I've just remembered a matter that demands my presence in Moscow immediately."

"But surely you could wait for morning to travel, sir. It's near to nine o'clock already."

"I'm quite aware of the time," he snapped. "But the sooner I attend to this business, the better it will be for all of us."

"Yes sir." Olga left to rouse the other servants. Tasha remained, wide-eyed and wondering, in the shadows.

Within half an hour, Prince Igor was riding at a furious pace in the direction of Moscow, rejoicing in the hope offered by his chance discovery.

Chapter Two

1862

More than a year passed before Prince Demidov finally summoned Tasha to Moscow. In the first days after he left Birchwood, Tasha had considered running away. But each time she thought of leaving the people she loved dearly, her heart was torn and she would put off flight. After all, she reasoned, there would be time enough to run away when the prince sent for her—in the meantime, she may as well enjoy Birchwood in the company of her dear friends.

As the seasons changed and still no word came from Moscow, Tasha's anxiety eased. She enjoyed her lessons with Monsieur Novotny, took leisurely walks in the forest, and spent happy hours with Yuri and Irina, Tanya, and, above all, doting Olga. In that year, she grew tall and slender, and developed the long, shapely legs and silky black hair of her mother.

Sometimes, when she thought about the prince, she assumed he had decided she was not worth the expense and trouble of sending her to Paris and that it was better to leave her at Birchwood. Other times she wondered, a bit guiltily, whether he could have been attacked by robbers the night he had hurried back to Moscow. But, she realized, someone at the estate would surely have received word if the prince was dead or missing.

Three days before Christmas, the delicious smells of spices, nuts, and freshly cut pine boughs filled the house. In the kitchen, Tanya was preparing gingerbread, tea cakes, and babalky, tiny loaves of bread that later would be fried with butter and onions as a tasty treat. In the parlor, Tasha directed Yuri as he hung pine boughs over the brocade draperies. Swept up in the holiday spirit, Tasha was unprepared for the message Olga waved as she hurried into the room.

"Tasha," the old woman cried excitedly, "it is from your father. He says we are to start for Moscow at once."

The girl dropped the branches she was holding, and turned to Olga with a determined look. "I'm not going. If he wants me in Moscow, he can come for me himself. But he won't find me here—I'll run away before I go anywhere with him."

"Hush, Tasha," the old woman said with distress. "You mustn't talk that way. You must do as your father bids. And it is my duty to see that you meet his wishes."

"Then I suppose you agree with his plans to send me off to Paris!" Her eyes flashed with hurt and resentment. "Olga, I dared hope that you, of all people —knowing how he ruined mother's life—would not stand idly by while he tried to ruin mine."

Olga threw up her hands in frustration. "What is this talk of Paris and of ruined lives? I hardly see how an invitation to Moscow for the holidays can ruin your life. True, the prince has been harsh in the past. But for heaven's sake, you must accept whatever amends he is willing to make. For the love of the Czar, child, when your father extends his hand to you, you must not commit the unpardonable sin of turning away."

Tasha stared at the old woman suspiciously. "You mean he makes no mention of sending me to Paris?"

"None. He simply bids you hurry to Moscow for the holidays."

"If his message is so innocent, why did he send it to you and not to me?"

Olga shrugged. "I suspect he feared that you would rip the letter to shreds before you even read it."

Tasha grinned maliciously. "Indeed, I would have. But now that you have softened the blow, I would like to read it for myself." She snatched the letter from Olga's hand and quickly scanned the lines. Casting it aside, she spoke in an agitated manner.

"It must be a ruse. He knows I would never come to Moscow if he disclosed his true plans. He thinks he will trick me into coming; then, when he has me in Moscow, he will whisk me off to Paris and I shall never see Birchwood again."

Olga clucked in dismay. "I am sure you are quite wrong, dear. Travel to Paris would be too difficult in the dead of winter. Besides, I hardly think you can enter a school in the middle of a term."

"Well, it makes no difference. Whatever his motives, I've no desire to go to Moscow. I would rather spend Christmas here, where I can enjoy Tanya's goodies. If he wants to make a show of paternal love, let him come to Birchwood for Christmas."

"Tasha," Olga pleaded, "I am an old woman, and God alone knows if I shall live to see another Christmas. If you will not think of your father, think of me. It would greatly please me to see the holy city once more before I am too old to travel."

Tasha's eyes clouded with tears, and her voice softened. "Dearest Olga, I never realized you pined so for Moscow. By all means, you must go and enjoy yourself. But," she continued resolutely, "I will spend Christmas at Birchwood."

At these words, Olga's eyes saddened. "Then I, too, shall remain at Birchwood. I have cared for you all your life, just as I cared for your mother before you. I cannot leave. Without you, I would not enjoy the journey for an instant."

Tasha hesitated, weighing her conflicting emotions. She burst into tears and threw her arms around the old woman. "All right, Olga, I will go with you to Moscow. I am so selfish—how could I let such devotion go unrewarded?"

They left for Moscow early the next morning. They traveled until late evening, stopping at an inn only when the horses became too weary to continue to struggle through the snow-covered roads. As dawn broke the following morning, they resumed their journey. It was the day before Christmas. The last rays of twilight were fading from the sky when they entered the curved carriageway in front of Prince Igor's mansion. The forbidding elegance of its marble facade was softened by the flickering glow of the gigantic lanterns that hung imposingly on each side of the arched doorway. The carriage had hardly stopped when a robust servant threw open the entrance doors. Lovely Christmas music filled the air.

"It's just as it was," Olga breathed, recalling Natalya Ivanovna's first happy days there. As they climbed from the carriage, she warned Tasha, "Now

43

mind you, be peaceful. Remember the spirit of Christmas."

Tasha nodded dutifully, and followed Olga up the short flight of stairs and into the grand central foyer. As a servant took their cloaks, the prince appeared.

He was more jovial than Tasha remembered, and he smiled with pleasure as he looked at her velvet dress trimmed with delicate lace at the neck and wrists. "My dear Tasha, you look the picture of Christmas," he cried, surprising her in a crushing embrace. He embraced Olga lightly. "Dear, dependable Olga, how good of you to accompany my daughter to Moscow. You have no idea how pleased I am to have her with me for the Christmas festivities."

Olga beamed with pleasure, but Tasha frowned suspiciously as the prince led them into the large, gaily decorated parlor. As they entered the room, a young woman with blonde curls and rouged cheeks ran up to the prince and clutched his arm.

Smiling, the prince turned to Tasha and Olga. "May I present my very dear friend, Anya. She has been a great comfort to me since the tragedy at Birchwood. And she has kindly consented to act as hostess for our Christmas celebrations."

"I am thrilled to meet Igor's daughter at last," the woman chirped.

Tasha stared at Anya coldly, her eyes studying the swelling breasts that threatened to pop out of her tight silk dress of the brightest vermilion. She wondered how the prince could so blatantly disgrace her mother's memory. But, remembering her promise to Olga, she swallowed the accusations rising in her throat.

Ignoring Tasha's obvious discomfort, the prince led her around the room, introducing her to several other guests present, his voice and manner overflowing with affected charm. Finally, he stopped before a lone young man, slouched in a gold velvet chair, sipping a glass of vodka. He did not appear to be enjoying the party. He wore the full dress uniform of a naval officer—dark green tunic with a standing collar and epaulets. His dark green trousers were trimmed with lavish gold braid.

"And this, my dear, is Lieutenant Nikolai Voronin," the prince informed his daughter. "We are fortunate to have the lieutenant with us until he departs for Russian America the day after Christmas."

The young man rose and bowed stiffly, while Tasha stared at him with silent curiosity. There was something strange about his appearance. His eyes—dark as her own—had an unusual shape, deep set and ever so slightly slanted at the corners. And his skin was dark and coppery, a tint she had seen on peasants who had worked long in the open potato fields.

"Tasha," Olga's insistent whisper interrupted her thoughts, "it is not polite to stare."

Nikolai grinned wryly. "I assure you, I am quite accustomed to it. After five years at the Naval Academy at Kronstadt, I've learned that Russians regard Creoles not only with curiosity, but sometimes with open hostility."

"What is a Creole?" Tasha blurted.

Nikolai answered simply, "It means I am of mixed blood. My father is a Russian, employed by the Russian-American Company, and my mother is an Aleut, a native of the islands that Russia claims as a part of Russian America."

"But why should anyone bear you ill will because of that?"

The young officer shrugged. "There are those who believe Russians should not mix their blood with the Aleuts or other native peoples. In Russian America it is different. Russian men have taken native women as wives for decades. No one looks down on them, or, thank God, their children. I shall be glad to return to my homeland."

He paused, and the prince quickly interrupted, "You can see, Lieutenant Voronin, my little Tasha

45

has an insatiable curiosity. Perhaps you will be so kind as to entertain her with tales of your country while I see to our other guests."

Nikolai nodded curtly, and indicated that Tasha take his seat. The prince led Olga away. With Tasha settled on the softly cushioned chair, he pulled up a side chair for himself and sipped his vodka, eyeing her over the rim of the glass.

"Tell me," he asked quietly, "what would you like to know about my country?"

His voice was pleasanter now, and Tasha was glad to be free, for the moment, of her father's overbearing presence. "I hardly know," she confessed. "My tutor, Monsieur Novotny, has taught me very little about Russian America—only that it is a vast land covered with snow and ice, full of strange animals, such as bears even greater in size than the ones in the forests around our country home, Birchwood. Also, that it is unbearably cold."

Nikolai laughed. "It is cold much of the year—just as in St. Petersburg and Moscow. But, I assure you, we do not suffer from a year-round freeze. Spring is always beautiful, and in summer, the days are often longer than the nights. And in the Aleutian chain of islands, the climate is normally quite mild. On Unalaska Island, where my mother was born, two kinds of orchids grow wild in the summertime!" He was warming to the subject now and seemed more at ease with her.

"Orchids! I thought they were a tropical flower. It does sound very nice. But tell me, isn't Russian America less, uh—that is, less civilized than Mother Russia?"

The young man shrugged. "That depends on what you mean by civilized. Of course, there are vast areas that have not been settled, or indeed explored, by the Russians. And the natives do not dress as people here do. But we have many churches, necessary because so many natives have converted to Orthodoxy."

He paused for a sip of vodka, then continued,

"Novoarkhangelsk, the capital, is not as large or as grand as St. Petersburg or Moscow, but it is nevertheless a city of some culture. We have schools, a college, a library, and any number of public gardens and teahouses. But of course you may judge for yourself—" he stopped abruptly and cleared his throat "—I mean, if we would ever have the pleasure of your company in Novoarkhangelsk, we would be happy to have your opinion."

Tasha stared at him steadily. "I think that is not what you meant to say, Lieutenant Voronin."

"Oh!" He flushed with embarrassment, and shifted in his chair. "But it is!"

Suddenly, Tasha had a strange thought as to why her father had made a point of leaving her with the young officer. "Lieutenant," she burst out, "I will not marry you, no matter what my father has told you."

His eyes opened in amused surprise. "Marry me? My God, I should hope not! I admit that you are attractive and intelligent but you're no more than a child and I've no intention of taking a mere girl for a wife."

Nikolai's genuine shock made Tasha realize the absurdity of her assumption. She stammered apologies. "I'm—I'm terribly sorry. Please forgive me, lieutenant. My father has been so anxious to have me out of his life that I'm afraid my imagination ran away with me. I hope I haven't offended you." She felt deeply ashamed, and did not know where to look.

"Not at all." His kind tone made her look up—he was smiling.

Encouraged, Tasha found herself spilling out her worries. "You see, last year, after mama died, my father talked of sending me to Paris for a fine education so I could attract a proper husband. He knew I wanted to remain at Birchwood—where I was born —but insisted that was out of the question. The strange thing is, he hasn't mentioned Paris for more than a year now, though when he summoned me to Moscow, I could not help but fear the worst." She lowered her voice and looked around cautiously. "I know it's a terrible thing to say, but I really do not trust him—my own father! I cannot help but feel he is plotting something, and I know I will hate it."

Nikolai nodded thoughtfully. "And you assumed I was somehow involved in his plot."

"Yes." Tasha nodded. "I hope you will forgive me. I do not usually judge people so quickly, and now that I am talking to you, I see you are not the sort of person who would conspire to make a girl unhappy."

"I certainly would not," he agreed. "But I must admit that I do not think you are wrong in your judgment of your father. I do not trust him either."

Her eyes widened questioningly. "What makes you say that?"

"Only my personal observation. Please—I must say no more." He studied the vodka remaining in his glass, then downed it in a single swallow. He sat silently, staring into the empty glass. Lifting his eyes to Tasha's, he asked, "How old are you, Tasha?"

"Fourteen."

"You seem a good deal brighter than I was at fourteen. Perhaps I do owe you a more complete explanation."

Tasha nodded eagerly and leaned closer to his chair.

"You must know that your father is a very powerful man, with influential friends throughout the Empire. While I was at Kronstadt, I received a message from the chairman of the Russian-American Company in St. Petersburg, instructing me to stop at Prince Demidov's home, here in Moscow, on my way back to Russian America. When I arrived—"

"My goodness, you two have certainly got your heads together," the prince's hearty bellow interrupted them. "But it's time that we pack ourselves off to church. You'll have sufficient opportunity to ask the lieutenant questions some other time, Tasha."

Drawing her to her feet, he placed an arm around her shoulders and steered her toward the parlor door.

Tasha hoped to find a seat in one of the sleighs beside Nikolai, so they could continue their conversation. Instead, she found herself wedged between Olga and the befurred Anya. Nikolai Voronin traveled in a second sleigh with the other guests.

"Tomorrow, when some of the commotion has died down, you must tell me all about Birchwood," Anya exclaimed, patting Tasha's arm.

"Certainly, madame," Tasha murmured, preoccupied with her thoughts about what Nikolai would disclose to her.

As they entered Krasnaya Square, Tasha blinked at the wondrous beauty of the Kremlin. Glistening under a thin layer of ice, with gold and silver onion-shaped domes variously rising above the walls, it appeared to be a celestial kingdom.

Even more awed was she at the sight of St. Basil's, the cathedral where the Christmas service was to be held. Its profusion of domes and pointed towers enchanted her eyes—so accustomed to the simple wooden chapel at Birchwood. Inside, the array of gold and silver icons, and the glittering vestments of the priest dazzled her. The swaying censers, the profusion of flickering candles, the powerful intonations of the priest, and the melodious chanting of the chorus lulled her into a peaceful reverie.

The Christmas mass lasted until well after midnight. When the congregation emerged into the biting cold air, fresh snow was falling, and every bell in the Kremlin was ringing, rejoicing in the birth of Christ. The prince led Anya and Olga, Tasha and Nikolai to a sleigh for the return to the Demidov mansion, while the other sleigh took the additional six guests to their respective homes. Caught up in the exhilarating holiday atmosphere, Tasha joined in singing a round of gay Christmas carols on the short ride home.

After they had removed their cloaks, the prince led

49

the small party into the salon. For the Christmas season, the entire room had been painted in bright red. White satin drapes caught with red sashes framed the main doorway and all the windows. A huge fir, laden with tempting candies, nuts, and spicecakes, towered in front of a window. As the party entered the room, two giggling servants scurried out, having just finished lighting hundreds of candles which were set at the very tips of the branches.

"How beautiful," Tasha breathed, gazing at the tree in delight.

"But this is only the beginning, my dear," the prince exclaimed. "Come, everyone, sit down." With a sweep of his arm he indicated the chairs grouped near the tree. "You, too, Olga—I would not forget the woman who cared for both my daughter and my dear, departed wife with such dedication. There are gifts for all."

As they seated themselves, he called to the servants to bring cognac for the men and wine for the ladies, Tasha included. Then, with an exaggerated theatrical manner, he distributed the gifts. Olga was thrilled to receive a large amber brooch in a hammered silver setting. Nikolai was given a warm fur cap and a new pair of valenky, the warm, felt boots so necessary in Moscow to ward off the bitter cold. Tasha thought the gift exceedingly generous, since Nikolai was little more than a stranger to her father. Her thoughts were interrupted by Anya's joyous squeals as she tore open her gift package.

Anya held up a sparkling ruby pendant. Surely, Tasha thought, there could be no larger jewel in all the world. Its gold setting contained at least twenty glimmering diamonds set midst an equal number of creamy white pearls. The velvet lining of the box also held a set of matching earrings, fit for a noblewoman.

"Oh, Igor," Anya exclaimed, rushing to plant a kiss on his lips, "you are, without doubt, the very soul of generosity. What can I give you to equal this exquisite gift?"

"I am sure you will think of something," he teased, crushing her to him as he warmly returned her kiss.

Tasha looked away. Her eyes filled with tears as she wished that, even once, he could have shown her mother such affection.

"And now, my dear Tasha, only you remain," the prince announced, as he pushed three huge packages toward her.

Blinking back her tears, Tasha turned to look at the packages. Gladly would she have hurled them back at the prince, but Olga's eyes caught hers—don't! she read in them. Meekly, she bent over the packages and tugged at the wrappings.

The first box contained a heavy brown woolen dress, trimmed with white collar and cuffs. The second one held a shimmering gold dress, with pearl buttons right down to the waist. The largest box contained a heavy, dark green cloak, trimmed in front with elaborate black satin frogs and lined with incredibly soft white ermine. An ermine muff and hat and a pair of green felt valenky completed the outfit.

"My, what beautiful clothes! You will certainly look like a princess in those," Olga nudged Tasha meaningfully.

"Yes, they are all quite exquisite," Tasha murmured. "Thank you, father." She stared at the fur muff in her lap.

From his seat across the room, with Anya perched saucily on his lap, the prince eyed the girl with mock concern. "I must say I expected your reaction to be more ecstatic. But I suppose you are tired after your long journey and all the festivities. I'll call Liza to show you and Olga to your rooms."

As Tasha rose to follow the servant from the salon, the prince's voice stopped her. "I do have one more surprise for you, my dear. We can discuss it in more detail tomorrow, but I'm sure you will be pleased to know at least this much—I have decided not to send you to Paris."

She whirled to face him, her eyes sparkling with

excitement. "Do you really mean it? Whatever made you change your mind?"

"I said we would discuss it tomorrow," he laughed. "But yes, I really do mean it. I trust the news will bring you pleasant dreams."

Tasha nodded happily as she turned back toward the door. Only the thinly-veiled sadness she glimpsed in Nikolai Voronin's eyes made her wonder if the news was really as pleasant as she wished to believe.

Chapter Three

1862

Despite her perplexity over the prince's announcement, Tasha slept soundly, overcome by exhaustion from her journey, the late celebration, and the tensions that had plagued her ever since she was summoned to Moscow. When she awoke at last, it was too late for even a light breakfast. She sipped a cup of tea, fresh from the heated samovar, while Olga helped her dress.

"Your father was very generous this year," the old woman remarked as she carefully fastened the buttons on Tasha's new gold satin dress.

"I suppose he was," Tasha replied noncommittally.

"And the dress is a perfect fit, too." Olga spun the girl around to admire it. Her eyes traveled over the slightly scooped neckline and she shook her head. "I wish it was a trifle more discreet, but I suppose the style is fashionable, and you are becoming a grown-up young woman."

"Compared to Anya, I suspect I'll look like a nun," Tasha laughed bitterly.

Olga sighed, "Well, it's not our place to pass judgment. Just try to see that you do nothing to embarrass me, or the memory of your dear mother, at dinner today."

"You needn't worry, Olga, I am anxious to get through the meal quickly, so I can learn why I am not being sent to Paris."

But there was no way to hurry the meal. First she, Olga, the prince, Nikolai, and Anya had to sample the zakooska, which were laid out on a special table in the salon. The rich assortment of appetizers included herring, dill pickles, caviar, pickled red cabbage, sausage, head cheese, cheese, freshly-churned butter, and Russian black bread. The men washed down their tidbits with vodka, while the women sipped peach brandy.

When they finally seated themselves at the elegant fruitwood dining table, the meal seemed interminable, as the servants brought course after course. First, they served cups of the clearest bouillon, accompanied by piroshki—deep fried pockets of dough stuffed with meat and eggs. Next came roast beef, then whitefish poached in wine and spices, all before the main course—a traditional Christmas goose stuffed with buckwheat groats and garnished with roasted apples. For dessert, there was a magnificent chocolate torte fragrant with rum, and finally, steaming tea served from the polished silver samovar.

At the conclusion of the meal, Anya announced that she intended to take a nap, and Olga agreed it seemed an excellent suggestion. There was an uncomfortable silence as Tasha stared expectantly at the prince. Finally, he caught her eye and smiled pleasantly.

"I suspect you are anxious to continue the conversation we began before you retired, Tasha. If you wish, I'll have Liza show you to my study; you may wait for me there. We'll have a pleasant chat after Lieutenant Voronin and I have taken our cognac in the parlor."

"If you'll excuse me," Nikolai interrupted, rising from his chair, "I think I am far too stuffed to enjoy your fine cognac, Prince Demidov. If you do not mind, I think I too will retire."

"Very well," the prince said as the rest of the party rose from the table. "I will enjoy a cognac in the study while Tasha and I talk." He gave Anya an affectionate squeeze as she passed him. "Rest well, little one. You may find yourself with little enough time for sleep later."

The young woman looked at him archly as she marched from the room. Tasha followed the prince to his wood-paneled study and sank into the large velvet chair he indicated by the fireplace. The prince strolled to his desk and poured some cognac from a crystal decanter before seating himself in a matching chair opposite Tasha.

He sipped his cognac, lazily rolling it around on his tongue, while he studied the girl. When he finally spoke, his manner was offhanded. "I was pleased to see you getting along so well with Lieutenant Voronin."

"He is a very likeable person," Tasha replied quietly. "And I found it interesting to learn about Russian America."

The prince smiled. "I'm glad you enjoy his company, since he will be traveling with you."

"Traveling with me?" Tasha became alarmed. "But I understood last night that I would not be going anywhere."

"I merely said you would not be going to Paris."

"And you also told me the lieutenant would be leaving tomorrow for Russian America." Her alarm turned to panic as she recalled the lieutenant's hastily swallowed statement of the night before.

"Precisely. And you are going with him."

Tasha blanched. "You can't mean that! Paris would have been enough. But Russian America is all the way across the ocean. It's in another world!"

"It is Russian territory," the prince replied calmly. "You said yourself you did not wish to leave the Empire. I thought you would be thrilled with this solution."

"But I had no idea you would think of sending me so far away—I won't go, no matter what you say."

The prince smiled again. "More than a year has passed since our last interview. I had hoped you would have matured more by now, but I see you are still the same headstrong girl."

"And what am I to do in Russian America? Marry some Indian and bear you Creole grandchildren that full-blooded Russians can look down on? I thought you were more concerned for my future, dear father." She spat out the words, causing the prince to spring to his feet, clenching his fists in anger.

"You had better hold your tongue, daughter. You're not too old to be whipped, even if it is Christmas Day. As a matter of fact, you will be going to the home of Monsieur Mikhail Lisovsky. I understand he is quite well off, so you should be quite comfortable. He is a—er—a distant relation of your late mother, and he especially requested that I send you to him."

"But I don't think mama ever mentioned a relative named Lisovsky."

"No doubt there were many people your mother didn't mention in the short span of years you shared."

Tasha shrugged. "I suppose. Still, it seems strange that someone so distant would care to see me. How can I be sure this Monsieur Lisovsky does indeed exist?"

"Surely you do not think your own father would be so unkind as to send you to a distant land without assuring your good care? At any rate, you may ask Lieutenant Voronin. He says he has met Monsieur Lisovsky on several occasions."

For a moment, Tasha was silent, stunned by the enormity of the news. Trying to compose her thoughts, she asked quietly, "Is it really necessary that I leave right away? Surely, we could delay the journey until I've had a chance to visit Birchwood once more."

The prince shook his head emphatically. "It is a long trip across Siberia, and you must reach Okhotsk in time to catch the summer ship to Novoarkhangelsk. It is imperative that you leave tomorrow with Lieutenant Voronin."

"But Siberia sounds so wild and forbidding. Is there no other way for me to reach Novoarkhangelsk?"

The prince sighed and spoke with exaggerated patience. "My dear daughter, Russia claimed Siberia hundreds of years ago, so it is hardly as untamed as you suppose. Besides, the lieutenant is quite capable of protecting you from any danger. As to your question, yes, there is one other way to reach the colony. The Russian-American Company sends a ship from Kronstadt once each year. But even you are bright enough to realize that you have missed that sailing by several months. The Neva and the Baltic Sea are quite frozen now."

Ignoring his biting tone, Tasha jumped to another question. "What is to become of Olga?"

"I assumed you would take her with you. I am prepared to pay her expenses for the journey. I certainly have no use for her."

"But she's well past seventy. I fear such a grueling journey may be too much for her."

The prince shrugged. "Then leave her behind, if you wish. No doubt I can find her a position with some other Moscow family."

"That would break her heart," Tasha protested. "What a poor reward after so many years of devotion to me, and to my mother's family before me."

The prince swallowed the last of his cognac and hurled the glass angrily at the fireplace. Shards of crystal flew across the carpet as the glass hit the marble mantel.

"Do as you wish about the old witch," he thundered. "I haven't the time to be bothered with these petty problems. But I'll tell you this, I'll not keep her in this house after you're gone." His fury mounted and he continued, "I want nothing here to remind me of that jade I had the misfortune to wed."

"Including me?" Tasha asked quietly.

"You, most of all," the prince replied with biting clarity. He stood and adjusted his waistcoat. "I think, Tasha, that our interview is ended. I have an appointment with Anya."

"Surely you recall that Anya has gone for a nap," Tasha blurted, unable to control her bitterness.

"Indeed I do." The prince's lips curled into a mocking smile. "And I intend to help warm her bed."

He left the room with a swaggering step while Tasha sat paralyzed in her chair. For several seconds she sat staring into the fire, blinking back the welling tears. She could not allow herself to cry. Tears would only confuse her, and she had to think clearly—of her own future, and of the few years of life remaining to Olga.

She kicked a sliver of glass across the floor, perplexed as to what her mother could have done to make the prince despise her so.

Still wondering about her own role in that unhappy marriage, Tasha left the study and climbed the marble staircase. As she passed Anya's room, she heard high-pitched exclamations of delight, punctuated by the prince's deep-voiced endearments. Passing her own suite, she went on to the door she knew led to Nikolai Voronin's room. Hesitating only a moment, she knocked briskly.

Instantly, Nikolai opened the door. He was dressed in a white frilled shirt, the gold-trimmed trousers of his uniform, and high black leather boots. Tasha knew at a glance that he had not been napping.

"I'm sorry to disturb you, lieutenant," she began nervously. "But I would like to talk to you."

He smiled compassionately. "You most certainly are not disturbing me. In fact, I was expecting you." With a gentle tug on her hand, he drew her into the room, then closed the door.

He seated her on a settee beside the fireplace, then filled a glass with cognac from a decanter sitting on the carved mantel. He spoke gently. "I can see by your face that your father has told you what I had intended to tell you myself last night." He handed her the glass. "Drink the cognac, it will help you feel better."

Tasha doubted that anything could make her feel better, but obediently raised the glass to her lips. As she sipped the smooth, amber liquid, she felt a flush spreading over her cheeks.

Nikolai sat beside her on the settee and watched approvingly. When she had emptied it, he took the glass from her and set it aside. "There, now you look a bit less faint. I suppose you wanted to ask me about Monsieur Lisovsky?"

Tasha nodded slowly.

"He is a very fine gentleman. If you will permit me to say so, not at all like Prince Demidov. I understand he has been with the Russian-American Company for nearly fifteen years. At any rate, he is an official of the company, and is well respected by the Russians and natives alike. From my own experience, he is a fair man, and very even-tempered."

"What about the rest of his family?"

Nikolai shrugged. "So far as I know, he has none. He must be nearly forty years old, but he has never married, even though I know of at least half a dozen women who have tried to snare him. I've heard rumors of some unforgettable love in his past, but of course that may be mere gossip."

Tasha shook her head uncertainly. "I still can't understand why this man would want to see me. Even if he is some distant relative, as my father claims, what possible interest could he have in me?"

"Well, in a few months' time, you can ask him yourself."

"*If* I decide to go with you," she said firmly, raising her dark eyes to meet the young lieutenant's.

His eyes expressed alarm. "But I don't see that you

58

have much choice. The prince would never consent to let you return to Birchwood. And if you did so on your own, he would soon find out and have you removed."

"But you could help me, couldn't you, lieutenant?" Tasha implored, grasping his hands spontaneously. "You could help me find a place to hide—a place where I would be safe and my father would never find me."

He shook his head. "And if I said I would? Do you think I could live with myself if I left you to fend for yourself all alone? Be sensible, Tasha. Russian America is not an inhuman place. It is a beautiful country. You can learn to love it just as I do."

"Of course you love it—it's your home! But Russia is my home. Birchwood is my home. I am sure I can never be happy anywhere else."

Nikolai's tone became firmer, and he squeezed her hands to emphasize his words. "I know it is painful, but you must accept the fact that Birchwood is no longer, and can never again be, your home. I agree that the prince has treated you unfairly, but won't you at least accept my protection on the trip to Russian America? I can assure you that life with Monsieur Lisovsky will be infinitely better than anything else the prince might plan for you. And if you find you are unhappy in Russian America, I believe Monsieur Lisovsky would find a way to return you to your homeland. And I confess," he added, brushing his fingertips down her cheek, "that I would dearly love to have your company on the journey through Siberia. Will you give me that pleasure, Tasha?"

"I don't know," she replied stubbornly. "I will have to give the situation more thought." But in her heart, she was already resigning herself to a long trip through unknown territory in the company of a man she hardly knew.

After wrestling all afternoon with the problem of what to do about Olga, Tasha finally decided to leave the decision to the old woman, and spoke to her. As expected, Olga insisted on going with Tasha.

"I've served the Nelidova women all my life," she answered simply, "and I've no intention of abandoning you now. Besides, it would never do for you to be unescorted while traveling with the young lieutenant, no matter how honorable a man he is."

"Olga," Tasha asked before they retired that last night in Moscow, "what do you know of this Monsieur Mikhail Lisovsky, to whose home we are being sent? My father says he is a distant relation of mama's."

The old woman winced at the mention of Mikhail's name, but a look of indifference quickly veiled her eyes. "I think I may have met him once, briefly. And I believe he wrote to your mother on at least one occasion."

"But how were he and mama related?"

"I couldn't say." The old woman spoke stiffly and turned away. "If we are to leave early in the morning, you had best get some rest." She extinguished the lamp on the nightstand and padded toward her own room.

Long afterward, Tasha lay awake, puzzling over Olga's reaction to the name Mikhail Lisovsky. She felt sure Olga knew more than she would say, and Tasha vowed that she would press her for more information before they arrived in Novoarkhangelsk.

Chapter Four

1862-1863

Early in the morning of the day after Christmas, Lieutenant Nikolai Voronin escorted Tasha and Olga from Moscow. Prince Demidov's carriage took the three to Krasnaya Square, where they waited for the coach which would take them along the post roads to Kozlov, Tambov, and on toward the Ural Mountains.

The prince accompanied them to the square, but when it became apparent the coach would be late, he announced that he had urgent business to attend to elsewhere in the city, and that he must leave them.

"I'm sure I can rely on you, lieutenant, to see the ladies safely aboard," he said crisply. "I trust I have provided you with sufficient funds to cover all foreseeable expenses, so there is really no need for me to wait here longer."

He took a step toward Tasha, holding his arms out as if to embrace her, but she moved away, refusing to let him touch her. She would not look at him. Without a word, the prince climbed into his carriage and directed his driver away from the square.

"Tasha," Olga whispered reprovingly, "what has become of your manners? Would it have hurt so much to bid your father goodbye?"

"Yes, it would have," she said sharply, wrapping her old gray woolen cloak tightly around her body. "I would rather die than let him touch me."

Olga smoothed the cloak over the girl's shoulders, clucking over a threadbare spot. "I don't understand why you wouldn't wear your new cloak. You look so lovely in it, and I'm sure it would be much warmer than this poor, worn thing."

"I could not bear to give him the pleasure of seeing me in it. I wouldn't want him to think his gift pleased me."

Before Olga could lecture her further, the coach arrived and Nikolai helped them inside. While he directed the loading of their baggage, Tasha examined the interior of the coach. It had room enough for six people, perhaps eight if none of them was too portly. With its brown horsehair upholstery, it was no match for the elegance of the prince's velvet-cushioned carriage. But it was fairly comfortable, and it would provide shelter from the winter winds that had begun to blow fiercely during their wait in the square.

Since it was the day after Christmas, most of the

city was still celebrating, so no other travelers turned up to share the coach with them. A moment after Nikolai climbed into the seat opposite Tasha and Olga, the driver clucked to the horses and they were off. Helpless to check the tears that suddenly flooded her eyes, Tasha pulled her hood down over her brow and sank into the corner of the coach. Before they had left the outskirts of Moscow, the swaying of the vehicle had lulled her to sleep.

When she awoke several hours later, she saw that Olga had dozed off beside her. Nikolai was engrossed in a book and seemed totally unaware of her presence. Looking outside, she saw that they were traveling through a blizzard. The countryside was blanketed in white, making it almost impossible to see the trees, the road signs, or even the road itself.

As she gazed out the window, the coach lurched deeply to one side and Tasha gasped aloud. When the coach steadied itself, Tasha turned from the window to see Nikolai studying her. Suddenly, she was glad to see him there.

"How can the driver see the road?" she asked.

"No doubt he can't see it at all." Nikolai did not sound disturbed.

"Then how will we ever get to Tambov? How can we know we won't be lost in the middle of nowhere?"

Nikolai shrugged. "Nothing is certain, of course, but I suspect the coachman has often driven this same road through blizzards before and will deliver us at the next posting station safely enough."

Tasha sighed and turned again to the view out the window. A birch bough appeared out of nowhere and cracked against the window. Tasha recoiled in alarm.

"Are you sure he knows the way?" she demanded in a quivering voice. "It doesn't seem likely that a tree would be so near the road, and so low!"

Nikolai closed his book and laughed. "Nor does it seem likely that we are actually traveling on the road-bed itself. Surely when you traveled from Birchwood to Moscow, you noticed that the roads had high ridges on each side."

When Tasha nodded, he continued patiently, "When there is a heavy snowfall, as we have today, it quickly drifts across the road, sometimes reaching as high as the ridges. Obviously, it would be difficult to guide a coach through snow that deep, so the driver drives it on top of one of those elevated sides."

"But what if we should slide off the sides and into the snowdrifts?"

Nikolai's eyes danced with amusement. "The trip will be difficult enough without you imagining catastrophes, Tasha. Perhaps you should let our coachman worry about the driving—you go back to sleep."

Tasha wrinkled her nose in annoyance and cast a glance out the window again. The beauty of the falling snow soon mesmerized her, and gradually she forgot her fears of becoming lost in the blizzard.

In the days and weeks that followed, Tasha began to feel toward Nikolai as she would toward an indulgent, older brother. Already by the end of the second day of the journey, much to Olga's dismay, she had dispensed with addressing him as Lieutenant Voronin, and simply called him Nikolai. He answered her constant stream of questions patiently, explaining as much as he could about the cities and steppes they passed through. Gradually, Tasha's bitterness at being uprooted from her home was replaced by a degree of exhilaration as she discovered new lands, new scenes and learned of the customs of other people.

At Kazan, while they waited to change coaches for the lap that would take them on toward the Ural range, she marveled at a tall tower rising from the plains bordering the city—a memorial to the Russians who gave their lives hundreds of years before in the battle against the fierce Tartars. Leaving Kazan, she breathed in the fragrance of the thick pine forests, allowing her mind to flash back only for a moment to the same pungent smell that had filled Birchwood a few days before Christmas. Within another week, they were climbing upward through the pine and birch forests of the Ural foothills. In a few days more, they had left European Russia behind and crossed the threshold of the singularly strange, enormous region called Siberia.

As the coach entered Ekaterinburg, the first city of any size on the far side of the Urals, Tasha's eyes widened and she sighed with relief. "Why, it looks like any other Russian city!" she exclaimed. "What lovely stone buildings! Siberia is not so uncivilized as I supposed."

Nikolai chuckled. "Ekaterinburg is not exactly in Siberia. But I think you'll find that other cities we'll be passing through are quite 'civilized,' as you put it. And Ekaterinburg may well be the most Russianized of all. It's a pity we don't have more time or I could show you the copper works, where all the Empire's copper coins are minted. There's a lapidary works here, too, where they polish opals, emeralds, garnets, topaz, lapis lazuli, and all the other precious stones found in Siberia. Some of the lovely jewels worn by your father's, uh, companion, probably originated here."

Tasha shrank at the reference to Anya, but she had no time to dwell on the woman as an unusual structure caught her eye. It was built of stone, with vaulted arches sweeping out from both sides and a profusion of square towers and spires rising from its roof. "Whatever sort of building is that?" she asked.

"That," Nikolai answered, "is a church."

Tasha craned her neck to examine the building more closely. "It doesn't look like any church I've ever seen. Are they not Christian here?"

"I assure you they are. You'll get used to seeing churches that look like that. Most Siberian churches are built in the Gothic style—I'm told it's quite popular in Europe. I'm sorry we won't have time to visit it. If we were traveling by horseback, we might be able to stop here for a day or two, but coach travel is so slow and we must push on toward Tyumen. I've been instructed to meet with a commissioner of the Russian-American Company there before continuing on our journey."

Four days later, after installing Tasha and Olga at an inn in Tyumen, Nikolai went off to locate the commissioner. He advised the women not to wait for him to have dinner, since he expected to be with the commissioner for a number of hours.

By the time Tasha and Olga were ready to retire, Nikolai still had not returned. Olga seemed unconcerned, but Tasha became more agitated as each minute passed. She lay awake for hours, listening for the sound of his return. When at last she heard him enter his room, which adjoined hers, she wished that she had fallen asleep earlier.

Nikolai Voronin was obviously not alone. The soft laughter of a woman accompanied the sound of his footfalls.

Tasha tensed in her bed as she heard a high-pitched giggle as a heavy burden—possibly Nikolai's heavy boots?—dropped to the floor. Within moments, Tasha could hear the bed creaking in a steady rhythm. The creaking seemed to go on forever. As the moments passed, it intensified, then suddenly stopped. Tasha could hear deep sighs through the paper-thin walls of the inn.

She lay awake for a long time afterward, waiting for the woman to leave Nikolai's room. But all remained silent, and when Tasha finally fell into a troubled sleep, she knew that the stranger was still sharing Nikolai's bed.

Early the next morning, Nikolai pounded on Tasha's door. "Time to get up," he called. "The innkeeper's wife will have soft-boiled eggs and fresh mare's milk ready for you in ten minutes."

Thinking her escort sounded far more cheerful than was proper, Tasha buried her head under her pillow and refused to answer. But Olga responded for her, and within ten minutes she had the girl dressed and stumbling sleepily down the inn's rickety staircase to the dining room. The old woman stayed upstairs to repack their belongings.

Watching Tasha yawn over her meal, Nikolai remarked with amusement, "You seem unusually tired. Did our good innkeeper forget to supply you with a bed?"

Tasha's eyes shot accusingly to his. "I am surprised you are not more tired yourself, sir," she replied tartly. "I'll wager you got even less rest than I."

"Well, it's true I returned rather late. But I hope you were not waiting up for me. I did warn you the commissioner might detain me for some time."

"It was hardly my fault if the activity in your room awakened me." Tasha trained her eyes on him meaningfully.

The young officer flushed momentarily, then quickly regained his composure. "You may still be too young to realize it, Tasha, but a man has certain needs that must be satisfied from time to time."

"My father has not neglected to make that fact abundantly clear to me."

"Then you can hardly blame me if I—" he stopped suddenly and shook his head in anger. "In the name of God, why am I explaining to you? You have no say over my life—or would you rather I used your body to satisfy my carnal urges?"

Tasha stiffened. Without thinking, she flung back her own angry question. "Is that thought so preposterous?"

"My lord, girl, you're hardly more than a child. Think of what you're saying!"

She tossed her dark hair defiantly. "I'll be fifteen this year. Some women marry when they're not much older."

Angrily, Nikolai scraped his chair away from the table. "This conversation is absurd," he said curtly. He jammed the chair back under the table. "I'm going to see about our baggage. When you've finished your meal, you and Olga can join me outside."

Watching him rush from the room, Tasha found that she had little appetite for food. She sat for a few minutes, toying with her eggs, wondering why she had responded to Nikolai as she had. Surely her remarks could not have been prompted by jealousy, or by any conscious wish to possess him. But, she suddenly realized, it did seem important that he think of her as a woman rather than a girl. Shaking her head, she pushed her meal away unfinished and trudged upstairs to find Olga.

During the next two weeks they saw sparsely scattered groves of stunted birch and other trees as they traveled through the flat, monotonous landscape of the Barabinsk Steppe. Nikolai and Tasha treated one another with cold formality, and each night Nikolai made it a point to entertain a young woman, often someone no more than two or three years older than Tasha herself. Though she burned with an inexplicable combination of anger and hurt at his behavior, Tasha made up her mind that she would never mention his indiscretions to him again.

As they left the steppe behind, the landscape changed to shallow hills covered with pine forests. After crossing the frozen Ob River, they passed through Tomsk, and wended their way through more hilly forests of pine and larch. As they traveled deeper into Siberia, their progress was slowed by the inefficiency of the post stations. Half the time, fresh horses or coaches were not available on the scheduled post-days, and Olga, Tasha, and Nikolai would be forced to wait a day or more in some small town, where only the humblest accommodations were available.

When Tasha complained about the inconvenience, Nikolai responded tersely. "So far, the trip has been easy. If you are complaining now, I hate to imagine how you'll plague me later on. Wait until we start on the Yakutsk-Okhotsk Track, where you won't even have the comfort of a coach."

After that, Tasha quietly contained any further comments about their accommodations. She was silent as they traveled through Achinsk, which separated eastern and western Siberia. Even when Olga commented on the town's beautiful cathedral square, she only nodded agreement and returned to her brooding.

Three days later, as they entered the city of Krasnoyarsk on the Kacha River, even Nikolai relented and tried to coax Tasha from her moodiness. Pointing to the steep clayey hills of reddish hue along the riverbank, he explained that the town had been named for their color. Olga, as if covering up for Tasha's impoliteness, expressed interest, but Tasha steadfastly refused to acknowledge the conversation. She was determined not to speak to Nikolai for the rest of the journey, no matter how many months they still had to travel together.

She could not then guess how glad she would be for his company and comfort in the days ahead.

Chapter Five

1863

They arrived in Irkutsk, near the shores of Lake Baikal, the largest freshwater lake in Europe and Asia, in late April. Nikolai announced they would have to remain there until the Lena River was free of ice and they could book passage northeast on a steamer to Yakutsk. To herself, Tasha wondered why they had made such a hasty journey if they were to be delayed at this point. But she bit back her angry questions and waited quietly while Nikolai booked rooms for them at a local inn.

This inn was larger and more comfortable than most of the places they had stopped at during the journey. Its spacious rooms had high ceilings, and were furnished with soft, capacious beds instead of the hard, narrow cots they found in the smaller towns. As it was quite near the Irkutsk bazaar, Tasha and Olga were free to examine the local wares while Nikolai entertained himself elsewhere. Tasha was fascinated with the way milk was sold at the bazaar. It was frozen in various size blocks, with a string threaded through one corner of each chunk. The buyer could simply dangle it from its string, to thaw at home at some convenient time.

After almost a week in Irkutsk, Tasha was bored with both the inn and the bazaar. It was near twilight one afternoon when she prevailed upon Olga to accompany her on a longer walk.

"Please, Olga," she begged, "I'm so tired of being cooped up in coaches and inns. Now that it's getting a bit warmer, a long, brisk walk would be good for both of us."

Olga shook her head uncertainly. "I don't like the idea of wandering too far from the inn without an escort. You never know when you might run into some untrustworthy character, in exile here from Russia."

"Oh, pooh, exiles are imprisoned under lock and key on the other side of the Angara River."

"The convicted criminals are in prison, child. But there are other exiles, too. Your life at Birchwood was too sheltered for you to know this, but many towns send exiles of their own to Siberia—men who drink too much or refuse to support their wives and children. I've heard tell most of them remain drunkards, willing to do anything for a taste of vodka or kvass."

"Well, a little drunkenness doesn't scare me! I'll not be forced to live like a prisoner in this inn." Tasha marched to the pine armoire and found her old gray cloak. "You may do as you wish, Olga, but I am going out."

"Can't you at least wait for Lieutenant Voronin to accompany you?"

"You know as well as I that Lieutenant Voronin may be gone until early morning. Besides, I think his company is worse than none at all." With a toss of her head, Tasha left the room.

Sighing, Olga hurried to find her cloak and caught up with the girl as she left the inn.

As they walked toward the banks of the Angara, Tasha realized with relief that more than half their journey was over. For the first time in weeks, her thoughts turned to Novoarkhangelsk and the man who was waiting for her arrival there.

"Olga," she asked quietly, "what does Monsieur Lisovsky look like?"

"How should I know, child?"

"You said yourself that you may have met him once."

"But that was a number of years ago. My memory is getting poor. Besides, people change over time. I doubt that he would look the same."

"At least tell me what he looked like then," Tasha persisted.

"Well, all right," the old woman sighed. "As I recall, he was quite tall and had fair hair. Other than that, there's little I can say."

"Was he handsome?"

"I suppose some people would think so."

"And how was mama related to him?"

Olga hesitated uneasily. "As I've told you before, I don't really know."

"After all the years you served with mama's family, you must remember some—"

"No," Olga answered shortly. "The Nelidov family is very large. I was never able to keep the distant relations straight in my mind."

Tasha grasped the old woman's hand and squeezed it gently. "Olga," she said softly, "why won't you tell me more? I can sense that you are keeping something from me, and I am beginning to suspect that there is some sort of scandal attached to Monsieur Lisovsky."

"Scandal?" Olga laughed nervously. "How silly. I'm

70

afraid you've let your imagination run away with you."

"If you would tell me what you know, I would have no need to imagine anything," Tasha prodded.

"I do know something more," Olga admitted slowly. "But it is not my place to tell you. Your dear mother confided in me only a few years ago, though I suspected as much from the beginning." She stopped abruptly, aware that the girl was studying her intently. "But, I've already said too much. Perhaps Monsieur Lisovsky will—"

Her sentence was interrupted as a man staggered from a shaded doorway. "Ho, what have we here?" he bellowed. "A pair of wenches to help warm a cold night." He threw his arms tightly around Olga and buried his face in her shoulder.

"Run, Tasha," the old woman hissed.

At Olga's words, the man lifted up his head and peered into Olga's face. "Why, you're nothing but an old hag," he spat, pushing her away with a burly arm. "I think I prefer the younger one."

Tasha stared at Olga, whose limp body had crumpled to the ground. Before she could move to help the old woman, the man had seized her and started pressing her down to the cold street. Tasha wrestled to free herself from his grip.

"I'll wager this is as good a place as any to sample your wares, missy," he whispered, grunting with exertion as he fought to pin her to the ground.

He straddled her as she twisted and squirmed, and started to tug at her skirts. The moment she regained her wits, she opened her mouth to scream. Instantly, she felt a blade of icy steel against her throat. "Now, you're going to be good and quiet, aren't you, little girlie?" he whispered. While one hand continued to hold the knife to her throat, the other struggled with his trousers and her skirt and petticoats.

Behind them, Olga had painfully struggled to her feet. Creeping toward them, she summoned all her strength and uttered a shrill, piercing scream. Dis-

71

tracted, the man turned around in a fury. "Scream will you, you rotten hag? We'll put an end to that." He leaped up from Tasha, and in a violent rage, plunged the knife into the old woman's chest. As Olga fell, he plunged the blade again and again into her chest though she now lay senseless.

Finding her voice, Tasha shrieked for him to stop. She was sickened at the grotesqueness of the scene. Straining her lungs, she screamed ringingly for help!

Olga's body now lay still where she had fallen. The man whirled around and waved his knife threateningly at the howling girl. Again he pushed her down and sat astride her, placing a filthy hand over her mouth as he roughly spread her thighs apart. Fumbling hurriedly, he exposed his member and was about to thrust it into the terrified girl when he hesitated and cocked his head as the sound of thudding feet approached. Cursing, he hurled his knife to the ground, pulled his trousers up, and disappeared into the darkness.

Tasha crawled to Olga's side. Taking the old woman's head into her lap, she bent over the bleeding body. "Olga, darling, Olga," she sobbed, "forgive me. Oh God! Please forgive me." Sobbing bitterly, her head fell against the woman's blood-soaked chest. After a moment, she thought she detected a faint heartbeat. As she lifted her head and gently stroked the beloved face, she saw that Olga was struggling to say something. Leaning closer to her pale lips, she heard her last whispered words.

"Mikhail Lisovsky is your—" The old woman trembled all over, then fell back lifeless.

For a stunned moment, the girl shook the frail body, trying to will it back to life. Then, as she realized she had lost her last precious link with the past, she clutched her closer and burst into passionate tears.

Several minutes passed before Tasha realized a crowd had gathered around her. Her cries had summoned help, but it was obviously too late for Olga.

Now the people stood back at a respectful distance while Tasha sobbed uncontrollably.

Finally, an old woman stepped forward. Placing her hands under the girl's arms, she pulled her to her feet and made her lean upon her, cradling her against her breast as she sobbed.

Patting Tasha soothingly, she whispered, "There's nothing more to do here, child. Come, we'll see you home. Where do you live?"

"I don't know," Tasha said piteously, for, in fact, she felt she no longer knew where home was. She had no home in Russia, and she was unsure of what Novoarkhangelsk would offer her. Then, realizing how foolish she must have sounded, she stammered an explanation. "I mean, Irkutsk is not my home, but we were staying at the Stanovoi Inn, near the bazaar."

The woman nodded and began leading her toward the inn. Tasha stopped suddenly and ran back to the crumpled heap that had been Olga. "I can't leave my Olga," she screamed.

"No, no, of course not," the woman said comfortingly. She nodded to two men, who immediately lifted Olga's body from the street. "We will bring her, too. Do come along now. You've suffered a terrible shock and you must get help and rest."

Tasha seemed not to hear, but followed the woman with dragging steps. She had taken only a few steps when the enormity of the tragedy struck her. Losing her balance, she sank fainting to the street. She felt as if she was suspended in a heavy mist. Dimly, she heard the woman's urgent voice calling out to someone named Sergei. The last thing she felt, before sinking completely into blackness, were a pair of strong arms enfolding her and lifting her up.

When Tasha began to regain consciousness, the strong arms were still supporting her. A familiar voice was thanking someone for bringing her to the inn. Then

73

she felt herself carried a short distance and laid upon a bed. She heard a hiss of steam and the tinkle of glass. In another moment, a strong arm was holding her up and the familiar voice was coaxing her to drink. From the glass held between her lips, she swallowed a small amount of tea strongly laced with cognac.

Slowly, Tasha forced herself to open her eyes and gradually, the dark, slanted eyes and worried expression of Nikolai Voronin came into focus.

"Oh, Nikolai!" she cried, throwing her arms around his neck and clinging to his heaving chest. Suddenly she realized that he was now the only person she could turn to, the only link between a shattered past and an uncertain future.

He set the glass on the small pine table beside the bed and tenderly wrapped his arms around her, stroking her silky black hair as she sobbed into his shoulder. Bit by bit, she quieted down and at last, she lifted her head and glanced tearfully around the candlelit room.

"Where is Olga?" she asked in a quivering voice.

"Olga is lying on the bed in my room. She's—" his voice cracked and he stumbled over the next words. "I'm afraid she's dead, Tasha."

"I know," the girl wailed, fresh tears spilling down her cheeks. "I know. And I am to blame. Oh, why did I have to be so stubborn?"

"Hush," Nikolai soothed, stroking her back affectionately. "You mustn't think about it now. Drink your tea. When you are feeling calmer, we can talk." He fluffed up the pillows behind her head and handed her the glass of tea.

For a few moments, Tasha concentrated on drinking the tea, relaxing as she felt the liquid warming her body. But the awful events of the evening soon crowded back into her thoughts. Quivering at the horrible memories, she looked up and met Nikolai's steady, sympathetic gaze. He was still sitting on the edge of her bed, and his nearness somehow made her feel more secure.

"How did you find me?" she asked.

"I returned to the inn, intending to treat you and Olga to dinner at a cozy restaurant I found nearby. I realized today that I have treated you rather poorly these past weeks, and I was anxious to make it up to you. At any rate, when I knocked at your door and received no answer, I became concerned. I was about to go out to the bazaar to look for you when I heard a commotion at the entrance to the inn. A man was carrying you, and some others were carrying Olga's body."

"Yes, they were very kind. If only they had been in time to save Olga."

"Tasha," Nikolai paused, unsure of how to phrase his question. "Your dress was torn. Were you—violated?"

She shook her head, blushing at the memory of the man straddling her. "No—but I would have been if Olga had not distracted the man. Nikolai, she gave her life for me! I don't think I am worth so great a sacrifice." Again she threw her arms around him, hiding her face in his shoulder and finding comfort against his warm body.

He was silent a moment, holding her tightly. When he spoke, his voice was filled with cold fury. "If only I could find the man who has made you suffer so. As God is my witness, I swear I would strangle him with my bare hands."

Shocked by the unfamiliar edge to his voice, Tasha sat upright and stared into his coal-black eyes, which were burning with uncompromising hatred. "Could you describe the man?" he demanded.

"No," she shook her head. "It was so dark, and I suppose I was too frightened to notice details. All I know is that he smelled terribly of liquor." She sank back against the pillows. "If only I had listened to Olga. She tried to warn me about the drunkards

75

lurking on the streets, but I thought I knew more than she did."

Nikolai pulled a down-filled comforter up and tucked it under her chin. "I think I am to blame most of all. I agreed to look after you and Olga, and it seems that I failed grievously. It was very wrong of me to let a petty disagreement interfere with my duty."

"No, Nikolai. I was wrong to question your needs. I'm sorry I have been such a nuisance to you."

He smiled sadly. "Well, let us not quarrel over who was at fault. But let me assure you, for the remainder of our journey, I shall give you much better care." His hand touched her cheek lightly as he stood. "I'll go to the kitchen now and see if I can get you a bowl of cabbage soup or some kasha."

"Please," she caught his hand and gazed up at him entreatingly, "don't go. I cannot eat. I cannot bear to be alone, even for a few moments."

"All right," he sat down beside her. "It won't hurt you if you don't eat tonight. But you'll feel better if you sleep. Do not worry, if you need anything, I will be right here."

Tasha closed her eyes and drifted almost immediately to the verge of exhausted sleep when she recalled Olga's dying words. Forcing her eyes open, she nudged Nikolai, who was brooding beside her. "Nikolai, I just remembered something. Before Olga died, she was going to tell me something about Monsieur Lisovsky. She said 'Mikhail Lisovsky is your—' but she never finished the sentence. Do you know what she was going to tell me?"

Nikolai brushed a wisp of hair from her face. "No, Tasha, I'm afraid I don't. All I know is what Prince Demidov told me—that Monsieur Lisovsky is a distant relation of your mother's. Go to sleep now. In a few more months we will be in Novoarkhangelsk and you can ask Monsieur Lisovsky himself how you are related."

His clear, unwavering gaze convinced Tasha that

he knew no more and she fell into a deep sleep, holding onto his large, comforting hand.

In the next few days Nikolai arranged for the funeral, and the burial of Olga, always being careful to remain close to Tasha. As the last spadeful of dirt fell onto Olga's grave, Tasha found that she had no more tears. In little more than a year, death had claimed the two people dearest to her heart. A sense of numbness seemed to be creeping through her, replacing the pain of loss. Now she felt only anxious to leave Irkutsk behind and move on to the future—whatever it might hold—that lay ahead.

The day after the burial, Nikolai announced that the Lena River was finally free of ice. They would leave that very afternoon on a short overland trip north to the place where the Lena became navigable. In another two days, they would be steaming northeast to Yakutsk, from where they would undertake the final and most arduous portion of the overland journey.

Chapter Six

1863

By the second day on the Yakutsk-Okhotsk Track, Tasha began to think Olga was fortunate indeed not to be with them. Nothing they had experienced in western Siberia had prepared her for the hardship of the wilderness trail. Journeying to Yakutsk up the Lena had been deceptively simple. Settled snugly in a small, comfortable cabin, Tasha had relaxed and expanded in the knowledge that her travels were nearing an end.

Now she wondered if she could survive to the end.

Her first clue to the difficult days ahead occurred after they had arrived in Yakutsk. Nikolai went directly to the bazaar, where he purchased waterproof cloaks and hoods for both of them, plus two pairs of thigh-high *sary*, the soft, waterproof Yakut boots made of horsehide.

"But I don't need any of these things!" Tasha protested. "I have cloaks, and hats, and a pair of valenky I brought from Moscow."

"Once we're on the track, you'll be glad for this protection," Nikolai warned her grimly. "Especially when we are caught in our first spring downpour."

Tasha was not pleased with the shapeless, unfeminine garments. She was even more repulsed when Nikolai described how the horsehide for the garments had been prepared—soaking it in sour milk, then smoking it, and finally rubbing a mixture of fine soot and fat into its surface.

But, as Nikolai had predicted, the rugged track made her appreciate the cloak and boots soon enough.

After one night in Yakutsk, Tasha and Nikolai went by barge to the *yarmaka*, a fair located on the flatland outside the city. There Nikolai engaged four packhorses, two riding horses, and a native guide, a Yakut tribesman of the area.

At her first glance at the horses, Tasha's eyes widened in dismay. They were so thin and emaciated she could not imagine how one of them could carry even a lightly-packed portmanteau, much less a grown man. "Surely we aren't going to burden these poor creatures with our weight," she exclaimed.

Nikolai shrugged. "They are the best available. You'll get used to it in time. Compared to most of the horses the Yakuts have to offer, this group is in fine health."

But Tasha was not able to adjust to the condition of the animals. She insisted on walking for at least half of each day's journey, just to give her horse a rest.

Most of the time she marveled that their guide, a copper-skinned, plumpish man with closely-cropped black hair and a dagger swinging from his belt, could even find the trail, so overgrown was it with weeds. At times the trail was blocked by huge, rotting tree trunks, forcing them to detour through the forest, or climb gingerly over the barriers, coaxing the horses to follow. Tasha enjoyed the sparkling air in the forests, and scattered forget-me-nots blooming along the trail cheered her up. But the simple joys of nature were not enough to compensate for the aching fatigue she felt at the end of each day.

For the first few nights they camped along the trail, huddling for warmth under layers of horsehide and fur. On the fourth night, as they prepared to make camp, several Yakuts approached, riding horses even more enfeebled than the ones Nikolai had purchased at the Yakutsk yarmaka. The Yakuts had fresh cream and sour cream, as well as a supply of freshly-slaughtered ducks and beef, all of which they were eager to exchange for packets of tea and tobacco that Nikolai had tucked away in his baggage.

Weary from the day of hard traveling, Tasha slumped down on a log, unwound the long leather strips that wrapped the sary close to her legs, and began massaging her aching limbs. Nikolai began to talk to the travelers in their own dialect, and Tasha paid no attention to them until she realized the native men were staring at her. Self-consciously, she looked at Nikolai questioningly.

"They have invited us to spend the night at their village, in one of their yurts," he said.

"What is a yurt?"

"Nothing mysterious. It is just a Yakut home. They say you'll be more comfortable there than here on the trail."

"Then by all means let us accept their offer." Tasha jumped to her feet. "How very kind of them to think of my comfort."

Nikolai laughed softly. "I can assure you they did not offer out of kindness alone. They expect to be paid well for their hospitality—with tea, sugar, vodka and tobacco. But it's true that you will be more comfortable there. So if you can force yourself to travel a little further, I suggest we go with them to their village."

Tasha nodded eagerly, and they resumed traveling until they reached the Yakut village after a short trek. The yurts did not resemble any houses that Tasha had seen, or could ever have imagined. They were clustered close together, and were somewhat pyramidal and tent-like in shape, with sloping walls made of logs or poles coated with clay on the outside. As they dismounted in front of the largest yurt, Nikolai caught Tasha's arm.

"I told them you are my wife," he whispered.

"You what?" Tasha stopped suddenly, feeling a flush creep up her cheeks.

"Shh." He wrapped an arm around her shoulders and pulled her closer to him. "Don't cause a scene. I thought it was the best thing to say to ensure that I could keep you close to me—and to be sure of keeping the young men away from you. It seems you've already fascinated a number of them." He glanced at the curious Yakuts crowding around them.

"Your wife? Couldn't you have said I was your sister?"

He grinned sheepishly. "I hadn't thought of that. Anyway, it's too late."

"What about our guide? Aren't you afraid he'll tell them the truth and prove you to be a liar?"

Nikolai flashed another mischievous grin. "What, didn't I tell you? He thinks we are married, too! Now come, we mustn't keep our host waiting."

As he took her arm and guided her through the entrance of the yurt, Tasha shook her head and smiled to herself. She felt strangely pleased with the idea of playing the part of Nikolai Voronin's wife. Despite her earlier determination never to marry, she had to admit that life could be pleasant with a man who treated her with as much tender consideration as Nikolai had shown her since their last days in Irkutsk. In less than a month, she would be fifteen —nearly a woman. Already she felt her body was like a woman's, with firm, still growing, breasts and gently rounded hips. Perhaps by the time they reached Russian America, she would be ready to think more seriously about marriage. And perhaps Nikolai would, too.

A voice speaking in a strange language jolted Tasha from her imaginings. A bronze-skinned woman with long black braids was motioning for her to be seated at a large, carved table. Following Nikolai's example, Tasha sat down and nodded agreeably as the woman placed cooked meat and fresh mare's milk on the table before them. The woman had obviously dressed in her finest to entertain the guests. Her sheer white blouse had long, flowing sleeves. She wore a long, dark skirt and a vest made of white squirrel bellies. Across the front of her head she wore a flat hat, a few pearls scattered amidst the festive embroidery decorating the brim. The woman's husband, seated at the head of the table, wore close-fitted leather trousers and a long leather tunic. Obviously, Tasha and Nikalai were being treated as honored guests.

As Tasha sniffed at her food, Nikolai leaned close to her and whispered, "You'd better eat it or you'll offend our hosts. The Yakuts have a proverb that says the highest destiny of man is to eat much meat and grow fat from it. Never mind what kind it is. Just eat it."

As if to prove the Yakut proverb, the hostess dished bowl after bowl of steaming meat from an iron pot suspended over the fire in the center of the yurt. After a while, convinced that she could swallow no more, Tasha declined another serving with what she hoped was a polite smile. But the men continued to eat, washing down their meal with *arigui*, a potent brew distilled from sour milk. The woman now sat down at the table and, as Tasha watched, took out a small pipe, filled it with tobacco and lit it with a straw she ignited in the flame of a candle.

While the hostess puffed and the men continued to eat and drink, Tasha glanced around the yurt. The table and chairs where they sat seemed quite out of place, since the dwelling had almost no other furniture, besides a few low wooden stools scattered around the room. Later, she learned from Nikolai that the dining set had been a gift from a Russian trader, in exchange for some particularly fine sable skins. The fireplace occupied the center of the yurt. Several children played on the earthen floor, oblivious to their elders. The walls were decorated with brightly colored curtains, and one wall was almost covered with a profusion of icons. Straw pallets near the walls served as beds, and as the evening progressed, the children, one by one, curled up on them to sleep.

After several hours of conversation, Nikolai nudged her and whispered that it was time to retire. They rose from the table and went to two of the pallets, covering themselves with furs provided by their hostess.

Reflecting on the evening, Tasha concluded that their Yakut host and hostess were friendly, generous people. Still, she felt out of place in their household —she could not even understand their language. Monsieur Novotny's French and English lessons did her no good here. She was fortunate to have Nikolai explain things to her. She was also glad to have his comforting presence beside her in the dimly-lit yurt. Just before Tasha fell asleep, as if sensing her feelings, Nikolai turned and threw a protective arm over her body.

The next day, after an early breakfast of native porridge, Nikolai, Tasha and their Yakut guide continued their journey. With each day, the track seemed to become more treacherous, winding for long stretches through dangerous bogs and swamps. At one of the hundreds of hazardous river crossings, one of the pack horses stumbled and broke a leg. Tasha felt heartbroken about the condition of the animal, and their guide immediately killed it. Later that evening, he prepared a horseflesh stew. Despite the weakness Tasha felt from the day's exertions, she found she could not eat.

Several days later, they lost another horse—the one Tasha sometimes rode—when it slid off the trail and became mired in a swamp, sinking ever deeper into the muck in its frenzied efforts to get out, until it finally drowned.

Somewhere in the gloomy, barren valleys of the Stanovoi mountain ridge, where the cries of wolves and wild dogs echoed ceaselessly, Tasha passed her fifteenth birthday. But she felt no cause for joy— when they reached the Sea of Okhotsk would be soon enough to celebrate.

Two months after leaving Yakutsk, Nikolai pointed out to Tasha the first signs that they were nearing Okhotsk. The clay became sandy, and soon the pine and larch were replaced by graceful willow trees, the only kind that could survive in this barren region.

When she first glimpsed the town and the shimmering sea beyond it, Tasha wept with joy and excitement. No matter how difficult the crossing to Russian America might prove to be, she was sure nothing could be more terrible than the two months they had just endured.

They headed directly for the waterfront. While Nikolai discharged their guide, paying him as previously arranged, and unloaded the horses that had survived the hazards of the trip, Tasha inhaled the tangy salt air. She gazed curiously at the ship anchored just offshore. It would, she thought, be beautiful on the ocean, its white sails billowing in the wind. She was unaware that Nikolai had finished his business until he came up behind her and affectionately squeezed her shoulder.

83

"Well, there she is," he said, his voice soft with admiration. "That is the brig *Ayan*—she will be our home for the next six or seven weeks."

"You speak of her like some beautiful woman with whom you have a love affair."

"She is like a beautiful woman, and so is the sea—moody and unpredictable, but controllable if you know her secrets. God, how I've dreamed of returning to the sea, through all my months at Kronstadt, and all my simple training missions on the Baltic." He laughed self-consciously. "But you must think me silly, carrying on like some lovesick cabbagehead over a ship. Come, we'll see if we can go aboard and find out when she sails."

Picking up their small amount of baggage, Nikolai hailed a rowboat and engaged the owner to row them out to the *Ayan*. When they reached the brig, a sailor called over the side, "Who goes there and what is your business?"

"Lieutenant Nikolai Voronin, bound for Russian America."

In a moment, a rope ladder was lowered over the ship's side and Nikolai guided Tasha up the swaying rungs.

"The captain's not aboard, lieutenant, but I've sent a man to fetch the mate," the sailor informed them.

Within minutes, a short, burly man appeared on deck and promptly gave Nikolai a sharp salute. "Lieutenant Voronin, glad to have you aboard, sir."

"Good to be aboard. May I inquire when we sail?"

"Well, sir, the ship is ready to go. Fact is, you were the last person we were waiting for. If the weather holds, I suspect the captain will set sail tomorrow."

"Excellent. Then we'll spend the night on board and be ready to go in the morning. Could someone direct us to our quarters?"

The first mate blinked at Tasha, as if seeing her for the first time. "I'm afraid I don't understand, sir.

We had word from Kronstadt that you would be joining us here, but there was no mention of a lady. This is a naval vessel, sir. We're packed with mail and supplies for the colony. I'm afraid we have no room for passengers."

Tasha's spirits collapsed. She was about to beg to be allowed to sleep on the deck, in the hold, or anywhere, when, putting an arm around her, Nikolai spoke to the mate in a conciliatory tone.

"Surely my wife can share my cabin. I'm anxious to take her home to Novoarkhangelsk with me. I'm sorry if I failed to mention that she would be traveling with me, but I can't see that we will inconvenience the captain or crew in any way."

"Your wife, did you say?" The mate appraised Tasha's young figure slowly.

"Yes, my wife. Bride might be a more appropriate term as we were married quite recently."

"Well, Madame Voronina, my congratulations." The mate broke into a smile. "I think you'll find this voyage quite a honeymoon!" He turned and led them below the deck to the cabin reserved for Nikolai Voronin.

Alone with Tasha in the small cabin, Nikolai shrugged and said, "Well, it seems that you'll have to continue to act the part of my wife. I hope you don't mind."

Tasha laughed. "Considering the alternative—being left behind in Okhotsk—I don't think I will mind at all."

"Oh, I would never have agreed to leave you behind—not after all you've endured getting this far."

"I don't know," she teased, "judging from your comments on the dock, I think if you had to choose between the sea and me, I wouldn't stand a chance."

With a sharp laugh, Nikolai turned to their belongings. "Then perhaps it's just as well I didn't have to make that choice! Now, if you would like to change into a fresh dress, Madame Voronina, I will be happy to keep my back turned. Then I'll take you ashore for a decent meal. I'll wager you'll be tired of hard-tack and dried beef soon enough."

Chapter Seven

1863

As the mate had predicted, the *Ayan* sailed with the morning tide. Standing beside Nikolai at the rail, watching the sailors scurrying to and fro, Tasha felt a sense of exhilaration. As they glided out to sea, Niko-lai pointed out a sandbar at the harbor entrance, ex-plaining that any ships that became beached on it were forced to wait for the tide to lift them free. The *Ayan* suffered no such fate, and they sailed smoothly out to sea.

In their cramped cabin that night, Nikolai insisted on sleeping on the floor, giving Tasha the narrow berth. She tossed through the night, thinking of his discomfort on the cabin's hard wooden floor. The fol-lowing night, she insisted that he share the bed, where he would be warmer and a little more com-fortable. When he refused, Tasha threatened to sleep on the floor beside him, leaving the bed unused. With a shrug of resignation, he gratefully crawled onto the berth beside her, and they were to share its confines for the remaining nights of their journey together.

Because the bed was so narrow—built to hold only one person—they had to sleep pressed closely to-gether to keep from falling to the floor each time the ship swayed. Tasha enjoyed Nikolai's physical near-ness, and the warm tremors his body sent through hers. Lying awake at night with his arm thrown protectively around her waist, she tried to imagine what it would be like to sleep with a man the way a wife slept with her husband. She wondered if Nikolai ever thought about her that way. If he did, he never showed it, for though he treated her affectionately and protectively, he was always very discreet with her.

During the day, Tasha spent most of her time on deck. Standing on the aft deck, wedged between the rail and the barrel of fresh water provided for the crew, she spent many hours contentedly watching the cresting waves. After the first few days, during which she endured their curious stares, the crew came to know that she was "Lieutenant Voronin's wife," so they paid little attention to her.

The *Ayan* was never out of sight of land for long during the voyage. Ten days after leaving Okhotsk, they passed the tip of the Kamchatka peninsula, the easternmost point of the Russian mainland. The ship sailed through the Lapatka Channel, with Kamchatka to the north and the Kuril Islands to the south, and thence into the North Pacific Ocean. Within five more days, they were in sight of the first of the long chain of Aleutian Islands—the beginning of Russian America.

Often, during her hours on deck, Tasha saw the white sails of passing ships, sometimes several in one day. Most of them sailed under a flag of red and white stripes with a star-studded field of blue in one corner. Although some of the ships passed quite close to the *Ayan*, neither crew would wave or show any sign of friendliness to the other, and Tasha asked Nikolai about the apparent hostility between the Russian and foreign vessels.

"They're hellships," Nikolai snorted in disgust. "Whalers from the United States."

"Why in the world do you call them hellships?"

"Because they're manned by such rotten devils, our governor found it necessary to cancel their shore privileges almost thirty years ago. But they still sneak onto the islands from time to time. Then they steal the Aleut and Eskimo food, fuel, and women—and leave the people to die from their disgusting diseases and stinking alcohol."

Tasha thought of the huge, beautiful creatures she had sighted occasionally in the ocean, their waterspouts blowing toward the heavens, and wondered how anyone could think of killing them. "But why do they hunt the whales?"

"For oil mostly, and for the bone. But they have no right to be in our waters. If I ever get command of my own ship, I'll blast every one of them back to their home ports!"

Quivering at the violent tone of his voice, Tasha remained silent and stared out to sea.

For the next two weeks the *Ayan* kept just south of the Aleutian chain, always in sight of land. Wrapped in fog for most of the trip, the islands seemed mysterious to Tasha. When the fog lifted to reveal patches of land, she glimpsed lush greenery, but a total absence of trees. On the fifteenth day, they passed Kodiak Island and headed across the Gulf of Alaska toward Novoarkhangelsk.

"If the weather holds and the winds are favorable, we should be arriving within ten days," Nikolai said spiritedly. "It will be good to be back home." His remarks threw Tasha into a reverie.

Studying her pensive face, Nikolai lightly squeezed her shoulder. Tasha had become accustomed to his touch since they boarded the ship, but she still wondered if all of his actions were meant to enhance his role as her pretended husband, or if he felt any real affection for her.

"You look very thoughtful," he teased, "I hope you're not already planning your flight back to Birchwood. At least give my homeland a fair chance before you condemn it."

"I will," she replied with conviction. "You may be quite sure I will."

The ocean was calm when Nikolai and Tasha went to sleep that night. They had taken a stroll on the deck before retiring, marveling at the magnificent display of lights flashing across the northern sky. Tasha had heard much about this wondrous phenomenon and was deeply thrilled to see the heavenly aurora.

By the time they went to their cabin, most of the crew had retired, leaving only a helmsman and a lookout on deck.

Tasha was sound asleep when a strange sensation awoke her. The *Ayan* trembled with a great shudder, as if something had rammed it with enormous force. She lay still a moment—perhaps she had been dreaming, as the ship now seemed to be moving steadily on. Then, the ship shuddered again, violently, and the cabin tilted precariously.

"Nikolai," Tasha cried, as she clung to him fearfully, "What is happening to us?"

He patted her reassuringly and mumbled, "It's only a storm, I'm sure. We've been fortunate not to have met one sooner. Go back to sleep. It will be over before morning."

"It can't be a storm!" she insisted. "We must have hit something—or something hit us. Would one of the hellships attack us?"

Nikolai mumbled sleepily and turned over. "Your imagination is too fertile, Tasha. We couldn't possibly have a collision—these waters are too well charted. The crew is most experienced. As for the hellships, I doubt that they'd risk the international repercussions of attacking us. Besides, they are not war vessels; they'd hardly be equipped to take us on."

As he spoke, the ship righted itself again. "You see, there is no danger." He brushed her forehead with his lips. "Now be still and go to sleep."

He snuggled close to her and closed his eyes to sleep. Just at that moment, it happened again. Within an instant, they heard crew members rushing through the passageway, shouting urgently, several voices speaking at the same time. "Sprung a leak, mates—looks bad—to the pumps—alert all hands."

Nikolai sprang out of bed. Since he insisted on keeping his trousers on while sleeping under his arrangement with Tasha, he was already half dressed.

Not bothering with a shirt or boots, he dashed to the cabin door. Pulling it open, he glanced back at Tasha. "I'd better see how I can help. They'll need all the hands available. You should be safe here for the moment. Stay here unless I come for you or send someone else for you."

She nodded in terror, then threw the blankets over her head as he closed the door behind him.

Alone in the cabin, Tasha waited fearfully, hearing the cries of the crew grow more frantic. She was sure the ship was leaning more and more to one side. Certain that it would be necessary to abandon ship at any moment, she got out of bed and groped in the darkness for a dress to slip over the petticoats she wore as a nightgown. The first dress her fingers found was the gold satin gown the prince had given her for Christmas. Without hesitation, she slipped the gown over her head and miraculously closed each of the pearl buttons.

She was crawling on the floor, searching for her shoes, when a violent lurch sent her sliding into the wall of the cabin. Stunned, she lay still, hoping that the ship would right itself. But this time, it remained at a precarious angle and Tasha felt her throat closing with panic.

Giving up her search for the shoes, Tasha slowly dragged herself toward the cabin door. With a hand on the doorknob, she pulled herself to her feet. She could not bear to wait any longer—she must find out what was happening.

She opened the cabin door and, leaning against a wall of the passageway, groped toward the ladder which she knew led to the deck. Icy water ran over her bare feet, making it difficult to maintain her footing and she slid to the floor time and again.

"Nikolai!" she screamed, "help me. Please come, Nikolai."

Tasha had her foot on the first narrow rung of the ladder, and felt the sodden bulk of her dress weighing her down, when she felt a hand grab her shoulder.

"Tasha, what are you doing here?" Nikolai shouted hoarsely.

Without answering him, she called out, "We're sinking, aren't we?"

He nodded gravely. "The ship's bow has been battered apart and the sea is coming in so fast, the pumps can't handle it. I was just coming for you. We'll have to abandon ship. We'll go up on deck for the lifeboats." He paused and surveyed her bedraggled dress. "Can you make it to the deck alone?"

She nodded in assent.

"Good. Go and wait by the first boat you can find. I'll be there in a moment. There are some papers in the cabin—relating to my commission—that I must save."

Tasha started up the ladder again, but stopped when she felt him touch her shoulder again. Turning her face, she felt his lips, dry and cool against her cheek.

"Be very careful, Tasha," he murmured. "Hold tight to whatever you can. I'll only be a moment."

She squeezed his hand in response and worked her way slowly up the ladder. Hauling herself through the opening to the deck, she saw the ship sloping sharply down toward the sea. On her hands and knees, gasping for breath, she crept over to its high side and struggled to her feet at the rail. Gripping the rail with all her strength, she shook with horror as she watched the *Ayan*'s great masts dip closer and closer to the sea.

When she looked over the railing toward the sea, she was even more terrified. Through the light fog that had descended since she retired, she saw a mammoth creature rising from the water, thrashing its mighty tail behind it. Its flukes smacked against the water as it advanced toward the ship.

With a sudden rush of clarity, Tasha realized what

was happening—but no, it couldn't be possible! The *Ayan* was not even a whaler—it had done nothing to enrage the creature.

As the behemoth reared again, Tasha stood paralyzed, her hands numbly clamping the rail. The last thing she saw before she felt herself hurled through the air were its enormous white jaws glistening against the midnight sky.

PART TWO
1863-1865

Chapter Eight
1863

Captain Russell Dawson squinted angrily into the last of the boats being hoisted up the side of the *Freedom*, the Yankee whaler under his command. "I send you out for whale and you come back with a waterlogged woman," he snorted. "What is the meaning of this, Mr. Northrup?"

Jared Northrup, the tall, well-built second mate of the *Freedom*, smiled and lazily pushed a shock of blond hair back from his forehead. "I hardly know myself, sir. Obviously, we lost the whale. Then we were feeling our way through the fog when we damn near ran into this young woman, clinging to a piece of wreckage."

"Well, who is she?"

Jared shrugged. "We have yet to find out. When we hauled her aboard, she was shivering something fierce. That water is none too warm, even if it is July."

"I don't need to be told about the temperature of the water, Mr. Northrup," the captain broke in. "I just want to know who the woman is."

"As I started to say, sir, we don't know yet. She is a foreigner, for certain—when I tried to question her, she would only repeat something that sounded like 'Ayan' over and over. Then she passed out."

"Ayan, eh? That's a Russian port on the Sea of Okhotsk. I've put in there a few times myself. No doubt she was aboard some Russian ship named for the city."

Jared shrugged. "Perhaps. We rowed about a bit, looking for other vessels, but in the fog it was next to impossible to see. The men were tired and chilled, so I directed them to return to the ship."

Captain Dawson snorted again. "Perhaps you should have spent your time looking for the whale you lost, instead of wasting it searching for foreign vessels. Three boats I sent out this afternoon and not one of you came back with whale. At this rate it will be another two years before we get enough oil to fill the hold." He turned disgustedly and started toward his cabin, but he stopped and turned back before descending the companionway. "Now, Mr. Northrup, what do you intend to do with this woman?"

Bending over the whaleboat, Jared tenderly lifted the unconscious Tasha into his arms. "Well, sir, I hardly think I can throw her back like some unwanted fish. Perhaps by morning she'll be conscious and we can find out where she came from. She may have washed overboard from a ship in the vicinity —this *Ayan* she mumbled about. When the fog lifts we may be able to see the ship."

"Well, do what you like, but I won't have her disturbing the order on this ship. Keep her away from the crew. After almost two years out of New Bedford, some of them would sell their soul for the chance to bed a woman. Better say good night." He strode briskly toward the stern and disappeared down the ladder leading to the captain's and officers' cabins.

Jared, carrying Tasha's limp body, followed at a distance. At the foot of the ladder, he turned down the passageway, away from the captain's cabin, and walked on to the next door. Shifting Tasha's weight to one arm, he opened the door and stepped into his quarters.

Like all the mates' staterooms, Jared's was small

94

and sparsely furnished. It contained only a narrow bunk, his sea chest, a chair, and a small table where he kept his daily journal. Whalers provided few luxuries, even for the officers, since their main space was reserved for the precious whale oil and bone. Still, the privacy of a second mate's stateroom was better than the crowded forecastle where most of the crew slept.

Jared lay Tasha gently on his bunk and lit a candle. Sitting on the edge of the bunk, he held the candle near her and drew in his breath as he took his first long, close look at the woman he had rescued. He was sure she would appear uncommonly beautiful once her tangled mass of black hair was properly dried and brushed. The candlelight accented her high cheekbones and her long, velvety lashes. Her face was tanned, as if she had spent long hours outdoors in the sun, but her satin gown, though somewhat the worse for its contact with the sea, told him she was no ordinary working woman.

As his gaze moved slowly over her body, Jared began to wonder if she really could be called a woman at all, or simply a girl on the very threshold of womanhood. Her breasts, outlined by the wet, clinging satin, were small and firm, and her hips, though slightly rounded, were still too narrow for a full-grown woman. But—he shook himself—he hadn't rescued this beautiful being simply to let her die of pneumonia.

Wearily he pulled her into a sitting position and unbuttoned the pearl buttons down her back. Handling her with gentleness uncommon to a weathered whale man, he gradually worked the gown down to her knees, pulling away her sodden petticoats and other undergarments at the same time.

When at last he had removed all her clothing, he dropped the garments to the floor and stared at her naked body, totally captivated by the beauty of what he saw. The skin that had not been exposed to the sun was smooth and creamy, and her muscles, conditioned by the rigors of the Yakutsk-Okhotsk Track, were firm.

His eyes traveled over her body, taking in every shadowy curve. An image of those long, slender legs wrapped around his loins came to him unbidden. Quickly, he expunged the vision, reminding himself that she was only a child-woman. In all likelihood, she was still virginal, and no matter how much he might desire her, his sense of honor would not allow him to take advantage of her in the present circumstances. Sighing in resignation, he rummaged through his sea chest for a shirt to cover her tempting body.

After enveloping her in one of his linsey-woolsey shirts, Jared wrapped the girlish body in a warm blanket and left her, still unconscious, on his bunk, while he went to the galley for a quick meal. He returned fifteen minutes later with a mug of broth that he hoped to coax the young woman to drink. At the door to his cabin he paused, listening to grunts coming from within.

It took Jared but a moment to sense the nature of the bestial sounds. He burst into the room and, enraged to find Norman Martin half out of his clothes, he hurled the hot broth into the crewman's face.

Martin howled in surprise and pain as the steaming liquid seared his face. He grabbed at his trousers, which were flopping around his knees. "What in tarnation did you go and do that for, Northrup?"

Jared stared coldly at the half-naked fellow. "What are you doing in my stateroom?" he demanded. "Your quarters are in the forecastle."

"Well, what do you think? I've come to collect my due. I helped haul the woman on board and it don't seem right that you should get all the pleasure out of the catch."

Glancing at the bunk, Jared saw that the blanket had been cast aside and his shirt pulled up above the girl's waist. His sense of decency totally outraged, he strode furiously to the cot and replaced the blanket over Tasha's shivering body. Then, turning swiftly, he slapped Martin's face so hard that the little man staggered backwards, tripping over his own feet and sprawling on his backside on the floor.

Panting with fury, Jared grabbed him by the collar and dragged him toward the door. "You slobbering swine," he spat, "What kind of man are you that you would think of taking a woman who has no way to protest?"

"Aw, it wouldn't hurt her none," Martin whined. "She's probably a whore, anyway. What other kind of woman would be parading around in a fancy gown in the middle of the ocean?"

Enraged at Martin's attempt to slander the innocent girl, Jared hurled the man against the wall of the passageway. "If I catch you near her again," he roared, "I will personally throw you overboard."

As Martin fled up the ladder to the deck, Captain Dawson poked his head out from his cabin. "Something wrong there, Mr. Northrup?" he queried curtly.

"No sir, everything's under control."

"Good. Remember, Northrup, I want no trouble about the woman."

Before Jared could reply, the captain's door slammed shut. Reentering his own room, Jared kicked the empty tin mug in disgust. A rustling sound from the bunk invaded his black mood, and he turned to see Tasha thrashing about. She was moaning something in a barely audible whisper.

Creeping closer and leaning down, Jared made out the words, "Nikolai! Nikolai!"

She seemed to be becoming more and more agitated, so he bent over her and placed his hands gently on her shoulders. "Nikolai," she murmured peacefully. Wishing to calm her, Jared coughed in response and he could feel her body relax, as if the realization of his presence comforted her. Through the shirt, her flesh felt as cold as the ocean.

He could think of only one way to warm her. Cautiously, so as not to disturb her, he slid under the

97

blanket and drew her body against his own. Gradually, her shivering stopped. Her breathing relaxed as her body absorbed some of his warmth. He began to feel desire for her throbbing through his groin and, groaning inwardly, he prayed for sleep.

"Blows! There she blows!" The lookout's cries woke Jared as the first rays of dawn filtered through the porthole above his bunk. Swearing softly to himself, he carefully slid his arms away from Tasha's sleeping body and got out of bed.

He had hoped the morning would be quiet, so he might have a chance to talk with the girl—assuming she understood English—and find out how she came to be floating in the ocean; perhaps take a crew out to search for her ship.

Now he might have to spend the rest of the day chasing an elusive whale. He could expect no sympathy from Captain Dawson, he thought grimly. No doubt the captain would have preferred that he leave the girl adrift on the ocean.

With a sigh, Jared looked once more at the sleeping girl. Revived by rest and the warmth his body had supplied, her cheeks now glowed rosily beneath her tan. She turned in her sleep and a lock of silky black hair fell across her face. Observing her form huddled beneath the blanket, Jared prayed the chase would be over quickly. The sooner he returned, the sooner he could learn her story.

Leaving the stateroom, Jared recalled his encounter with Herman Martin the night before. Without hesitation, he secured the door, then hurried to the deck to direct the lowering of the whaleboat which he commanded.

It was early afternoon before Tasha awoke. She stretched drowsily and thought of Nikolai. In a moment, the unfamiliar feel of Jared's rough shirt startled her into full wakefulness, and her eyes flew around the small chamber. Instantly, she knew this was not the cabin she shared with Nikolai aboard the *Ayan*.

She sat up quickly and examined the oversize, loose garment she was wearing. It was uncomfortable against her bare skin. Her rumpled golden dress and undergarments lay in a heap on the floor. How, she wondered, had they been removed from her body? No matter how she racked her brain, she could not remember undressing. Why was she now wearing a man's shirt? And whose was it?

Painfully, Tasha pulled herself to her feet. Her head throbbed with dizziness and her stomach felt hollow. Supporting herself against the wall, she crept to the porthole. All she could see was the calm Alaskan Sea. Its gentle blue waves offered no answers to the fearful questions filling her mind. She stumbled to the door and for several minutes vainly struggled to release the handle. When she failed, a wave of panic overcame her as she realized she must be the prisoner of some unknown man on a strange ship.

At first she thought of screaming, but, remembering her unusual attire, fought back the desire to do so. She could not greet strangers dressed in this fashion.

She picked up her dress. It was in tatters. Her captor, she reflected bitterly, must have been exceedingly anxious to get her out of it.

A quick survey of the stateroom eliminated any hope of an immediate escape. The porthole was too small to admit even her slender body. Besides, if she did manage to wriggle out, she didn't know how to swim.

There seemed no alternative but to wait. Dismally, Tasha sat down on the bunk, pulling the blanket tightly around her, to await the return of—she wished she knew!

Chapter Nine

1863

Several hours later, Tasha again looked out at the rippling sea through the porthole. She was beginning to feel mesmerized by the motion of the gentle waters when she heard a sudden clattering on the deck overhead, followed by gruff voices as they descended to the stateroom level. She strained to understand their unfamiliar words. What language were the voices speaking? It was hard to tell at first.

Suddenly she froze, gripped by a frightening realization: they were speaking English, but it was not the cultured, gently-inflected rhythm she had learned from Monsieur Novotny. These inflections seemed flatter and harsher than what she would expect from proper folk. Her mind raced, trying to make sense of it. If they spoke English, but not in the cadences of the British, they could only be Americans! And the only American ships she had sighted from the *Ayan* had been whalers. Was she being held prisoner aboard one of the hellships?

Tasha shuddered, imagining all the horrors the name "hellship" brought to mind. What would happen to her—indeed, what may already have happened to her?—at the hands of the devils on board?

Totally unnerved by her fears, she sprang away from the porthole as she heard the sound of a key turning in the door behind her.

To Tasha's relief, the man standing in the doorway did not look at all like a devil. His wind-swept hair was bleached almost white by the sun and salt spray. His blue eyes sparkled with interest and compassion as his gaze met hers.

He was tall and slender, but with broad, muscular shoulders, and Tasha had no doubt that he could easily overwhelm her if she refused to do his bidding. She returned his gaze warily, shrinking back against the cabin wall.

For a long moment, Jared stood in the doorway, as his eyes traveled over her body, which was barely traceable under the shirt he had dressed her in. His gaze lingered on the shapely legs revealed below the shirt's hem. Seeing her flush with embarrassment, he smiled indulgently and looked away from her, allowing her a moment to regain her composure. He cleared his throat, stepped into the stateroom, and closed the door behind him.

"Well," he said quietly, "I'm glad to see you have rejoined the world of the living. I'm sorry I wasn't here when you regained consciousness, but I hope you found my quarters comfortable enough."

As he took a step toward her, Tasha retreated and pressed herself against the wall. He seemed friendly enough, but perhaps he only wanted her to let down her guard. His voice was a pleasant baritone, coaxing her to trust him, yet she could not help feeling she would be a fool to trust anyone aboard a hellship.

If only she could know what had happened while she was unconscious! At least then she would know what to expect of him. But, she thought with sudden bitterness, could there be any doubt? Here she was, locked in his quarters, dressed in his shirt, her own gown in tatters—it could all mean only one thing.

There was no way she could change whatever had already happened, but, she decided with sudden determination, he would have to kill her before he succeeded in abusing her again!

Jared stopped only a step away from her, noting her obvious fear and the way she stiffened when he addressed her. "You have nothing to be afraid of," he said reassuringly. "But perhaps you cannot understand me. Do you know English?"

"Of course I speak English," she said smartly, exploding with the tension that had gripped her all day. "Do you think me so provincial that I can speak only my own language? Tell me, sir, do you speak Russian?"

Jared laughed heartily. "It seems you've not only recovered your health, but your spirit as well. I'm glad to see that. A simpering, delicate flower of a woman would soon wilt on board a whaler. And I myself would find such a woman intolerable."

Tasha contemplated him quizzically, abandoning all wariness as anger overcame her. "But it seems you did not find me intolerable last night. Or was that simply the craving of a man long starved for a woman?"

When Jared stared at her speechlessly, Tasha pointed meaningfully at her shredded dress, still lying on the floor. "You needn't try to explain. The state of my gown says everything."

Jared's eyes widened in incredulity as her accusations became clear. The day's chase had been fruitless. He was tired, and anxious to return the girl to her own ship. She had already caused problems with his crew, the captain, and, to be truthful, his own emotions.

He had rescued her from the ocean—and from worse—but instead of gratitude, she greeted him with bitterness and accusations. He found himself wishing he hadn't bothered to save her.

When he spoke, the undercurrent of anger in his voice was clear. "I rescued you from the ocean's depths and this is how you thank me."

"Rescued me?" Though alarmed by his obvious anger, Tasha was determined to face up to him. "The last thing I remember, I was sleeping peacefully aboard the *Ayan*. Is that what you rescued me from, kind sir?—peaceful rest aboard a safe ship? As to any thanks, I believe you have already collected more than your due."

Her acerbic tone, together with his own fatigue, combined to drive all sensibility from Jared's mind. He had saved her, nursed her, protected her honor

102

from the likes of Herman Martin—all the while fighting his own fugitive desire to possess her magnificent body, and she had the audacity to accuse him of raping her!

Overwhelmed by boiling rage, his hands shot out, grabbed the neckline of the shirt he had spared for her use, and ripped it straight down the middle.

Her bared breasts heaved violently as she tried to back away from him. Never had he seen anything more exquisite than her pink-tipped mounds and he reached out recklessly to grab one of them in his large, leathery hand. Tasha resisted, struggling to lash out at him as he crushed her body against his.

"Well," he growled, "since you are convinced that I possessed you last night, it can hardly matter if I take you now. Or perhaps that is precisely what you wish—to taunt a man into helping you realize the fantasies you have dreamed about in your pure little virgin's bed."

He pitched her quaking body down on the bunk, and pressed his flesh tightly against hers. Tasha squirmed beneath him, trying to escape his vise-like grip. As he brought his mouth roughly down over hers, she moaned, as though in acceptance, but as his lips touched hers, she bared her teeth and bit piercingly into his full lower lip.

"Christ!" Jared shouted, recoiling in pain. "Who in hell do you think you are?" He raised his hand, intending to punish her outrageous behavior, when the taste of blood on his tongue returned him to sensibility.

He stared at her a moment, his face paling, then limply dropped his hand. "Dear God," he whispered, "what am I about?" Quickly throwing the blanket over Tasha's naked, shivering flesh, he rushed to the far side of the stateroom. He threw himself down on the sea chest and buried his face in his hands. His shoulders heaved as he tried to bring himself under control.

When he finally began to speak, he did not turn to face her. Tasha had to strain to hear his barely audible words.

"Can you possibly forgive me? I know the way I behaved just now is inexcusable, but—please try to imagine the torture you have put me through since last night. Despite your alluring beauty, I have done nothing more than rescue and protect you, though I suppose you could not help but assume the worst had happened. I beg you to reserve further judgment until I've told you how you came to be in my quarters."

Tasha was silent for a moment, and Jared felt encouraged to slide around on the sea chest until his eyes could meet hers directly. Succumbing to the earnest pleading she read within their troubled depths, Tasha nodded slowly.

Briefly, Jared described how he had found her adrift in the ocean, clinging to what he thought was a scrap of a ship's railing.

When he mentioned the word "Ayan" and asked if that had been her ship's name, Tasha nodded. "Yes, the brig *Ayan*, bound from Okhotsk to Novoarkhangelsk—New Archangel, I suppose you call it. But," she paused to gaze at him skeptically, "do you know how I came to end up in the sea?"

Jared looked disappointed. "I'd hoped you could explain that. Were you washed overboard, perhaps? Did your ship encounter a storm? Neither possibility seems likely, since the sea was reasonably calm last night. But for the life of me, I can't come up with any other explanation."

Shaking her head, Tasha tried in vain to remember what had happened.

"At any rate," Jared continued, "by the time we got you back to the *Freedom*—that's the name of this whaler—you had passed out."

He glanced at her mound of clothing on the floor. "I'm sorry if I offended your sense of modesty by removing your clothes, but if I'd left you in those wet things you could have frozen to death, or at the very least, fallen ill with pneumonia."

Noting Tasha's bashful blush, he quickly added, "Please rest assured, I did not molest you in any way, though I must admit—restraint was difficult. I had hoped that by this morning you would have recovered enough to discuss your plight with me. But I was called out while you were still asleep, and I thought it best to let you rest."

Tasha studied him carefully, searching for anything in his manner that might indicate he had fabricated the story. He returned her gaze unwaveringly, his eyes entreating her confidence.

"If all that you say is true," she ventured cautiously, "and if I am really not a prisoner, then why did you find it necessary to lock me in?"

Jared cleared his throat uneasily. "Believe me, I only intended to lock others out. Some of the members of the crew have far less control over their urges than I."

"Oh." She flushed and sat up slowly on the bunk, drawing the blanket around her as she drew her knees up, rested her chin on them, and lost herself in thought for a few moments. "If only I could remember!" she wailed. "Is there nothing else I said—no further clue?"

Jared grimly shook his head.

For several minutes Tasha stared at her knees, evaluating all that Jared had revealed to her. Finally she spoke, slowly and uncertainly. "You say I was grasping a section of railing?"

He nodded. "That's what it appeared to be."

"Is it common for such things to be floating in the ocean?"

"Not at all, except in the rare instance of a shipwreck. And I haven't heard of any wrecks in these waters all season."

"Then do you suppose the rail came from the *Ayan?*" She was surprised at her own detachment as she tried to piece together the mystery.

Jared shrugged. "I hardly know what to suppose. I can't imagine how the *Ayan* could have sunk last night. The sea was calm, and I assume the captain had charts of the region, so he would have avoided any possible obstacle. You're sure that you couldn't have fallen overboard? Or could someone have pushed you? Did you have a serious disagreement with anyone aboard the ship—any enemy?"

Tasha laughed huskily. "If someone wished to be rid of me, do you suppose he would have thrown me a piece of wood to keep me afloat? No, I had no enemies aboard the *Ayan*. For the most part, no one paid me much attention. Except, of course, for Nikolai."

"Nikolai?" Jared pounced on the name. "You mentioned that name in your delirium last night. Think hard! Can his name help you recall what happened?"

She screwed her eyes tightly closed and tried to recapture her last encounter with Nikolai. In her mind she saw herself struggling up the ladder to the *Ayan*'s deck; Nikolai, who was standing in the passageway, came forward, his dark eyes filled with concern, and then—"He kissed me," she whispered incredulously.

"What?" Jared sprang to his feet, strangely disturbed at the thought of some Russian stranger, this Nikolai, touching this innocent, vulnerable girl whom he had rescued and protected. Had the man taken other liberties with her?

"He kissed me," Tasha repeated quietly, and then, for the first time, her heart felt wrenched by a hollow fear that she would never see Nikolai again.

"Where? Where did he kiss you?" Jared was pacing the small stateroom now.

"On the cheek."

"No, no! I mean where were you when he kissed you? Were you aboard the *Ayan*?"

"Yes." Suddenly her mind fastened on another detail of the memory. "We were in the passageway below deck, and water was swirling around our feet.

Not just a little water. It kept getting deeper and deeper!"

Jared nodded, encouraging her to go on. "And then what happened?"

She shook her head hopelessly and kneaded her small fists against her temples in agitation. "I don't know. I can't remember."

Still pacing, Jared tried to revive her memory. "If there was water in the lower passageway, the ship must have been sinking. Was there any problem with her during the voyage?" When Tasha shook her head again, he frowned in puzzlement. "Then why would she be sinking? Unless—" he paused and shook his head, "—but that's too preposterous even to imagine."

"What is too preposterous?" Tasha asked anxiously.

Again he shook his head. "Never mind. I'm sure you'd laugh at me for considering it possible."

"I hardly think I'm in a position to laugh at any possibility."

"It's just that I was recalling a case more than forty years ago, when the *Essex* was stove by a whale."

"Stove? I don't understand."

"Rammed. It sank, in fact. It's a common enough occurrence with our little whaleboats, but so far as I know, the *Essex* is the only ship that was ever stove. She was out of Nantucket, and only five men survived the disaster. All five of them are still alive today, but of course they've given up whaling—" his voice trailed off as he noticed Tasha staring at him with wide, terrified eyes. "I'm sorry, I didn't mean to frighten you—" he began.

She cut him off with a violent shake of her head, and sat perfectly still, as if in a trance. In her mind, she saw again white jaws flashing against the midnight sky; again, felt her hands grip the rail as she stared in horror. Her heart pounded at the sudden, vivid memory and she screamed in agony. "That's it! The *Ayan* was stove by a whale!"

Jared stared in disbelief, sure that the frustration

of not being able to remember made her desperate to accept whatever explanation was presented.

"Calm down, and think again," he said gently. "Surely you are mistaken."

She shook her head emphatically. "No, I'm certain of it. I felt the creature hit the ship—it woke me up. And then it hit again and again, as if, for some reason, it was furious with the *Ayan*."

"But if you didn't see it, how can you be sure it was a whale?"

"I did see it! Now I remember. Nikolai had sent me up on deck to prepare to abandon ship. While I was waiting for him at the rail, I saw the whale rise out of the water and come charging at the ship, as though it would punish us for invading its domain!"

Thunderstruck, she cried, "But surely I am not the only person you rescued. There must be others from the *Ayan* aboard this ship."

Slowly, Jared shook his head from side to side.

"Perhaps another of your whaleboats recovered someone and you simply haven't heard yet."

Again, he sadly shook his head.

"But there have to be other survivors!" she cried. "Did you see nothing on your expedition today? No trace of a Russian ship or her crew—no debris to mark the *Ayan*'s grave?" Her voice was trembling so she could hardly speak.

He answered uneasily. "We went off in a different direction today, and the whales we pursued gave us little chance to watch for other ships. The fog was so thick last night it was only through blind luck that we found you."

Tasha's slender body shook with sobs as she cried in a muffled voice, "Oh Nikolai, have I lost you, too? Dear God, am I to be denied every person I dare to love?"

Tears of desperation burned her cheeks and she turned away from Jared to beat her fists against the wall, reaping some small measure of solace from the long-denied outburst.

Watching her agony, Jared felt his own heart constrict in sympathy. He walked to the bunk, sat down beside her, and gently turned her head until it nestled against his chest. Wrapping his arms around her, he rocked her tenderly, brushing his lips against her hair.

"Don't," he murmured. "Don't torment yourself. Perhaps boats from another whaler picked up other survivors from the *Ayan*. Even now, this Nikolai may be safe aboard another ship."

"No," she protested, muffling her sobs in his shirt. "He did not survive—I can feel it."

"Hush now. It is too soon to say that. Perhaps in another day or two we can learn more from other passing whalers. Until then, it will do no good to grieve. For the present, you must depend on me. I will take care of you and see that no further harm befalls you."

"You?" she sniffled. "How do I know I can depend on you—a stranger? I don't even know your name."

"I am Jared Northrup. Second mate of the whaler *Freedom*, out of New Bedford. Now, since it appears you are to be my guest for a time, suppose you tell me your name?"

"Natalya Igorovna Demidova. But everyone calls me Tasha. Or, perhaps I should say," she paused and drew a long, rending sigh, "everyone *called* me Tasha."

"Why do you say *called?*"

"Because there is no one any more to call me anything. Mama is dead. And Olga. My father has banished me from his life. The dear friends I grew up with are far, far away, and now even Nikolai is gone!" She collapsed in a fresh spate of sobs, burying her face in Jared's shoulder.

"Well, now I will call you Tasha," he soothed. "Don't worry, we'll get you to New Archangel. Surely there must be someone waiting for you there."

"Yes. There is a Monsieur Lisovsky—a relative of mama's. But I don't even know him, so I can hardly guess if he will welcome me with open arms—or indeed, if I will be pleased to stay with him."

Tasha threw her arms around Jared, clinging to his

109

comforting warmth as she continued to sob. She hardly noticed as the blanket slipped away from her shoulders. But Jared was painfully aware of her naked breasts pressing against his thin shirt, and he suppressed an agonized groan of passion as he tried to concentrate on comforting the girl.

Her body seemed to sear his like a hot iron and he felt his manhood straining to be free of his trousers. Part of his mind warned him to flee from the stateroom before he did something he would later regret. But when he began to unwind his arms from her, she only clung to him the more, and he hadn't the heart to leave her alone.

Without thinking more about his plight, he gently raised her tear-dappled face and tenderly kissed each of her swollen lids. Her sobs subsided as his lips lightly touched her nose, and she held her breath, perhaps waiting for his mouth to steady her trembling lips.

Jared hesitated, fearful of another attack from her tiny teeth; then brushed his lips quickly across hers. To his surprise, her mouth turned to follow his. In the next moment he was tasting the full sweetness of her delicately curved lips.

Breathlessly, Tasha marveled at the effect of his body touching hers. She felt her skin glowing, as if thousands of tiny fires had been ignited beneath its surface; yet, at the same time, she shivered as she would from the cold. She felt her nipples stiffening against his chest, and a pleasant tingling had begun in her groin. In all the nights she had lain close to Nikolai, never had she known even a hint of the sensations that were now flooding her body, growing more and more insistent as her lips opened to Jared's hungry mouth.

At the same time, Jared felt his own desire rising to an uncontrollable pitch. He had meant only to comfort and calm her, but feeling her body molded against him, he was suddenly swept away by his surging passions.

Tasha felt herself falling backwards on the bunk, seemingly suspended in space, unable and unwilling to change the course of events. Then she was lying on the narrow bed and for a moment Jared's chest seemed to crush her breasts. Still kissing her, he shifted his weight until they lay side by side—as their tongues met, sighs of languid pleasure escaped them both.

He moved a hand to fondle one of her small, firm breasts, drawing a finger lightly back and forth over its nipple until it stood fully erect. Tasha whimpered a meek protest as he took his mouth away from hers. But the whimper quickly turned to moans of pleasure as his tongue moved teasingly down her neck, along the hollow between her breasts, then back up to the crest of first one breast, then the other. She slid her hands through his straight blond hair, instinctively holding his head to her breast, helplessly yielding to the surging riot of pleasure and desire pulsing through her body.

Jared suckled at each engorged nipple in turn, while his hand began to creep lower on her body, past her slender waist, across her flat, smooth belly, stopping at the delta throbbing between her thighs.

Jared's fingers caressed her virginal recesses ceaselessly, sending tremors of voluptuous excitement up her spine until her body craved for fulfillment. Suddenly Tasha tensed, realizing for the first time the seriousness of what was happening. She felt afraid of the unknown . . . afraid of what Jared—still hardly more than a stranger—would think of her after he had used her body to slake his desires.

She felt his warm breath in her ear as he whispered, "What's the matter, love? Don't be afraid. I'll be gentle. I won't hurt you." His fingers continued their exploration and she felt her body dissolving as he asked, "Don't you want me, Tasha?"

She shook her head mutely, confused and unsure how to respond.

Abruptly, he took his hand away from her. Tasha

111

drew her breath in at the sudden cessation of pleasure. "I don't know," she stammered huskily. "I don't know what to say. I don't know what to do. I'm so afraid."

"You needn't be," he murmured comfortingly. "I'll take care of you. Trust me. Just tell me what you want."

His lips covered hers again and he pulled her close. Feeling his strong body pressed against hers, Tasha had no doubt of what she wanted at that moment.

Jared raised his head to gaze into her dark eyes, searching for her answer. Her gaze wavered as she fought her conflicting emotions, and her throat and mouth felt suddenly dry. His eyes told her he would not force her, yet she sensed he would be terribly disappointed if she refused him now. And her own disappointment would not be small.

Unable to utter the word they both ardently wished to hear, she tilted up her chin, about to nod assent, when the stillness was shattered by a sharp rap at the door. Both Jared and Tasha swung their eyes to the door, not daring to breathe as they waited for the intruder to leave.

When Jared did not answer, the knock was repeated and the third mate's voice announced, "All hands on deck, Mr. Northrup. Captain Dawson's boat just came back with whale—a good-sized bowhead. They're already breaking out the cutting stage."

Jared groaned in pain as he pulled himself away from Tasha's body.

"Did you hear, Jared?" the mate's voice came again.

"I heard you," Jared muttered. "Damned whales don't know when to keep out of sight."

He swung off the bed and turned to look ruefully at Tasha. "You might as well get some sleep," he sighed. "I'm not likely to be back before morning."

Chapter Ten

1863

A strange emptiness crept over Tasha as Jared closed the door behind him. Not bothering to light a candle, she wrapped herself in the rough blanket and paced in the darkening stateroom, mulling over the events of the evening. If the third mate had not knocked, she would, at that very moment, be beneath Jared, experiencing for the first time the full meaning of womanhood. Would he have been gentle with her, as he had been in the earlier moments? Or, once having gained her consent, would he have been brutally rough, as he had been in his angry moments at the beginning of the evening?

Now, having been granted a reprieve from her decision, would she still make the same choice if he asked her again? Would he ask her again? Could she say no? Did any part of her even wish to say no?

The image of Nikolai, kissing her in the passageway of the *Ayan*, flashed through her mind, and she felt a sharp pang of guilt. She had learned of his probable death only moments before, and already she had begun to disgrace his memory. But could he possibly blame her after all the opportunities he had allowed to pass, when he could have claimed her as his own? Could anyone possibly blame her for responding to something that seemed so right and inevitable?

Thinking of Nikolai, and then thinking again of Jared, confused her.

In the last months, as she traveled with Nikolai, she had slowly come to believe that she was in love with him. Except for their one misunderstanding, which now seemed buried in the distant past, she

113

had learned to know him as a gentle, considerate person, deeply concerned with her welfare. Indeed, during her masquerade as his wife on the *Ayan*, she had begun to fantasize about really becoming his wife some day. A future with Nikolai had begun to seem secure and pleasant.

But now Jared had uncovered a completely unknown part of her nature, and she wondered if she could ever again feel content with another man. How could she understand the feelings he had aroused within her? Could it be passion? In her sheltered life at Birchwood, she had always supposed that only men experienced passion. As far as she knew, her mother and Olga had never felt the need to be with men. And she suspected that her father's friend Anya had acted as she did only to secure lavish gifts from him, not from any physical needs or desires.

But if she had not felt passion, what had she felt? Could it be love? Could she have fallen in love with someone she hardly knew—even while she believed she loved someone else?

Tasha closed her eyes, and imagined Jared's mouth on hers. Once again she felt his firm, muscular body pressed full-length against her quivering flesh, his hardness pulsating against her belly. In her own loins she felt a warm throbbing, as she thought again of his gently probing fingers.

"Oh Jared!" she moaned, throwing herself on the narrow bunk, "what kind of demon are you, that you have already enslaved both my mind and my body? What strange powers do you and your hellship hold? Will you also have my heart—or do you possess it already?"

She buried herself beneath the blanket, seeking the escape that only sleep could bring. The bed, though built for only one person, seemed strangely empty.

Whatever the explanation for her feelings and actions, she knew that Jared had a power over her that no other man had ever exerted. Something in her could hardly wait for her next encounter with

114

him and his ability to render her utterly pliable—to make her own desires match his.

Tasha's emotions raged within her for hours until at last they exhausted her, and she slept.

A gnawing pain in her stomach awakened Tasha and she realized she had not eaten in more than a day. She opened her eyes, slowly sat up on the bunk, and looked around the stateroom, now flooded with daylight. As he had predicted, Jared had not returned.

She swung her legs to the floor and stood up. Weak from hunger, she swayed unsteadily for a moment, then slowly walked to the stateroom door and tried the handle. To her astonishment, the door opened. In his agitation the night before, Jared had forgotten to lock it.

As she opened the door a crack, a delicious aroma floated in from the passageway. Tasha sniffed, trying to identify the smell. It was unfamiliar, but that hardly mattered. It was definitely food, it made her mouth water, and she intended to find its source. There was only one problem—she had nothing to wear.

Closing the door quickly, she looked around the room for something to cover her nakedness. Her dress and undergarments were hopelessly shredded. Jared had destroyed the shirt of his she had worn the day before. The blanket was not large enough both to cover her and tie securely in place. Then her eyes fell on the sea chest and she raced across the room to lift up its heavy lid.

Beneath a razor and a few other toilet articles lay a neatly folded, striped shirt and a pair of rough, blue trousers. With a cry of relief, Tasha pulled them out of the chest and struggled into them. Like the shirt she had worn the day before, this one almost reached her knees and the cuffs dangled below her wrists. After rolling the sleeves up to a manageable length, she stepped into the trousers and stuffed the shirttails into them. Quickly buttoning the front of the trousers, she bent to roll up the legs.

The moment she moved, the pants slid down from her waist and dropped to the floor. Even with the extra bulk provided by the voluminous shirt, her slender hips could not support the trousers.

Glancing despairingly into the sea chest for some other, more suitable clothing, Tasha's eyes spotted a small sewing kit. Delighted, she found a threaded needle and, pulling the trousers back up, quickly sewed a deep tuck on each side of the waistband. She was about to leave the stateroom when the door opened and Jared entered.

His clothes were splattered with oil, and his face was drawn from a strenuous, sleepless night, but after one look at Tasha he threw back his head and laughed heartily.

"Just what is so amusing?" she demanded.

He choked back his laughter. "You, my love. Have you any idea how comical you look."

She tossed her head and looked down at the shapeless outfit. "Well, I couldn't go out looking for food without any clothes. And I do have to eat, you know." She stared at Jared meaningfully.

"I'm sorry," he sighed, "I couldn't get away to bring you anything. I hardly got a bite myself all day. Did you manage to find something for yourself?"

"Not yet. I was just about to go out. Something out there smells wonderfully like food."

He nodded. "The smell is coming from Captain Dawson's cabin—salt pork and beans."

"Well," she wrinkled her nose impishly, "whatever it is, at least it smells better than you. What is that awful stench?"

"Whale oil and smoke, mostly, and no doubt a bit of blood and guts. I had intended to change clothes when I got down here, but," he patted her buttocks playfully, "you seem to have helped yourself to my last clean shirt and trousers."

She shrugged. "I didn't mean to pry into your personal belongings. But I had to have something to wear."

"That point is debatable—but," he walked toward his sea chest, "if you'd been patient and looked a bit further, I think you could have found more suitable attire."

He knelt beside the chest and pushed aside several layers of belongings as he dug to the bottom. Finally, finding what he wanted, he tugged it out and held it up before Tasha's eyes. It was an emerald green silk gown with a low, square, ruffled neckline and more ruffles at the hemline and cuffs.

The sight of the exquisite gown set off a confusing chain of questions in Tasha's mind. Why did Jared have a woman's gown in his sea chest? Was it for his wife? His lover? His fiancée? Had it been left behind by some previous visitor to his stateroom? If she had submitted to him last night, would she have been one of a series of quickly forgotten conquests?

"Well," Jared teased, throwing the gown at her, "you certainly don't seem too pleased! Perhaps you prefer wearing men's clothing after all!"

"No, I—" she faltered. "It's just that I'm afraid the gown is intended for someone else—and perhaps your wife would not be pleased to give up her present for a Russian girl."

"Wife, did you say?" Jared's laughter filled the stateroom. "What makes you think I've been fool enough to marry anyone? But you're right, the gown was intended for someone else. I bought it for my sister, Clarissa, when we put in at San Francisco last year. However, I'm sure she would agree that you are more in need of it at the moment, just as I am in great need of my shirt and trousers."

Stepping over to Tasha, he took a small knife from his pocket and quickly sliced through the stitches in the trousers, releasing the tucks she had hastily sewn at the waistline. The trousers instantly fell to her feet, and Tasha turned away, blushing in embarrassment.

"I believe you've made your point," she said softly. "But would you do me the courtesy of allowing me to dress in privacy?"

117

Jared grinned. "That hardly seems necessary after the various states of dress—and undress—in which I've seen you. But to appease your sense of modesty, I'll turn my back till you've gotten into the dress."

While Jared stood facing the wall, Tasha quickly pulled his shirt off over her head, and stepped out of his trousers and into the dress. After several moments of fumbling with the tiny buttons at its back, she lamely admitted, "I can't get it fastened. Could you help me, please?"

"I don't know," he teased, "I'm not very good at doing buttons with my eyes closed!"

"Oh, you are impossible! Come help me before I throw your precious shirt and trousers into the sea!" She picked up his clothing and rushed threateningly toward the porthole.

Catching her lightly by the waist, Jared laughed. "All right, you little imp. Now hold still while I button you up."

At his touch, Tasha quivered and dropped the pile of clothes to the floor. She stood quietly, holding her long black hair above her head, to allow him to see the buttons. Feeling his fingers at her back, she longed to turn, throw her arms around him, and press her lips to his. She wondered if her nearness was stirring him, and, if so, would it be more than just a passing diversion?

Standing behind her, Jared gazed longingly at Tasha's smooth, creamy skin. More than a head taller than she, he could see right over her shoulders. The fabric of the dress, which was cut for a fuller-bosomed woman, swung away from her body permitting an enticing glimpse of her small, firm breasts. Watching them rise and fall as he leaned over her shoulder, Jared longed to cup them in his hands and caress them as he had the night before. He bent down to fasten the buttons at her waist, marveling at its delicate size. His two large hands could easily span it, though she was not even wearing a corset.

God, why did she have to be so damned beautiful?

All day, as he had chopped away at the whale blubber and watched over the men boiling it down into oil in the try-pots, he had not been able to get her out of his mind. If the third mate had not knocked when he did last night, he would surely have taken her—it was inevitable. How would he then have faced himself, and her, in the morning? The girl was too innocent to be seduced by some stranger on a whaler. She deserved more than a passing liaison that would be forced to end when they reached New Archangel—and he was far too foot-loose to be able to offer her more. Yes, it was for the best that they had been interrupted. But, how to resist her in the weeks that lay ahead?

Jared finished buttoning the dress and stood for a moment, his hands resting lightly on Tasha's shoulders. He felt her tense under his touch, waiting for his next move, and he sensed that she would submit to him without a struggle. If he remained there any longer, feeling and seeing and smelling her delicate young body, he would certainly lose control.

Dropping his hands, he turned and strode to the door. "Stay here," he whispered hoarsely as he let himself into the passageway. "I'll bring you something to eat. It's not safe for you to go wandering around the ship."

Tasha stared after him in confusion. Her eyes fell to his clean clothes, now forgotten on the floor, and she shook her head slowly. He had seemed so playful and friendly. What had she done to bring about his sudden change in mood?

Jared returned a few moments later with a plate of food for her. Before leaving again, he tersely informed her that Captain Dawson refused to interrupt his whaling run for her, but had agreed to deliver her in New Archangel after the northern whaling season was finished and the *Freedom* was heading south again.

He did not return to the stateroom again that day, or even that night. In the morning, he brought Tasha

119

a mug of strong coffee and some hardtack, but he appeared strained.

"I thought you would return last night," Tasha said timidly, as she broke off a piece of hardtack and dipped it into her coffee.

"I was on night watch," Jared replied gruffly.

"All night? That seems an unfair task for one man."

"No. Not all night. But it was a clear, pleasant night so I decided to sleep on deck."

"Oh." She tried to conceal the hurt in her voice and leaned forward to set the mug of coffee on Jared's desk.

Her dress drooped away from her bosom as she moved and Jared groaned inwardly at the tempting sight of her ivory breasts. "Can't you do anything to make that dress fit you better?" he snapped.

"Well, yes. I suppose I could take it in a bit."

"Then I suggest you do. Your appearance is nothing short of scandalous."

Scalded by his tone, Tasha stammered, "I didn't want to ruin something that didn't belong to me."

"For God's sake, woman," Jared thundered, "think what you're doing to me! It's driving me to distraction, falling out of that dress the way you are. Do something about it!"

"Oh!" Tasha flushed with embarrassment and hurried to the sea chest to find the sewing kit. "I'll take care of it at once. I had no idea—" Jared stalked out of the stateroom while Tasha struggled to open the dress's buttons.

In the next several days, Jared Northrup spent very little time in his room. Except for a few days when he was out in one of the whaleboats, he brought Tasha three meals each day and tried to see to any of her other needs. But now he seldom sat in the room to talk with her, and he never allowed himself to touch her. He was kind, and amiable enough, but noticeably detached.

For the first few nights he would not even sleep in

the room with her, saying he preferred the open deck. But as they traveled further north, through the Bering Straits and into the Arctic Ocean, he admitted the deck was too cold at night. Still, he never returned to his quarters until late at night, after Tasha had retired. And then he always slept on the floor, leaving Tasha by herself in the bed.

Alone for most of each day, Tasha pondered Jared's strangely aloof attitude. Was there something about her that he found repulsive? Some flaw in her body? Something about her Russian heritage? Why had he been so tender, so intimate and loving on that first night—and so cold and distant now?

Several times when he slipped into the stateroom late at night, thinking her asleep, Tasha lay awake, aching to have him lie beside her, to have him brush kisses across her face, to feel his comforting arms around her again. Some nights she had to bury her face in the mattress to keep herself from crying out, from begging him to bring to full flower the sensations he had given her a small taste of.

But she resolved never to beg him for anything. She would continue to be gracious and grateful to him for rescuing her from the sea. But, no matter how her pulse quickened whenever he entered the stateroom, she would not let him know her true feelings.

Chapter Eleven

1863

It was Sunday, more than a month after Tasha's rescue from the sea. Jared had already eaten dinner with the other mates in the captain's cabin, and now he sat moodily in his stateroom, watching Tasha devour the portions he had brought her.

Even with the barrier he had created between them, his desire for her had not diminished. Worse, it was stronger than ever. He wondered if she had any idea of his torment. Since she had altered the dress, it fit her perfectly, accenting each graceful curve. Her hair, burnished by frequent use of the hairbrush she had found in his chest, flowed over her shoulders. It had the soft, inviting texture of black velvet. How he longed to bury his hands within that hair, and to crush her to him!

He fervently hoped they would soon have their full catch of bowheads. Then the *Freedom* could sail south, and he could leave the little temptress in New Archangel. Surely, once she was off the ship, he could get her out of his mind.

The lookout's shrill cry interrupted his musing. "Blows! There she blows! There she whitewaters!"

"Where away?" came Captain Dawson's muffled cry.

"Three points off the lee beam, sir!"

Jared's hand was on the door handle in an instant.

"Jared?" Tasha's soft voice stopped him, and he turned to see her dark eyes pleading. "Do you think I could go up on deck while you're out?"

He shook his head adamantly. "Absolutely not! It wouldn't be safe."

"But if all the men are off in the whaleboats, who can possibly bother me?"

"They won't all be gone. There are always the ship-keepers—the cooper, the blacksmith, and a few others—to tend to things while we're gone. I wouldn't want you up on deck if I'm not there to protect you."

"But you never take me up there! Even when you *are* around to protect me. I think you're ashamed you fished me out of the sea!" She pushed out her lower lip in a hurt pout.

Jared sighed irritably. "I haven't time to argue now, Tasha."

"Then at least promise to take me on deck when

you return, Jared. I need fresh air and exercise. I'm beginning to feel like a caged animal down here."

He glanced quickly around the small stateroom and knew she was not exaggerating. He would go insane if he had to stay there for days on end. "All right," he sighed, "we'll discuss it when I get back." Quickly he stepped into the passageway, locking the door and hurrying to the ladder before Tasha could argue any more.

From the port, Tasha watched as four whaleboats went after the spouting, blue-black form of a giant bowhead whale. She could see Jared standing on a small platform in the stern of the lead boat, handling the steering oar with one hand, and gesturing to his crew with the other. Through him, she felt the thrill and terror of the chase as they bore down on a beast that seemed to dwarf their frail boat.

She saw the harpooner struggling to the small platform in the bow of the boat, his weapon raised above his shoulder. With a quick, graceful thrust, he sent the harpoon flying into the whale's back. The creature reared from the sea in sudden fury, thrashing its tail violently. Tasha was sure it would overturn the small whaleboat. Then it lurched forward, swimming away furiously, pulling the whaleboat along behind it. Tasha turned away from the port, unable to watch as the whale towed Jared's boat to what she felt sure would be inevitable destruction. By the time she had the courage to look out again, the boat was no more than a small speck, barely discernible in the distance.

It was near dark when Tasha heard the stateroom door being unlocked. When she saw Jared framed in the doorway, she flew into his arms and astounded him with an energetic kiss on the lips.

Tasha felt a flush spreading over her face as Jared gently untwined her arms from his neck, pushed her into the stateroom, and closed the door.

"To what do I owe this rare greeting?" he asked, his eyes glittering with amusement.

Embarrassed, Tasha turned away. "I—I was just glad to see you return unharmed. I watched some of the action from the port, and I was sure that the monster would take you so far you would never find your way back."

Jared laughed. "That sometimes happens, you know. He gave us quite a ride, all right, but it was nothing we couldn't handle. That's one whale that won't be towing any more whaleboats."

"You destroyed him?" Tasha wondered why her voice cracked, why she felt sympathy for a creature that might have been the very one that wrecked the *Ayan.*

"Of course we finished him! That's what we're out here for. Don't tell me you think I'm a murderer for that?"

"No." She laughed self-consciously. "Of course not."

Jared shrugged. "I can see why Captain Dawson doesn't like women on his whalers. I guess all this killing and cutting up could offend a lady's sense of decency. Anyway, I just came down to see if I could get you something. Mr. Andrews's boat just brought in another bowhead, so with two of them to take care of I'll probably be on the cutting stage all night, and most of tomorrow, too."

Tasha squared her shoulders and turned to face him. "I'm coming with you."

"What?" Jared shook his head incredulously. "I don't think you know what you're saying. Just a minute ago you were upset about us killing the whale and now you want to watch us hack it up!"

"I just want some fresh air! You promised to take me on deck when you returned."

"I did not *promise* you anything. Listen, Tasha, I just don't think this would be the best time for you to be wandering around."

"I don't intend to wander around. I do have enough sense to keep out of the way, you know. And this would probably be the best possible time for me to go on deck. The men will all be so busy none of them will even have time to notice me."

Jared hesitated, considering her logic. Then he shrugged and sighed. "All right. I won't argue with you any more. I haven't got the time, and I can see you won't listen, anyway. Just be sure to stay out of the way. Stay away from the cutting stage. It gets pretty slippery from all the grease, and well—I might have second thoughts about fishing you out of the ocean a second time. Also, keep away from the try-works once they start boiling the blubber—a splash of hot oil could give you a nasty burn."

Tasha nodded obediently, trying to picture in her mind what the cutting stage and try-works would be like.

Going to his sea chest, Jared pulled out a bulky denim jacket and threw it around her shoulders. "Here, you'd better take this. You'll get cold standing in the night air. If you tire, you'll have to find your way down by yourself. I won't be able to stop work and escort you."

He led Tasha above and to the forward deck under the curious glances of the crewmen who were hurrying to erect the cutting stage over the side of the ship. The stage was a narrow platform suspended over one of the dead whales, which was securely chained at the *Freedom*'s side. The other whale floated a short distance from the ship, a marker flag flapping above its massive shape. Behind the foremast, they passed the try-works, a kind of brick-enclosed stove that held the fire and cauldrons. When they reached the foredeck, Jared stopped and indicated a spot by the rail.

"You will be out of the way here, but you should be able to see everything if you're interested. Now I must get to work." He headed for the cutting stage, then turned to give her one final warning. "I almost forgot, whatever you do, keep out of the way if the captain gives the order, 'Splice the main brace'."

As Tasha regarded him quizzically, he explained, "That means he's going to pour a glass of grog for every man—and no one in his right mind comes between a sailor and his grog!"

Whistling, he turned and sauntered aft, climbing over the ship's side to the now-completed cutting stage. Captain Dawson and Mr. Andrews, the first mate, were already at work with long-handled cutting spades, chopping the whale's head away from its body. Tasha swallowed hard as she watched a dark cloud of blood spreading through the water alongside the *Freedom*.

Turning to wave to her, Jared picked up a cutting spade and began to slice into the blubber on the whale's body. Some of the crew members attached a hook and chain to the first piece of blubber that loosened. Others strained at a winch to which the chain was attached, hauling the strip of blubber up to the deck. The whale's carcass began to turn over slowly in the water as its blubber was stripped away. Jared continued to slice at the blubber, so it came away in long, spiral strips, like apple peel falling away from a knife.

Pausing to mop his brow with his forearm, Jared glanced at Tasha, standing rigidly by the rail. Even in his bulky jacket, her feminine form was apparent. Her hair was rumpled by the breeze, and against the backdrop of the darkening sky she looked like some tempting sprite.

He knew that all the men envied him, that they whispered among themselves about the second mate's luck in having a wench in his stateroom, ready for him to bed whenever he pleased. If they could know he had not even taken her once, they would laugh him right off the ship. If only he didn't feel so damned responsible for everything that happened to her!

"Mr. Northrup!" Captain Dawson's gruff voice cut in on his thoughts. "Do you intend to work or dream away the rest of the night?"

"Sorry, sir." Still gazing back at Tasha, Jared turned

to continue cutting. The cutting stage was already slick with splattered grease and his foot slipped. Struggling to regain his balance, he lost his grip on the awkward cutting spade. Its blade slashed into his leg before the tool bounced off the stage and into the ocean.

Convulsed by the searing pain that shot up through his leg and into his body, Jared fell to the stage, clutching its edge just in time to save himself from following the spade into the water.

"Jared!" Tasha cried as she rushed from the bow. She already had one leg over the side of the ship, ready to climb onto the stage, when a strong grip stopped her.

"Stay here, missy! I'll bring your man back to you." She turned her head and recognized the third mate, who had passed the stateroom door at the precise moment she had kissed Jared that evening.

"We can't have both of you overboard," he said as he gently pushed her back and climbed over the side.

Tasha nodded numbly, gripping the rail as she watched the man hurry to where Jared lay.

He threw Jared's arm around his neck and pulled him to his feet. Gritting his teeth, Jared hopped along beside the man as the mate guided him as far as the rail. Two members of the crew reached over to help him to the deck, where Jared collapsed in pain, gripping his bleeding leg.

The men scattered as Captain Dawson barked, "There's plenty of work to be done yet, men. No sense everyone stopping just because we've lost one. You, Adams," he called to the third mate, "take Mr. Northrup's place on the stage." He paused to glare at Tasha for a moment. "See if you can get him below and out of the way, girl." With an irritated snort, the captain turned back to the whale's carcass.

Kneeling beside Jared, Tasha cradled his head in her lap. "Jared," she sobbed helplessly, her own tears falling freely across his ashen face, "are you badly hurt?"

Attempting a smile, he replied, "I suspect I'll live."

He leaned forward to examine his leg, and seeing the blood still gushing out, lay back and pulled his shirt over his head.

"Here," he said, handing the shirt to Tasha, "tear it into strips for a bandage, until we can get below and take a better look at it. Tie it tightly so it stops the bleeding."

As Tasha struggled to do his bidding, he pulled his trouser leg over the wound, wincing as the fabric caught the raw tissue.

Tasha's gentle fingers pushed his hands away. Then she eased his trouser leg higher and began binding the ugly gash. As she knotted the ends of the bandage, he smiled wanly. "All right now, if you can help me up we'll go below and see about the damage."

With one arm wrapped around Tasha's shoulders and the other hand grasping the rail, Jared struggled to his feet and hopped bravely toward the stern, trying to keep his weight off his injured leg.

As they neared the ladder, Jared stopped, leaned against the rail, and took a deep breath. "We'll have to move away from the side of the ship now," he mumbled, "and I won't have the rail to hold onto. Do you think you can stand to support a bit more of my weight?"

Tasha nodded, tensing her muscles in preparation. As they moved from the rail, her frame sagged beneath the added burden, but she bit her lip in determination and continued to edge slowly toward the companionway.

Sensing her struggle, Jared tried to place some weight on his injured leg, but as he stepped down, a flash of white-hot pain shook his body and he leaned heavily on Tasha's shoulders. Straining under the sudden shift in weight, Tasha stumbled and fell face forward onto the deck, bringing Jared sprawling beside her.

"Oh, Jared, I'm so sorry!" she cried tearfully. "Here,

let me help you to get up." In vain, she tugged at his arm.

"No," he mumbled, clenching his teeth against the pain. "I'm too heavy for you. Next thing you'll be injured too—if you aren't already."

"But we must get you to your quarters!"

He began to crawl, slowly and painfully, over the remaining distance to the companionway. Reaching the hatch, he maneuvered his sound foot onto the top rung of the ladder, then, step by step, haltingly descended to the passageway and crawled to the door of his stateroom.

Inside the room, he managed to pull himself halfway up onto his bunk, murmuring his thanks to Tasha as she strained to help him the rest of the way.

After making sure he was as comfortable as possible, she lit a candle so she could unwind the makeshift bandage. At the first glance, she gasped in alarm —the bandage was soaked through with dark red blood.

Jared forced a smile and squeezed her hand weakly. "Go to the galley—above the captain's cabin—for some hot water to cleanse the wound," he directed. Tasha was at the door when he added, "But first, there's a flask of rum in my sea chest. Could you bring it to me?"

She nodded silently and searched in the chest until she found the flask. She supported him in a half-sitting position while he gulped three long swallows of the strong liquor, then hurried out to find the galley.

When she returned, carrying a pot of boiling water and some clean linen towels she intended to use for fresh bandages, Jared's eyes were closed. The half-empty flask lay on its side next to the bunk.

Fearing the worst, Tasha rushed to him with a cry of anguish. But as she lay her head on his chest, a shallow movement assured her that he was still breathing. With a sigh of relief, she began removing the bloody bandage. Now that Jared lay resting, the bleeding had ceased. Tasha expected him to thrash in pain as she pulled away the last bit of bandage. However, he continued breathing peacefully, numb to her touch.

As she washed the wound, cleaning away the bits of dried blood and scraps of fabric, she discovered it was not as deep as she had at first feared. Still, it looked ugly, and she worried about the chance for infection. She picked up the rum flask and opened it. For a moment, she hesitated, then she shrugged and poured a liberal dash of the alcohol over the wound before binding it up with clean linen.

Tasha threw the soiled bandages and reddened water out the port, then turned to look at Jared. His bare chest and arms still glistened with sweat from the exertion of getting to his stateroom, and his trousers were streaked with whale blood and grease. She decided to return to the galley for more fresh water to bathe him.

Tenderly, Tasha washed his face, pushing aside his thick blond hair as she bent to plant a tender kiss on his forehead. She worked downward, bathing his arms and chest—thrilled to feel his taut, firm muscles beneath her hands—and when she reached his waist, barely hesitated a moment before slowly inching off his stained trousers so she could finish bathing him.

Only when she had finished cleansing Jared and covered him with a blanket, did Tasha pause to look at herself. With dismay she noted that her dress—the one Jared had bought for his sister—was blotched with bloodstains. Removing the dress, she sponged the spots over and over until they disappeared. She draped the dress over the chair by Jared's desk, hoping the water itself would not damage the emerald silk.

Exhausted from her efforts and the emotional impact of the accident, Tasha sighed and looked longingly at the bunk. After all the nights Jared had slept on the floor, allowing her the luxury of the whole bed, she should now do the same for him. But—she had lost so many loved ones!—surely it would not bother him if she lay still beside him during the night.

Blowing out the candle, Tasha slid beneath the blanket and snuggled against Jared.

The stateroom was still dark when Tasha felt Jared begin to move beside her. She held her breath, afraid that she had moved in her sleep and somehow disturbed him. He rolled toward her, folding her in his arms, and she felt the thick, curly hair of his chest tickling her cheek. She could sense that his breathing was stronger than a few hours earlier.

"Jared," she whispered, "are you all right?"

"Mmm. Wonderful," he murmured, rubbing his face in her silky hair.

"Should I get up so you can rest more peacefully?"

"No." His arms tightened around her. "Don't leave me."

She felt herself beginning to melt in his embrace, willing to accept whatever might follow. His hands massaged her back, running lightly and quickly along her spine until she shivered with pleasure. Reaching lower, he grasped her buttocks, gently kneading them as he drew her groin closer to his. She parted her lips as his mouth met hers and she felt his tongue, still holding a mild flavor of rum, enter her mouth. Without thinking, she responded, flicking her own tongue into his mouth, making him groan with pleasure.

She slid her arms beneath his, circling his back and pulling his chest tighter against her breasts. Her breasts seemed to be pulsing, tingling, burning with the need for him. She felt an even stronger heat throbbing in her groin as he rubbed himself back and forth across her smooth, soft belly, making her aware of his hardness. His hand slid between her

131

legs, stroking her quivering thighs for a moment, then creeping higher to explore her moist pulsing pocket of desire.

She gasped and squirmed away as his fingers found her most sensitive spot, but he coaxed her back to him, planting a path of fiery kisses on her throat, her breasts, her belly. He ended with a quick kiss at the dark delta of her thighs before bringing his mouth back to hers, drowning her moans of newly discovered passion.

He rolled atop her, sliding his legs between hers. Tasha instinctively raised her knees, opening herself to him as she felt his manhood between her thighs. He entered her slowly, gently. His arms tightened their embrace as, with a single, forcible thrust, he pierced the veil of her virginity. Tasha bit hard into her lower lip, unwilling to cry out her pain, but tears coursed down her cheeks in the darkness.

Feeling her tense beneath him, Jared whispered, "Relax, my love. The pain lasts only a moment. Relax and feel the wonder of love." His tongue found her tears, licking them away from her cheeks as he began to rock to and fro over her, moving gently within her.

Tasha sighed in relief as the pain began to subside.

Now a new sensation began to grow in her groin. At first it was only a warm, pleasant tingling, but soon became a craving that surged and struggled within her. With quick sighs of pleasure, she arched her buttocks upward, straining to meet him. She and Jared were no longer two separate bodies. They had become one entity, moaning ecstatically, moving voluptuously—giving and receiving pleasure at the same time. Eagerly, her lips accepted his mouth again and she absorbed not only his kisses, but, she felt, his whole being.

When Jared finally fell away from her, Tasha stifled a whimpered plea for more. She molded herself against his chest, listening to the loud thumping of his heart as she rubbed her face in his fur and inhaled the scent that was his alone. He crooked an arm around her back, burying his own face in her hair, kissing it softly in the warm aftermath of love.

In a few moments, his breathing became more relaxed, and Tasha knew that he had fallen asleep. She felt secure and at ease in his arms, as if she had waited all her life for the security of his embrace. On reflection, she knew she did not regret any of what had just happened. But she wondered if Jared would regret it—or even remember it. Could he have acted out of a delirious dream—perhaps a reaction to his wound? Or, had he at last unmasked his true feelings for her? And if so, would he admit to those feelings when they faced one another in the morning?

Chapter Twelve

1863

Jared opened his eyes as the early morning light streamed into the stateroom. As he turned his head, he felt Tasha's silky hair against his cheek. Her delicate form nestled against him brought back warm memories of their lovemaking. Still, for all the sweetness of their union, he could not help but regret that he had taken her. She was not some dockside slut to be enjoyed by every passing sailor, and he knew he had been wrong to succumb to the temptation.

It was too late to change what had happened, but he would have to try somehow to keep her from misinterpreting the incident. He could offer her nothing—though she deserved so much.

Sleeping peacefully, her face bathed by the soft light she looked more innocent than ever. Yet last night she had proven herself to be a woman in the most wonderful sense.

He flexed his arm beneath her, trying to ease the numbness resulting from holding her all through the night. At his movement, her eyes flew open and she regarded him shyly, as if searching for something in his eyes.

"Good morning, Jared," she murmured sleepily. She snuggled closer to him, luxuriating in the pleasure she still felt. "Did you sleep well?" she asked timidly.

"As well as could be expected with an aching leg." He tried to sound offhanded, hoping to prevent any discussion of their lovemaking.

"Oh." She had hoped he would say he had slept wonderfully, that he would somehow allude to their union. She could not hide the disappointment in her voice. She stretched slowly to disguise her uneasiness. "I'm so hungry."

Jared nodded. "Then perhaps you could go and find us something to eat. I'm famished, too. The rest of the crew should still be occupied with the cutting-in and trying-out, so there shouldn't be anyone around to annoy you."

"If you wish. I'll go now." Tasha slid from the bed and went to get her gown.

Watching her through half-closed eyes, Jared marveled at the power her slender body had over him. He had known scores of women—some of them breathtakingly beautiful, and all of them of a more mature and voluptuous build than she—but none had fascinated him like this guileless girl.

He had spent countless evenings swapping stories of amorous conquest with the other mates, but he knew he would never tell anyone about his moments with Tasha. There was something too precious—almost sacred—about them. The others could tease him and fantasize as they wished about the Russian wench in his stateroom—he would neither confirm nor deny their conjectures.

After watching her struggle for a few moments with the buttons at the back of her dress, Jared commanded softly, "Come here, I'll do that for you."

Shrugging, she went to perch on the edge of the

bunk, and he started to work the buttons. When she felt his fingers at her back, she began to tremble. Determined not to let him know her feelings, she squared her shoulders resolutely and stiffened her spine. The moment she felt him close the last button, she jumped from the bed and hurried to the door. "I'll be just a few minutes," she called back over her shoulder as she left the stateroom.

As soon as she left, Jared felt overcome by a great sense of guilt. He should have maintained control over his passion. He should have remembered all his reasons for staying away from her these last weeks. Oh, if only she had not insisted on sleeping alongside of him!

Surely she was not so ignorant that she could not have guessed what might happen! Or had she remembered their first evening together and—wished it to happen?

It's useless, he thought. How it had come about made no difference. The truth was, he was more experienced than she and he alone was responsible. But he had to make her understand that they were not in love with each other. It would be hard enough for her to face the future, having surrendered her virginity—he did not want her pining away in New Archangel for a man she mistakenly considered her first love. For the rest of the voyage, he would have to be more careful, to protect her from both his desires and from her own confused emotions.

Tasha returned, carrying steaming plates of rice and salt junk, the heavily salted beef that was a staple on most whalers. "We were in luck," she smiled, trying to mask her sadness, "the cook had just fed the men on deck and was glad to dish out the leftovers to me." She wrinkled her nose over the plates. "I'm afraid it makes for an unappetizing breakfast, but I suspect it will fill our stomachs."

Jared was sitting up in bed, his back propped against the wall. She handed one plate to him, then seated herself at his desk with the other. They had just begun to eat when there was a sharp rap at the door.

"Who is it?" Jared called.

"Captain Dawson. I'd like a word with you, Mr. Northrup."

"By all means, sir. The door's open."

As the captain entered, Tasha scurried across the room to sit on the sea chest, leaving the chair free for him. He nodded curtly to her, then sat down and faced Jared.

"You'll forgive me for not rising, captain," Jared said, running his fingers through his hair to tidy it, "but I've not yet had the opportunity to dress, and I still haven't determined how much weight this leg will bear."

Captain Dawson waved aside his apologies. "No need to explain, Mr. Northrup. I merely thought I'd stop in and inquire about the wound."

"I appreciate your concern, sir, and I can assure you I'll be back fulfilling my duties in short order. I believe Tasha treated the wound quite capably."

The captain's eyes darted to Tasha, perched on the sea chest, quietly eating her meal. Turning back to Jared, he gave the young man a pensive stare. "What puzzles me, Mr. Northrup, is how such an accident could befall a man of your experience and competence."

Jared shrugged. "Well, I suppose even the most experienced whaleman has a careless moment now and then."

The captain raised his eyebrows and hardened his voice. "Let us hope not, Mr. Northrup! If I, for example, were to have a careless moment, we might all pay with our lives! For similar reasons, I cannot tolerate carelessness in my officers and crew."

"I understand, sir," Jared said quietly.

"However, I would prefer to think of this incident as a bit of ill fortune—brought about by our passenger here. I've always said women are bad luck on whalers, and I see now that my suspicions have been confirmed. I will never allow another woman to board my ship under any circumstances."

"I hardly think, sir, that we can blame Tasha for my accident."

"Mr. Northrup!" Captain Dawson interrupted, "When I want your opinion, I will ask for it. However, we needn't concern ourselves overmuch with the question, for our guest will be leaving us soon enough. We'll be sailing back south in a few days. The first whale yielded almost eighty barrels of oil, and the second also looks to be well above average size. With that kind of catch, I think it's wise to sail south before the ice begins to close in."

"Yes, sir."

The captain rose. "Perhaps when your little visitor is gone, you will be better able to concentrate on your work, Mr. Northrup. At any rate, I suggest that you make every effort to recover quickly, since I will be forced to record a deduction from your lay of the profits for each day's work you miss. Good day." Without even a backward glance at Tasha, Captain Dawson left the stateroom.

For a moment, Tasha sat in stunned silence, absorbing the captain's words. Then, forgetting all her earlier resolutions, she set her plate aside and flew to Jared's side, where she buried her face in his chest.

"Oh, Jared!" she sobbed. "Does Captain Dawson really intend to get rid of me?"

Jared chuckled. "I would hardly put it that way, Tasha. I'll agree the man is a bit harsh, but he's hardly an executioner."

"You know what I mean," she cried. "Do you think he'll force me to leave the *Freedom?*"

"I think he intends to leave you off in New Archangel, as we always knew he would."

"But I don't want to go to Novoarkhangelsk!" she wailed.

"Don't be silly. Of course you do. If I recall correctly, that is precisely why you were aboard the *Ayan.*"

137

"No, no," she protested. "I never wanted to go to Novoarkhangelsk. It was my father's way of getting rid of me because he hated my mother and he hates me. I don't even know anyone in Novoarkhangelsk."

"But apparently someone there knows you. You did tell me you were expected." He grasped her shoulders, gently pushing her away from him and looked into her troubled eyes. "Be sensible, Tasha. You can't just stay aboard the *Freedom*."

"Why can't I?" she started to sniffle.

"Because a hellship is no place for a lady. Just yesterday you were complaining about how cramped and bored you were staying in this stateroom all the time."

"But Jared, that was before!"

"Before what?" he demanded harshly, inwardly cringing at his own cruelty.

"Never mind," she whispered hollowly, "if you don't know, there's no sense in my saying more."

Jared looked away, unable to bear the hurt look in her eyes. "Tasha," he said slowly, "last night should never have happened. I'm sorry, I shouldn't have—"

"Don't!" she shouted, jumping off the bunk and going to stare out the port. "Don't destroy it completely. Let me have some sweet memory, even if I was wrong to hope you cared as much as I."

"Tasha," Jared sighed, struggling to pull himself to his feet. He hobbled toward her, wincing as the pain shot up his leg. "Try to understand. You are very beautiful, and I do care a great deal for you."

"If you cared for me, you wouldn't be so anxious to be rid of me!" she snapped.

"That is where you are wrong. For weeks, I've struggled against my desires for you, wanting to spare you the very pain you are feeling now. Last night I lost that struggle—and I will regret it for the rest of my life. I still desire you, but I won't allow myself to ruin any more of your life."

"It seems to me you are already doing quite a fine job of ruining it!"

He put his hands gently on her shoulders. "Can't

138

you see that I have nothing to offer you? I'm a whale-man. I'm married to the sea, and there's no room in my life for another. Our voyages sometimes last three or four years. You're too delicate to come with me, and too young and beautiful to sit at home waiting. You need to grow, and live, and enjoy the company of many people. You need to go to New Archangel, to be among your own people."

"How can you presume to tell me what I need? I'm not a girl any longer! I'm a woman! I'm old enough to know what I want and what I need!"

Jared smiled sadly. "You are most certainly a wom-an, Tasha. A wonderful woman. No one knows that better than I. But you still have a great deal to learn about life—even about love."

"Well, it's clear that you won't be the one to teach me!" She whirled away from the port. "I doubt that you know anything about love. In fact, I suspect that you've spent too many months in the Arctic waters—your heart seems to have turned to ice!"

Looking straight ahead, she stomped from the state-room, slamming the door behind her. Only when she reached the deck, did she surrender to the tears brimming in her eyes.

The voyage south, through the Bering Straits, around the Aleutians and into the Alaskan Sea, took almost a month. To Tasha, it felt like a lifetime.

At first she was determined never to return to Jared Northrup's stateroom. But after her first cold, wet, al-most sleepless night on deck, huddled among some coils of rope, she doubted the wisdom of her decision. Rising stiffly in the morning, she stumbled down the companionway leading to the officers' quarters.

She hesitated outside of Jared's door, then slowly opened it and looked in. To her relief, Jared was no-where in sight. As she let herself in, her relief quickly changed to anger. If he was strong enough to be up and about, she thought bitterly, he could have come looking for her and spared her the night of agony.

Her discovery supported her new conclusion that he did not truly care for her. She should have remembered the vow she made as a child at Birchwood—when she had resolved never to marry. Now she was certain that love was only an illusion—an illusion men used to get what they desired. At least, she thought with a sad sigh, she had learned the lesson early. She would never again allow herself to fall prey to any man.

Jared did not return to the stateroom until evening, when he hobbled in with a dish of salted codfish and potatoes. He smiled at her and asked, "Are you feeling better?"

Tasha thought she saw a shade of compassion in his blue eyes, but she quickly turned away, refusing to let him catch her off guard. She stared at the wall while he stared uncomfortably at her back.

"I suppose you're hungry—" he ventured awkwardly.

Still she refused to give any indication that she heard him.

He slammed the plate down on the desk and opened the door to the passageway with an angry jerk. "Dammit!" he muttered, barely controlling the frustration in his voice, "then don't talk to me. I certainly won't beg for your conversation! The food is there. Do what you like with it." He slammed the door and Tasha could hear him stamp angrily away.

"Here's what I'll do with your food!" she screamed, rushing to the desk to pick up the plate. A few furious strides brought her to the port, where she heaved the food out into the sea. She whirled and sent the empty tin plate flying toward the door. It hit the door at shoulder level—Jared's shoulder level exactly—and clattered to the floor. Tasha sat down on the bunk, a satisfied smile spreading across her face.

Jared did not return to the room that night. Nor the following night, nor any of the remaining nights while Tasha occupied his bunk. He would bring her the meals each day, setting the dishes down on

140

the desk before leaving the stateroom—but he never spoke a word to her.

For her part, Tasha averted her eyes whenever he entered, and refused to eat until he had left. She would not have him think she was grateful for the food. After all, even an imprisoned criminal was accorded meals as a basic right.

One evening, just as Jared opened the stateroom door to bring in Tasha's supper, Captain Dawson called to him from the passageway. "Mr. Northrup, I would have a word with you."

"Certainly, sir," Jared stepped back into the passageway and closed the door. Creeping to the door, Tasha strained to hear their conversation.

"We're only a few miles from Kodiak Island," the captain began. "I intend to put in there tomorrow."

"You're the master, sir. I hardly think you need consult me on the matter."

The captain cleared his throat irritably. "Nor do I, Mr. Northrup. I merely thought to inform you since it seems a good opportunity to dispose of our passenger."

"Your pardon, sir, but the girl was not bound for Kodiak. She was headed for the capital, New Archangel."

"They're both part of Russian America. What difference does it make?"

"A difference of several hundred miles, sir," Jared replied coolly. "That seems rather a great distance for a young girl to travel alone. Particularly when she is not acquainted with the area."

Captain Dawson snorted. "Let her own people worry about getting her to their capital. I'm not running a ferry service and I can't be responsible for every wandering waif who catches your eye!"

"But you've already assumed responsibility for her by allowing her on your ship. Suppose this Lisovsky to whom she was being sent is a close friend of the Russian governor's? It would hardly do to offend him, which abandoning the girl on Kodiak would surely do."

141

"I hardly see that it makes much difference, Northrup. The governor of Russian America has already cancelled shore privileges for American whalers in New Archangel. In fact, I doubt that it would even be safe for us to sail into New Archangel's harbor."

"I'm sure it would be, if we made it known we had a Russian citizen on board. The governor might consequently be so pleased with our gallantry that he would open the harbor to us in the future."

"Hmmm . . ." The captain pondered Jared's statement. "You are very persuasive, Mr. Northrup. Are you sure you're not just trying to buy more time with the wench? I imagine she makes a rather pleasant plaything for a hot-blooded young man such as yourself."

Jared's voice was controlled. "I can assure you, sir, that I am every bit as anxious as you to be rid of her. Perhaps even more anxious."

"Very well, Mr. Northrup. I'll give the order to make sail for New Archangel. But if there are any incidents, I shall hold you personally responsible."

"Fair enough, sir." Jared turned and walked back to his stateroom door, opening it just as Tasha jumped back.

He flashed her a wry grin. "Listening, eh?"

Suddenly all the anger and hurt that had been brewing in her for weeks erupted, and Tasha broke her self-imposed silence. "You may tell your captain," she spat, "that Kodiak is close enough! I wouldn't want you to be troubled any longer than necessary—and I won't be used as a pawn to curry favor with the governor of the colony."

Jared gritted his teeth. "You are expected at the home of a Mr. Lisovsky in New Archangel, and I intend to see you safely delivered. I only hope the poor man is prepared for the likes of you! Now eat your supper. It's already getting cold." He dropped the dish on the desk and stomped out of the stateroom.

Nine days later, in midafternoon, Timothy Adams, the third mate, knocked timidly at the stateroom door. "Captain Dawson requests your presence on deck, miss. We're nearing Sitka Sound, and he thinks you might be needed to speak Russian if we're challenged."

"You mean he orders me on deck to be used as a peacemaker, don't you?" Tasha responded bitterly as she opened the door.

"I—I didn't say that. I'm just repeating the captain's request," the man stammered, his face turning almost as bright as his carrot-colored hair.

"Never mind," Tasha said, taking pity on the young mate. "I'll be up immediately. Anything to speed the moment when I can be free of this ship." She followed Timothy to the companionway and climbed to the deck, where Jared and Captain Dawson were waiting.

"Well, young lady," the captain greeted her, his tone more jovial than she had ever heard it, "we'll soon have you installed in your home."

"It's not my home, sir," she replied briskly. "My home is near Moscow."

"Harrumph." He turned away from her irritably. "I would think a woman in your position could try to be a bit more grateful. Damned Russian baggage!" he growled.

Ignoring his remark, Tasha turned away. She positioned herself at the rail a short distance from both men, and got her first breathtaking view of the island she thought marked the end of her journey.

As they entered Sitka Sound, Mount Edgecumbe on Kruzof Island towered over them to the left, its pine-covered slopes capped with glistening snow. To the right, on Baranov Island, rose another range of high mountains. In the distance, at the foot of the mountains, she could just discern the buildings that had to be Novoarkhangelsk. A domed spire, topped by a gilded cross, stretched joyfully above the town.

143

Tasha's heart lurched as she recognized the symbols of a Russian cathedral, and for the first time since boarding the *Freedom*, she felt a pang of homesickness, a yearning to be in the company of Russians, to eat Russian food, and to share in Russian customs.

Perhaps, after all, she might feel at home in this strange land so far from Birchwood.

At the same instant, she felt a pang of regret, remembering how Nikolai had longed for her to love this land as he did. Was it possible he could somehow have survived the wreck of the *Ayan*, and was even now waiting somewhere in Novoarkhangelsk? More likely, his body was at the bottom of the ocean, never to be seen again.

"Kto edet?" The harsh voice of the harbor pilot, demanding the identity of the strange ship, intruded upon Tasha's musings. Following the direction of the voice, she looked down and saw an old man seated in a small, three-seater boat that looked like it was made of animal skins, his rifle poised in a ready position as he challenged the *Freedom*.

Overwhelmed with joy at hearing her native tongue, Tasha waved energetically and responded without prompting from Jared or the captain. *"Ya Russkaya, Natalya Demidova. Noojno yechats na Gospodin Lisovskye"* [I am a Russian, Natalya Demidova. I must go to Mr. Lisovsky's].

"Eh?" The pilot regarded her quizzically, unsure whether to believe her words. She spoke Russian well enough to be a native, but what was she doing aboard an American whaler? He shrugged to himself. Regardless of her identity he had orders not to guide any hellships into Novoarkhangelsk harbor, and he was not one to disobey orders.

He called back to her in Russian, explaining that he could not take the *Freedom* in, but if she truly wished to visit Gospodin Lisovsky, he would ferry her to the dock himself.

"Otleechno!" [excellent!], Tasha replied, satisfied that she would be rejoining Russian society and leav-

ing the *Freedom*, with all its confounded inhabitants, behind. Turning to Captain Dawson, standing at the rail with Jared, she announced coolly, "If you will be so kind as to order a ladder lowered for me, captain, I shan't trouble you further. The gentleman has kindly offered to see me to the town, so I won't require your services any longer."

"The hell you won't!" Jared snapped as he leaned forward. "You aren't leaving my sight until I see you delivered to this Lisovsky fellow."

"Oh, but I'm afraid I shall have to leave you. The pilot has just explained to me that the *Freedom* will not be permitted in the harbor. And I am the only person to whom he offered the comfort of his boat."

"For God's sakes, Mr. Northrup," the captain interceded, "why can't you just let the girl go and say good riddance?"

"Your pardon, sir, but it's a personal matter. A question of honor, as I see it."

"Oh, I see." Captain Dawson sighed as he studied first Jared, then Tasha, through narrowed eyes. "Very well, Mr. Northrup, if you can persuade our Russian friend to transport you, you have my permission to accompany the girl. But the *Freedom* will go no nearer the town. I've no desire to sample the governor's cannon, nor to remain in unfriendly waters through the night. We will sail by sundown. See that you are back before then."

"Aye, sir." Jared turned and ordered the lowering of a rope ladder. Before Tasha could protest, he climbed down and into the pilot's waiting *bidarka*, then stood aside to assist her.

The pilot looked dubiously at his extra passenger, but did not challenge him. Tasha stared at the approaching shoreline, refusing to acknowledge Jared's presence. Let him accompany her if he wished! He would look a fool when they arrived in Novoarkhangelsk and he could not even speak with any of the inhabitants! And how would he convince anyone to return him to his ship? Picturing him gesticulating

145

helplessly to some boat owner, she smiled in smug satisfaction.

"So, you're pleased to be arriving here," Jared said, noting her smile.

"Oh, yes," she replied, "I am very pleased, indeed."

As the pilot directed the bidarka toward the landing dock, Tasha surveyed the large buildings to her right. They were constructed of massive cedar logs, riveted to the top of a rocky point, surrounded by water on three sides.

Guiding the boat to the dock, the old man explained that the buildings were the army headquarters and Governor Ivan Furuhelm's residence, named Baranov Castle in honor of the colony's first governor.

As the boat scraped alongside the high pier, Jared jumped out and offered Tasha his hand. Ignoring his offer, she scrambled onto the pier unassisted, turning to thank the pilot for her passage and to request directions to Mikhail Lisovsky's home. She surmised that Monsieur Lisovsky was well-known in Novoarkhangelsk, since the old man gave her directions immediately. Jared stood back, an amused smile playing on his lips as the two conversed in Russian.

With a wave of farewell to the pilot, Tasha turned and began walking up the graveled Governor's Walk, Novoarkhangelsk's main boulevard, the pilot had informed her.

"Suppose you tell me where we are going," Jared said, his long, relaxed stride easily matching Tasha's small, hurried steps.

"I am going to Monsieur Mikhail Lisovsky's!" she replied curtly. "I haven't the slightest notion where you are going. I don't need you, Jared Northrup, so why don't you go and amuse yourself elsewhere?"

"I am curious," he said, his voice tinged with laughter, "to see this Monsieur Lisovsky. I hope he realizes just what he is in for with you."

"I can't see that that is any of your affair."

"Perhaps not," he shrugged. "But I'll come along just the same."

"Perhaps you are simply coming along to demand the return of your sister's dress," she said sarcastically.

"The dress is yours, Tasha," he replied quietly, a slight note of hurt in his voice. "Under the circumstances, I'm sure Clarissa would consider me quite a boor if I were to demand its return."

In silence, they passed Baranov Castle, the government office building, and the bakery, from which the delicious aromas of various breads and sweet rolls floated out on the October air. It was warmer than at Birchwood in the month of October, but without a coat, barefoot, and wearing only the emerald silk dress, Tasha shivered in the crisp breeze. She felt that people were staring at them as they passed the row of shops in the center of town, and she quickened her step in embarrassment.

Stopping at the corner of a side street, she gazed for a moment at the end of the boulevard, where the cathedral rose above a green square. Like all of the buildings they had passed on the boulevard, it was built of wood. Smaller in scale than the grand cathedrals of Moscow, it brought back pleasant memories of the wooden chapel at Birchwood. An exquisite wrought iron clock hung at the base of its tower, and as she stood watching, the six melodic bells in the spire chimed the hour. It was four o'clock.

Turning into the narrow side street, Tasha walked to the second house on the right, just as the pilot had directed her. It was a sprawling, two-storied log structure, almost as large as Birchwood. But with its unfinished log sides, it looked much more primitive. She stood at the foot of the stairs leading to the first door, staring up uncertainly at the polished brass knocker. She could feel Jared watching her, and she would not give in to the sudden urge to flee from the strange house. Besides, she was anxious to get inside and warm up.

Swallowing hard, she ran up the six steps to the door, raised the knocker and rapped it twice against

147

the massive wooden door. Within seconds, a brusque-looking old woman opened the door and eyed Tasha curiously.

Tasha returned the woman's gaze, wondering whether to address her in Russian or French. Assuming Monsieur Lisovsky was of the upper class, and that his household followed Moscow and St. Petersburg customs, she chose French, and asked, "Is this the home of Monsieur Mikhail Lisovsky?"

The woman studied her for a moment, repeating Tasha's words to herself. "*Da,*" she finally answered in Russian.

Switching to Russian, Tasha asked if she might see the master, to which the woman replied that he was having tea at the moment and could not be disturbed. Perhaps, she suggested, dubiously eyeing Tasha's bedraggled dress, the young lady would care to call tomorrow, at a more appropriate hour.

"But I can't call tomorrow!" Tasha wailed, succumbing to the pressures of finding herself friendless and homeless in a strange land. "I haven't any place to stay!"

The woman shrugged, as if the problem did not concern her, and began to close the door.

"Wait!" Jared called, vaulting up the stairs to wedge his booted foot in the door. "The young lady is Tasha Demidova. Perhaps you should announce her to Monsieur Lisovsky."

Although she was unable to understand Jared's statement, the woman did recognize the name. She cocked her head expectantly at Tasha, and Tasha nodded energetically, pointing to herself as she repeated, "*Da, da, Tasha Demidova!*"

At that moment a pleasant, mellow voice came from within the house, demanding in Russian, "What *is* the disturbance out there, Xenia?"

"Tasha Demidova! Tasha Demidova!" the old woman cried excitedly.

"What?" The voice came nearer and a tall blond man Tasha judged to be in his forties appeared behind Xenia. "Tasha?" he asked, his blue eyes showing stunned disbelief.

She nodded hesitantly, fearful that something about her appearance offended him and he would reject her.

"Tasha!" he repeated joyously, pushing aside Xenia as he rushed to embrace her. Exuberantly, he kissed her on each cheek, then crushed her to his chest. "My God, girl, I never dreamed you might still be alive. It's been almost two months since we received news of the *Ayan*'s disaster. And word was that there were no survivors. I never dared hope you would still turn up!"

He stepped back, holding her at arm's length while his eyes traveled searchingly over her features. "But I should have known at first glance who you were. You look exactly as I remember your dear mother."

Tasha thought she detected a special softness in his tone when he mentioned her mother, and she could not keep herself from asking, "Were you close to my mother, sir?"

The man hesitated before answering in a barely audible whisper. "Yes, Tasha, for a time I like to think we were very close."

Satisfied that he was leaving Tasha in good hands, Jared began to back down the stairs. His movement caught Lisovsky's eyes and the older man chided Tasha gently. "My dear, it seems we've been terribly impolite, discussing personal matters. Won't you introduce me to your companion?"

"Oh," Tasha mumbled awkwardly, "he's an American. The man who rescued me from the ocean." Why, she wondered, did she feel compelled to admit that?

"American, eh?" Lisovsky said, now speaking in fluent English. "I do business with people in San Francisco from time to time—we ship them ice, strange as it sounds. You're not by any chance connected with the American-Russian Commercial Company?"

149

"I'm afraid not, sir," Jared replied. "I'm a mate aboard the whaler *Freedom*."

"Oh. A whaleman." Lisovsky was visibly disappointed. "I don't suppose I need tell you your kind are not very popular in this town."

"Indeed, sir, I'm well aware of that."

"Nevertheless," the Russian continued in a brighter tone, "it's clear we have judged at least some of you too harshly. If you rescued Tasha, I suppose you must have some redeeming qualities. Won't you come in and have a glass of vodka while I find a way to thank you more properly?"

"I appreciate your offer, sir," Jared replied sincerely, "but I really must get back to my ship. Seeing Tasha safely delivered, and knowing she is in good hands, is thanks enough for me."

While Lisovsky puzzled over the younger man's words, Jared turned to Tasha. He raised her hand and pressed it lightly with his lips. "Until we meet again, Tasha."

"I doubt that day will ever come," she said coolly.

"But I am very sure it will come, little one." He squeezed her hand meaningfully. Then he nodded amiably to Lisovsky, galloped down the steps, and sauntered away, whistling.

Mikhail Lisovsky watched him, a thoughtful frown creasing his face. Tasha looked away, blinking back the tears that inexplicably filled her eyes.

Chapter Thirteen

1863-1864

After the discomforts of the wilderness trails and the cramped ship's quarters, the Lisovsky home seemed a paradise to Tasha. Despite its somewhat primitive exterior, the decor of the interior compared favorably with the finest homes in Moscow. It was lavishly and comfortably furnished and staffed by a group of Creole servants.

Xenia, the housekeeper who had greeted Tasha at the door, bustled off to order a hot bath for the girl, while Mikhail led her into the drawing room, where a gleaming brass samovar bubbled with welcoming tea.

"To think you are here at last," he said, handing her a glass of tea in a filigreed holder. "After I had despaired of ever knowing you."

Tasha laughed self-consciously. "Well, I had certainly despaired of reaching you. Although at first," she admitted, relaxing under his warm smile, "I was not at all sure I wished to come to Novo-arkhangelsk."

"Why was that?" Lisovsky asked gently.

Tasha shrugged. "I thought it was a trick of papa's, just to send me away. I could not imagine why you would want me here. And I hated leaving my home."

"Did your father mistreat you?" Lisovsky's eyes sparked, though his tone remained steady.

"Not exactly," Tasha replied slowly, suddenly unsure of what to say. "I suppose we simply did not understand one another. After all, we saw very little of each other. I grew up at Birchwood, while he spent most of his time in Moscow. Still," she continued cautiously, "I always had the feeling he was unkind to mama."

Lisovsky's expression became stormy, and he pressed his lips tightly together.

Sensing that it would be best to change the subject, Tasha asked quickly, "But why *did* you send for me?"

He blinked at her, as if jolted from a trance, then, choosing his words carefully, said, "Your mother was very special to me. After I learned of her death, I was anxious to meet you—to have some part of her near me."

Tasha nodded seriously. "Olga told me you were a distant relation of mama's."

"Yes." He hesitated. "We were distant cousins. You may call me 'uncle,' if you wish."

"Uncle Mikhail," Tasha softly tested the name, then nodded happily. "Yes, I like that very much."

"Good," Mikhail smiled broadly. "I hope you will consider this your home, Tasha. You are free to stay here as long as you wish—but I hope that you will never choose to leave."

In the next months, Tasha relaxed and enjoyed the excitement of becoming acquainted with her new home. She soon learned that Novoarkhangelsk had over two thousand residents and was a thriving, industrious community. The Russian-American Company had originally founded the city as a center for the hunting of otter, seal, and other fur-bearing animals, and it still carried on a prosperous fur trade. But it had also become a mining center and the first center for steamship building on the western coast of America. Workers in the city constructed everything from the frames of the ships to the engines, and sold many of the completed steamers to companies in the United States. In addition, the Russian-American Company carried on a lucrative ice-trading business, shipping hundreds of thousands of pounds to California each year.

Most days Mikhail left Tasha to amuse herself while he was busy with company meetings, overseeing shipments, checking books, or planning for future shipments. He clearly loved both his work and his location, and Tasha could not help but find his enthusiasm infectious. While the last days of fall lingered, she spent hours strolling in Novoarkhangelsk's spacious public gardens, located only a few blocks from the Lisovsky house, where she enjoyed the season's late-blooming roses and bright, hardy chrysanthemums. Occasionally, despite Mikhail's warnings not to wander too close to the Indian village, she ventured beyond the gardens to the winding paths along the Kolosh River. There, among the towering pines and cedars, and the ferns and mosses that carpeted the forest floor, she felt most at peace.

To Tasha's delight and amazement, winter in Novoarkhangelsk was milder than any she had ever before experienced. Even the occasional light snows did not accumulate in drifts against the houses, but melted and disappeared within a day or two after falling. Mikhail explained that much of the colony experienced dreadful winters, such as she had always supposed plagued all of Russian America, but Novoarkhangelsk was blessed with the combined warming effects of the Japan Current and the protection offered by several small islands to the west.

That December, Ivan Furuhelm—a Finnish mining engineer who had governed the colony for the past four years—retired, and was replaced by the Prince Dmitri Maksutov and his youthful wife, Adelaide, the daughter of his English instructor at Kronstadt. Soon afterward, Tasha was thrilled to be invited to accompany Mikhail to Baranov Castle for a holiday ball.

As they entered the castle, her eyes widened at the sight of the huge brass chandeliers and elaborate brass hinges on the doors. She followed the other ladies into the drawing room to sample the fresh caviar and salmon, the vodka punch and other appetizers set out on long tables before the mirror-lined walls.

At the same time, the men were sampling zakooska in an adjoining salon, so without Uncle Mikhail, Tasha found herself among strangers.

The other ladies smiled indulgently at her, openly appraising her youth. Then they turned to gossip among themselves, as if she no longer existed. Listening to the women titter about their husbands and lovers, Tasha began to feel more and more misplaced. A strange emptiness swept over her, and for the first time since her arrival in Novoarkhangelsk, she thought longingly of Jared. Where was he at that moment, she wondered? Probably on some tropical island, being entertained by a Polynesian beauty.

She refused to think more of him—these women

were fools, she thought, to chatter so much about men. Still, she could not shake off her mood of depression, even when the ladies joined the men for dinner.

She was quiet throughout dinner. Mikhail attributed her silence to nervousness at attending her first ball and remained unconcerned. He spent his time exchanging pleasantries with the woman seated on his right, and with another seated across the table from him. At the dinner's conclusion, as the dancing was about to begin in the spacious ballroom, he graciously turned to Tasha and requested the honor of the first dance.

"Oh no, uncle," she pleaded. "I am really a most unaccomplished dancer. I'm afraid I'd embarrass you. Besides," she laughed nervously, "I wouldn't want to make enemies of all the women who are vying for your attention this evening."

"Nonsense," he laughed heartily. "If you can't dance, it's time you learned. I've waited years for the joy of leading you out on the dance floor, and I won't be put off. The other women will simply have to wait their turn—I'm tired of their pursuit of me."

Reluctantly, Tasha followed him onto the polished parquet floor. At first he held her lightly, but as the music intensified and other dancers crowded the floor, he gradually pulled her closer. For a moment Tasha imagined she felt his hand trembling against her spine, but she pushed the thought from her mind, convincing herself that her own uncertainty was playing tricks on her.

"You look very pensive, my dear," Mikhail whispered, catching her eyes with his penetrating gaze. "Is something wrong?"

"No, it's nothing. I was just wondering—" she stammered and flushed, "—but it really is none of my business."

"What is none of your business?" he gently prodded. "If I can relieve your bemusement, I will be happy to do so."

"I was just wondering—how is it, Uncle Mikhail,

154

that you never married? It is obvious to me that it has not been for the lack of willing women." She looked away nervously, afraid that her question might have offended him.

He hesitated, studying her closely as his blue eyes took on a faraway look. "No," he answered slowly, "it was not for any lack of willing women, but for the lack of one particular woman. The one woman I wanted would not have me, and I will not dishonor her memory by choosing another."

Tasha drew in her breath sharply, upset by the pain she read in his eyes. "I'm sorry," she choked, "I was rude to ask. But I think she must have been a very foolish woman not to want you, Uncle Mikhail. I'm sure she regretted her decision in the end."

Mikhail smiled and squeezed her waist affectionately, "Thank you, my dear. Your opinion in the matter is more precious to me than you can imagine."

He was silent for the remainder of the waltz, and Tasha could not bring herself to intrude any further upon his thoughts. When the musicians paused, she pleaded fatigue and begged to be allowed to sit down, urging him to enjoy himself without concern for her. Mikhail disappeared into the crowd, searching for some champagne, and she watched the other dancers whizzing by.

As Nikolai Voronin had explained to her in Moscow almost a year ago, the social system in Novoarkhangelsk was of a less rigid order than that of European Russia. Creoles held government and company posts that were as high or even higher than those held by the full-blooded Russians, and were considered social equals. Though many Russians and Creoles were fluent in French, and even English, Russian was the accepted language in society here.

Tasha sat for more than half an hour, watching her Uncle Mikhail dance by with numerous, adoring women. He seemed oblivious to their charms. She was beginning to feel like a detached observer when she heard a deep voice asking her to dance.

She looked up into the smiling, handsome face of the new governor. He reached down and grasped her hand, pulling her to her feet.

"Oh, but I couldn't," she gasped.

"Of course you can. I saw you dancing earlier with your uncle. And I always insist that all of my female guests share at least one dance with me."

Not wishing to offend her host, Tasha allowed him to steer her into the crowd.

"I'm sorry our gathering has not pleased you, little one," the prince said.

"Oh, but it has," Tasha protested weakly.

The prince smiled. "You needn't be so diplomatic. I've been watching you, and I would say you seem bored."

"Not bored," she countered quickly. "It's very exciting seeing the castle and being among all these people. But," she admitted, "I do feel a bit out of place. I know so few people here, and so little of what and who they talk about."

Prince Maksutov nodded. "That is the curse of being young and attending your first ball in a new city. But I can assure you, when you meet a young man who strikes your fancy, you will find yourself ready to dance till dawn."

Tasha cringed, but bit back the urge to tell him she would never meet such a man. Her reaction did not go unnoticed and the prince chuckled as he watched her.

"It's obvious you doubt my words. But perhaps the hazards encountered in your trip have left you somewhat cynical. Your uncle tells me you were shipwrecked and then had to spend some time on an American whaler. I hope the whalemen did not mistreat you in any way?"

His tone was sincere, and Tasha flushed uneasily as she quickly answered. "No. The quarters were cramped and uncomfortable, but nothing more harrowing than that."

"Good. Then perhaps we should simply attribute your doubting nature to your youth." He paused, then changed the drift of the conversation. "Your uncle has also told me you are fluent in English. No doubt you have heard that my wife is British. I am sure she would be most interested in arranging a visit with you, for the pleasure of chatting with another woman in her own language."

"I would be most pleased to talk with the princess at her convenience," Tasha murmured humbly.

The music stopped and the prince led her to the carpeted area bordering the dance floor, bowing graciously as he took his leave of her. The remainder of the evening passed in a blur, until Tasha gratefully accepted Mikhail's suggestion that they return home.

That night, for the first time since her arrival in Novoarkhangelsk, Tasha had trouble falling asleep. She lay awake, pondering Mikhail's pained revelation, and wondering about the woman who had affected him so deeply. It was hard for her to accept the fact that a man could suffer as much as a woman from the whimsical workings of love, but she could not doubt the truth of Mikhail's story.

Her uncle's revelation strengthened her resolve never to marry. Coupled with the memories of her mother's unhappiness, and her own short, disillusioning encounter with Jared, this new knowledge made her even more sure of her decision.

Perhaps she could admit to loving kind Uncle Mikhail—in the way she had always wished to be able to love a father—but there could be no place in her life for *romance*. But why did Jared's face—his hair bleached almost white from the sun and salt spray, his blue eyes laughing—haunt her as she finally drifted into sleep?

Tasha never was to have her discussion with the governor's wife.

Princess Maksutova was taken ill and died of a bronchial infection soon after the ball, bringing all dinners, receptions, and other social events at Baranov Castle to an abrupt halt.

As time passed and his grief lessened, the prince began inviting a few of Novoarkhangelsk's prominent citizens, among them Mikhail Lisovsky, to the castle. But there were no more gala social functions announced, and although sad about Princess Maksutova's death, Tasha was relieved to be spared further social obligations at Baranov Castle.

She preferred to stay home, curled up in a large leather chair in Mikhail's study while losing herself in one of the books from his extensive library. Other evenings she played the rosewood piano in the drawing room, amusing herself and delighting the household with the pieces she had learned as a child at Birchwood.

One rainy evening in April, as she finished a particularly intricate piece by the composer Glinka, Tasha was startled to hear someone applauding behind her. She turned to see her uncle, his eyes beaming with approval.

"I don't know how the household got on before your arrival, Tasha," he said, coming forward to rest his hands lightly on her shoulders. "This piano has always sat silently—just another useless piece of furniture for Xenia to polish. But you have brought it to life, as you have given life to everything and everyone within my house—and most of all, to me."

Touched by his pronouncement, Tasha looked away, blinking at the candlelight flickering across the keyboard. "Uncle Mikhail, you mustn't flatter me so. I give you no more than you have given me; indeed, I fear it has been far less."

"No, dear child," he whispered, squeezing her shoulders affectionately, "I am sure you can never fully realize just how much joy you give me by your very presence and by your generous affection."

Tasha swallowed a lump in her throat, wondering again what kind of woman could have denied him her affection. Forcing a smile, she looked up at his frilled white silk shirt, the freshly pressed blue suit, set off by a gold brocade waistcoat, and changed the subject. "You're going out, I see."

"Yes," he sighed apologetically. "I hope you don't mind being left alone with the staff for yet another evening. The governor asked me to join him and a few others for billiards, and I felt it would be indelicate to refuse the invitation."

"Please don't be concerned about me, uncle. I'm satisfied to stay home and entertain myself."

"But I *am* concerned. You should be out among people your own age, not hidden in this house with the servants."

"I grew up in a house where servants were my only friends. I was very happy there. And," she added sincerely, "I am very happy here."

Mikhail smiled fondly and, with a gentle finger, raised her chin to gaze into her eyes. "Grew up, did you say? My dear little Tasha, despite all you have been through, you are still hardly more than a child. A lovely, beautiful, enchanting one. Very much like your mother the last time I saw her." A special softness came over his face as he mentioned her mother, and for a moment he gazed at Tasha silently. Then he shook his head and shrugged. "But then, I suppose I shall always think of you in that way."

His lips touched her forehead in a gentle kiss. "I'd best be off. Perhaps in the summer, when the rains have diminished somewhat, we can host our own party to see that you are properly introduced to society."

Tasha frowned at the suggestion, but Mikhail was gone before he could see her reaction. She played a little longer, but had lost her ability to concentrate on the music and seemed to strike one discordancy after another. Finally, she selected a book of verse from Mikhail's library, and went upstairs to soak in a hot bath.

Bathed and dressed in a snowy white flannel nightgown, Tasha bid good night to Theodosia, the elderly

Creole who served as her maid, and climbed into the high, canopied bed. The moment she snuffed out her bedside candle, the rain outside seemed to intensify, pelting her window furiously. The boughs of the old cedar tree outside her room tapped against the glass. The velvet draperies rustled as the April wind whirled through the cracks in the casement windows.

Shivering, Tasha closed her eyes and tried to close her ears to the sounds of the storm. She had never been afraid of storms, but at that moment she desperately wanted someone to cling to, someone who could comfort her with his strength. Irritated by her inexplicable fears, she tossed fretfully, trying to rationalize what was bothering her. By now she should have been accustomed to the rainy weather, since it had rained several times a week since her arrival in Novoarkhangelsk. Her mood must be due to something else—but what?

She buried her head beneath a pillow, trying to shut out the world so she could sleep. And then she knew what was bothering her. In her mind she saw Jared leaning over her, his eyes half-lidded as he bent to caress her breasts with his tongue. She felt his hands move down her body, tracing the smooth curve of her hips before sliding inward to tantalize her more.

"Don't," she groaned into the pillow.

"What's the matter, love? Don't you want me?" His voice seemed as clear as if he was actually there.

"No! No! I don't want you! I never wanted you!" she muttered against the mattress. "Why can't you leave me alone? Can't you understand I don't want you plaguing me any longer?"

She tossed in the large bed, squeezing her eyes tightly shut and shaking her head to try to dissolve the vision. Jared's flushed, passionate face disappeared. Then it reappeared, but the deep blue eyes, instead of glistening with joy and desire, held the hurt expression she had read in Uncle Mikhail's eyes the night he told her of his lost love.

"Don't try to deceive me!" she continued her anguished soliloquy. "Don't try to make me think you care. I won't pity you. I won't admit to loving you, just so you can use me and then cast me aside. I never wanted you in my life, Jared Northrup, and I don't miss you now that you are gone!"

Abruptly the face disappeared. But the clouded, sorrowful eyes seemed to float over her, refusing to release her, even when she finally fell into a fitful sleep.

Tasha had been asleep less than a hour when Mikhail Lisovsky came home. He stumbled up the stairs, swallowing a belch brought on by too much vodka and pickled herring. He had lost steadily at billiards that night, confirming the feeling he had on the way to Baranov Castle that he should have stayed home with Tasha. But, as he had gazed at her in the drawing room, he had sensed that her company would be too painful for him that night, too reminiscent of her mother's, and so he had purposely stayed on, downing toast after toast of vodka.

Still, he had been unable to stop thinking about her, even in Prince Maksutov's billiard parlor. The girl seemed to grow more irresistibly beautiful and more like her mother every day. When he had received the letter from Prince Demidov, almost two years ago, he had been ecstatic to learn of the child's existence. But he had never dared to imagine what a perfect replica of Natalya Ivanovna she would be. Sometimes he wished she looked less like her mother. There were moments when the resemblance pained him too much.

Reaching the top of the stairs, Mikhail ambled toward his bedroom. He stopped with his hand on the doorknob, turning to look longingly across the hall to Tasha's room. Perhaps he would just look in on the child and see that she was tucked in properly. After all, it was his right as a father—a right he had been denied for too many years.

He tiptoed to the door of her room and slowly

turned the knob. The hinges creaked slightly as he pushed it open, and he stood still, afraid of waking her. In the starlight, he could dimly make out her form in the bed. Slipping through the doorway, he crept closer to study the sleeping girl. Her long, shining black hair spilled over the comforter and spread across the pillow like a length of black satin. Long, thick lashes lay darkly against her ivory cheeks, and her lips were pursed appealingly.

Gazing at her, Mikhail smiled. What a creature of beauty he and Natasha had created. Seeing Tasha, he could not regret what had passed between them that night in Zelenograd more than sixteen years ago. If only the days and years afterward had been different. If Natasha had consented to become his wife, perhaps she would still be alive today, alive to share with him the joy of watching their daughter grow into an enchanting young woman.

Ah, Natasha, he thought wistfully, how I long for your touch, even after all these years. We had only a single night together, but that night has sustained me all through the years. His mind flew back over the time, and he envisioned her as she had been that night at the inn, tempting and innocent.

His attention returned to Tasha as she shifted in her sleep and sighed, suddenly pushing away the comforter to reveal her firm, young breasts rising and falling beneath her white flannel nightgown—the same kind of gown that he remembered Natasha wearing. The alcohol he had consumed made him feel unusually relaxed.

Impulsively, Mikhail reached over and gently cupped one of her breasts. To his surprise, she moaned acceptingly and, still sleeping, opened her arms in seeming welcome. Suddenly, seeing only his beloved Natasha, the woman who had haunted his dreams for more than sixteen years, Mikhail carefully lowered himself to the bed and cradled her in his arms. Once again he felt the young man en route to Siberia, embracing the girl who had instantly captured his heart.

In her sleep, Tasha snuggled against his chest, molding her body closely to his. Her response produced in Mikhail a fire demanding release. He closed his eyes and kissed her, and her lips parted readily. His groin throbbed uncontrollably and he rolled her onto her back, sliding his hands down her slender side, then crouched above her as he fumbled to loosen his clothes.

Opening his eyes, he began to untie the ribbons of her nightgown, trembling in his eagerness to possess her. Slowly he began to peel away her gown, pausing to gaze again at that beloved face. Then, leaning closer to plant a warm kiss on her brow, he froze—the face below him was very like Natasha's, but it was too young! Every feature, every nuance of coloring, was Natasha's—but it was not she!

He blinked repeatedly, sure that his eyes and mind were playing tricks on him. It had to be Natasha! No one else on earth possessed that flawless beauty. No one except—

Groaning in horror at what he had almost done, Mikhail slid off to one side, praying the girl would not awaken. With shaking hands, he pulled the comforter up to her chin, trying to ignore the insistent pulsing that continued in his groin.

Turning away, he fled to his bedroom. He locked the door behind him, as if afraid the image would pursue him, and stood shuddering in self-disgust as he reviewed the last moments.

How could he have come so close to taking his own daughter? Was it not enough that he had taken her mother without benefit of marriage, causing her years of unhappiness?

In all the years before he had met Natasha, and in all the years since, no other woman appealed to him as she had. Indeed, compared to her, the others had merely diverted him. But now it seemed it was not even safe for his own daughter—*her* daughter—to sleep in the same house with him. What kind of monster was he?

For months he had waited excitedly for Tasha's arrival. When she finally joined his household, he had been certain his life was complete. Now his feelings had suddenly changed! He felt sure she could not continue to live there. For her sake, he could not face the risk of again losing control over himself. Perhaps it would never happen again. Still, having her forever near him would put a great strain on their relationship, perhaps destroying the warm affection that had developed so wonderfully between them. He must remove her from the house!

But where could he send her? The answer came to him instantly: the bishop's school. She would be a boarding student. Yes, that would surely be the best solution. She would be near enough to visit occasionally, but far enough away to remove temptation. He would be able to see to her welfare without endangering her virtue. And by the time she finished her education, she would no doubt be ready to marry and start a life of her own.

Relieved by his decision, Mikhail undressed and prepared for bed. But one thing continued to puzzle him. Why had Tasha responded to his touch as if she was already acquainted with, indeed craved, the intimate attentions of a man? She was not yet sixteen and consequently must be ignorant of the ways of physical love. Of course, he consoled himself, she had not really responded—she had been asleep; unaware of her actions. Had she awakened, no doubt she would have been terrified by the mere thought of a man touching her so intimately. In her sleep she had merely reflected an underlying, passionate nature, inherited from her mother. After all, Natasha had been totally innocent on that long-ago night in Zelenograd, and yet she had responded with unmistakable passion.

Mikhail sighed. If only Natasha had accepted his proposal. Her loving caresses would have been enough to satisfy him forever. If she had consented to share his life and his bed, he could never have ended up desiring their daughter.

Chapter Fourteen

1864

Mikhail Lisovsky rose early, anxious to talk with Tasha and reveal his plans for her future. Remembering his moments in her room, he wanted to resolve the problem as quickly as possible, before he could be tempted again and his terrible secret became a sordid reality.

In the back of his mind, he was still disturbed by the girl's response to him last night. Was it possible she had been awake? Could she have known he was there, or was she dreaming of someone else? And if she was dreaming, were her dreams of a real person, someone with whom she had actually experienced something, or were they only a young girl's romantic fantasies?

He was sitting in the sunny breakfast room, drinking his third cup of strong black coffee, when he heard Tasha descend from her bedroom. She rushed into the room in a bubbling mood, showing no sign of emotional trauma from the previous night. Her light blue cotton dress, sprigged with darker blue flowers, brought an air of springtime into the room, seeming to dare the rains to begin again. Passing Mikhail's chair, she bent to plant a good morning kiss on his forehead before seating herself in a chair opposite his at the small table.

Looking at her young figure, innocently displayed beneath her modestly cut dress, Mikhail could not resist a smile. By daylight she looked like a sweet young girl, not the seductive temptress he had imagined last night. "You certainly seem happy this morning, Tasha."

"Indeed. Since the rain has stopped, I think I shall go for a stroll in the gardens this morning. It seems ages since I've been there."

"Well, don't expect to find too much in bloom this early in the year. We've hardly passed winter." Picking up a small brass bell beside his plate, he rang, and a serving maid immediately appeared with a plate of sweet rolls and a glass of tea for Tasha.

Watching her closely as she selected a roll filled with sweet, creamy cheese, he asked, "Did you sleep well last night?"

"Very well," she answered a bit too quickly to be convincing.

Mikhail frowned. "I'm relieved to hear that. You see, I looked in on you when I arrived home, and your sleep seemed rather fitful."

Tasha bent her head over her plate, hoping to hide the flush she felt spreading across her face. "Well, perhaps I was just having a dream when you looked in, although I don't recall any. At any rate, I must have slept well—I feel marvelous today."

"Good." Mikhail cleared his throat nervously, unwilling to pursue the subject further. "There is something I wish to discuss with you, Tasha."

Troubled by his serious tone, she raised her eyes to search his. "Not about the ball you mentioned yesterday evening? I don't want to sound ungrateful, Uncle Mikhail, but I'd much prefer not to be introduced to society just yet."

"No, not about the ball. I've given the idea some thought, and I quite agree it's too early to push you into the social whirl."

Tasha sighed in relief and gave him a warm, appreciative smile before taking a sip of tea. "Then what is it? Does it concern me?"

He nodded. "I would say it concerns you most of all."

Mystified, she stared at him over the steaming glass. "Please don't keep me in suspense any longer."

"Very well." He cleared his throat again. "It is time

we gave some consideration to your education. Since the 40s, when Governor Etolin and his wife were here, a thorough education has had special importance to all the residents of Novoarkhangelsk."

"Dear Uncle Mikhail, surely my father has informed you that I have already received an excellent education. Mama found a marvelous tutor for me, and I was very diligent in my lessons. But," she paused and gazed at him curiously, "perhaps you think there is something missing in my education. Do I embarrass you in some way by my lack of learning or culture?"

Mikhail laughed nervously. "Not at all, child. But we can never come near to learning all that the world has to offer. Here in Novoarkhangelsk, most young people attend school until they are seventeen years old. Besides, going to school would give you a good opportunity to meet other young people."

"As I told you last night, I'm not at all anxious to meet other young people. Please believe me, uncle, I am quite content to stay here."

"Nevertheless, Tasha, you are too young to know what is best for you. In a few years you will be thinking of marriage, and you will be glad to have had the opportunity to meet a variety of people to help you choose more wisely."

"I don't intend to think of marriage ever," Tasha stated firmly. Then, seeing Mikhail's shocked expression, she softened her tone and explained. "Why should I want to marry? Mama was not happy in marriage. I'm sure my father was not. And you seem quite content never to have married."

"But my dear child, I would happily have embraced marriage with the right woman. You mustn't close your mind on the subject at such an early age. With an attitude such as that, when the right fellow comes along, you'll be too proud to admit it and then, believe me, you will be miserable for the rest of your life."

Tasha shrugged diffidently. "The relationships I

167

have witnessed speak much more powerfully than your words, Uncle Mikhail," she said quietly.

Mikhail sighed. "Tasha, you are making this much more difficult than need be. You must believe me, I have only your welfare at heart. The bishop maintains a fine boarding school in the northwest part of the city. I intend to speak to him today about enrolling you there."

With shaking hands, Tasha set down her teacup and pushed her chair back from the table. She stared at him with widened eyes, as if begging him to retract his words. It was bad enough that he wanted her to attend school. But sending her to boarding school was tantamount to banishment. And he seemed so anxious to do it right away, as if her presence suddenly displeased him.

Forcing herself to swallow the lump in her throat, Tasha tried to keep her voice steady. "A boarding school? Do you mean I would be required to live there? That I would no longer reside in your home?" Despite her efforts, her voice quivered on the last word, and a tear slid down her cheek.

"You make it sound too harsh, Tasha," he said in a consoling voice. "Of course you would stay at the school during the term. During vacations you would return here. This is your home. Rest assured I have no intentions of giving your room to anyone else."

"Then why must I stay at the school at all? If I must enroll in a school, surely I can learn just as well at one where I could come home every night."

He shook his head. "Boarding school means you stay there, Tasha, as long as school is in session. Trust me, it will be a good experience for you, living with other young people. Besides, there will be many rainy nights when I'm sure you wouldn't want to venture out to come home. You'll see, sharing your life with others will be immeasurably better than rattling around in this old house, where I must leave you alone so often."

Dashing away her tears with the back of her hand,

Tasha jumped up from the table and began pacing in the small breakfast room. She bit her lower lip, feeling a mixture of anger and confusion. How could he so calmly announce that he was sending her away, twisting the simple facts to make it sound as if he had only her best interests at heart? Did he really think she could be so easily deceived?

"I don't understand you!" she cried in frustration. "When I arrived in Novoarkhangelsk, you said this was my home for as long as I wished and you hoped I would never leave. Only yesterday evening, you were telling me what a joy it was to have me here. And now, this morning, you're plotting first to remove me from your house and then to marry me off. Why do you suddenly want to be rid of me?"

"I don't want to be rid of you. Yesterday I spoke selfishly, from my heart, about the happiness you have brought into my life. Today I speak from my mind, thinking of what is best for you."

"But you're not thinking of what is best for me!" she screamed. "If you wanted what was best for me you would think of my feelings! But you seem intent on pushing me out, just as my father forced me out of Birchwood!"

Ignoring his pained grimace, she continued, "I thought that you actually cared for me. All these months, I believed you really wanted me in your home. I've allowed myself to be taken in, to feel content here. But now I find that you are just as deceitful and loathsome as my father!"

A heavy silence fell upon the room. Her words tore into Mikhail's heart and he could bear it no longer. "Tasha," he whispered in a strained voice, "I *am* your father!"

She stopped pacing, whirling to face him, sure she could not believe what she had just heard. For a long, long moment, she stared at him. Unable to face her any longer, he nodded confirmation and buried his face in his hands.

Tasha went to the window to collect her thoughts.

When she finally spoke, her voice was cold and hard. "You must be lying! Prince Igor Demidov of Moscow is my father. Mama told me so herself."

"Your mother was protecting you," Mikhail sobbed, "keeping a secret that even I did not know until a few years ago, when Prince Demidov wrote to me with the evidence. Prince Demidov was your mother's husband, but I am your father."

Still refusing to face him, Tasha pounded her little fists against the windowsill. "But that's impossible! If mama was married to the prince, she wouldn't—"

"That's not the way it was, Tasha," Mikhail cut her off. "Your mother and I had a brief relationship before she was married to the prince. It was in the betrothal period."

A cold, convincing realization suddenly nudged Tasha's brain. She remembered the note she had read on her mother's dressing table a few months before her death, and how she had puzzled over the prince's words, "Let us hope this one is truly mine."

"So that is why the prince was so cruel to my mother," she whispered. "And why he obviously detested me. He *knew* all along I was not his child."

"Apparently he knew from the first. It seems you were born too soon after their marriage." Mikhail came up behind Tasha and placed his hands on her shoulders. "I'm sorry, my dearest Tasha—for everything; your mother's unhappiness, the prince's mistreatment of you both; especially, that you had to find out this way."

She turned on him angrily, brushing his hands away as she snapped. "Sorry! What good does that do? Being sorry won't bring mama back or erase the pain she suffered for years! How could you abandon her when she was carrying your child?"

"Please, believe me, Tasha. I had no idea I had left her with child. I did ask her to marry me, but she would not break off her engagement to the prince."

He chose his words deliberately, not wanting

to make Natasha sound unfeeling or without a sense of honor. "She felt she had made a commitment to the prince and it was her duty to see it through. Unfortunately, neither of us had the foresight to imagine that my seed had already taken in her."

"And so," she whispered bitterly, "you went on your way, never bothering to consider her welfare again."

"No, Tasha," Mikhail shook his head sadly. "I went on my way, but not a single day or night passed that I did not think of her, yearn for her, and even regret what had passed between us. I did write to her once, begging for a reunion, but when I received no answer, I assumed she was happy and that further interference from me could only bring her pain."

"But she wasn't happy! Even as a child, I could see that her life with the prince was pure misery. And it was your fault! If you hadn't planted your seed in her, perhaps the prince would have treated her with more consideration. Perhaps he would even have loved her and she would have had some chance for happiness."

"Tasha! Tasha!" he cried, covering his ears in anguish. "Those very thoughts have plagued me ever since Prince Demidov wrote to me, obviously anxious for me to take you off his hands. Why do you suppose I haven't told you sooner that I am your father, even though I ached to call you 'daughter'? It was because I feared you would despise me and revile me, just as you are now doing, when all I want is your love and understanding!"

Bursting into tears, Tasha sank into a chair and hid her face against the table. "I want to understand!" she sobbed. "I want to love you—I have no one else! But I keep thinking of mama and how she suffered."

Mikhail pulled his chair close to hers and placed his arm around her shoulders. Her body shook with sobs. To his relief, she did not shake him off. He let her sob out her grief and hurt and disillusionment, and he felt his own tears tracing salty paths down his cheeks. Finally she raised her head and regarded

171

him with tear-swollen eyes. Taking a sniffling breath, she asked in a shaking voice, "Did you love her?"

His eyes told her the answer even before he spoke. "I loved her from the first moment I glimpsed her. I continue to love her still, and shall do so until the day I die."

Her voice becoming firmer, Tasha continued her questioning. "But if she was already engaged to the prince, how did you—" She paused, uncertain of how to phrase the all-important question. Taking a deep breath, she began again. "Did you possess her against her will?"

He hesitated. How many times had he asked himself the same question, only to conclude that she had had ample opportunity to resist, yet she had responded to him with a desire equal to his.

"No, Tasha," he replied steadily, "I did not rape your mother. You are so young I cannot hope for you to understand—that is one reason I had intended to put off telling you this until you were a few years older—but sometimes love and passion are so powerful that they take control of a person's whole being. It is only afterwards that the mind recalls us to our responsibilities, just as your mother later remembered her duty to her betrothed."

An image of her own young body, writhing ecstatically beneath Jared's on his narrow bunk, flashed through Tasha's mind. No, she thought ruefully, I am not too young to understand. No doubt you would be shocked to discover just how fully I understand the power of passion.

"So," she asked slowly, "do you think that mama also loved you?"

"Yes," he nodded, "for a time, at least, I am sure she loved me. Perhaps her pride would not allow her to admit it, but I'm sure you know your mother was not the type of woman who would give herself to a man she did not love."

Tasha nodded in agreement, wondering if she herself was the type who would give herself to a man she did not love. Had she loved Jared? Did she love him still?

She stared across the room at the velvet-flocked wallpaper. How different their lives would have been if her mother had met Mikhail before being promised to Prince Demidov.

Tasha tried to imagine her mother in this house, dressed stunningly in an ice-blue satin gown for a ball at the castle. She tried to imagine her strolling with Mikhail, through the city's public gardens, their hands clasped. Under different circumstances, she would gladly have accepted Mikhail Lisovsky as her father. He was handsome, considerate, amiable. He had all the qualities she would have desired in a father but never found in Igor Demidov.

Thinking again of all Mikhail had told her that morning, and of his past allusion to a lost love, she blurted, "Was mama the one—was she the reason you never married?"

"Yes," he replied, taking her hand gently in his. "No other woman could compare to your mother, and I have always felt it would be useless to let any woman try."

For a few more moments they were silent, then, gently squeezing her hand, Mikhail asked, "Can you ever forgive me for the harm I have done to your mother and to you?"

She shrugged uncertainly. "I don't know. I'm sorry, but I just don't know. I can understand, I think, but forgiveness is something else. Right now, I am very confused and upset."

He smiled patiently. "Then perhaps it would be best if I left you alone to sort out your thoughts. I have business to take care of at the company headquarters, so I probably will be away for the rest of the day."

He went for his hat, and before leaving, returned to the breakfast room. "I won't pressure you, Tasha. You must be guided by your own feelings. But I must tell you that I love you with the greatest love any father could offer a daughter, and I hope that you can find it in your heart to love me."

From the window, Tasha watched him walk down the steps and away, toward the government buildings. His usually proud bearing was gone, and his shoulders seemed slumped in dejection. Instead of his usual, lively step, he dragged his feet, as if it was an effort to walk.

She did not doubt that he loved her, and yet her emotions were in such turmoil that she was at a loss to know how she felt toward him. As Mikhail disappeared around the corner, she turned from the window and went to the drawing room. Filling a glass with fresh tea from the samovar, she sat down beside the fireplace and again burst into tears.

Chapter Fifteen

1864

Tasha had been in the drawing room almost an hour, her plans for an outing in the gardens washed away with her tears, when Xenia bustled into the room.

"Gospoja, Tasha," she said excitedly, "there is a gentleman to see you."

Without even looking up, Tasha replied, "I don't know any gentlemen in Novoarkhangelsk, and I don't wish to meet any today."

"Ah, but you do know this one," Xenia cajoled, "and I think you would like to see him."

Raising her tear-stained face to Xenia, Tasha snapped, "Can't you see I'm in no condition to entertain anyone? For heaven's sakes, please tell whoever it is I'm indisposed and send him away."

From beyond the doorway, a cheerful voice intruded, "Now that's a hell of a way to treat a fellow who's just paddled countless miles in a bidarka for just one glimpse of you."

"Jared?" Tasha jerked her head toward the door, unable to believe her ears.

With a jaunty grin, he bowed low. "I'm afraid so, love."

"Jared!" she shrieked ecstatically, bolting from the chair and flinging herself into his arms.

Over Tasha's shoulder, Jared caught the eyes of the housekeeper, who was shaking her head in consternation. With a broad smile, he returned Tasha's embrace, swinging her off her feet and twirling her around.

"I told you that we would meet again," he said as he set her back on her feet and stood back to look at her admiringly. "But after your parting words, I hadn't expected you to be quite so pleased to see me."

"But I *am* pleased to see you," she murmured, rubbing her cheek against his chest. "So very pleased."

At the sound of a cough behind her, Tasha turned. "Haven't you work to attend to elsewhere in the house, Xenia? I would like to speak privately with the gentleman."

Xenia shrugged and muttered, "First you don't want to see him, now you want to be alone with him. There is no way of understanding you young people. And it hardly seems right for me to leave you here unchaperoned."

Tasha stamped her foot impatiently. "Gospodin Northrup and I shared a room much smaller than this on his ship—without any chaperone. Now be gone. And close the door as you leave."

The housekeeper looked skeptically from Jared to Tasha, but, seeing the determination in Tasha's eyes, she obeyed, sighing loudly as she closed the door.

"Now," Tasha began, pulling Jared toward the settee, "you must tell me how you came to be here."

Raising her chin in his hand, Jared gently kissed each of her red-rimmed eyes. "First," he whispered, 'you must tell me why you have been tormenting those beautiful eyes."

She looked away. "I'd prefer not to talk about it just now."

"But I insist. I could never live with myself if I thought you were unhappy. Was I wrong to bring you here?"

She shook her head helplessly. "I suppose not—I don't know. I was very happy until today. Now I am so confused I just don't know what to think. I don't even know who I am, really."

Frowning, Jared sat down on the settee, and pulled her into his lap. "What do you mean, you don't know who you are?"

"All my life I've thought I was Natalya Igorovna Demidova, the daughter of Prince Igor Demidov of Moscow, but today I learn that I am actually Natalya Mikhailovna Lisovskaya, the daughter of Mikhail Lisovsky."

"But does that really change who you are?" he asked, gently running his fingers across the back of her neck.

She frowned, thinking over his question, then answered slowly, "I suppose not. But this discovery is so upsetting."

"Why? Because you've found out you're not a princess?"

"Of course not! That never mattered to me. I've never felt like much of a princess, anyway."

"Then what is so upsetting? If I were you," he continued practically, "I would be overjoyed to learn that Lisovsky was my father. He seems like a fine person —much better than your prince in Moscow, from what little you've told me of the past."

"He is a better person," Tasha nodded, "and if I had to choose between the two there is no question that I would choose Mikhail Lisovsky. But—"

"But what?" he prodded, lightly pressing his lips against her temple.

176

"I just can't forgive him for what he did to my mother."

"What do you mean?" Jared frowned. "Did he rape her?"

Tasha shook her head emphatically.

"Did he desert her when she was with child?"

Again she shook her head. "Not exactly. He asked her to come with him, but she was already betrothed to my father—I mean the prince—and she refused. And at the time, neither of them knew she was pregnant with me."

"Then I fail to see what there is for you to forgive. I'll grant you that he should never have taken her when she was engaged to another man. But if he did not rape her, then she is as responsible as he. The situation is unfortunate, but I think you should not judge Lisovsky too harshly."

Tasha frowned dubiously. "Do you question my mother's innocence?"

"No, love, I am sure she was at least as innocent as you."

For the second time that morning, Tasha vividly recalled her intimate moments with Jared. Blushing, she looked away from him.

"I wish I could talk to mama about this," she moaned.

"But you can't," Jared stated flatly. "So you must simply decide for yourself whether you can trust Lisovsky to have told you the truth."

"I do believe him. But it upsets me so to know how mama suffered, and why."

"Do you suppose that he did not suffer at all?"

"No. I am quite sure he suffered. Even before he knew of me he suffered, because he missed mama so."

Jared pressed her head to his chest, burying his face in her hair as he murmured, "I am quite sure he suffered too, love. In fact, I think he has suffered more than enough for whatever wrong he has done. If I

177

were you, Tasha, I would not cause him more pain by rejecting him now. I think he needs your love very badly—and he deserves it."

Tasha was silent, allowing him to rock her on his lap, enjoying the warmth of his body, the sound of his heart thumping beneath her ear. Everything Jared said made sense. He was able to analyze the matter with the necessary detachment of one who was not personally involved. But could he really understand her turmoil, and her father's emotional pain?

As if sensing her question, he lifted his head and spoke softly. "I think I can understand, better than you might imagine, just how your father must have ached with longing for his beloved."

Tasha stiffened and sat up to look him in the eye. "So, you do have a sweetheart," she said accusingly. "Why is it that in all our time together you never told me?"

He grinned mischievously. "I doubt that you would have believed me."

Suddenly feeling uncomfortably out of place on his lap, she jumped to her feet and walked to the samovar. Pretending nonchalance, she began to fill a glass, watching the flow of the amber liquid as she tried to regain her composure.

"Still, you might at least have told me. After all—" she stopped, thinking of that night on his bunk when she had willingly surrendered her virginity to him and wondering if, even back then, there had been someone else.

Swallowing hard, she forced herself to continue in a cool voice. "Is she someone you met on one of your whaling voyages?"

"Yes." He could hardly control the undercurrent of laughter in his voice.

"I suppose it is really none of my affair, but do you intend to marry her?"

"If she will have me."

With shaking hands, she stirred a generous portion of honey into her tea. She turned to face him, her voice unconvincingly casual. "I seem to recall you once told me you were already married to the sea—that there was no place in your life for another woman."

He shrugged and raised his bushy blond eyebrows. "Apparently I've changed my mind. Or perhaps I should say, I've had a change of heart," he chuckled.

"I'm afraid I fail to see the wit in your statement," Tasha said bitterly. "I've already had quite a trying day, so I hope you'll forgive me if I am not amused. Perhaps you will be so kind as to tell me why you have come to see me."

Jared smiled expansively. "But certainly, my love."

She frowned. "Under the circumstances, I think that form of address a bit misplaced."

"But you *are* my love. You don't think I'm fool enough to paddle all the way from the other side of Kruzof Island in a bidarka just to say hello to someone I don't care for?"

Tasha shook her head in confusion. "Please stop—You have my head spinning. How can you say you love me when you've just finished telling me about that other woman—the one you intend to marry?"

"Did I say there was another woman?"

"You said—" she hesitated, perplexed. He had said there was a woman he missed, someone he wished to marry. But if there was no other woman, he could only mean—! No, that was impossible. It wasn't *her* he cared for. She had heard him tell Captain Dawson how anxious he was to be rid of her. But, then what was he doing here, in her father's drawing room, after being free of her for more than half a year?

Carefully setting her glass down on a side table, she walked to the settee and sat down beside Jared. She took his warm hands in her icy, shaking ones, and stared into his laughing blue eyes. "Jared, I beg of you, don't play games with my heart," she whispered hoarsely.

As his gaze met hers, the laughter in his eyes drained away, to be replaced by gentle concern and a spark of smoldering passion. "Tasha," he whispered, "love is too sacred to lie about. I've missed you far too much for this to be a joke, and I'm certain that I want you for my wife."

She continued to stare at him in bewilderment, trembling as he squeezed her hands. "I've missed you too, Jared," she finally whispered. "But I've been so afraid to admit it, even to myself. You know, you never so much as hinted that you cared for me."

"Hinted?" He laughed shortly. "My God, girl, did I have to spell it out for you? The problem was that you never believed it. Almost everything I did was out of concern for you, but you always acted as if you despised me!"

"Oh, no, Jared!" she protested. "I never despised you. But I thought you—" She cut herself short with her own nervous laughter. "How silly we both were! And what a lot of time we've wasted! But now that we understand one another, we can begin to make up for all that. Will you take me back aboard the *Freedom* with you?"

He shook his head, grimacing as her laughter turned to a frown.

"But you must!" she pouted. "I don't think I could bear to be separated from you again. And I promise not to complain about the cramped quarters."

He held up his hand to stop her. "Have you forgotten Captain Dawson? He still has not changed his opinion on the merits of having women on board, and I doubt that he'd be pleased by your presence."

"Couldn't you sneak me aboard?"

"Hardly. And when we are married, I won't want to keep you in hiding. I'll want to proclaim our marriage to everyone we meet. Besides, I think we're forgetting something. You can't simply abandon your father now. I think it would break his heart."

"Then perhaps you could just stay here. The *Freedom* can get along well enough without you, and there's plenty of room for you to live in this house. I'm sure Uncle—my father," she stammered slightly over the word, "would not mind."

Jared shook his head. "Your father has already made it clear he is not particularly fond of whalemen. It's unfortunate so many of my countrymen have given us a bad name. I'm afraid it's true that many whalemen have cheated the Aleuts and Indians in Russian America, getting them drunk on cheap liquor while they stole their women and supplies. And I doubt that any Indians would have developed syphilis if the whalemen hadn't brought it. It's obvious to me your father would not be pleased to have me join his household just yet.

"As to jumping ship, that would be a foolhardy thing to do. My fortune is tied up in that whaler. If I leave now, I'll forfeit my share of the profits, and I won't have a thing to offer you. It would be better to wait until we return to New Bedford and I collect my due. Then I'll be able to approach your father with an honorable proposal of marriage. I'm sure he will be more inclined to honor my request for your hand if I show myself to be a responsible provider. Perhaps it would be best if you told him nothing of our plans until I return."

"But when will that be?" Tasha wailed.

He shrugged. "My guess is the summer of next year. We've been out three years already, and if we have a good season this summer, the hold should be full. After we return to New Bedford, I'll collect my due and then ship out again, probably aboard the *Freedom*. Except then, I *will* jump ship when we reach the Aleutians. I'll arrive here with half my fortune, prepared to collect the other half," he kissed her forehead meaningfully.

"You make it all sound so simple, but I'm not sure I can survive without you for a whole year. And what if something happens to you in the meantime?"

"Nothing will happen, Tasha. I've been a whaleman for eight long years, and I'm tougher than any stupid ocean beast. Of course I'll miss you, but it will be easier to bear if I am certain that at the end of that time, I can claim you as mine. That was the worst torment of these last months—not knowing if you would accept my proposal."

He paused and gazed into her eyes. "But perhaps you'll tire of waiting. Perhaps you will still change your mind. You must have hundreds of others clamoring for your hand."

She smiled shyly. "You needn't worry. There is no one else. There couldn't be anyone else, Jared. But it will be a lonely year without you."

He traced a teasing line of kisses from her temple to her ear and whispered, "Then you must go out and enjoy yourself. Go to every ball and party to which you are invited—and I'm sure there will be scores. You are much too young to languish in a cold house while I am out adventuring on the high seas. You can even flirt a bit and practice your feminine charms while you still have your freedom. Once we are married I'm afraid I shall be a very jealous husband."

She giggled as he playfully nipped her ear, then turned her face to meet his. Hungrily, she parted her lips, inhaling his mouth, his breath, the love that he had finally confessed. Thrilling as she felt him shudder with pleasure, her tongue traced teasingly along his teeth. In response his tongue found its way into her mouth.

Sighing with rapture, she leaned back against the flaring wing of the settee, pulling his lean, warm body with her. His fingers slid to the tiny buttons at the front of her dress. Her breasts strained against her undergarments, yearning to be free. Deftly he undid her bodice, then the ribbons of her camisole.

She moaned softly as his warm hand pushed away the restraining garments and cupped one of her breasts. In a moment, his other hand was cupping her other breast. Then he began to knead the nipples until they became hard. He bent his head to suck tenderly at one of the throbbing mounds, his tongue tracing quick, tantalizing circles around the erect nipple. Burying her fingers in his golden hair, she leaned back, as all the desire she had denied for months released itself, rocking her body with delicious tremors.

As his mouth returned to hers, her frenzied fingers unbuttoned his shirt, pulling it wide open so she could feel the soft hair of his chest tickling her breasts. Her hands slid under his shirt and around his bare back, becoming reacquainted with his firm, taut muscles as she pulled him closer.

"Oh Tasha!" he sighed, his breath warming and tickling her ear, "you are hardly more than a child, and yet you are more woman than any other."

"I am your woman, Jared," she responded simply. "Take me. Take me now and let me show you how completely I am yours."

Trembling with anticipation, he threw up her skirts and petticoats and his hands touched the quivering flesh of her naked thighs. In his eagerness to reach the moist, warm delta hidden within, he accidentally ripped her lacy pantalettes.

"It doesn't matter," she breathed in his ear, her own anticipation transforming her voice to a husky whisper. "Don't stop now, dearest Jared!"

To his delighted surprise, he felt her fingers opening the buttons on his trousers. Without hesitation, her hand darted inside, grasping his ready hardness, then encircling it and massaging it while he panted with unbridled pleasure. In response, his fingers found her center of sensitivity, which he stroked repeatedly until she was squirming and whimpering.

Together they slid lower on the settee, so that she was lying on her back with him atop her. Lodging himself between her thighs, he slid into her easily. She muffled her gasps of joy against his broad shoulder. This time she knew it was no dream. He was here, bringing her ecstasy beyond all of her dreams. This time she knew he wanted her, not just for the pleasure of the moment, but forever.

Encouraged by that knowledge, Tasha abandoned herself to the tide of passion surging through her.

She twined her legs around his back, raising her buttocks to receive his thrusts, every one penetrating deeper within her and sending ever-stronger shivers up her spine and through her whole body. Just when she thought her own body could not bear any more pleasure, his passion culminated and her joy intensified in a final explosion of unbelievable ecstasy.

After a few moments, he eased himself away from her, kissing her one, last, lingering time. With a hasty look at the drawing room door, he began to button up his trousers and shirt.

"I think you had better put yourself in order, too," he suggested. "What if one of the servants, or your father, should walk in?"

"My father is gone for the day," she said languidly. "And none of the servants are likely to disturb us." Nevertheless, she sat up, straightened her skirt and petticoats, and began retying the ribbons on her camisole. She had just done the top button of her dress when Xenia burst into the room.

After a brief glance at Tasha's tousled hair and flushed face, and an accusing glare at Jared, the housekeeper waved her feather duster and announced, "You go on with your talking. I have my work to do in here."

"Xenia!" Tasha exclaimed in outrage, embarrassed at the thought of what the old woman might have witnessed had she entered just a few moments earlier, "haven't you been instructed to knock before entering a room?"

Xenia shook her head. "For twelve years I have been housekeeper here, and Gospodin Lisovsky has never told me to knock. And you," she regarded Tasha through narrowed eyes, "are too young to be keeping secrets with gentlemen."

Sighing in exasperation, Tasha rose indignantly. "Well, never mind, dust away. The gentleman and I are going for a stroll in the gardens."

With a toss of her head, she walked to the door, motioning Jared to follow, and leaving Xenia to stare open-mouthed after them.

Except for the topiary section, where conical-shaped evergreens and fastidiously sheared hedges were on view, Novoarkhangelsk's public gardens offered little to see in April. The rosebushes were still brown from the ravages of winter, and no other flowers had yet pushed up through the cold ground. Oblivious to the limited horticultural offerings, Tasha and Jared strolled hand-in-hand along the garden's pebbled paths. The day was chilly, but beneath her sealskin cloak she still glowed with the warmth of their love-making. For a long time she said nothing, not wishing to disturb the unspoken communication they shared.

Finally, as she led him away from the garden toward her favorite woodland path, she asked, "How long can you stay in Novoarkhangelsk?"

He grimaced. "I won't be staying at all."

"What?" She stared at him, unbelieving. "Now, don't tease me, Jared!"

"I wish I were teasing," he answered miserably, slipping his arm around her waist and pulling her close to his side.

"But you can't have paddled from Kruzof Island only to leave so soon!"

He nodded. "I've got to get back to the ship. You know how impatient Captain Dawson is. He said he'd stop only long enough to take on supplies and make some minor repairs. I don't think he would be pleased to wait for me. And if I miss the sailing, I can never hope to collect my lay. You do understand how important it is, for us, don't you?"

Nodding glumly, she turned aside to hide the tears that sprang to her eyes.

"Anyway," he bent to kiss the back of her neck, "the trip has been more than worth it for me. Knowing that you will wait, that you are mine—after all the nights I've lain awake wondering if you would have me.

185

That will make everything worthwhile. I just hope my visit does not cause you too much pain."

She laughed, blinking away her tears. "Your visit has brought me nothing but joy, Jared. I shall treasure these moments until the day we are reunited."

Circling his neck with her arms, she pulled his head toward her until their lips met. Their kiss was long and tender, filled with all the gentleness and mutual concern of true love, with only a slight taste of the passion that would have to smolder until their reunion.

Laughing lightly, Jared pulled away and gazed into her dark eyes, his own shining softly. "I almost forgot," he murmured, sliding his hand into his trouser pocket, "I brought you something else to treasure until my return."

He took her left hand and slid an exquisitely carved white ring onto her third finger.

Tasha gasped, examining the minute details of the carving. The polished white ring consisted of two narrow bands which were joined by a twining vine of tiny primroses. Amid the flowers were carved the initials "TD" and "JN." "It's exquisite," she breathed. "Where in the world did you get it?"

"I didn't get it, love," he replied, his eyes dancing merrily. "I made it."

"You made it!" she repeated incredulously. "Those big, clumsy hands made this beautiful piece of jewelry?"

"May I remind you," he teased, playfully pinching her cheek, "that not an hour ago you did not seem to think my hands at all clumsy! But, yes, I made it. It's scrimshaw, an art every whaleman learns his first year out. It's a great way to pass the time between whale sightings."

"But how did you make it?"

"I carved it from a piece of whale's tooth."

"And how ever did you guess the right size?" She twisted the ring around on her finger.

He shrugged and laughed. "Must have been fate, Tasha, my love."

"Well," she smiled mischievously, "I'll be proud to wear it, but there is one problem."

"What is that?"

"You've got my initials wrong. As I told you earlier today, my name is Tasha Lisovskaya."

"Well, Miss Tasha Lisovskaya," he replied with a light slap on her rump, "I shall just have to carve you another. It will give me something to do during the long winter. But don't get too accustomed to being called Lisovskaya. I intend to change your name to Northrup soon enough."

"Tasha Northrup," she repeated dreamily. "Tasha Mikhailovna Northrup." She giggled. "If I have any more name changes I shall have to be baptized all over again!"

"Well, whatever you call yourself, you shall never escape me. Now come, give this poor sailor a kiss before he returns to the sea."

Her eyes clouded over again. "I wish you didn't have to go, Jared. Let me at least walk with you to your bidarka."

"No," he said emphatically, then softened his tone as he gestured down the woodland path. "It's only a short distance; I hid it in the bushes near the end of the shoreline promenade. But I'd rather say our good-byes here. If I have to watch your tears as I leave, I'll end up bawling myself, and next thing I'll be crashing the damned bidarka against the rocks and you'll have a dead fiancé."

"All right," she whispered, wiping her tears against his jacket. "Hold me, Jared. I need a long embrace to carry me through the months to come."

He wrapped his arms around her, smoothing her hair as he pressed her head against his chest. Reaching up, she twined his hair around her fingers and slowly pulled his mouth down to hers.

With a sigh of regret, he finally took his mouth

187

away, lightly brushing her nose, her forehead, and each moist eye.

"Be brave, Tasha," he whispered in her ear. "Think of me. Pray for me. Remember, I love you. And be kind to your new-found father."

Before she could swallow the lump in her throat, he was gone. Blinking in the bright sunlight, she looked along the path, but it was already empty. Taking another path, she quickly scrambled up to the bluff that overlooked the shoreline. She scanned the water until she saw a small, Indian-made craft, looking so fragile and tiny as it bobbed in the waters in the shadow of Mount Edgecumbe.

As if sensing her presence, Jared turned and gazed at the bluff until he caught sight of her frantically waving. He waved back in answer, then turned his full attention to his paddling.

"I love you!" Tasha screamed. Her words came back to her, reverberating off the mountains that surrounded her, and she wondered if he heard her over the crashing waves and the cawing of the gulls.

She watched the boat until it disappeared beyond the bulge of Mount Edgecumbe, then slowly began to retrace her steps toward the garden, and then to the house. Thinking of her precious moments with Jared, she understood suddenly all that her father must have suffered—to have discovered ecstasy, only to be robbed of it for the remainder of his life.

She wondered: What would happen if Jared had planted his seed within her and then something prevented him from returning, and she bore his child. If, at some future time, their child was to meet him, would she want the child to despise him? She knew the answer immediately: She would want the child to love Jared just as she loved him. Realizing that, all the hurt and resentment she had felt that morning drained away, to be replaced by deep sympathy for the man she now knew was her father. She knew then that when he returned home that evening, she would proudly and lovingly call him "papa."

Chapter Sixteen
1864-1865

It was late afternoon when Tasha returned to the house. Xenia let her in, eyeing her curiously, and informed her that Gospodin Lisovsky was not yet home. Tasha let the old woman take her cloak, then hurried up the stairs to her bedroom.

For several minutes, she sat on her bed, examining the intricate detail of the ring Jared had carved for her. She wanted to show it to everyone, to proclaim how caring and talented her beloved was, how much he must love her to have done the painstaking work required to create the ring. But she knew she could not tell anyone just yet.

As Jared had pointed out to her, her father, like most residents of Novoarkhangelsk, was not exactly fond of whalemen. He would probably not be too pleased to learn she had met with Jared and that they had planned their marriage without consulting him.

It would surely be better to wait until Jared returned to present his own case to her father. When he arrived with his carefully-saved profits accumulated from his voyages, her father would have to agree that he was a responsible young man, and worthy of her hand. So, for the present it would be best if no one knew about the ring.

Still, she was determined not to be without it for one moment until their reunion. Going to her cedar bureau, she opened the top drawer and looked over the satin ribbons she used to tie back her hair. Her fingers pulled out a deep blue ribbon. Yes, it was perfect, she thought, almost the color of Jared's eyes. Taking the ribbon, she quickly threaded it through the ring and then tied it securely around her neck. Beneath her dress and camisole, the ring dangled between her breasts, close to her heart, dispelling at least some of the emptiness she had felt as she watched Jared's bidarka move out to sea.

After vigorously brushing her hair, Tasha descended the stairs to wait for her father. As she reached the foot of the stairs, Xenia bustled by and gave her an approving nod.

"Da, you look much better now, with your hair neatly combed. I won't ask what you and the young gentleman were doing to get you into such a state as I found you. But I must warn you such situations only lead to trouble—and you're too lovely a girl to be throwing your life away because of some foolish thing you did as no more than a child!"

"Xenia!" Tasha exclaimed. "What ever are you talking about?"

The old woman shook her head and clucked her tongue. "I only hope you are really as innocent as you would have me believe."

"For heaven's sakes, Xenia, must I remind you that you're the one who insisted I see the young man? I told you at the time I did not wish to be disturbed."

"I know, I know." Xenia rolled her eyes heavenward. "I just pray to the Almighty Father I won't live to regret it."

"And I suppose you intend to tell Gospodin Lisovsky about my visitor and all that you imagine occurred?"

"Oh no," Xenia said quickly, crossing herself as she hurried toward the kitchen. "I don't wish to be held responsible. I just hope no ill comes of the incident."

Smiling, Tasha turned toward the drawing room. She could bear the old woman's reproof so long as she did not have to worry about her carrying tales of Jared's visit to her father.

Within a few moments, Tasha heard the front door open and Mikhail Lisovsky entered the house. As Georgi, his manservant, was taking his coat, he glanced up and saw Tasha approaching from the drawing room.

Smiling nervously, he said, "Good evening, Tasha."

"Good evening, papa," she replied quietly.

Mikhail's eyes widened in shock, and Tasha hurried to explain. "I hope I have not offended you. It's just that, after this morning, it seems a bit awkward to call you Uncle Mikhail. However, if you would prefer—"

"My dear child," Mikhail silenced her with a hearty embrace, "you make me very happy. You mustn't think I'm upset. You just caught me off guard. After this morning, I hadn't expected you to be quite so ready to accept me."

"I acted very foolishly this morning," she said meekly. "You've suffered long enough and I realize now that I love you too much to want to cause you more suffering."

With glistening eyes, Mikhail looked down on his young daughter.

She seemed to have matured in the hours since he had seen her. He wondered what could have brought about the change, then shrugged in simple gratitude that it had occurred.

Sniffing the air, he changed the subject. "I smell borsch and piroshki. Let's see if supper is ready." Taking her arm, he led her into the dining room and seated her at the pine table.

As a servant cleared away the soup dishes, Tasha buttered a second slice of gray bread and looked across the table at her father. "What did you find out about the boarding school?" she asked, willing now to accept anything that would fill the hours until Jared's return.

Mikhail coughed uncomfortably and waited for the serving maid to set a plate of lamb and potatoes in front of him before replying. "It seems I've been too wrapped up in my work these last years to pay attention to all that's been happening in the town. Perhaps I paid little attention to the schools, since I had no children here. At any rate, it seems the boarding school was turned into a seminary a few years back.

And since you are neither a young man nor likely to be entering the priesthood, you will be pleased to learn I will not be enrolling you there."

Tasha smiled. "Then are there other schools in Novoarkhangelsk I might attend?"

Her father nodded. "There are other schools, but for the present I think we shall put off enrolling you. The current term will be over in less than two months, and we can consider the matter anew in the fall. But, as you pointed out this morning, you are already well-educated and perhaps you need no further training."

He had given the question serious consideration during the day, and decided not to force his daughter into anything. Besides, if she could not board at school, the major advantage of enrolling her was eliminated. Of course, he could send her to another boarding school in the Empire, the Smolny Institute in St. Petersburg, perhaps. But he did not think he could bear to send her so far away. He still felt a bit uneasy about a possible repetition of last night's events, but he desperately hoped he would be able to control himself now that their true relationship had been revealed. For one thing, he resolved, he would be extra careful not to drink himself into insensibility.

For another, he would make every effort to find his daughter a suitable husband, someone who could convince her that she did, indeed, wish to marry. He did not know that Jared Northrup had already accomplished that feat.

"Whatever you think is best, papa," Tasha responded demurely, again making him wonder at her change of attitude.

In the next months, Tasha spent many days at the public library, which had an excellent collection of books and periodicals. It didn't matter that the periodicals were all at least a year old, being brought by steamer from St. Petersburg or Okhotsk once a year—they still contained much fascinating information from other parts of the continent. She immersed herself in the works of Pushkin and Lermontov, as well as the newer novelists, Tolstoy, Dostoyevsky and Goncharov, and found that she was as contented as could be, except for Jared not being there.

Often, as she hurried through the streets trying to avoid the island's frequent rains, she would pass Indians from the Kolosh village on Novoarkhangelsk's northern boundary. Both the men and women habitually dressed in faded blue blankets, the women's often embroidered with beads and mother of pearl. Rings and shell ornaments dangled from the pierced ears and noses of many Kolosh, and Tasha noted with interest that some painted their faces black. Her father explained that they did so in memory of dead relatives.

Every night, just before sundown, a bell was rung at the Novoarkhangelsk stockade. At its tolling, all the Kolosh still within the town hurriedly completed their business and rushed through the gate to return to their village. Under penalty of imprisonment, the Kolosh were not permitted to be within the limits of Novoarkhangelsk after sundown. Once, early in the city's history, the savages had burned the settlement and massacred its residents. Ever since, the Russians had been careful to keep them strictly controlled.

To Tasha, the restrictions seemed harsh. Still, she had to admit that she would be frightened were she to meet a Kolosh with a grotesquely painted face and nose pierced by a shell in the dark of night. And she supposed the Russians had at least improved their lot by bringing to them religion, erecting a church for their worship, and opening a school for their children.

Summer brought an abundance of blueberries on the wild bushes covering the mountain slopes, and Tasha spent many afternoons gathering the luscious fruit to enjoy at breakfast and for desserts. The season also brought renewed social activity, with numerous invitations arriving at the house for Tasha and her father.

Since Tasha had already attended one ball as Mikhail's niece, the two puzzled at first about how to present her now that she knew herself to be his actual daughter. Finally, they agreed to explain that Mikhail had decided to adopt his "niece," since both her parents had died some years earlier. That explanation, they felt, would protect Tasha's position in society, while allowing her to freely call Mikhail "papa."

Welcoming a way to fill the months until Jared's return, Tasha accepted every invitation they received. Mikhail was delighted to see his daughter's transformation from a brooding recluse to a gay socialite. With her witty conversation, ready smile, and tantalizing appearance, she quickly became one of the most popular young women in Novoarkhangelsk, and was surrounded by men at every event they attended.

Mikhail noted with pride that his daughter would have no difficulty finding a fine husband among her many admirers. In fact, he felt more than pride—he also felt relief. There had been no repetition of that close encounter in her bedroom, but he was nevertheless haunted by the constant fear that he might someday let down his guard.

From time to time, Tasha would consider telling her father about Jared. But she was convinced that Jared was right to suggest she await his return before revealing their engagement.

Amused by the way her father encouraged her to meet all the young men, Tasha responded to each introduction graciously, secure in the knowledge that Jared would be returning for her before one of them could become troublesome. As an extra precaution, she flirted a little with all of them, and showed none even the slightest preference.

The various social events helped to fill the afternoons and evenings, but nothing could ease the emptiness of the nights, when she would lay awake, pressing

194

Jared's ring against her breasts while she longed for his comforting presence beside her.

From the day he had given it to her, Tasha had worn the ring constantly. When her dresses were too revealing to conceal the satin ribbon around her neck, she would remove it and weave it through the ribbons that tied her camisole, refusing to be without it at any time.

Since she thought it safest not to confide in anyone, Tasha wouldn't even let Theodosia help her to dress or undress, lest she discover the ring. Having heard whispered rumors from Xenia about goings-on in the drawing room on a particular day, Theodosia began to fear that Tasha was hiding something shameful. But as the months passed and Tasha's well-fitted gowns revealed no change in her slender outline, the maid, though perplexed, sighed in relief.

In the fall, Prince Maksutov, who had returned to Russia after the death of his young wife, came home to the colony, accompanied by an attractive new wife, Maria. Baranov Castle again became the hub of Novoarkhangelsk's social life, with the governing couple hosting an endless succession of balls plus a state dinner every Sunday. The new Princess Maksutova was only nineteen years old, and her warm, open manner quickly endeared her to the residents of Novoarkhangelsk. People of all rank were entertained at her parties, and she never refused a request to dance, no matter who asked her.

On New Year's Day, the prince and princess hosted a lavish masquerade ball for two hundred guests. Tasha and her father were invited. In the mirrored drawing room a towering evergreen was hung with gifts, one for everyone in attendance. Tasha was examining her gift—a tiny ceramic bell delicately painted with a winter scene reminiscent of Birchwood —when her father approached with a smiling, masked stranger.

"My dear, I would like to introduce Lieutenant

Yuri Zarevsky. Lieutenant Zarevsky is a naval officer employed by the Russian-American Company."

Smiling mechanically, Tasha offered the lieutenant her hand. "How very nice to meet you, Lieutenant Zarevsky."

He bent to kiss her hand, tickling it with his thin, black, meticulously-groomed moustache, then straightened up, his dark eyes full of challenge. "Please call me Yuri. And if you will permit it, I shall call you Tasha. I have been watching you all evening, and I feel I already know you well."

Despite his courteous words, there was a touch of mockery in his voice that repelled Tasha. She would have liked to reply that she would prefer to be more formal, but not wishing to embarrass her father, she lowered her eyes and murmured, "As you wish."

The young officer smiled broadly, as if to indicate he had won a major victory. Still holding her hand, he pulled her firmly toward the ballroom. "I hear the music beginning again. Perhaps you would honor me with a dance." He turned to Mikhail. "If you have no objection, sir."

"None at all," Mikhail replied heartily. "You young people go and enjoy yourselves!"

Sliding his arm around her waist, Yuri guided her toward the ballroom. "I assume," he bent to whisper in Tasha's ear, as if they were already intimate acquaintances, "that you also have no objection."

"If Princess Maksutova has the generosity to dance with whomever asks her," Tasha responded icily, "I feel I should follow her example."

"Oh ho!" Yuri chuckled, pulling her close as they glided onto the dance floor, "I see you are full of spirit, as I suspected. Good! I like a bit of challenge in a woman—as long as she remembers her place."

"And just what do you consider a woman's place?" Tasha asked irritably.

"You will learn in good time, never fear," he said, adding sardonically, "yes, little tigress, I may be just the man to tame you!"

196

Foolish man, Tasha thought. Only one man will ever have power over me. And only because I love him. Thinking of Jared brought a dreamy smile to her countenance, which the lieutenant immediately assumed was for his benefit.

"See," he whispered, "you are already responding to my irresistible charm."

"Forgive me," Tasha retorted, "I'm afraid my mind was wandering." Changing her expression to a stern frown, she studied her dance partner coolly.

He was a head taller than she, with broad shoulders and a narrow waist. His dark hair glistened beneath the chandeliers, and even behind his mask, his eyes shone with unadulterated self-assurance. By most women's standards, she supposed he would be considered attractive. In fact, several heads turned as they whirled smartly around the dance floor. But the way he looked at her, as if by a simple nod of his head he could secure complete possession of her, made her shudder in revulsion.

"And how," he asked, "did such an enchanting princess come to be in this godforsaken land?"

"I live here!" she bristled, "and I would hardly call Novoarkhangelsk godforsaken! I find it quite charming. Furthermore, it seems clear that Princess Maksutova, who is far more enchanting than I could ever hope to be, is also pleased to be living here."

"Ah, but she has a reason. She chose to come here for the joy of being with her husband." He shrugged. "But perhaps you will find a husband to take you away from here one day. With your face and physical attributes," he squeezed her slim waist suggestively, "the task should not be difficult."

Ignoring his last remark, Tasha asked, "Since you hold our town in such low regard, why are you here?"

"Out of simple duty, nothing more. I've been assigned here for a few months, strictly as an observer. In the summer, I shall be sailing for Kamchatka, where the company hopes to expand its fur-trading operations."

Tasha nodded absently at his explanation, hoping she would not run into him at too many more social events. As the musicians stopped playing, she started to move away from him, only to feel his strong grasp around her waist.

"I had hoped to continue dancing with you, Tasha. I'm quite sure the orchestra will not tire for at least another hour."

"You're very flattering sir, but I could not possibly be so selfish as to deny the other women present the unbounded pleasure of your company. Besides," her eyes hurriedly scanned the room until they found Ilya Kostronov, another acquaintance, "I'm afraid I've already promised this dance to another, and I take great pains to keep my promises."

Leaving him dumbstruck at having failed to impress her, she floated across the room and tapped a surprised but delighted Ilya on the shoulder. For the remainder of the evening, Tasha managed to elude Yuri Zarevsky. She was not always so fortunate in the months ahead. He seemed to appear at almost every social event to which she was invited, and was most persistent in his attentions to her.

Mistakenly interpreting their verbal sparring as lighthearted, flirtatious banter, Mikhail watched the couple with pleasure, thinking what a fine husband Yuri Zarevsky would make for his daughter. He was impressed with the young lieutenant's wit and his self-assurance, and he assumed Tasha felt likewise.

To her despair, Mikhail began to entrust her to Yuri Zarevsky's care at each party where they met, until it seemed that the lieutenant had a monopoly on her company.

Her one consolation, as June approached, was the certainty that Yuri would be departing for Kamchatka before the summer's end, and by that time, Jared would have arrived to proclaim her his own.

On reflection, Tasha admitted to herself that Yuri would not be so unpleasant if he did not constantly exercise such a high opinion of himself. He was undeniably intelligent, and handsome in much the same way as she remembered Prince Demidov. But he also possessed the same mocking smugness that, even as a girl, she had found so repulsive in the prince. Perhaps if he did not remind her so much of the prince, and if her heart was not already committed to Jared, she might have judged him less harshly. She knew most of the other young women in Novoarkhangelsk envied her all the time he spent with her.

But she knew she could never bring herself to care for him, and would gladly have traded her time with him for time with any of the pleasant, unassuming young men she had met before his arrival in Novoarkhangelsk.

Chapter Seventeen

1865

Early in June, on the evening of Tasha's seventeenth birthday, she and her father enjoyed a quiet dinner at home. It seemed strange to her that they had not received a single invitation for that evening, but she was relieved that she was at least to be spared Yuri Zarevsky's pompous presence.

After dinner, as they sipped their tea in the drawing room, Mikhail presented her with an ivory satin gown that was cut fashionably décolleté at the bodice. Green satin trim accented the neckline, the waistline and the hem, giving the gown a simple elegance.

Before she had finished exclaiming over the dress, he slid a thin box into her hands, opening it to reveal a shimmering emerald pendant—perfectly matched to the trim of her gown—suspended on a delicate gold chain.

"Oh, papa," she cried, throwing her arms around his neck as tears sprang to her eyes, "You have made this my most perfect birthday ever! If only—" She stopped herself, on the verge of mentioning Jared. She was expecting him now at any time, certainly by September at the latest.

"If only what, child?" Mikhail asked, lifting her chin to look into her tear-filled eyes for the answer.

She shook her head quickly, as if to nullify the true reason for her tears. "If only I could have come to live with you sooner."

Mikhail's eyes clouded, and his mellow voice became husky as he replied, "Yes, if only you and your mother could have joined me years ago. If only I could have brought happiness to both of you."

Clearing his throat briskly, he pulled away from her. "Now then, suppose you go on upstairs and put on all this finery. We won't know if it really is beautiful until you have modeled it."

"All right." Tasha gathered up the dress and necklace and gave him a quick kiss as she hurried toward the door. "Wait here," she called over her shoulder. "I'll only be a few moments."

"Take your time, daughter," he replied amiably. "I'm sure your beauty will be a picture worth waiting for."

In her room, Tasha quickly undid the flowered broadcloth dress she had worn to dinner. Nervously, she untied the satin ribbon holding her ring and laced the ring through the ribbons of her camisole, thinking how perfect this birthday would be if only Jared would arrive that very evening. She slid into the new gown, fumbling with the tiny buttons and loops.

She had managed to fasten almost half the buttons when there was a knock at the door, followed by Theodosia's timid voice, "May I enter?"

"Yes, certainly." Tasha presented the woman her back as she entered the room. "These buttons are impossible! Could you finish them for me?"

"But of course." Theodosia's nimble fingers quickly matched loops to buttons, and she turned Tasha around to admire the full effect. "That Gospodin Lisovsky certainly does have taste when it comes to choosing a gown."

Tasha nodded, opening the catch on the emerald pendant and fastening the necklace around her neck. "Indeed he does." She studied her reflection in the mirror—was that stunning woman herself?—wishing Jared could be there to see her. "But what was it you wanted, Theodosia?"

"Oh," the servant replied, picking up a hairbrush, "Gospodin Lisovsky sent me up to see to your hair."

Tasha frowned, looking in the glass at her well-brushed hair. "I can't see why it is necessary to do anything further with my hair. Are we going out?"

"No." The servant shuffled nervously. "He simply said I should do something with it befitting the gown."

With a sigh, Tasha took a seat in front of her dressing table so that Theodosia could dress her hair. Half an hour later, her hair elaborately coiled atop her head, Tasha was ready for her father's scrutiny.

Mikhail was standing at the foot of the stairs. He looked up at the sound of her soft steps. "Yes," he nodded exuberantly, his eyes lit with pride and love, "the gown does you justice. And you it. You look even more enchanting than I had imagined."

"Thank you, papa." Tasha's cheeks turned rosy under his gaze. Her eyes moved questioningly to the closed double doors of the drawing room. "I suppose you got bored waiting for me. I'm sorry I took so long."

"Well," he took her arm and pulled her toward the drawing room doors, "I would judge you more than worth the wait. Now, I wish you would play something for me—I'm sure the piano is lonely for your touch."

Tasha smiled, happy to be able to please him. But her smile became a gasp of surprise as her father threw open the doors and she surveyed the scene inside the drawing room.

"Happy Birthday!" fifty voices shouted in unison.

She turned questioning eyes to Mikhail, who smiled sheepishly. "I could not resist a small celebration in your honor. After all, you are the one thing in my life of which I am most proud."

Touched, Tasha smiled and squeezed his hand. "It's very sweet of you, papa. And to think I never suspected a thing!" Advancing into the room, she accepted the good wishes of her friends and acquaintances.

She had greeted only about half the guests when a great sheaf of variously-shaded purple and white flowers was thrust into her arms.

"Orchids!" Tasha exclaimed, laying her warm cheek against the cool blooms. "How very beautiful they are! I'm so grateful."

"I hoped you would be pleased," said a familiar voice.

She looked up into the face of Yuri Zarevsky. "I had them brought over from Unalaska Island especially for this happy occasion," he explained.

He appeared very pleased with himself. Tasha flushed, embarrassed, and angry with herself for showing it. "Really you shouldn't have gone to the trouble," she murmured. "Please excuse me now while I greet my other guests."

More than an hour passed before Yuri Zarevsky caught up with Tasha again. Standing by a window during a momentary lull, she felt a strong hand grasp her elbow. "You're a bit flushed from the noise and the excitement," he whispered. "Perhaps you could use a bit of fresh air."

Caught off guard by Yuri for the second time that night, she agreed. "Yes, I think I would welcome the change."

"Then you must allow me to escort you outside." He deftly led her around the room and through the terrace doors. Several of the older women present nodded approvingly to one another as they watched the couple leave.

A golden sliver of moon was just sailing behind a cloud. Yuri drew Tasha to the edge of the terrace, sliding his arm around her waist. "You haven't truly thanked me for the orchids yet," he whispered, as his hand crept slowly from her waist to brush, then cup her breast.

Throwing off his hand, Tasha stepped back. "If you don't mind," she said in an icy tone, "I would prefer to say thank you with my lips!"

"Ah yes, your lips!" With a rapid movement he seized her shoulders and pressed his mouth firmly against hers.

Aghast, Tasha strained against his chest, trying to escape his hold. But the further she pulled her head back, the closer he followed, keeping his mouth to hers. She kept her lips taut and unyielding, refusing to respond, until at last he released her.

"You are no gentleman!" she cried, whirling away from him to return to the drawing room.

Catching her shoulder in a vise-like grip before she could move more than a step, he bent to whisper in her ear, "But it pleases me to see that you are very much a lady. You give no part of yourself lightly. I would not have my wife behave in any other way."

Outraged by his actions, Tasha flew across the terrace without hesitation. Her rage prevented her from realizing what he had said. Calm yourself now, she instructed herself—you owe him nothing. But she failed to notice when Yuri left the room with her father a few minutes later.

By the time Mikhail and Yuri returned, Tasha had downed several glasses of champagne in an attempt to quell the rage still burning within her. How dare Yuri Zarevsky force himself on her? Did he think he could win her favors with a mere bundle of flowers? If *only* Jared were there. He would defend her honor in no uncertain terms—he would make it quite clear to whom she belonged. Feeling a light hand on her shoulder, she turned to face her father.

"Are you enjoying yourself, my dear?" he asked with a conspicuous note of pleasure.

"Oh yes, papa!" she replied with false brightness, not wishing to burden him with her true feelings. "It's a wonderful party!" She pointedly ignored Yuri, who was standing directly behind Mikhail wearing an unbearable expression of—victory?

"Good! Good!" Mikhail chortled. "I myself have just had a very pleasant conversation with our friend Zarevsky." He winked knowingly at the younger man as he said this. "And it seems to me that this evening, with our dearest friends conveniently assembled here, provides a fitting occasion for our announcement." He was positively beaming at her.

Tasha stared at him uncomprehendingly, a sense of fear growing in her breast. Mikhail, overflowing with his own joy, didn't take notice of Tasha's reaction. Withdrawing from his pocket the small copper bell he used to summon the servants during meals, he held it high above his head, ringing it repeatedly until he had the attention of all the guests.

"My dear friends," he bellowed, "I wish to make an announcement to you that brings me complete joy. Not only is this celebration in honor of the birthday of my dear niece and adopted daughter, but it has also become the happy occasion of her betrothal!"

A murmur of excitement and approval swept through the room as Yuri Zarevsky stepped boldly to Tasha's side and placed his arm nonchalantly across her shoulders. The same matrons who had watched them earlier in the evening again nodded knowingly, and several young women shot Tasha envious glances.

Numb with sudden realization, but unwilling to believe that her father's announcement could be anything more than a joke, Tasha felt the color drain from her face as she froze between her father and Yuri.

When the crowd had quieted down, Mikhail continued. "That is right. Lieutenant Yuri Aleksandrovich Zarevsky has asked for Tasha's hand. And I, as her guardian, have given my heartfelt consent."

As Mikhail concluded his statement, the guests started to come forward to congratulate the couple.

Tightening his arm around her shoulder, Zarevsky chided Tasha in a whisper. "Come now, Tasha, try to appear a bit more thrilled for the benefit of our well-wishers."

Suddenly recovering her spirit, Tasha turned to him in fury, and warned him in a voice sputtering with rage, "I will never, under any circumstances, marry you, Yuri Zarevsky!"

Then, turning to face her alarmed and confused father, she shrieked, "How could you? How could you abandon me this way? And I believed all this time that you loved me!"

"Tasha!" Yuri commanded, digging his fingers into her shoulder. "Behave yourself! I will not have you making a scene!"

"You, sir, will not have me at all!" she screamed. She tore herself from his grasp and with arms out-stretched, pushed her way through the people crowding around. The stunned guests fell back, allowing her a wide berth as she stormed out of the room, heedless to her father's voice calling after her in anguish.

Chapter Eighteen

1865

It was past noon the following day before Tasha ventured downstairs in search of her father, intending to inform him most emphatically that she would never marry Yuri Zarevsky.

The night before, after hastily bidding his guests good night, Mikhail had pounded on her bedroom door for more than an hour, demanding that she explain herself. But Tasha had steadfastly refused to answer him as she knew she was incapable of thinking, or even speaking, clearly. I will deal with this outrage in the morning, she swore to herself.

Muttering to himself, Mikhail had finally stomped off to console his wounded pride with some cognac, leaving Tasha to pace until dawn when, succumbing to the physical and emotional exhaustion of the night's events, she fell across her bed and slept.

She found Mikhail in the study, slumped over his desk, the half-empty decanter of cognac at his elbow. For a moment she considered leaving him there, and postponing the discussion for a few hours. But, no, the matter could not wait. Every hour was precious, now that Jared was due to return shortly.

Touching his arm softly, she whispered, "Papa, are you awake?"

Mikhail groaned, then slowly lifted his head and regarded her through weary, bloodshot eyes. "You caused me a great deal of embarrassment last night, Tasha. I am at a loss to understand your behavior."

"If you had consulted me before making your announcement," she replied quietly, "you could have spared us both embarrassment. Why, papa? Why did you presume to offer my hand in marriage without so much as asking about my feelings on the subject?"

His eyes opened wide. "But I thought your feelings for Yuri were evident! You've spent more time with him these last months than with any of your other suitors. In fact, not an hour before I announced your engagement, I saw the two of you going arm-in-arm to the terrace. I assumed you would reserve such tete-a-tetes for the man who had a special place in your heart. And Yuri Aleksandrovich himself led me to believe he had already received your consent. He beseeched me most earnestly to give the two of you my blessing."

"Then he lied to you!" Tasha hissed. "He never proposed to me, and I find it beyond belief that he cares for me at all. Yuri Aleksandrovich Zarevsky is too immersed in himself to care for any woman, except perhaps as a bauble to show off to his acquaintances."

"Tasha!" Mikhail said, his voice tinged with fatherly reproof. "You judge the young man too harshly! Perhaps he was afraid to confront you directly with his proposal. Even the bravest men have been known to become faint-hearted when seeking the love of a beautiful woman.

"I can understand, now, how your pride was wounded by the devious manner of his proposal. But I think if you reflect on the situation, you must admit that Yuri would make a fine husband, one any young woman would be proud to claim. Incidentally, he told me before leaving last night that, despite the scene you caused, he still considers you his betrothed."

"How magnanimous of him!" Tasha spat bitterly. "He will have to be informed that *I* do not consider myself betrothed to him!"

"Think on it before you say that again, Tasha. Didn't you see the wistful expressions on the faces of your women friends—obviously every one of them envied your good fortune in snaring Yuri Zarevsky."

"Then they are welcome to him. They can take him and divide him up between them, for all I care!"

"Tasha!" Mikhail was now pleading with her. "There is something else to consider; after last night, it is unlikely that any other young man will ask for your hand. Few men want an unmanageable wife, no matter how great a beauty she may be. Furthermore," he paused meaningfully, "if you reject Yuri, he could make life rather difficult for us."

"I don't see how. In a few weeks he will be leaving for Kamchatka."

Mikhail sighed wearily. "But he can do enough harm before his departure to last a lifetime. You see, when he honorably declared his intention to marry you, I felt it only fair to reveal to him that I am your actual father. He accepted the fact without passing any judgment. But if you reject him, he might use it against us. Novoarkhangelsk is a very staid community. The good people of the town might not so readily welcome you into their homes if they learn you are a bastard. And the company has a very strict moral code. My position could be endangered if news of my past indiscretions leaked out."

"Papa," Tasha cut in sharply, "I find it hard to believe that the company would punish you for an indiscretion committed more than seventeen years ago—before you had even entered their employ. As for myself, I don't care a bit what the rest of the town thinks."

Taking a deep breath, and making the decision before prudence could stop her, she continued bravely, "There is one other man who knows you are my father and is not disturbed by the fact. We love one another and we intend to be married."

He looked at her in shocked surprise. "Who is this man?" Mikhail demanded. "Why have you not told me about him sooner?"

"His name is Jared Northrup," Tasha answered calmly, "and I did not inform you sooner because he wished personally to ask you for my hand, just as Yuri did—only Jared had the courtesy to gain my consent first."

"Jared Northrup?" Mikhail repeated the name, trying to place the man to whom it belonged. "An American?"

She nodded. "Yes, papa. He is the man who rescued me when the *Ayan* sank."

"The whaleman?" He stared at her incredulously. "You don't mean you expect me to consent to your marrying a whaleman?"

She shrugged. "He doesn't intend to remain a whaleman, papa. And I love him. Surely you would not deny me a future with the man I love, not after the way you suffered without mama."

He waved her words aside. "Do not confuse the issue, Tasha! Your mother and I were a different matter entirely. For one thing, both of us were older than you—more able to recognize and deal with love. No doubt you've allowed your gratitude to this Northrup to blind you."

"No!" Tasha protested. "Gratitude has nothing to

208

do with my feelings. We never even discussed marriage when I was still aboard his whaler."

"Then when did you discuss it? Do you mean to say you entertained the young man since your arrival in Novoarkhangelsk—without my knowledge."

"He was here in the spring of last year and we made our plans then. We did not willingly deceive you, papa, but you were not at home when he called. And we had only a few brief hours, as he had to return to his ship immediately.

"I would have told you, papa, but Jared and I thought it better to await his return this year. Knowing your low regard for whalemen, Jared said he could present a stronger case to you if he had in hand his earnings from his whaling voyages."

"Or so he told you," Mikhail said dubiously. "When, precisely, did you say he would return?"

Tasha shrugged. "Sometime this summer, whenever the *Freedom* puts in to the Aleutians."

"I see," her father continued. His tone was now kind, but condescending. "Has it ever occurred to you that he will not return at all? Perhaps he did not make an attempt to speak to me because he had no intention of marrying you. Americans—whalemen in particular—cannot always be trusted. For all we know, the man may even have a wife back in some Yankee whaling town."

"He doesn't, papa!" Tasha declared vehemently. "I know him, and I trust him completely. Doesn't the fact that he rescued me and brought me here in the first place prove that he is an honorable man?"

Mikhail shook his head. "Rescuing you was a brave and decent act—I'll grant that even some whalemen are capable of decency. As for bringing you to me, it was as good a way as any for him to be rid of you, yet know where to find you if he desired a bit of dalliance."

Tasha's voice rose with barely controlled anger. "You accuse me of judging Yuri Zarevsky too harshly, yet you readily slander the man I've told you I love!

209

He *will* return to marry me! He has already given me a ring as a token of his love."

"What kind of ring?" Mikhail asked quickly.

Reaching within her dressing gown, Tasha pulled out the scrimshaw ring suspended on the blue satin ribbon. "See for yourself. He carved this ring for me himself, from a bit of whale's tooth."

Mikhail fingered the ring, turning it round to scrutinize the intricate carving. "Ah, yes. Scrimshaw, I believe they call it. The whaleman's art. It's very clever, my dear, but hardly a fitting symbol of devotion. I'm told the average whaleman carves scores of scrimshaw pieces in a voyage. It's simply a way to pass the time, and the materials are readily available."

Deeply hurt at her father's words, Tasha snatched the ring back and placed it again beneath her dressing gown. "Must you find fault with everything he has said or done for me?" she sobbed.

Rising stiffly from his desk, Mikhail tried to put a comforting arm around his daughter, but she pushed him away and stumbled, teary-eyed, to a window, refusing to look at him.

"Tasha, Tasha," he chided gently, "how can I make you understand that I have only your best interests at heart? It would tear me in two to see you heartbroken when your Jared does not return. I know too well the agony of life alone, and I cannot idly stand by while you throw away a golden opportunity. I still believe it would be best for you to marry Yuri Aleksandrovich. I am convinced he cares for you, and he can offer you a secure future."

"But, papa, I do not care for him. I despise him!"

"You are too upset right now. When you think about it, you will see that marrying Yuri is the best course. You are young, Tasha. You can learn to love him and build a happy marriage."

Her voice was steely with determination as she answered, "I will not marry him, papa! I cannot!"

"Why can't you, Tasha?" he cajoled. "You have yet to give me an acceptable reason."

She hesitated, wondering if she dared give him the one reason that would surely silence him and end the argument forever. Yes, she would dare—to gain her freedom. Turning slowly, she looked into his eyes and pronounced in a steady voice, "I cannot marry Yuri Zarevsky because it would represent the basest act of deception on my part."

As her father raised an eyebrow questioningly, she continued, in the same steady, even voice. "No doubt, Lieutenant Zarevsky expects a virgin bride. I fear I would disappoint him, for I am not a virgin."

An expression of deep pain clouded Mikhail's eyes, and Tasha looked away, unable to bear the sight. For several seemingly endless moments, he said nothing. Then, as if in a daze, he turned back to his desk, sank into the heavy, leather chair, and, in a low, shaking voice, asked, "Do you know what you have said, child? Please tell me it is just a joke—a ruse to make me rest my case."

"It is no joke, papa. I am quite serious."

"But how? Were you raped?"

"No, papa, nothing like that. I lay with Jared, and though I am sorry it brings you such grief, I am not sorry I did it."

"Jared!" Mikhail thundered, rising again to pace in the study, "now I understand perfectly. He plied you with promises of marriage, simply so he could rob you of your most precious possession. Great God in heaven, girl, now I'm more certain than ever he will not return. He's already taken all that he wanted. A scrimshaw ring was a small price to pay for what you gave him!"

"How can you be so certain?" she replied coldly. "Unless, perhaps, the circumstances you describe applied to your relationship with mama. Is that how it happened, papa? Did you take what you wanted without intending to return to her? Did you lie to me when you told me how I came to be?"

Freezing in his steps, Mikhail paled. Then he strode across the room, grabbed Tasha roughly by the arms,

211

and, in an unfamiliar tone, growled, "Never, never again let me hear you speak that way about what passed between your mother and me!"

"Then don't speak disparagingly about my relationship with Jared!" she shouted. "You expect me to understand the love and passion you felt for mama. You expect me to forgive all the pain it caused. Yet you can't seem to understand that Jared and I feel that same love and are driven by that same passion. I'm not a child, papa. I'm a woman, capable of all the emotions of a woman."

Sighing, Mikhail relaxed his grip. "But you are so young, Tasha, so vulnerable. I want only to protect you—to shield you from the suffering your mother endured."

"Then surely you can see it would be wrong for me to marry Yuri Zarevsky."

He shook his head. "I don't know what to think. Your revelations have thrown me quite off balance. I need time to think things out—to decide what is the best course for all concerned, but especially for you, Tasha. I hope what has passed between us since yesterday evening has not made you doubt my love for you. You are still more important to me than all else."

His words and manner touched her, and she felt contrite for lashing out at him. "I believe you, Papa." Tasha stood on tiptoe to kiss him lightly on the cheek. "And you mustn't think, even for a moment, that I love you any the less. I'll leave you alone with your thoughts now—in time, I am sure you will be able to see things through my eyes."

She walked from the room, confident that the crisis had passed, and ascended to her bedroom. So soundly did she sleep that she did not hear a certain visitor arrive in the foyer below, nor did she hear the heated discussion which ensued between that visitor and her father.

When Mikhail knocked at Tasha's door it was almost seven in the evening. "Have you forgotten the ball at Baranov Castle?" he called. "We should be leaving within the hour."

Stretching sleepily, Tasha noted the relaxed quality of his voice, and immediately assumed that he had decided the matter in her favor. Otherwise, he would surely sound agitated, anticipating another painful argument with her.

"If you don't mind, papa," she called back, "I think I would prefer to stay home tonight."

"And what if I were to say I wish you would accompany me?" he called. "Would you change your mind on my account?"

Tasha knit her brows, considering the implications of his question. If he could change his mind about whom she should marry, she could certainly change hers about so simple a matter as going to a social event. It might be a bit awkward, if they were to see some of the people who had witnessed the scene at her party last night, but with her father's support, she could weather their stares. Besides, Jared would be arriving any day, and once they were wed it would not matter what anyone else said or thought.

"You know, papa," she replied gaily, "I feel quite refreshed already. If you'll send Theodosia, I'm sure I can be ready within the hour."

"Good, good," he responded, "the prince and princess might be offended if you did not attend. I'll call Theodosia for you." She heard his steps retreat down the hall.

An hour later, gowned in delicately-tinted rose moire, Tasha was seated in the carriage beside her father for the five-minute drive to Baranov Castle. She fidgeted, wondering why he did not tell her the outcome of his considerations. His manner was amiable as ever—leading her to conclude that he would agree to let her marry whomever she wished. Yet, if that was the case, why would he not come out and simply tell her? Perhaps, she consoled herself, he was waiting for the right moment.

As they were climbing the steps to the castle, Mikhail placed his hand on Tasha's arm. "I think I should tell you that Yuri Aleksandrovich came to call this afternoon."

Tasha made an effort to appear distracted. "Whatever did *he* want?"

"He wanted to know if you were feeling better, and to inquire about plans for the wedding."

"And did you tell him I will not be marrying him?"

"Not precisely," Mikhail admitted sheepishly. "But I think I have found a solution that will suit all concerned."

"Any solution that involves marrying Yuri Zarevsky will not suit me," Tasha rasped angrily and started back toward the carriage. "You have deceived me, papa."

Rushing to bar her way, Mikhail grasped both her hands. "Hear me out before you pass judgment, Tasha. I began by telling Yuri I am still very pleased at the prospect of your marrying him. But I added that I felt you were still too young to take that step and suggested that the marriage be postponed until next summer, when you would be more mature and better able to cope with the responsibilities of marriage."

"But I've told you I will not marry him!" Tasha protested.

Mikhail silenced her by placing a finger on her lips. "I haven't finished, Tasha. On reflection this afternoon, I decided that if your Jared does return, proving himself a man of honor, I will not stand in the way of your marriage. Postponing the marriage to young Zarevsky will give your man a chance to fulfill his promises. In the event the whaleman does not return for you—and I must admit I still have my doubts—you may find that your feelings toward Yuri have changed. Then, if you wish, you can marry him and enjoy a secure future."

In a lower voice, he added, "As for your lack of virginity, we can attribute it to the ferocity of the wreck of the *Ayan*. At any rate, we have until next summer to consider that problem."

"We won't have to consider it at all, papa," Tasha said confidently. "Jared will return, and I shall marry him. I wish you could simply accept that fact, but I know that you will see soon enough. But," she paused and studied him worriedly in the light that flickered from the beacon at the top of the castle, "what explanation will you give Yuri when he returns from Kamchatka and finds me wed to another?"

Mikhail shrugged. "In the event that happens, I will think of something and I will take full responsibility. Now," he took her arm and led her back up the steps, "shall we join the other merrymakers?"

"Yes, papa. I am beginning to feel quite merry myself."

She entered the ballroom feeling relieved. Her father had accepted her love for Jared—even if he still could not accept Jared's love for her—and when Jared returned, he would permit their marriage. She felt she could ask for no more. It didn't matter that he had not relayed to Yuri her unconditional refusal, for she was confident she would never have to face the prospect of marrying him. So sure was she now that her future with her true love was secure, she was unusually quick to accede to Yuri's request for a dance. He simply didn't matter anymore.

Chapter Nineteen

1865

Yuri Aleksandrovich Zarevsky seated Tasha at the long dining table in Baranov Castle, then seated himself in the chair beside hers. Responding to Tasha's bright smiles and charming chatter, he had been unusually solicitous all evening, holding her tenderly as they danced, stopping to rest when she claimed fatigue, summoning a waiter with champagne if she complained of thirst, and never leaving her side for the entire evening.

The other guests, many of whom had attended Tasha's birthday celebration, eyed the couple approvingly and gossiped among themselves. No doubt, they whispered, Tasha's outburst the night before over her engagement announcement had been the result of a lovers' quarrel; she obviously was very happy with the young lieutenant; and didn't the two make a lovely couple?

While the other guests were seating themselves for the midnight supper, Yuri looked at Tasha through half-closed eyes. "I am indeed fortunate," he murmured.

"In what way?" Tasha asked innocently.

"Why, to claim you as my fiancée, of course."

"Such flattery, Yuri! Novoarkhangelsk has scores of women more worthy of your affection than I."

Yuri pursed his lips in pretended thought. "More worthy, perhaps. But none more beautiful, or more sought after by the young gentlemen. I wonder," he paused reflectively, and the briefest hint of mockery flashed through his eyes, "just why you are so popular."

"I'm sure I couldn't say." Tasha bent over her *baklazhannya ikra*, a first course of eggplant and tomatoes, not sure of his meaning.

Both remained silent through the soup course, and Yuri did not speak again until they had almost finished their *kotleta pojarski*, a delicately breaded chicken dish. But despite his silence, his knee spoke to her insistently, nudging her again and again until Tasha wished the meal would be over so they could return to the ballroom where the surveillance of others would make him behave more circumspectly.

Dabbing the corners of his mouth with his napkin, Yuri leaned toward Tasha and whispered, "You know, the grandeur of this house never ceases to impress me.

Isn't it amazing that something so splendid exists in this wilderness? I've been told there's even a theater under this roof."

"But surely you knew that," Tasha said, expressing surprise. "You don't mean to say you have been in Novoarkhangelsk almost six months, appeared at virtually every ball or tea party, and never attended one of the performances?"

"I'm afraid that is the case. But then, I don't suppose the material is of quite the quality offered in Moscow or St. Petersburg."

"On the contrary, it is usually excellent. Just last month papa and I saw a thrilling performance of a play written by the Frenchman, Molière."

"Imagine that!" Yuri feigned incredulity, then sighed. "Well, I should hate to travel to Kamchatka without being afforded one last glimpse of culture. I hear Petropavlovsk, where I am to be stationed, is a dreary place. Would you be good enough to show me the theater?"

Tasha hesitated. "I don't know. I'm afraid there may not be another performance before you leave Novoarkhangelsk."

"But we could make our own performance."

"What do you mean?"

"Simply that we could slip away after the meal, so that you could personally show me the theater." His knee nudged hers again.

"But I'm not sure that would be proper. At any rate, the theater would be dark."

"Surely you're not afraid to take me there? You act as if you are afraid to be alone with me, but you must know in your heart I wouldn't do anything to harm my betrothed." Again the trace of mockery flashed across his face. "You must know that I would want you to be as pure on our wedding night as you were the day I met you."

Bridling under his tone, Tasha sat up straighter and met his gaze. "Very well, beloved," she murmured with a meekness she did not feel. "If you so urgently desire to visit the theater, I shall certainly honor your request. But we must be quick—if papa notices we are gone, he may worry."

"Yes," Yuri mumbled, "he does seem quite protective. He thinks of you as a child, though it is plain you are a woman in every way."

They finished dessert, a torte richly laced with rum, and, as the other guests drifted back toward the ballroom, Yuri guided Tasha toward the door. Passing her father, he smiled serenely and said, "Tasha would like a bit of fresh air."

Nodding assent, Mikhail followed the other guests back to the ballroom, certain, after the force of her recent arguments with him, that his daughter could take care of herself.

Outside, the sky was still gray. A light drizzle was beginning to fall, so Tasha hurried as she led Yuri up the castle's rear stairway to the theater on the third floor. To her surprise, as they climbed the stairs, a manservant hurried past them down the stairs. He seemed to nod at Yuri as he went by.

"I hadn't thought—" Tasha said as they neared the door, "but, in all likelihood the theater is locked since there was no performance scheduled tonight."

"Oh, I'll wager it is open," Yuri countered playfully. He reached out and opened the door easily, bowing low as he stepped aside for Tasha to enter.

She hesitated on the threshold, suddenly very uncomfortable. "Perhaps it would be better for me to stay here, to be sure the door does not blow shut. With the light from the sky, you may be able to get an impression of the size of the theater."

"Don't be a ninny," Yuri complained. "It's beginning to rain harder, and you'll be drenched if you stand here. Your gown will be ruined. For some reason, you act as if you are afraid to be alone with me."

A loud clap of thunder accentuated his words. Tasha jumped in alarm and Yuri took advantage of her fright to pull her into the theater, closing the door firmly behind them.

"You see," Tasha declared breathlessly, "it's too dark to see a thing in here."

"Well, it's clear we can't go back out now," Yuri said. "Let's sit down until the worst of the rain is over." He edged over to a velvet-cushioned seat, dropped down onto it, and pulled Tasha into his lap.

With a cry, she tried to jump up, but he held her firmly by the waist. "If you don't mind," she said slowly, "I will find my own seat."

"Come now," he purred, planting a warm, wet kiss on the back of her neck, "isn't it rather harmless for you to sit on the lap of your fiancé?"

"I think," she replied, "that betrothal should not involve unwarranted privileges. We are not yet married, you know!"

"Indeed we are not," his tone hardened, "but you have offered far more to others without the bonds of marriage."

Tasha stiffened. "You dare to slander my good name!"

"On the contrary. I do not censure your past indiscretions. I simply demand my due—what you have already given to others certainly belongs to me as your betrothed."

Roughly he inserted a hand beneath her moiré bodice, ripping her camisole as his hand closed around her breast.

She squirmed, biting his arm in protest. "You are grossly mistaken in your assumptions, sir!"

Yuri laughed harshly, pushing her face away from his arm as he proceeded to probe deeper within her gown. "Yes, I would have thought so, too, had I not heard the news from your own mouth."

"What are you talking about?"

"Your argument—or should I say confession?—with your father this afternoon. No doubt you did not hear me enter the house, but I clearly heard every word you said. I seem to have arrived at a most propitious moment—just as you were announcing to your father that you are not a virgin."

Tasha gasped. "You eavesdropped! But how could Xenia have allowed you?"

"Poor thing, she was quite as horrified as I to hear your sordid declaration. It took her several moments to regain her composure and suggest that I return at a later time. By then, I had learned all."

His other hand had thrown back her skirts and was creeping up her thighs. She tried vainly to squirm away. "Though you are not the pure maiden you pretended to be last night, I still intend to marry you. I'm told the women on Kamchatka tend to be fat and ugly and I'll need an attractive piece of flesh to provide me with some diversion."

"Find yourself another," Tasha hissed, "for I shall never consent to share your marriage bed!"

Yuri laughed ominously. "There you are mistaken, my dear. You *will* share my bed, both in marriage, and before."

"No!" she shrieked, furiously pounding his chest as his hand crawled higher between her thighs, then patted its target possessively.

"It will do you little good to scream," he counseled. "The noise of the storm and the music at the ball below will simply overwhelm your feeble sounds. Why not submit to me as you did to—what was the name I heard today—Jared?"

The utterance of her beloved's name gave Tasha sudden strength. She freed herself from Yuri's probing hands and stumbled up the aisle toward the door. In the darkness, her hands found the handle, but before she could push open the heavy door, Yuri's hands were at her shoulders, dragging her away. He shoved her to the floor.

"You ungrateful little bitch!" he snarled. "I offer to marry you—you, the bastard of some St. Petersburg slut—and you proceed to humiliate me before a crowd. Now I learn that you are no better than your mother—a trashy harlot who could not even wait to be wed to get herself bedded. Well, my dear," his tone became more threatening, "since you did not wait, why should I? I will have my duel"

Sobbing, Tasha started to crawl away between two rows of seats. He caught the hem of her skirt, and with a tug, ripped it from her bodice, leaving her half naked. He chuckled. "What a pity that your stubbornness should ruin this expensive gown."

He lunged at her, pinning her to the cold floor as he clawed away the rest of her clothes. His mouth closed greedily over one bared breast, while his hands tore the pins from her hair.

Helplessly caught beneath him, Tasha lay rigid as he moved his mouth to hers. His kiss was brutal, bruising, as if he wished to imprint an indelible mark on her. His moustache bristled against her tender skin as he pressed his mouth harder and harder against hers. Now, while the fingers of one hand held her by the hair, his other hand roved down her body, pushing away torn sections of cloth until she was entirely bare.

Moving carefully, Tasha managed to free one arm. She moaned as if in submission and slid it around his back, as if to embrace him.

"That's better," Yuri murmured approvingly. "Soon you'll be bouncing in ecstasy, wondering why you were ever foolish enough to lay with some coarse, inexperienced American boy. Then you will beg me to marry you, as you will want me to take you again and again, until eternity."

Again, a helpless sound escaped her, and she parted her lips to accept his hungry tongue. He settled himself on top of her more comfortably, finding the right balance of his weight to hers. Freeing her other arm, she wrapped it around his back, pulling him closer.

Satisfied that she was now fully subdued, Yuri released her hair and used both hands to roam over her body. His hand slid past her waist, lifted her buttocks and forced her belly firmly against his fully tumescent manhood, throbbing within his trousers.

He released a tell-tale sigh and, in that instant, her hands moved quickly upward and raked his cheeks with her nails. With a howl of fury, he sat up in a straddling position, resting his weight on her groin.

"So you want to play rough!" he snapped, his open hand smashing across her cheek in a stunning blow. "As you wish. It matters little to me, for I shall have you, no matter how!" His hand fell again, delivering an equally stinging slap to her other cheek.

While Tasha fought for air, he quickly undid his trousers and shook them down. Catching both her wrists in one hand, he jerked them above her head, then dropped his full weight upon her again. He pushed his knees between hers, using his free hand to force her thighs open wider. Grunting, he rammed himself deep into her, ignoring her pathetic cries of anguish.

Her body was not ready for him—could never be! —and the pain of penetration was more searing than that first time when she had so willingly surrendered herself to Jared. Sobbing, she raised a foot and tried to kick him in the back, but he caught her leg and forced it down. Raising himself slightly, he spread his legs, pressing hers together between them, creating even greater pain inside her. Unable to throw him off, or to hear the agony of her useless resistance, she swallowed any further protests, afraid they might drive him to greater brutality, and lay mutely until he shuddered out his last rush of desire and collapsed over her.

Raising himself after a few moments, he nuzzled her ear and whispered, "That is how a man makes love. It will give you something to dream about until I return next summer to claim you as my bride. Of course, I still intend to marry you. I have wanted you from the moment I glimpsed you at the New Year's ball, and I will not be content until you belong to me.

"Besides, I am an honorable man. Surely, you cannot think I would take a woman and then desert her. As I told you before, I will need some diversion on Kamchatka, and your beauty and intelligence might even prove to be an asset to my career as well."

Ignoring her strangled cry of outrage, he continued. "You are still my betrothed. And I think, on reflection, you will realize that you have little choice but to marry me. No other man will want to wed a woman who has already been taken by another. I am your only hope in that respect."

That is where you are wrong, Tasha thought. Jared will marry me, despite what you have done. She bit back the urge to spit that fact in Yuri's face, as it seemed he had not lingered outside her father's study long enough to know that Jared was returning. How triumphant she would feel next year, when Yuri arrived from Kamchatka expecting to collect a submissive bride, only to find her happily married to someone else!

Yuri rose up, took off the jacket of his uniform, and dropped it over her. "Put that on and I'll take you home," he commanded coldly. "Your gown has not survived our rendezvous, so you cannot return to the ball."

The main floor of the castle was alive with lights and the sounds of laughter as Yuri guided Tasha down the hill to the Governor's Walk. His carriage was waiting there, revealing to her how meticulously he had prepared his approach. Of course, she thought bitterly, he had all afternoon to attend to all the details, even to bribing a servant to unlock the theater.

She hunched herself into a corner of the carriage, and would not look or speak to him as they rolled through the quiet streets of Novoarkhangelsk. When they stopped before her father's house, Tasha pushed aside his proffered hand, leapt unassisted to the street, and hurried up the stairs to the door.

She let herself inside and ran on tiptoe up the stairs to her room and slammed the door behind her. Unbuttoning Yuri's coat, she flung it to the floor in disgust and collapsed against the bedstead, shaking uncontrollably in anger and humiliation. Kicking the offensive coat beneath the bed, she slipped into a dressing gown and went to rouse Theodosia, asleep in the room adjoining hers.

Shaking the servant awake, she said, "I want a hot bath at once!"

Theodosia sat up and rubbed her eyes. "At this hour, Gospoja? It's the middle of the night. There won't be any bath water heating on the stove at this hour."

"Then set some to heating!" Tasha snapped. "I can't retire without a hot bath!"

Shuffling to her feet, Theodosia reached out a hand to press Tasha's forehead. "Are you feeling all right?"

"No," Tasha admitted, her voice cracking, "I am feeling positively miserable. I sorely need the curative effects of a bath."

"Very well," Theodosia nodded, "you shall have it. Go and lie down while I heat the water."

Tasha returned to her room and sank limply across the bed. But, exhausted as she was, in mind, heart and body, she could not drift into sleep. She felt despoiled, and she knew she could not sleep without washing away the substance of Yuri that clung to her skin like an embalming fluid.

Some of it, she felt, could never be washed away, because it seemed to have pervaded her very soul.

When the bath was ready, Tasha sank into it gratefully and waved Theodosia away.

The servant looked at her worriedly. "Are you sure you won't be needing me any more?"

"I'm sure." Her tone was gentler as she felt the cleansing water enfolding her body. "Go back to bed, Theodosia. I'm sorry to have disturbed you."

On her way to the door, Theodosia stopped to pick up the tattered remnants of Tasha's clothing. A look of horror gripped her face. Glancing at Tasha, she saw that her mistress was staring at her in exasperation. Hurriedly, she dropped the remnants on a chair, mumbled good night, and left.

Tasha stayed in the bath until the water grew cold. Her mind groped for ways to repay Yuri for his cruelty. Her first impulse was to dress again, ride back to Baranov Castle, burst into the festivities, and reveal to everyone present what the animal had done to her. Instantly, she dismissed the thought, not wishing to disgrace her father, and really feeling too weary to go out again.

Next, she considered talking with her father privately, urging him to do what he could to disgrace Yuri. But she rejected that course of action just as quickly, in favor of letting Yuri suffer the shock of finding her wed to another. How much sweeter her revenge would be if he passed a whole year away, thinking all the while that he had her within his power, only to learn of her own triumph upon his return.

She climbed wearily into bed, praying that Jared would arrive soon.

Chapter Twenty

1865

As the sun crept below the canopy of her bed, Tasha stretched luxuriously. For an instant she grimaced, remembering her experience with Yuri the night before. But she couldn't bear to think about it and quickly thrust it from her mind.

Jared would be coming soon and her father had consented to their marriage—nothing Yuri Zarevsky said or did could change that. In fact, she thought confidently, as she swung her feet to the floor and got out of bed, she would allow nothing to darken the future.

Wearing a bright yellow muslin gown, her hair

brushed and gleaming as it curled over her shoulders, Tasha descended the stairs for breakfast. Her father rose as she entered the room, smiled affectionately, and pointed to a chair across from his at the cozy breakfast table.

"You look lovely this morning, my dear," he said as he bent to kiss her cheek. "I'm pleased to see you looking so well. Yuri Aleksandrovich informed me he escorted you home as you were feeling ill last night."

A frown fleeted across Tasha's brow. "Yes," she answered dutifully, "I wasn't well, but I am much improved this morning."

"Good." Mikhail tapped the shell of a soft-boiled egg, then paused to look at her gratefully. "I was heartened to observe your gracious treatment of Yuri last night."

Again Tasha frowned, thinking of the treatment she had received in return, but she answered evenly, "I felt I could spare a little kindness, now that I know I won't be forced to marry him."

Her father raised his brows. "I hope you did not tell him as much."

"No, papa. I let him believe what he wished. Nevertheless, the knowledge is a relief to me, and I thank you for your leniency."

"I hope my decision results in the happy outcome you expect," he said, turning his attention back to his plate. "I would be loath to see you disappointed."

"Everything will be all right, papa. You'll see."

He shook his head gravely. "I sincerely hope so, Tasha. I really do. Incidentally, Yuri told me he gave you his coat to protect you against the rain last night. He'll be over later to get it."

The arrogant fool, he thinks he has an explanation for everything, Tasha mused. How would he explain the marriage of his fiancée to another man? "Very well," she murmured, "I'll have Xenia see that it is pressed before he arrives."

They continued to eat in silence, until they were

interrupted by a slight commotion in the foyer. An excited exchange of words between Xenia and a man could be heard. After a few minutes, Xenia entered, looking flustered, and turning to Mikhail, said, "Your friend Gospodin Sukenak is here. I've told him you are at breakfast, but he refuses to leave. He insists he has some very exciting news that you will want to hear."

Mikhail nodded. "Then by all means show him in, and instruct Tanya to bring him some tea. We've almost finished here, anyway."

Xenia bustled out, muttering to herself, "Absolutely disgraceful . . . interrupting people at meals . . . some old friend . . . should have the courtesy to call at a more sensible hour."

She returned a moment later, followed by a short, balding man with a drooping gray moustache, whom Tasha had met on several occasions. He nodded amiably to Tasha, then abruptly addressed her father. "I'm sorry to disturb you, Mikhail Pavlovich, but I felt this news was much too important to wait."

"Think nothing of it, Semyon Borisovich," Mikhail waved him into a chair and waited while he sipped the tea Tanya had set before him. "Now, tell me, what news has excited you so?"

Semyon hesitated, looking sideways at Tasha. "Perhaps the girl would not be interested," he suggested. "It's not the sort of thing a lady would concern herself with."

Relieved to break away, Tasha rose. "I've other things to do in the house. If you'll excuse me, papa?"

"Of course, my dear. Close the door as you leave, will you?"

She nodded to Semyon, and started for the door.

"A very lovely young woman you have there, Mikhail Pavlovich," the visitor observed appreciatively.

"Thank you, dear Semyon. Now then, the news?"

Closing the door, Tasha could not resist lingering a moment to try to catch some hint of the news that had prompted a visit at so unlikely an hour. What she heard compelled her to stay on outside the door, straining to catch every word.

Semyon cleared his throat importantly. "There's a whaler docked in our harbor. A Yankee whaler."

Tasha's heart stopped. He had come for her! He had come, bringing his whole ship with him!

"A Yankee whaler, hmm?" her father said. "That is a bit unusual for Novoarkhangelsk, but hardly worth disturbing the early morning hours over."

"But that in itself is not the news, Mikhail! The news was carried by the ship, the *Arctic Princess*, I think they call her."

Tasha's spirits sank, then rose again quickly. It was not the *Freedom*, but Jared had not been certain he would be aboard the *Freedom*. He had said "I'll ship out again, *probably* aboard the *Freedom*." Perhaps he had come on the *Arctic Princess* instead.

"Get to the point, man," Mikhail urged. "Precisely what news does the *Arctic Princess* carry?"

Semyon hesitated, which gave his words, when he finally spoke, extra impact, "There is a Confederate cruiser on the prowl in these waters—hunting out and sinking whalers."

"But that's preposterous, man! Just last week I received word from the American-Russian Commercial Company office in San Francisco that the War Between the States is ended. The last of the Confederate armies surrendered in April."

"That may be, but apparently the Confederate navy has not yet given up. According to the captain of the *Arctic Princess*, this cruiser has sunk no less than twenty vessels already. Burned them right there in the Bering Straits. The *Arctic Princess* just managed to escape under cover of fog, and sailed here seeking sanctuary."

Mikhail chuckled grimly. "It's a strange day indeed when a Yankee whaler thinks to find sanctuary in our port. Did no one tell the cruiser the war is over?"

"I understand several whaler captains attempted to,

but the master of the rebel vessel, called the *Shenandoah*, refused to believe them—thought it was just a Yankee trick to save their skins. Says he won't rest until he's tracked down and destroyed every last vessel in the Arctic whaling fleet."

Mikhail whistled softly. "Well, we've always wanted to be rid of the scourge of the hellships. Still, this seems like a terrible way to go. With all that oil on board, I imagine they take to the flames quite readily."

"No doubt about it," Semyon agreed. "They say you can chart the course of the *Shenandoah* by following the burning hulks of the whalers." He sighed. "God, what an agonizing way to die!"

Stunned by the conversation she heard within the room, Tasha collapsed against the door. It couldn't be true! No one, not even a warship's captain, could be that cruel! And the whalers were private ships, not war vessels. Jared had never even mentioned anything about a war to her.

Unable to contain herself, Tasha pushed open the door and confronted her father and Semyon. They looked at her ashen face in alarm.

"I'm sorry," she faltered. "I could not help overhearing your conversation. These whalers that were destroyed," she plunged ahead breathlessly, "would you know if one called the *Freedom* was among them?"

Semyon shrugged. "I've no idea what their names were. As I've told your father, no less than twenty have been destroyed, and it matters little to me what they were called. One hellship is the same as another."

Agitated further by his uncaring, offhanded reply, Tasha demanded, "Is this *Arctic Princess* still in port?"

Again Semyon shrugged. "I suspect so. She just sailed in this morning, and since the governor didn't see fit to give her a cannon blast right away, she's probably still afloat." He chuckled at his own cleverness. "Why all the interest in whalers, girl?"

Without bothering to answer, Tasha turned and ran from the room. She brushed past a startled Xenia and sped out the front door, not even stopping to take a shawl to protect her against the morning chill.

In the breakfast room, Semyon turned questioning eyes to Mikhail, who cleared his throat and explained lamely, "She spent some time aboard the *Freedom* after the wreck of the *Ayan*. Naturally she feels some bond to the vessel that rescued her from the sea. And," he added almost as an afterthought, "she fancies herself in love with one of the *Freedom*'s crew."

Tasha raced down the Governor's Walk, toward the towering masts of the *Arctic Princess* which she could see rocking in the harbor. At the edge of the dock she paused to catch her breath, panting from a combination of exertion and the fear gripping her chest. As she stood gasping, her hair disheveled and fluttering in the breeze, a group of sailors gathered at the bow of the whaler to admire her.

"Hey, Russian girl," one of them called boldly, "how'd you like a free tour of a real American whaler?"

"And sample the best that some American whalemen have to offer," added another with a ribald laugh.

Tasha bit back an angry retort, realizing she would have to flirt and act sweetly if she wanted to get any information from them. With a winning smile, she lifted her face toward the deck. "You're all very kind," she called in English, letting her dark lashes flutter against her flushed cheeks, "but the truth is, I've already seen as much of a whaler as I care to. I spent several months aboard the *Freedom*, from New Bedford. Perhaps some of you know the ship."

"*Knew* her would be a better way of saying it," one of the group called. "You won't be spending no more time on that ship. I can guarantee it."

"Why so?" Tasha asked ingenuously, trying to ignore the sudden stab of pain in her chest.

Oblivious to the way the color had drained from

Tasha's face, the sailor continued, "Because it's sunk, she is. Burnt up right out in the straits. So, if you've a hankering to go whaling again, I suggest you come with me." He winked impishly. "I could show you a real good time."

"No, I—" Tasha stopped, straightened up, and blinked back her tears. Even if the *Freedom* had gone down, there was no reason to believe Jared had gone down with it. At least—not just yet. She forced herself to continue her questioning. "Did you know any of the *Freedom*'s crew? I mean on this voyage, this year?"

A tall, sandy-haired young man, with rough-hewn features painfully reminiscent of Jared's, stepped forward. He spoke more quietly than the others. "I was acquainted with some of the crew, ma'am. We had a gam a few weeks back and I spent some time aboard the *Freedom*. Not ten days before the *Shenandoah* got her."

"A gam?" Tasha asked lamely, now stalling, fearful of what she might learn about Jared.

He nodded. "A 'gam' is a visitation between two ships. Helps pass the time between sightings. Their captain, Mr. Dawson I believe it was, came aboard the *Arctic Princess* and some of us fellows went over to the *Freedom*. Oh," he bowed and smiled broadly, "in case you're wondering, I'm James Sanders, first mate of this vessel."

Tasha smiled politely. "Pleased to meet you, Mr. Sanders." She was silent for several moments, staring at the water lapping against the side of the ship, putting off the inevitable question.

"Ma'am," James Sanders ventured, leaning over the rail to study her worried face, "was there someone aboard the *Freedom* you wanted to ask about?"

She nodded, admitting to herself that of course she had to ask. "Jared Northrup," she said in a slightly quavering voice.

James Sanders's mouth fell open and he struck his forehead with his open palm. "Of course!" he exclaimed. "I should have known!" Then, looking down at Tasha's perplexed expression, he said, "Wait there a moment." He scrambled over the side of the ship and dropped onto the dock beside Tasha.

She stared at him uneasily. "May I assume then that you know Jared?"

"I do," he nodded enthusiastically, "and I should have known you as well. He spent almost the whole time I was aboard raving about his Russian beauty. I'll bet you're Tasha."

Tasha swallowed hard. "So he *was* aboard the *Freedom*."

Realizing the impact of his remarks, James wrapped a comforting arm around Tasha's shoulders. From the deck, his shipmates hooted, but he quieted them with a rough wave of his hand.

"Perhaps there's some place we could talk," he suggested. "If we stand here, I'm afraid those fools on deck won't give us much peace."

She nodded assent. "I suppose we could go to one of the teahouses. But what is there for us to talk about? Perhaps it would be better for me to be alone."

"I think," James said quietly, "you should not be alone right now."

"Perhaps you're right," Tasha sighed. "If you have the time to spare, I'd be grateful for your company, Mr. Sanders."

Silently, she led the way to the teahouse beside the public gardens. Only after they had seated themselves at a small table and were holding steaming glasses of tea, did Tasha permit herself to think again of Jared's fate.

"Mr. Sanders," she asked softly, "what happened to the crews of the ships burned by the *Shenandoah*?"

James Sanders hesitated, staring into his tea. "I can't really say, ma'am. Soon as word spread about the *Shenandoah*, our captain got us out of those waters. That's how we ended up in New Archangel."

"But can't you surmise what happened?"

He cleared his throat uneasily. "Well, this is a pretty unusual case. Being that the *Shenandoah* is a warship, I suppose she could either have made the crews prisoners of war or—" he took a swallow of tea, leaving the sentence unfinished.

"But if this warship burned more than twenty ships, she couldn't have taken all the crews prisoner, could she? I've only been aboard two ships in all my life, but I know the space is very limited. No doubt the *Shenandoah* barely had room for her own crew, plus whatever cannon and ammunition she carried. Am I right?"

His look did nothing to refute the logic of her words.

"Mr. Sanders," Tasha pressed on, "have you heard of any survivors from the burned ships?"

He shook his head. "No. I heard no such reports."

"Then in all likelihood we can assume that the crews were—" her last words were swallowed in her sobs. Heedless of the curious glances from patrons seated nearby, she lay her head on the table and wept uncontrollably.

James Sanders watched Tasha helplessly, feeling tears brimming in his own eyes. He wished he could comfort her, but he knew any words of consolation from him would seem hopelessly hollow. He sipped his tea, waiting for Tasha's tears to end.

She lifted her head and stared beyond him with reddened eyes. "I'm sorry, Mr. Sanders, but I simply cannot control myself. My future burned with the *Freedom*. Perhaps Jared did not tell you, but we were to be married this year."

"He did tell me," James whispered. "I had the impression he told everyone. He seemed very proud of it. His only worry was that your father might not approve."

Tasha sighed and said, "And now he will never know that only yesterday papa gave me his blessing." She gulped down her tea, which had grown tepid while she cried, and pushed herself away from the

233

table. "I think we should go now, Mr. Sanders. I have taken too much of your time."

He escorted her from the teahouse, pausing at the arbor leading to the gardens. "Perhaps a walk in the gardens would help," he suggested, offering his arm.

Tasha forced a smile, but turned away. "I appreciate your concern, but I'm not sure I will ever walk in the gardens again. Anyway, I know I could not bear to today." She looked up and saw his troubled frown. "It's all right," she added quickly, "you couldn't have known. This garden is where Jared and I said goodbye, only, at the time, I didn't think it would have to last us till eternity." Blinded by new tears, she stumbled on the path. James gently grasped her elbow to steady her.

"I'm sorry, ma'am," he mumbled. "I know it seems so unjust, but then war always is."

"But Jared was not involved in any war!" she exclaimed. "He never even mentioned a war to me."

"The fact is, to those of us who had been away from home whaling for a few years, the war seemed far away. The only time we thought about it was when we went home and had to worry about being waylaid somewhere off the Atlantic seaboard by a rebel raider. There were a few other raids in the Atlantic Ocean, but never any in the Pacific, and nothing like the *Shenandoah* anywhere."

"What is so special about the *Shenandoah?* How could she take so many ships?" Tasha asked, hoping that conversation would help to keep her from crying.

"The *Shenandoah* is a steam-powered ship," James explained. "She's got sails too, I hear, but the steam gives her the upper hand. Whalers have to depend on the wind for speed. Rumor has it she can travel well over three hundred miles in a day. She's fully armed, too. No whaler could be a match for her, and she's yet to encounter any other kind of ship. Still, sooner or later, the United States Navy is bound to catch up with her, and when that happens I'll wager they treat her captain and the crew no better than they would a band of pirates."

Tasha shrugged. "No matter. It is already too late for me."

"Believe me, Tasha, I wish the *Arctic Princess* could have taken the *Freedom*'s place. The *Shenandoah*'s captain ought to be hanged, if for no other reason than the grief he's caused you."

"It's not your fault," Tasha said softly, "so you mustn't be concerned. Thank you for being so kind to me. If there's nowhere else in the town you wish to visit, I'll walk you back to your ship."

"That isn't necessary. I'm sure I can find my own way."

"Please," she persisted, "it will give me something to do for a bit."

"Very well." James took her arm and allowed her to lead the way back to his ship. At the dock, he paused. "Take good care, Tasha," he whispered. "In time, the world will look brighter." Kissing her quickly on the forehead, he climbed up the side of the *Arctic Princess* and disappeared over the top.

Tasha began the seemingly endless walk back to her father's house. In recent days, she had always hurried back to the house from any outing, anticipating that Jared might be waiting for her. Now there was no reason to hurry. Jared would not be there. The future, so bright only hours ago, now loomed before her like a dark void.

Passing Baranov Castle, she looked at the massive timbers and the copper spikes that joined them to the rock formation below. She had thought the love she shared with Jared was like that structure—monumentally steadfast—and it still was. Only now she shared that love with a ghost. Never again would it be brought to full, joyful consummation. Only the ring he had lovingly carved, and the memory of their short, precious moments together remained.

Instinctively her hand flew to her chest to clutch the ring to her heart, as she had so often during the months of their separation. Her fingers faltered, patting the smooth fabric of her bodice, searching for the small lump of whale's tooth that was her most treasured possession. It was gone!

As her mind retraced the awful events of the night before, she realized the ring had not been with the torn camisole when she undressed to bathe. In her general outrage at Yuri, she had failed to notice it was missing. And the morning's events had left her little time to consider such details.

She stopped in the street and turned back toward the castle. There was only one place the ring could be. She quickened her step, hoping she could slip into the theater without being observed. On the third stair leading up to the theater, a glint of gold caught her eye. Bending down, she saw it was a button she had torn from Yuri's coat as she pulled it angrily around her. No doubt he would enjoy knowing he had left behind a symbol of his foul victory. Viciously, she kicked the button, sending it clattering down the hill toward the army headquarters.

To her relief, the door to the theater was still open. Apparently Yuri had not thought it worthwhile to pay the same servant he had bribed to open the door to return and lock it. Once he had what he wanted, he did not care if he left any evidence.

Opening the door, she stood still while her eyes became accustomed to the dim light. The light filtered through a single curtained window high up on a wall, casting a ghostly glow over the theater.

Leaving the door ajar, she crept down the aisle, stopping at the third row of seats, where she dropped to her knees. Running her hands across the polished cedar floor, she found several patches of fabric, torn from her gown, her petticoats, and her camisole. She crawled a bit further between the rows of seats, until her hand hit something hard. Dear God, thank you, she prayed. She carefully picked up the ring, which was still attached to a bit of ribbon.

Sliding the ring lovingly onto her finger, she mur-

mured, "I, Tasha, take you, Jared, forever and ever!"
Dropping her arms onto the seat nearest her and placing her weary head on them, she wept bitterly.

In midafternoon, feeling as if there were no more tears left within her, Tasha left the theater and headed toward her father's house. Glancing back at the harbor, she saw that the *Arctic Princess* was still there, and for an instant she allowed herself to imagine that the three tall masts swaying above the dock belonged to the *Freedom*. But she pushed the thought from her mind, vowing never to allow herself to entertain such fantasies.

As she pushed open the front door of the Lisovsky house, Xenia bustled out to meet her. A worried frown creased the old woman's face as she studied Tasha's tear-streaked cheeks and disheveled appearance.

"Lieutenant Zarevsky is in the drawing room with Gospodin Lisovsky," she said. "He has been asking about you."

"Oh." Tasha started up the stairs toward her room. "If he asks again, you might tell him I have a headache—probably a recurrence of the ailment that forced me to leave the ball early last night. I'll send Theodosia down with his coat."

Without giving Xenia time to protest, or question her appearance, or her whereabouts all day, Tasha continued up the stairs. Dragging the coat from beneath her bed, she called Theodosia and instructed her to press and return it. Then she sank across the bed, lost in sad reverie.

She wondered what sort of discussion Yuri was having with her father. No doubt the cad was feigning heartfelt concern for her condition and accepting her father's expressions of gratitude for taking care of her last night. If only her father could know how Yuri had taken care of her last night!

Absently toying with the scrimshaw ring, Tasha smiled grimly to herself. Perhaps she should honor Yuri Zarevsky with her presence in the drawing room after all. It would be gratifying to see him squirm when she told her father how he had ravaged her. What sweet revenge it would be if Lieutenant Yuri Aleksandrovich Zarevsky were forced to depart for Kamchatka in disgrace and humiliation.

Gradually, the smile faded from her lips. Her father, she knew, would be hurt and deeply ashamed to learn he had been so wrong in his assessment of the lieutenant. Yuri, most likely, would threaten to reveal the circumstances of her birth to protect himself from exposure. To Tasha, it no longer mattered what society might think, but her father would be hurt and ridiculed, and perhaps his position with the Russian-American Company would be jeopardized, as he feared.

Suddenly the idea of revenge seemed to lose its sweetness. She must spare her father, and keep the secret of Yuri's heinous act to herself. She could glean some small satisfaction from knowing that Yuri would leave for Kamchatka and she would not even bid him farewell. And in the year he was away at Kamchatka, she would somehow convince her father she could not marry him.

Inexplicably, she wondered suddenly if her mother had ever bade her father farewell. But their situation had been so different from hers, she told herself quickly. Her parents had loved one another, and her father had not raped her mother. On the other hand, neither she nor Yuri cared for one another, and Yuri had most definitely taken her against her will.

Still, it was possible that both situations were alike in another, horrible way. Yuri may have planted his seed within her, just as her father had unknowingly planted his within her mother. No, she insisted to herself, it was *not* possible. She had lain with Jared twice and had not come away carrying his child, though now she almost wished she had. It was unlikely that Yuri could have left her with child.

Still, the thought refused to leave her mind. It hovered at the back of her brain. She could not dispel the idea. Gradually, it grew from a vague possibility to a probability, and finally to a certainty; she could almost feel the seed taking root within her. How often had she heard the older women whisper sagely, "A woman knows. She knows when she is pregnant, even before any of the signs."

At that moment, while the pain and grief of the day swirled around her, Tasha became sure of it: She was carrying Yuri's child!

A wave of revulsion swept over her. If Yuri sailed for Kamchatka the next week as planned, the child would be born long before he returned. Then, she suspected, he would refuse to marry her, claiming that she had tainted herself with another man. And no one else would consider marrying a woman with an illegitimate child. If she did not swallow her pride and marry Yuri right now, before he departed, the child—her child—would be fatherless.

Tasha shook her head in confusion. Her own life, she felt, had ended with Jared's, but she had to consider her father. And if she remained there, and bore a child out of wedlock, he would suffer undeservedly. By marrying Yuri now, she could avert that pain. She knew it would please her father to see her marry Yuri. He would be content that she had made a good match, and since she would be far away with her husband on Kamchatka, he could never see how unhappy she was. Yuri, knowing the child was his own, would surely treat it kindly. Thinking of the misery Prince Demidov had brought her childhood, Tasha knew how important that could be.

Then again, even for the sake of an innocent child and her loving father, could she contract marriage with a man who had abused her so ruthlessly?

Sighing with the weight of her final decision, Tasha dragged herself to her feet, opened the door, and started down the hallway toward the stairs. In the foyer below, she heard her father's voice. Apparently, he and Yuri were parting.

If she remained silent, she would not have to face

239

them. The front door was opening now, and in an instant Yuri would be gone. She forced herself to move to the head of the staircase. Never in her life had she felt such fatigue.

"Papa," she called weakly, the strain of the moment evident in her voice.

Both men raised their eyes. For an instant, she thought she saw concern in Yuri's eyes, but it made no difference, for her decision was made. Advancing halfway down the staircase, she gained the necessary strength to say confidently, "Papa, I have given this matter much thought, and I have decided—if you consent, and if he will have me—I would like to marry Yuri Aleksandrovich this year and go with him to Kamchatka."

PART THREE

1865-1867

Chapter Twenty-one

1865

Mikhail Lisovsky sat on the edge of his daughter's bed, holding her hand in his. "Are you sure, Tasha?" he asked gently. "I won't blame you if you change your mind, even at this late moment. You would probably be the subject of all kinds of gossip, but that is unimportant. All that matters to me is that you be happy."

Tasha patted his hand and smiled weakly, blinking back her tears. That evening, she would be exchanging the marriage vows with Yuri Aleksandrovich Zarevsky, and tomorrow she would sail with him for Petropavlovsk on the Kamchatka peninsula.

"It's all right, papa," she whispered. "It was my decision, you know. Everything will be fine."

Mikhail sighed and shook his head. They had planned all the details of the wedding in only five days, and in that time he had had little opportunity to talk privately with his daughter. He was still perplexed by her hasty decision, but she refused to explain it, stating simply, "It is done and I shall become Yuri's wife."

All week she had seemed distant, as if in a trance. Now he studied her glazed eyes, and voiced his concern. "I still do not understand it. You were so set on marrying the American; so vehemently opposed to Yuri. Why the sudden about-face? It's just that I hope you won't regret it."

She shook her head. "There is nothing to regret, papa. My beloved Jared is dead. His ship was one of those burned by the *Shenandoah*."

"Oh, Tasha!" he threw his arms about her and clutched her to his chest. "How you must be suffering! Why didn't you tell me sooner?"

She shrugged. "There was no point in telling you. Nothing can be done for him now."

"But why rush into marriage with Yuri? Perhaps, in your grief, you could not think clearly. If you are marrying Yuri to salve your aching heart, you may regret your decision once your grief has faded."

"My grief will never fade," she whispered, then added in a falsely light tone, "but you do surprise me, papa. What has become of the man who so joyfully announced my engagement?"

Mikhail smiled ruefully. "He has become terribly worried about the happiness of his only daughter."

"Then stop worrying. Yuri is a fine man. I judged him too harshly at first. We will make a good life together, and of course you must come to visit us sometimes, to see your grandchildren." She did not feel any of the joy she tried to inject into her voice, but she could not bear to see her father looking so sad. If he shed even one tear, she was sure she would collapse in her own despair.

"Very well, then, I'll leave you to rest and prepare for the evening." He rose and started for the door, stopping before he stepped into the hall. "I've had you such a short time, Tasha. I shall miss you more than you can imagine. But if I can feel that you are happy, your absence will be easier to bear."

Slipping from the bed, she ran to embrace him. "You shall have me always, papa, just as I shall always have you. Mere distance will not change what is in our hearts!"

"You're right." He smiled fondly and kissed her forehead. "And for a young girl you are wise beyond your years."

As he entered the hall and closed the door, Tasha

wondered just how wise she really was. Was it possible she would regret her decision to marry Yuri Zarevsky? He had been unusually polite and solicitous all week, and she had found his company at least tolerable. But would that change once she had spoken the vows and become his property? You must stop thinking like this, she cautioned herself, and called Theodosia to help her begin preparing for the ceremony.

There had been no time to have a wedding dress fitted, so Tasha had chosen a plain white satin gown with a long train, which she had embellished with intricate, white satin embroidery. Its long sleeves were closely fitted, accentuating her slender arms. The neckline was high in front, but dipped low and square in back. A tiny golden cross on a delicate gold chain, a gift sent by Yuri that morning, lay against the white satin of her bodice. As always, she wore Jared's ring concealed within her garments. When she took a deep breath, she could feel it pinch against her breasts. She knew that when she said her vows that evening she would be thinking only of Jared.

The bells of St. Mikhail's cathedral were chiming six o'clock as Tasha, seated in the carriage beside her father, rode into the small cathedral square. Before descending from the carriage, she sat staring pensively at the paneled painting of St. Mikhail which hung over the cathedral door. Perhaps, St. Mikhail —her father's patron saint—would provide a special blessing for this hapless union.

Smiling at her father, she allowed him to help her from the carriage, and they walked to the open door of the cathedral. She never ceased to be dazzled by the cathedral's silver lamps and chandeliers, and the white and gold altars. Although the outside of the cathedral was crude by Moscow standards, the interior, filled with priceless icons, artwork, and sacred articles from the Russian mainland, was as luxurious as any cathedral in Russia. How often, during Sunday

243

masses, had Tasha dreamed of being married here!
Only, in her dreams, it was Jared, not this smiling,
dark-haired stranger, who had stood at the other end
of the aisle.

Studying Yuri from where she stood in the outer
vestibule, Tasha had to admit he was a stunning figure in his green and gold-braided full-dress uniform.
His black moustache was a thin line above his smile.
His hair was highlighted by the flickering candles positioned throughout the cathedral. His eyes roamed
over Tasha eagerly, as if he had not already sampled
what she had to offer.

Normally, Tasha would have blushed to have a man
appraise her so openly, but she felt curiously detached. Throughout the ceremony, which lasted for an
hour and a half, Tasha felt as if the entire experience
did not really concern her. It was as though someone
else was about to become Yuri's wife. Standing before
the bronze, open-work doors leading to the inner
sanctuary of the main altar, she felt oblivious to the
intonations of the priest. The chanting of the all-male
chorus, hidden behind the altar by a carved screen,
seemed to be coming from some immeasurable distance.

Without thinking about them, she murmured the
correct responses and performed the prescribed movements for marriage. But all the while she was studying
the silver images of the saints inlaid on the bronze
doors, and marveling at the workmanship in the ren-
dering of the Last Supper which was suspended over
the doors. Each face in the picture was painted on
ivory, and every figure was draped in a robe of silver.

When the ceremony ended, Tasha dutifully took
Yuri's arm for the walk back up the aisle as the chorus
chanted a recessional. On the square outside the
cathedral, they accepted the kisses and congratulations of a throng that seemed to include all the residents of Novoarkhangelsk.

After the last well-wishers delivered their kisses and
hugs, Yuri helped Tasha into a carriage, which led the

way to Baranov Castle. Princess Maksutova, who loved to entertain anyway, had insisted that their wedding reception be held there.

Seating himself beside her in the carriage, Yuri put his arm around Tasha's shoulders. "You could appear a bit more ecstatic," he whispered, "after all, you are the one who insisted we marry at once."

Tasha grimaced. "Forgive me, sir. The rush of events has left me in a daze."

"No doubt you'll snap out of it at the reception," he laughed. "If not, I have a surprise for you later that will surely make you feel less dazed. For the moment though, try at least to wear a smile for the benefit of our guests."

"As you wish, master." She parted her lips in a thin smile.

"Master," Yuri chuckled. "I like that. It's good to know you realize your place." He bent and brushed his lips against her cheek. "Perhaps someday you will explain to me what brought about your change of heart."

They rode the rest of the way in silence, while Tasha began to wonder about the surprise her husband planned for her.

She had little time to think about it at the reception. More than two hundred people were crowded into the drawing room, sampling the tea, coffee, chocolate, champagne, and the exquisite, tiered bridal cake. Most of the ladies wore pastel muslin dresses with white satin shoes and silk stockings. Their gloved hands kept their fans in constant motion, as they tried to keep cool, and to preserve their coiffures against the heat and jostling of the crowd.

It was traditional in Novoarkhangelsk for a bride to open the wedding ball by dancing with the highest officer present, so Tasha led off with Prince Maksutov, who held the rank of captain in the Imperial Navy.

"It seems I have been proven right at last," the prince smiled.

Tasha cocked her head quizzically. "Proven right about what, sir?"

"Don't you remember your first ball, when I told you that one day you would meet someone special? At the time you seemed to doubt my words, but now everyone can plainly see you have found exactly the right man. My warmest congratulations. I hope you will find as much happiness as I have with my Maria."

"Thank you." Tasha stared across the floor at the man who was now her husband and knew that the prince's wish could never come true. Even if they declared a truce in their treatment of one another, she and Yuri could never share the easy companionability of the prince and his lovely Maria. During the last week, she had thought she might learn to tolerate him, but in the carriage riding from St. Mikhail's she had begun to doubt that assessment.

At the conclusion of their dance, the prince surrendered Tasha to Yuri, who in turn surrendered her to an endless stream of gentlemen, young and old, anxious to enjoy a last dance with their favorite before she traveled back to Siberia.

Tasha flirted gaily with each of them, willingly prolonging the time until she would be alone with Yuri. Now that she was his, he seemed less possessive, more willing to share her company with other men, thinking, no doubt, that when they left the ball he would have her to himself for all time.

It was after midnight when Yuri reclaimed his bride from her admirers. Whisking her across the floor, he whispered, "The dancing will continue till three in the morning. Perhaps it would be wise for us to leave now."

"But it may be our last ball for months," Tasha protested. "From what you've told me, Petropavlovsk has little to offer in the way of social amenities. Couldn't we stay until the end?"

"Our ship leaves early in the morning," Yuri said, "and we have things to do before then. Besides," he laughed harshly, "our guests might think it strange if we are not anxious to be alone on our wedding night.

Such behavior might set some mouths to gossiping about your virtue—or lack of it."

Tasha tossed her head. "I couldn't care in the least what they think."

"But *I* could care," Yuri replied in a steely voice. "I'll not have anyone believing I chose a woman lacking in virtue. Since you are my wife now, you must honor my decisions. I have decided it is time to leave. Besides, aren't you anxious to see the surprise I have arranged for you?"

"Not particularly!" she retorted bitterly. "After the surprise you gave me last week, I've no desire for any further surprises you might devise."

"Oh, but I can assure you this one is quite different. I think it will please you immensely. Shall we go, then?"

Tasha sighed in resignation. "It seems I have no choice in the matter. Would you permit me to say goodbye to my father? There may be no time in the morning, and I know he is going to be terribly lonely after I am gone."

"By all means," Yuri smiled broadly. "I've no intention of coming between you and your father." He danced her toward Mikhail, to whom he announced, "It seems it has been a long day, and the bride has begun to weary. By your leave, sir, I believe we should be departing. The morning sailing of the *Chaika* will come all too soon."

"Indeed it will," Mikhail agreed. "And I suppose it would be too much for me to ask you to visit me before you embark tomorrow. A newly-married couple has more important things to concern themselves with than a doddering old father."

"Not doddering, papa," Tasha quickly cut in. "A very dear father, whom I shall miss very much."

His eyes were moist as he turned to her. "Ah, Tasha, you have given my life new meaning in the months we shared. Through you, I have been able to see and love once again all the best qualities of your mother. Thank you, dear daughter, for giving me back a part of my life that was lost for so many years."

"Thank *you*, papa, for giving me your home, your love, and your understanding." Her voice was heavy with unshed tears as she threw her arms around his neck and buried her face in his shoulder.

Mikhail, blinking back his own tears, patted her back and chided softly, "Hush, child, you mustn't cry at your wedding reception. People will think you are not happy. And you are happy, aren't you?"

"Yes, papa," she replied.

"Of course you are," he said, as much to convince himself as her. "I shall always treasure your love, Tasha, but there is a new man in your life now and you owe your first allegiance to him." He grasped her shoulders and gently pushed her away from him. "Go with your husband now, and begin your new life."

Tasha gave her father one last kiss, then turned to her waiting husband, who took her arm and quickly led her outside, where a carriage waited for them in the crisp June air. In silence they drove to a one-story log house, much smaller than her father's house, where the carriage stopped.

Swinging his new wife down from the carriage, Yuri remarked, "How fortunate for us that my friend Dmitri has not yet returned from his voyage to Kronstadt. We will savor our wedding night in privacy here in his home."

Tasha nodded, wishing with all her heart that they were spending the night in her father's house, where she thought Yuri would be less inclined to treat her harshly. Now that she had actually married him, she knew it would be a sin to deny him his conjugal rights, even if there was any chance he would honor her wishes.

Yuri opened the door and pulled her into the house. A lamp flickered in the small sitting room, where two crystal goblets and a decanter of wine waited on a small table.

"You seem very quiet, my dear wife," Yuri murmured with a touch of cynicism. "Perhaps a glass of wine will loosen your tongue." Strolling to the table, he filled both goblets and handed one to her.

He clinked his glass against hers and murmured, "A toast, to the years we shall share."

Raising her glass automatically, Tasha drank. She watched her husband cautiously over the rim of her goblet.

His dark eyes met hers, and Yuri snorted, "You needn't regard me as if you fear I shall pounce on you without warning."

"Your previous actions were warning enough," she murmured.

"Ah, but I've been to confession since that time, and I've vowed to mend my wicked ways. Your body is seductive, Tasha, but I think it demeans us both for me to have to resort to force."

"A pity you did not feel that way before!" she replied bitterly. "Now that I have spoken my vows, I am compelled to fulfill them, regardless of my own feelings in the matter."

Yuri chuckled. "Then it appears you did not marry me out of affection and longing for my caresses. Of course," he shrugged, "I suspected as much, though I am still puzzled as to why you changed your mind."

She turned away from him. "As you surmised, it was not for love of you or of anything you can offer me. Let us simply say I wished to please my father. For some unaccountable reason, he considers you worthy to be my husband."

"I think," Yuri murmured, "that your father's opinion had little to do with your decision. But, right now, your reasons are unimportant." He crossed the room and stood behind her, placing his hands possessively around her waist. She felt his breath hot against her ear as he whispered, "You are mine now, and that is all that matters."

Tasha stiffened as his hands roamed upward, cupping her breasts, then squeezing them. With one hand, he quickly unfastened the back of her dress, while his other hand moved upward to pull the front of her bodice away from her heaving bosom. His fingers slid into the warm cleft between her breasts as he hurriedly untied the ribbons of her camisole. For a moment he stared over her shoulder at her creamy flesh and smooth, pink nipples. Then he turned her toward him, holding her at arm's length to appraise her quivering form.

"The last time I could only feel you, and had to imagine to myself how tantalizing you looked," he murmured hoarsely. "But tonight I intend to fully examine my property."

Embarrassed by his frank stare, Tasha wrenched away from him and, turning her back to him, attempted to pull her clothing up over her breasts. Roughly, he grabbed her shoulder and spun her back toward him.

"Considering our intimate knowledge of each other," he growled, "and your own past indiscretions, it seems a bit late for shyness. I was willing to take you as you were, knowing you were not a virgin. I expect you, in turn, to give me whatever I ask."

Hooking his thumbs under her camisole, he quickly peeled it down, freeing her breasts for his inspection. He pulled her closer and attempted to work her undergarments further down her body. His eager fingers slid beneath her camisole, then hesitated as they closed around something concealed within the garment. He bent over her as he drew the scrimshaw ring into the light.

"What is this?" he demanded. "Some childish trinket?"

Tasha nodded, hoping he would accept that explanation.

Sensing her uneasiness, Yuri ripped the ring away from her camisole to examine it more closely. He drew in his breath as he noted the initials in the English alphabet. "Where did you get this?" he demanded.

Tasha was silent, wondering what to say that would enable her to preserve her one memento of Jared.

"Answer me!" Yuri thundered, slapping her face so hard that she staggered backwards a few steps.

Bringing her hand up to her stinging cheek, Tasha stared at him defiantly. When she spoke her voice was cool. "It was a gift from my father. Now give it back to me." She held out her hand.

"A gift from your father!" Yuri spat. "You must think me very stupid if you suppose I would believe that. If it was indeed a gift from Mikhail Pavlovich you would wear it openly on your hand, not concealed within your clothing. And it is no more yours than mine. May I remind you that you have chosen to become my wife, which makes all your property mine. Now," he grabbed her shoulders, digging his nails into her flesh, "suppose you tell me where you really got it?"

Wincing, she stared back at him, her eyes flashing bold resistance. "I've already told you. From my father."

"And I have told you I do not believe you. Since you wear it concealed and close to your heart, I can only assume it was a gift from a lover. Perhaps you thought to make a fool of me by marrying me and continuing to carry on an affair with another!"

"Don't be absurd!" Tasha replied through clenched teeth. "How could I carry on an affair with someone in Novoarkhangelsk when we are leaving for Kamchatka tomorrow?"

"Perhaps he sails with us. Or perhaps you intend to return here from time to time, under the pretense of visiting your beloved father. Which form of deception did you plan to use?"

"Neither!" she insisted. "I do not love you, Yuri Aleksandrovich, and I doubt that I ever shall, but I swear to you there is no one else!"

"You say there *is* no one else. But perhaps I would not be wrong to assume there *was* someone else. After

251

all, there is still the question of your surrendered virginity."

For the first time, Tasha's gaze wavered, and she bit her lower lip nervously. He could think what he wished, but she would never discredit Jared's memory by discussing him with Yuri.

"Aha!" Yuri exclaimed triumphantly. "I see that I have struck the truth. You do not love me, but you did love this other man. Who was he?"

Tasha shook her head. "It doesn't matter."

"It does matter! I want to know the identity of the man who took what was rightfully mine. Every man has the right to expect the gift of his wife's maidenhead on his wedding night. I have been denied that right, and I demand to know who cheated me."

"How can you pretend to be so righteous!" Tasha snapped, "when you took me yourself before we were wed? You knew I wasn't a virgin, but you chose to marry me anyway."

"What I did is immaterial at the moment. I have asked you a question and as your husband I demand an answer! What was the name I heard you tell your father that day? Jared, wasn't it? Who is this Jared?"

"I told you it doesn't matter!" Tasha shrieked in fury. "Would you seek out a ghost and do battle for the right to my virginity?"

"A ghost," Yuri repeated quietly. He grasped her chin and peered into her eyes. "The man is dead?"

"Yes, dead," she choked. "Does that satisfy you?"

He shrugged, releasing her chin in disgust. "Not entirely. Not while you still hold his memory warm against your heart."

Before Tasha could protest, he raised his arm and flung the ring across the room, into the fire blazing in the fireplace. With a cry of pain, Tasha rushed after it and sank to her knees beside the grate. She would have plunged her hands into the fire to retrieve the ring if Yuri had not grabbed her arms and dragged her away.

"You little fool!" he muttered, grasping her hands

and waving her golden wedding band before her eyes. "This is the only ring you need concern yourself with now! I will not tolerate a wife who pines for another man, living or dead! I am your master now! You shall keep no trinket that reminds either one of us of the men from your sordid past!"

Tasha struggled in his grasp, until he thrust her against a wall and pressed himself tightly against her, making it impossible for her to escape. He brought his mouth down upon hers, bruising her tender lips. His powerful thighs flattened hers against the wall, and his hands slid up to massage her breasts. His fingers were hunting for the pins in her hair when someone knocked at the door.

Yuri lifted his head and flashed Tasha a lazy, self-satisfied smile. "I believe that is the surprise I promised you. Come along and see." He wrapped an arm around her shoulder and pulled her toward the door.

"Please, Yuri," Tasha pleaded, trying to hang back so she could pull up her dress. "I'm hardly dressed to receive guests."

He laughed. "I can assure you our guest will find nothing amiss in your appearance. I would say you look exactly as a young bride should on her wedding night." With that he opened the door and waved in the guest.

A voluptuous woman in her mid-thirties entered. Her long, thick, reddish-brown hair swirled around her sensual face. The woman casually threw off her shawl to reveal a low-cut, formfitting red dress with a laced-up front. The laces were dangling loosely, revealing that she wore no undergarments.

"Sorry to be late, sweetheart," she said to Yuri, giving him a peck on the cheek, "but there were more requests for my services than usual at the barracks tonight." She glanced at Tasha's bared bosom and cocked an eyebrow toward Yuri. "But it appears you may not be needing me tonight after all. Perhaps the lady is less averse to your charms than you thought."

"Nonsense, Marta, I've promised my wife a sur-

prise tonight, and I intend to keep my promise."
Clapping an arm around each of them, he pulled the
two women toward the bedroom. Once inside, he took
a key from his pocket, locked the door, and, ignoring
the mystified look on Tasha's face, turned to the
woman he called Marta. "Make yourself at home," he
said suggestively.

The woman giggled. "I thought you'd never get
around to it. And this damned dress is frightfully
tight; I can scarcely breathe."

"Then you must allow me to help you," Yuri smiled.
With one quick movement he reached out and pulled
the loose end of the lacing. The dress opened, and
Marta took a deep breath, allowing her bosom to
spill out of the constricting material.

"Ah, that's much better," she purred. Then, to
Tasha's horror, she proceeded to strip off the dress
and stood naked in the bedroom. She was too flabby
to be very alluring, but it was obvious she must have
once had an exquisite figure.

Seemingly oblivious to both of them, Yuri was removing his own clothes. He stopped when he heard
Tasha's strangled gasp. "My dear, innocent, young
wife," he said in mock concern, "I hope this arrangement does not offend you in any way. Personally, I
considered it a sort of wedding gift to you. Since
you made it obvious you did not enjoy our last session of lovemaking—not to mention your preference for a dead man—I thought I would spare you
the agony of sharing my bed tonight. Since Marta
here is more than willing, I believe the arrangement
should suit all of us."

Tasha stared at him dumbfounded. The other woman was already bouncing playfully on the bed. "You,
sir, may do as you please. Marta is welcome to you, as
I have no desire to sleep with you! But you surely
cannot expect me to stand by and observe you in the
act of infidelity."

Yuri shrugged. "I'm afraid I do. After tonight, Marta
will no longer be available to me. I will require your

wifely services from time to time aboard the *Chaika*, and on a fairly regular basis once we reach Kamchatka. And I shall expect you to submit with at least a modicum of regard for my desires. Perhaps you can learn something of how to please me by watching Marta, who is quite accomplished."

Lifting her chin and staring at him unblinkingly, Tasha declared, "I will not permit you to treat me in this manner!"

Smiling wryly, Yuri replied, "I can't see that you have much choice." He threw aside his trousers and underwear, and dove onto the bed beside Marta. Tittering, she rolled into his embrace, then slid upward on the bed until she could push one of her large breasts into his mouth. He sucked it greedily, massaging her other breast with one hand, while his other hand pinched and kneaded her buttocks.

Marta squealed in delight and wiggled closer to him, boldly reaching down to squeeze his stiffening manhood. Groaning with pleasure, Yuri pushed her onto her back, rolled atop her and plunged inside her. With a series of pleased whimpers, Marta rocked beneath him, flailing her legs ecstatically with every thrust.

Trapped in the room with them, Tasha felt her stomach churning. The episode sickened her, but she could not tear her eyes from the couple writhing on the bed. Finally, they lay still, and their regular breathing told Tasha they had drifted into sleep. Stealthily, she crept to the door and tried to open it. She checked the pockets of Yuri's discarded clothing, but could not find the key. On reflection, she could not recall him returning it to his pocket. What could he have done with it?

Tasha tiptoed toward the bed, searching for a glint of metal. Gently she lifted the corner of the pillow, hoping to find the key concealed beneath it. Instantly Yuri's eyes flew open and he grinned at her wickedly. "Looking for something?" he whispered. "Or were you perhaps preparing to join us in bed?"

She backed away, as if burned by his words, and

he laughed harshly. "I see my first assumption was correct." He raised an arm and opened his fist, revealing the key. "Perhaps this is what you seek?"

Tasha lunged for his open palm, but he, anticipating her move, quickly closed it and buried it beneath Marta's bulging buttocks. "Be patient, little wife," he mocked, "the door will be opened in time for us to reach the *Chaika*. But I see no reason for you to exit sooner." Reaching up with his free hand, he twined it tightly in her hair and pulled her face down to his. "Now, will you honor your new husband with a goodnight kiss?"

For answer, Tasha spat in his face, rejoicing as her saliva spilled down his nose and streaked across his cheek.

"You little bitch!" he growled, his hand tightening painfully around her neck, then flinging her to the floor. "You had best learn to obey me or you will find that life can be very hard indeed! Tonight you can shiver on the cold floor for all I care." He turned away from her angrily and snuggled against Marta.

Huddled on the floor, massaging her aching throat, Tasha bit back her sobs. She refused to let him know how he had hurt her. Inside her, she felt a resolve growing: she would never allow this man to bend her to his will.

A week earlier she had thought herself beyond feeling, except for a stubborn love for Jared's memory and for her father. But now she knew she was capable of another emotion: hate. She hated Yuri Aleksandrovich Zarevsky with all her heart.

Chapter Twenty-two

1865-1866

Tasha awoke as a boot jabbed her ribs. Her eyes traveled from the leather-clad foot to the unsmiling face of her husband. "Up, bitch!" he commanded. "The *Chaika* departs in less than half an hour."

She stretched her cramped, stiff muscles, but made no move to sit up. "The *Chaika* can depart without me," she said coldly. "I've no intention of going anywhere with you, Yuri Zarevsky!"

"I've no time to discuss your intentions, *Madame Zarevskaya*," he emphasized her name sarcastically. "Nor do I care to hear more of your insolence. Now," his boot jabbed her ribs more sharply, "I suggest you get up immediately!"

Tasha stared at him, unmoving, challenging him to make her obey.

For a moment he stood over her, his feet planted on either side of her slim waist, his eyes flashing a warning. Then he leaned over and grabbed her wrists, jerking her to her feet.

"By God!" he roared, "you'll do as I say!" Sitting on the edge of the bed, he held her locked between his legs as he furiously pulled up her camisole and dress, still hanging loose from the night before. "You can change aboard the ship," he muttered. "Your Theodosia will be there with your trunks." He raked his fingers through her hair and jerked her toward the bedroom door. Only then did Tasha notice that the door was ajar. The red-haired Marta was gone. With regret, she realized she had missed a chance for escape.

At the sitting-room door, Tasha turned and looked sorrowfully toward the fireplace, now dark and cold.

"I told you there's no time to dawdle!" Yuri roared, yanking her roughly toward the front door.

"I—I thought I might have dropped something in the sitting room last night," she stammered.

"Dropped something?" He laughed shortly. "If you are referring to that silly trinket, by now it is nothing but a charred piece of rubbish, to be swept up with the other ashes."

Dragging her outside, he almost threw her into a waiting carriage, then clambered in beside her. As they rode to the dock, he threw an arm around her shoulders and pulled her close, waving like a happy bridegroom to anyone they passed. "You would do well to imitate me," he whispered.

Tasha stared straight ahead, refusing to acknowledge him.

At dockside, the *Chaika* was aswarm with sailors preparing her for the voyage. Tasha glanced around looking for a chance to escape, but Yuri, sensing her thoughts, never loosened his grip on her arm. As the carriage that had brought them rolled away, another arrived, and Tasha's heart jumped when she saw her beloved father descend.

"Papa!" she screamed imploringly.

Yuri tightened his grasp on her elbow as her father came toward them. "Now don't make a scene," he whispered in a warning tone. "It would only embarrass everyone, including your father. And it would gain you nothing, except for a few well-placed slaps in the privacy of our cabin."

She was about to retort angrily when her father reached them and heartily embraced them both. "How are the newlyweds?" he asked. "I couldn't let you go without a last fond farewell."

"Very thoughtful of you, Mikhail Pavlovich," Yuri said stiffly, pulling away from the embrace. Tasha clung to her father as if she would never let go.

"Well, Tasha," Mikhail spoke cheerfully. "You're off on another adventure. I'll wager there are few girls your age who have traveled as many miles as you have."

"I don't want to travel any more, papa," she wailed. "I want to stay in Novoarkhangelsk with you. You are my only family, and this is my home."

Mikhail shot a flustered glance at Yuri. "Nonsense, child. Your home is with your husband, and he is your family now. And in no time at all the two of you will have created more family than you can handle— if you haven't already begun." He chuckled, but stopped as Tasha continued sobbing.

"I think your daughter is suffering a bit of a letdown after all the excitement and the tension of the wedding night," Yuri explained. "No doubt she'll feel better after we've sailed and she's had the benefit of the fresh ocean air."

"You may be right," Mikhail said, gently pulling away from Tasha's clinging embrace. "Perhaps I did you both a disservice by coming here. I'm afraid I've upset my daughter unnecessarily."

"Not at all," Yuri said magnanimously, pulling Tasha close to his side. "But I think we must be boarding now. The ship is due to depart at any moment."

"Of course. I won't detain you longer. I sent Theodosia with the trunks earlier this morning, so I assume she is already aboard." Mikhail kissed Tasha quickly on the forehead, then stepped back and watched as Yuri led her to the ship.

On board, Yuri steered her toward the companionway leading to the passenger's cabins. "You will find the departure less painful if you go below immediately," he advised. Tasha thought she detected a note of sympathy in his voice, but she dismissed it, assuming it was solely for the benefit of the other passengers and crew who might overhear them.

She replied coolly, "I prefer to watch until my home is out of sight."

"As you wish," Yuri said, leading her to a spot by the rail. He stood behind her, resting his hands lightly on her waist, as the crew weighed anchor and the *Chaika* slid away from the harbor and into the straits.

Silently, Tasha watched Novoarkhangelsk shrink in the distance until only the golden spire of St. Mikhail's and the massive outline of Baranov Castle could be seen. Then the *Chaika* rounded the edge of Mount Edgecumbe, and even those landmarks were lost from view.

Satisfied that she could no longer escape from him, short of throwing herself into the ocean—an act he doubted she was desperate enough to try—Yuri left her at the rail and went below to their cabin.

Tasha stood at the rail for hours, watching the foggy forms of the Aleutians drifting by. At dinnertime, Yuri came and, against her will, guided her below to the common dining room, where he cheerily introduced her as his bride. Remembering another voyage, when Nikolai Voronin had pretended she was his wife, Tasha ate in sullen silence. She found herself wishing the *Chaika* would meet the same fate as the *Ayan*, however unlikely that might be. After dinner, Yuri led her to their cabin, pushing her inside and locking the door behind him before he went back up to the deck.

The *Chaika* was considerably smoother and swifter than the *Ayan* had been. The *Chaika*, like the already-infamous *Shenandoah*, was a steamer equipped with sails for supplementary power. Tasha thought it ironic that she should be sailing to Siberia on the same type of vessel that had put an end to Jared's existence, but she had little interest in the actual operation of the ship.

During most of the voyage, Yuri simply ignored her. He allowed her on deck during the mornings and afternoons, but locked her in their cabin each evening after dinner. Most nights, he did not return until long after midnight, when Tasha was already asleep. He woke her by pushing her aside roughly to make room for himself in the bed, but he never tried to make love to her.

Though she did not ask him about it, Tasha assumed that he had found a mistress on board. Far from distressing her, the thought of her husband with another woman relieved her. She only hoped the woman would be staying in Petropavlovsk, thus freeing her from any distasteful marital obligations.

Midway through the trip, nature provided her with the usual sign that she was not carrying Yuri's child after all. Her earlier premonition, distorted by grief and confusion, had been erroneous.

At first she was relieved, knowing she would not

have to bear the child of a man she hated. But her relief was quickly swallowed in despondency as she realized there had been no real necessity for her to marry Yuri. Had she only known, she could have waited the year her father proposed. In that time, she could surely have found some way out of the marriage—perhaps Yuri would have tired of waiting for her and married someone else. Now the vows were spoken and recorded, and she was trapped. In the few days since their marriage, she had often regretted the hasty decision she made, even were she to have been pregnant. Now, she feared that decision would prove to be the worst mistake of her life.

On the fifteenth day out of Novoarkhangelsk, the *Chaika* came in view of the Kamchatka peninsula. By midafternoon, they were steaming into Avacha Bay, preparing to dock at Petropavlovsk. Yuri joined Tasha at the rail in the final moments of the voyage, presenting to onlookers a picture of husbandly pride.

As they steamed into the harbor, Tasha sighted a mountain slightly north of the city spewing forth flame and smoke. She jumped back from the rail in fright, and instantly felt Yuri's arms around her waist. "It's the volcano, Koryakskaya Sopka," he whispered matter-of-factly in her ear. "I hear it erupts regularly, but it has never been known to cause any disturbance or damage to the city. Geographers have counted more than one hundred volcanoes on Kamchatka, though less than a quarter of them are active."

Surprised by his air of friendliness, Tasha relaxed and leaned against him, watching in fascination as the mountain spewed forth its lava. As the eruption subsided, her eyes drifted to the beach, where groups of walrus and seal sunned themselves on the warm, offshore rocks. As the *Chaika* neared the shore, she could see otter swimming in the bay, teasing the seals that slipped into the water for a cooling dip.

As her gaze took in the playful animals, the green

pasture surrounding the city, and the abundance of birch trees beyond the shore, Tasha imagined for the briefest moment that she could find happiness on this wild peninsula. Then she felt Yuri's hands around her waist, and she reminded herself she could never be happy while she was forced to live with him.

Perhaps, for a while, she would pretend to be the submissive wife. He would react with pleasure and surprise, assuming he had mastered her. When the right moment came, after he had learned to trust her docile nature, she would find a way to be free of him forever.

Stiffening with resolve, Tasha pulled away from her husband and turned toward the companionway. "I suppose we'll be landing soon," she said offhandedly. "I'd best go below and see that Theodosia has packed our belongings."

Yuri nodded absently. "See that you are not gone for long. I'm anxious to disembark."

When Tasha returned, the ship had anchored, and she looked out over the city in dismay. Fewer than a hundred squat log houses were scattered along the shoreline. Most had roofs made of straw or bark; a few of the larger houses were distinguished by red-shingled roofs. In the midst of the cluster of houses stood a small, octagonal wooden church, with a tiled roof and a bulging green spire.

"Surely this is not *all* of Petropavlovsk!" Tasha cried.

Her husband smiled. "I'm afraid, my dear, this is indeed the whole city. One could hardly expect more, since the Russian population is scarcely three hundred, and the Koryaks—the natives of the region—are not civilized enough to be counted as inhabitants."

Tasha glanced at Yuri uneasily. "And of these three hundred, how many are criminals, exiled by the Czar?"

"None," he laughed, taking her arm and helping her into the boat that would row them ashore. "Our

Czar is compassionate. He considers Kamchatka too far to send even the worst of criminals. Only the Empire's hardiest adventurers come to this peninsula."

"And yet we are expected to live here?"

Yuri shrugged. "Perhaps not for long. In time, I expect to be promoted to a more significant position. No doubt, we shall eventually settle in St. Petersburg, where I expect to gain a position on the Russian-American Company's board of directors.

"For now, we shall have to make the best of the situation. Kamchatka may be crude, but it is rich in soft gold." In answer to the question he read in her eyes, he explained, "Furs. The area is full of otter, sable, silver fox, blue fox, beaver. It is my job to see that these resources are exploited more fully. If the Kronstadt approves my work, you and I shall have a bright future."

Tasha stared silently at the town. If the other towns she had visited on her travels through Siberia had seemed small and provincial, Petropavlovsk was hardly more than a primitive settlement. Far from any post roads or trading tracks, this scattering of cabins was totally isolated from the rest of the Empire. By comparison, Novoarkhangelsk, which she had previously considered remote, might have been the capital of the universe.

They left the boat, and Yuri led her up the dirt street that served as the main thoroughfare. Passing the church, Tasha noted its dilapidated state. She was relieved when Yuri stopped before one of the newer, larger, red-roofed houses, and announced that this was to be their home. It had been recently vacated by an official of the company who had been called back to St. Petersburg. Though a mere cabin, it was more appealing than most of the dwellings they had passed in their trek through town.

To her astonishment, Yuri whisked her off her feet and carried her over the doorsill into the house. He laughed as he set her down in the small, carpeted parlor, then announced briskly that he was off to pay his respects to Captain Soutkovoi, the captain of the port of Petropavlovsk.

"Should I accompany you?" Tasha asked innocently. It occurred to her that it might be prudent to cultivate the captain as a friend.

"That's not necessary," he replied. "It would be better for you to see to your house, Madame Zarevskaya. Theodosia should be along with the trunks soon—I left directions to the house with two members of the crew who offered to carry your things." Without further words, he left Tasha to examine her new home.

The house was a single story, and consisted of a high-ceilinged parlor, a dining room, a kitchen and two bedrooms. An attempt had been made to create a home-like air through the use of Oriental rugs and ornamental wallpapers. In the parlor were a sofa, three easy chairs, and, on a side table, a dusty brass samovar. The dining room contained a heavy oak table and chairs; the bedrooms wide cedar beds, serviceable chests of drawers and tall wardrobes.

In the very center of the house rose a *pechka,* the large, brick heating oven commonly found in Russian peasant homes. The pechka had a system of flues and pipes that wound into each room of the house, thereby warming the entire building.

By the time Tasha had finished inspecting the house, which did not take more than a quarter of an hour, Theodosia and two burly sailors arrived, carrying Tasha's three trunks of clothing and personal belongings. As soon as the men departed, the women began unpacking and storing things, taking a minute to add a personal touch to the little house here and there. When Yuri returned an hour later, the brass samovar was already polished and steaming with fresh tea.

Much to Tasha's surprise, her husband continued to treat her with the indifference he had shown aboard the *Chaika*—with one exception. His mistress had ap-

264

parently continued west aboard the *Chaika,* so now he made conjugal demands on Tasha from time to time. She gave herself to him as one fulfilling an obligation: readily, but without joy. He, in turn, took what he wished without treating her harshly, but without showing any regard for her own feelings or desires. There was no pretense of affection between them, but there was at least no open hostility.

During the daytime, while Yuri investigated the fur business in Petropavlovsk, Tasha was free to explore the town and nearby areas. While the summer weather lasted, she and Theodosia spent many afternoons climbing in the green hills, picking gooseberries, raspberries, and whortleberries, or making posies of roses, tiger lilies, and Solomon's seal, which grew wild in huge clumps.

On Sundays, after mass in the small church, Yuri and Tasha would join other company employees and their wives on fishing excursions in the bay. The herring and oversize crab they snared provided the fare for luscious picnic suppers on the beach.

The leaves began to fall in October, but surprisingly, the weather continued warm through November. When the snows came, they were heavy and deep, and snowshoes or dog-sledges became the only practicable modes of travel. Yuri kept four dogs and one sledge, which was small, light, and high, and could carry only two riders at a time. On warm days, bundled up in bear skins and fox furs, Yuri and Tasha frequently joined a caravan of other couples into the interior of the peninsula, sometimes passing wild sheep, bear, or reindeer as they sped by.

Sled travel terrified Tasha, who feared she would fly out into the snow when they bounced over hills. She heard stories from some of the women about sledges overturning on icy mountain stretches, forcing their drivers to hang onto anything they could reach, while being dragged over the ice and snow, lest the nearly-wild dogs abandon them in the wilderness. Each time she mounted the sledge, she envisioned

herself being dragged along in the snow, her face
coated with ice; or, worse still, unable to hold on, being left behind and devoured by wolves. But when
she voiced these fears to Yuri, he simply called her
childish and insisted that she accompany him. If
other wives rode with their husbands, he said, she
could do the same. If she was to be an asset to his
career, she must follow the dictates of society.

After the rides, the party usually gathered at the
home of Captain Soutkovoi, who had the largest
drawing room, boasting the only piano in Petropavlovsk. There they ate and drank, and smoked until
near dawn. Many of the Siberian women, like the
Yakut hostess of Tasha's earlier travels, smoked as
freely as the men. Even those who had been raised in
European Russia enthusiastically lit up *papyrosa,* or
Russian cigarettes. But, no matter how Yuri encouraged her to try, smoking was one custom Tasha refused to adopt.

By springtime, Sunday evening gatherings at the
captain's house had become a weekly event. Early in
May, shortly after the last of the ice had melted in
Avacha Bay, the first ship of the season docked at
Petropavlovsk, and Captain Soutkovoi and his wife arranged an evening of special entertainment. After
dining, the guests, including Yuri and Tasha, and the
crew of the ship, assembled in the drawing room to
observe a group of local Koryaks perform a Kamchadale dance.

The native women wore long silk dresses. The men
wore *narkas,* shirts made of reindeer skin, and *kam-
legas,* garments made of various animal skins stripped
of fur. While the Koryaks began chanting "an-kelle,
an-kaget," three of the women in their group stepped
forward, waving silk scarves before them. Rhythmically swaying their hips, they danced into the center
of the room, rippling the buoyant scarves teasingly
in front of their bodies. As the tempo of the chant accelerated, they rolled their heads from side to side,
then forward and backward. Continuing to sway and

gyrate, each of them shuffled toward a man in their group and waved the scarf before him invitingly.

Grasping the loose ends of the scarves, the three chosen men rose to accept their partners, moving in time to the chant. The woman would turn away from her partner from time to time, as though rejecting him, but after several beats, would dance back, moving even closer to him each time, and becoming increasingly more seductive with each return. Slowly, the women sank to their knees and arched backwards, supporting themselves with their palms on the floor. The men followed them to the floor, leaning over them in a rhythmic representation of lovemaking.

As the chanting continued, more Koryak couples joined in the dance, and even the Russian spectators, infected by the excitement, began to chant "an-kelle, an-kaget." Tasha, who had carelessly taken more vodka than was her custom, started to chant with the others, unconsciously swaying with the rhythm of the words.

Suddenly, one of the Koryak men presented himself to her, ceremoniously waving a scarf in invitation. Laughing, Tasha grasped its corners and stepped onto the dance floor with him. Yuri, engrossed in conversation with the captain of the ship, did not notice his wife's indiscretion.

Abandoning herself to the pounding beat of the Koryak dance, Tasha rolled her head around her shoulders, her body writhing and gyrating in the same manner as the native women. Concentrating on the encouraging smile of her dark-skinned partner, she did not notice that she was the only Russian woman dancing. She sank to her knees and arched backwards, smiling seductively as her partner leaned over her. As their bodies moved forward again, the chant crescendoed and her partner leaped to his feet and turned his back to her.

Glancing at the couples beside her, Tasha saw the other men do the same. In the next instant, the women jumped to their feet and mounted their partners' backs. Seeing her own partner waiting, Tasha gamely followed their example, hoisting her bulky skirts and petticoats out of the way to free her legs.

The spectators hooted their approval loudly, and Yuri, still deep in conversation, looked up casually to determine the cause of the commotion. Seeing Tasha astride a Koryak's back, exhibiting her legs to the best families in Petropavlovsk, his face paled in anger.

"Natalya!" he barked, using her given name for the first time in their relationship, as he pushed his way toward her.

Surrounded by the other dancers, with the sounds of "an-kelle, an-kaget" ringing in her ears, Tasha did not hear him. Her partner turned abruptly and, with Tasha still astride him, followed the other dancers through the drawing room and out of the front door of the Soutkovoi home.

Yuri stormed after them, overtaking them as they entered the avenue of white poplars leading from the captain's door. Enraged, he tore his wife from the man's back and flung her to the ground. The Koryak turned to regard him in perplexity, and Yuri's fist crashed into his jaw.

"You filthy savage!" Yuri snarled. "I suppose you think yourself very clever, trying to steal my wife from right beneath my nose!"

The Koryak raised his hand to his jaw, staring at Yuri in confusion. On the ground, struggling to regain her composure, Tasha saw her husband's fist close again and she scrambled to her feet, catching his arm in mid-air.

"Yuri, don't, please!" she gasped. "The man meant no harm."

He shoved her away. "Be quiet, you slut!" he spat. "I'll deal with you later!" As he turned to raise his fist again, two men rushed out of the captain's house toward them.

"Enough, Yuri," one of the men whispered. "I doubt the man intended to abduct your wife. Let him go." The man then addressed the Koryak in his own tongue, apologizing for Yuri's behavior and instructing him to leave. Shrugging, the Koryak followed his companions down the avenue of poplars.

"You mustn't blame him, Yuri," the man explained. "It's their traditional way of dancing, however obscene it appears to civilized folk. The man was only trying to be friendly."

"A bit too friendly for my tastes!" Yuri replied.

His friend shrugged. "Still, there's no harm done. We've simply had confirmation of something we already knew—that you have an uncommonly desirable wife. You're a lucky man, Yuri Aleksandrovich. Now, come and rejoin the party."

Shaking his head, Yuri grasped Tasha's arm. "No, I've no more taste for partying tonight. It seems my wife requires some instruction. Perhaps the Koryaks do not know any better, but a Russian lady should know how to comport herself. Good night to you." He nodded gruffly to the men and dragged Tasha away from the house.

At the entrance to their own house, Yuri flung open the door and delivered a stinging blow to Tasha's back as he pushed her inside. "You little slut!" he growled. "What could you have been thinking to behave so indecently?"

Tasha stared at him boldly. "How dare you complain," she chafed, "when you are always telling me I should join in the activities of the other women? You are the one who dictates my behavior, hoping to use your 'good and beautiful' wife to secure yourself a promotion in St. Petersburg."

"Mind your tongue!" he barked. "You are just as anxious as I to leave this godforsaken town! And I never meant for you to join in the savage activities of the heathen Koryak! I expect you to behave like a well-bred Russian woman—did you see any of them participating in that disgusting dance?"

"I—I didn't notice," she stammered.

"Well, you should have! Had you taken the time to look, you would have seen that none of them were indulging." He snorted in disgust. "You pretend to be such a lady, refusing even to light a *papyrosa*, then you exhibit yourself in some copulative dance in front of all the guests at the captain's house!"

"You needn't put it that way!" she cried defensively. "You heard your friend say there was no harm in it, that the dance was merely a Koryak custom."

"Perhaps there is no harm done in the Koryak's eyes, but don't think your reputation is the same as it was in the eyes of civilized society. I will not stand for it, Tasha! I won't have you wrecking my career through your mindless behavior."

Without warning, he snatched her up into his arms, and strode into their bedroom. Tossing her onto the bed, he slammed the door.

"Now," he muttered, pulling off his trousers and throwing her skirt and petticoats aside, "I will give you a lesson. In our society, a woman does not ride on a man's back, a man rides a woman while she lies on her back. And I, dear wife, will be the only one to ride you!"

Mounting her, he took her brutally, oblivious to her sobs of protest. When he was finished, he pushed her roughly aside, unmoving as her body slid limply off the bed to the floor, where she lay in pained silence. He waited until he judged her nearly asleep, then yanked her back onto the bed and ripped off her rumpled clothing.

"Hellish slut!" he muttered. "I'll teach you to desire other men! Almost a year I have had you, and you have never honored my attentions with more than indifference. Yet, the moment my back is turned, you begin a lewd exhibition with a stinking savage, shaming us both before all polite society. Don't try to deny that you wanted the fellow—I saw the wild look on your face as you rode on his back, waving your naked limbs in Captain Soutkovoi's face. You were imagining yourself lying with him—imagining that filthy Koryak inside you!"

"That's not true!" she cried.

270

"Don't add lying to your other sins! I know what I saw. Well, if you want to be taken savagely, I will be glad to oblige you."

He thrust his shaft into her so furiously she had to bite her lip to keep from screaming. "Never again," he grunted as he pierced her again and again, "let me catch you casting eyes at another man or, by God, I shall punish you beyond your wildest expectations."

After one final, brutal thrust, he lay still atop her, panting and heaving. Within moments, he was sleeping, pinning her to the bed with his weight. She had no choice but to lie, still and aching, beneath him. No night had ever seemed as long to her as this one, and she closed her eyes only when the early morning light illuminated the face of her husband, a sight she could not bear to look at. As the sun rose, she fell asleep.

Chapter Twenty-three

1866

Tasha awoke to the sight of Yuri stuffing clothing and belongings into a trunk. She blinked in numb bewilderment. If he was leaving, she was glad, and it was of no concern to her where he might choose to go.

He stopped his packing to confront her with a dark frown. "In case you are wondering, I am sailing today for St. Petersburg. The *Constantine*, the ship that arrived yesterday, carried a message from the company, requesting my presence. She sails for St. Petersburg before noon."

Tasha met his stare, registering neither surprise nor concern.

"I suppose you expect to accompany me," he continued, incensed by her blank stare, "but that is out of the question. Early yesterday evening, before your

271

little exhibition, I had planned to surprise you with the trip. But you have made it obvious that I cannot trust you to behave properly. You might drink too much and feel obliged to demonstrate the Kamchadale dances to St. Petersburg society. You would make me the laughing stock of the empire!"

He turned away from her in disgust and continued packing. "Perhaps if you remain here for the year, without my company, you will come to appreciate your good fortune in having me as your husband. And perhaps you will learn to act in a way befitting the wife of an official of the Russian-American Company."

Goaded to anger, Tasha replied bitterly, "But won't the company directors wonder why you did not bring your trinket—to display before them and win their favor?"

He shrugged. "If asked, I shall tell them you are with child, and hence unable to travel. We've been wed almost a year, so they would not be surprised."

She could have told him then that she was, in fact, with child. She had known for almost three months, but had put off telling him. Now she did not care if he ever knew, or ever saw the child. In fact, she hoped he would never return.

Facing him boldly, she asked, "Aren't you afraid I might be with child when you return? Since you have so low an opinion of my character, do you not suppose that, in your absence, I might avail myself of other men in Petropavlovsk—perhaps even the very Koryak you accuse me of desiring?"

Yuri slammed the trunk shut and charged toward her, regarding her with narrowed eyes. "I have indeed given the matter thought, and it has occurred to me that since you are yourself a bastard, such leanings might be in your blood. Therefore, I propose to spare us both undue grief and concern by leaving you in the care of Father Iosaf. The Koryaks will not approach you there; they have superstitious fears about the powers of a priest. And it seems unlikely that any Russian men will touch you—not because of the

272

priest, but for fear of contracting any diseases you may have picked up in your carnal wanderings."

He tossed her a red satin dressing gown. "Here, cover your nakedness. I intend to take you to Father Iosaf immediately."

She stared at him coldly. "Would it be so great a sacrifice of your time to allow me to dress properly?"

"Yes," he spat. "The good father can provide you with clothes suitable to your needs—perhaps he will let you wear a cast-off cassock while you tend to his cooking and scrub his floors."

"And what will become of Theodosia?"

"She will stay here and tend this house until I return for you both. No doubt the company has new plans for me—if your reputation does not precede me to St. Petersburg and ruin my chances. Now, will you put on the dressing gown, or would you prefer to go to the priest naked?"

For answer, Tasha hurled the gown in his face, bolting for the bedroom door. His hand shot out and grabbed her wrist, wrenching it mercilessly as he jerked her back toward him. Cursing her stubbornness, he pushed her arms through the sleeves of the gown and wrapped it loosely around her body, knotting the sash at her waist. His hands strayed within the satin folds to trace the curves of her breasts and buttocks, caressing her for a moment like one hesitant to leave his beloved. Then he swung her roughly into his arms and stalked from the house.

Heedless of passersby, who stared at the sight of the woman in a dressing gown struggling in his arms, Yuri carried Tasha directly to the door of Father Iosaf's house. He pounded on the door until the priest's stockily-built housekeeper opened it.

Eyeing them suspiciously, the woman announced that the father had no time for idle talk, as he was preparing to say the morning mass. Her gaze took in Tasha's disheveled hair and red dressing gown, gaping open at the neckline, and it was clear she assumed the younger woman was not the kind who attended mass. She cleared her throat and informed them that as it was too late for confession before the morning mass, perhaps Father Iosaf could arrange a special hearing afterwards.

Dropping Tasha on her feet, Yuri grunted, "She'll have plenty of time for confession in the months to come, since I intend to leave her here."

The housekeeper gave them a flustered look. "I'm sure you're mistaken if you think the father would allow that. I assure you, it is quite impossible. How would it look to have a woman of her kind living right here in the house of the priest?"

"Despite what you may think," Tasha bristled, "I am not a woman of 'that kind,' as you so delicately put it. I am—"

"The lady is my wife," Yuri cut in smoothly. "I simply wish to leave her in Father Iosaf's care while I am forced to journey to St. Petersburg."

The woman raised her eyebrows dubiously. "Can you not leave her in her own house? Is she not to be trusted?"

"It has nothing to do with trust," Yuri snapped. "As you can plainly see, my wife is a woman of striking beauty. Many men have shown an interest in her and, left alone, she could not possibly have the strength to fight them off. Under Father Iosaf's protection, I can be sure she will come to no harm."

"I don't know if Father Iosaf will agree," the woman argued. "It seems to me you could hire a guard to stay with the lady. This is highly irregular."

At that moment, Father Iosaf, a tonsured, middle-aged priest of medium height and plump build, bustled in from an adjoining room, on his way to the church next door. He stopped when he saw the three people at the door and addressed his housekeeper in a resonant voice. "Is there some problem, Lyudmila?"

The woman stepped back from the door, allowing the priest a full view of Tasha and Yuri. "I'd hoped to spare you some trouble, Father, but this man is determined to leave his wife at your house."

Father Iosaf stepped nearer, appraising Tasha's appearance, and smiling slightly as she blushed and pulled her dressing gown closer. He nodded. "It can be arranged."

Lyudmila looked shocked, but he brushed past her as the chimes in the church steeple rang. "Leave the woman here," he told Yuri. "You can walk with me and explain the situation on the way to the church. My flock is waiting. Lyudmila," he called over his shoulder as he led Yuri away from the door, "give the girl some tea and see that she is comfortable until I return."

Clucking in dismay, the housekeeper led Tasha into the small parlor and bade her to sit. "A woman in the priest's house," she muttered as she went to the samovar. "As God is my witness, no good can come of that!"

Tasha smiled bitterly. "You are a woman, and Father Iosaf seems to have suffered very little from your presence!"

Lyudmila looked at her sharply, cautioning her not to make light of the situation. "But I am too old and too well-fed to present a temptation. You, on the other hand—" she paused and shrugged, eyeing Tasha with a combination of contempt and envy. "Well, even a priest is first of all a man. It is foolish to tempt any man. And to come so attired!" She raised her eyes heavenward in a mute plea.

"My mode of dress was not of my choosing," Tasha cried defensively. "My husband, in his haste to see me delivered to this house before his departure, did not allow me time to dress." Her voice was tinged with sarcasm as she rose and moved toward the door. "Since it is clear you do not approve of my presence here, I shall simply leave."

"That you shall not do." Lyudmila hastened to plant her bulky frame in front of the door. "Father Iosaf has bid you stay, so I can not allow you to leave. Besides, it would be sinful to have you parading around the streets in that garb. What if someone saw you leave this house looking like that?"

Sighing, Tasha went back to the sofa. Lyudmila was more than twice her weight, and she had no doubt the woman would use force to detain her if necessary. Suddenly she felt very tired. Perhaps it would do no harm to wait for the priest to return.

Father Iosaf returned an hour later. Helping himself to a cup of tea, he informed Tasha that Yuri's ship had already departed. "Such a fine young man," he murmured, "and obviously quite concerned about you. I assured him I would take special care of you in his absence." His eyes rose shiftily above his teacup, roving over her figure, which was accentuated by the flowing folds of satin. "I used to look at the two of you leaving Sunday mass together and think, What a perfect couple! Such a pity you must be separated for a time. But it will give me a chance to become better acquainted with you. I like to get to know my parishioners well."

Something in his tone made Tasha shudder involuntarily, though she felt sure the priest could mean her no harm.

He rose stiffly and started for his room. "If you will excuse me, I have some studying to do. Lyudmila is exceptionally busy today, but perhaps tomorrow she can go to your house and bring you several changes of clothing."

"Tomorrow?" Tasha repeated in dejection, pulling the top of her dressing gown more tightly closed.

"Yes, tomorrow. It hardly matters since she and I are the only ones here with you. I shan't mind if you do not dress for dinner." He smiled broadly. "In fact, you look quite presentable as you are. You mustn't feel embarrassed in my presence. Think of me as a father, or a brother—a member of your family—with whom you can feel quite open and intimate." Chuck-

276

ling over some private thought, the priest proceeded to his study.

The day dragged on as Tasha moved restlessly about the parlor. Several times she thought of trying to escape out the front door, but Lyudmila always appeared, as if by magic, to discourage her with her bulky form. She read from various religious books scattered about the room, but found them unable to hold her interest. Father Iosaf belonged to the Black order, which was pledged to celibacy, so, unlike members of the White order, he had no wife and children. The house offered nothing and no one to amuse Tasha.

At dinner, and again at supper, Father Iosaf seemed preoccupied and silent. Several times, Tasha thought she caught him staring at her bosom, but she dismissed the thought, telling herself it was a product of her own self-consciousness about her improper attire. She was well aware of rumors that the priest hoped to become the next Archbishop of Yakutsk, and she felt sure he would do nothing to impair his chances for promotion. After supper, she retired early to a room maintained for the present Archbishop's infrequent visits to Petropavlovsk.

Tired of the dressing gown, Tasha dropped it beside the bed and slid, unclothed, between the sheets. Lying in bed, listening to the sounds of Lyudmila and Father Iosaf moving around the house, she determined that she would not wait until tomorrow for fresh clothing. Her mind was made up. She would not remain a prisoner! When the house was quiet and she was sure its inhabitants were asleep, she would slip out and run the distance to her own house, where she could plan her escape from Petropavlovsk.

Now that spring had come, more ships were sure to be docking in Avacha Bay. She and Theodosia would board the first one that arrived, no matter where it was bound. Anything would be better than waiting in Petropavlovsk for the husband she despised to return.

The house became quiet and Tasha was anxious to leave. Still, she forced herself to lie still a bit longer so she could be sure both the priest and Lyudmila were fast asleep. The silence remained unbroken, so at last she pushed her blankets aside and placed her feet on the cold, wooden floor. Poised on the edge of the bed, she froze in fear as she thought she detected a sound at her bedroom door. Her eyes tried to pierce the darkness. Candlelight suddenly spilled in and the hinges creaked as the door opened a crack.

Stunned, Tasha remained seated on the edge of the bed, her creamy flesh echoing the glimmer of the candle as Father Iosaf entered the room and closed the door behind him.

"Hush, child, don't be frightened," he whispered as he advanced toward her, "I've come to help you."

"Help me?" Tasha repeated weakly. Was it possible the priest knew how she had suffered with Yuri and was going to help her flee from Petropavlovsk? Confused and—realizing her state of undress—embarrassed, she pulled a blanket around herself.

Father Iosaf came closer. In the candlelight, his face glowed demonically, and Tasha shrank back, certain she could not want whatever help he might offer her.

A pudgy hand, damp with perspiration, shot out and snatched the blanket away from her. "Don't cover yourself, my child," he chided. "Let your body appear in the glorious design created by the Almighty Father." He held the candle closer to her, undisguised lust springing to his eyes as they traveled over her firm, smooth flesh. With a moan of despair, Tasha tried to turn her head away from his lecherous eyes, but he caught her chin, squeezing it as he turned her face around to meet his gaze. "I am a man of God," he said softly. "You must know you cannot hide your sins from me. Look at me, Tasha. Only I can guide you to salvation."

Holding her eyes locked in his gaze, he continued, "Your husband today gave me the sad news that your eyes—and yes, even that beautiful, treacherous body you display so proudly—have strayed. He reports that you have lusted after other men, you have lain in their arms, even accepted them into your body. No," he lay a finger across her lips as she opened her mouth to speak, "do not protest. It is known that the body of a woman is as weak as it is soft."

His hand slid down to cup her soft breast for emphasis, lingering to squeeze it, before traveling lower on her body. Tasha's flesh seemed to shrink away from his touch. Still, she remained paralyzed, too much in awe of the holy powers of a priest to cast his hand aside.

Father Iosaf's eyes glazed over as his fingers grazed the dark delta above her thighs. "Since your husband has entrusted you to my care, I have decided to help you both by exorcising your carnal desires!"

Tasha felt her throat constrict and her heart beat wildly in panic. She glanced uneasily at the flickering candle. "What do you intend to do?" she asked hoarsely.

His smile became more indulgent. "Nothing that will cause you pain. Lie back now. If you follow my directions, I think you shall find exorcism to be quite a pleasant experience."

When she hesitated, regarding him skeptically, he gently but firmly pushed her down on her back. "Father," she pleaded, vainly reaching for a blanket again, "in truth I have no need of exorcism. I do not desire any man." She almost added "not even my husband," but swallowed the phrase, fearing he would call such an attitude a sin that required further ministrations.

"Do not lie, child!" he intoned sharply. "God does not look kindly on those who try to deceive their confessor. Now," he positioned a pillow over her face, "you must hide your eyes for a moment, as there are certain holy signs the uninitiated must not be allowed to see."

Tasha lay tensely, listening to the rustle of his cassock as he moved beside the bed. The church, and those who found their vocation in it, had always held an aura of mystery for her. But, even so, she could not resign herself to the strange nature of this encounter. In her mind, again and again, she saw Father Iosaf watching her at supper, giving her looks which, from any other man, could only be interpreted as lustful. But he was a priest! It was not possible that—. The memory of Lyudmila's statement cut short her thoughts: "Even a priest is first of all a man."

Filled with sudden foreboding, Tasha slid her head from beneath the pillow. She expelled a strangled gasp at the sight that greeted her eyes.

Father Iosaf stood before her, completely naked. His plump flesh sagged disgustingly, but his manhood stood swollen and erect. No longer able to doubt what he intended, Tasha sat up in panic. "No!" she sobbed.

"Be still, child, the rite is far from complete," he whispered, as he swung a leg up to straddle her. His voice was hoarse with desire. The sight of his nakedness had dispelled whatever awe Tasha had felt for the priest. Instinctively, she jerked up her knee and drove it between his legs with more force than she imagined she possessed. Howling in pain, Father Iosaf collapsed at the foot of the bed. His hands reached out angrily for her, but the blinding pain made him too weak to hold her. Pushing him roughly aside, Tasha caught up her dressing gown from the floor and threw it on as she fled from the room. She stumbled through the parlor and reached the door leading to the outside just as Lyudmila, roused by her master's cry, bustled into the hallway.

As Tasha bolted into the street, she heard the housekeeper cry, "Where are you, Father? What has happened?"

Clutching the troublesome gown tightly around her, Tasha flew through the empty streets of Petropavlovsk. Only when she reached the door of her own house did she pause to look back towards Father Iosaf's. No one was in pursuit.

No doubt, she mused, the priest was in too much pain, and Lyudmila would be too concerned with helping him to think about her. For the moment she was safe, but she could not help fearing what the morning might bring. Her gaze rose to the harbor, and as the lighthouse beam swept across the water, her heart leaped with hope. A ship rocked in the water—a ship that could, that must, take her to freedom!

Exultantly, Tasha pounded on the door until Theodosia shuffled from her bed.

"Who is out there?" Theodosia called fearfully.

"It's me, Theodosia, let me in," Tasha panted breathlessly.

"Gospoja Tasha?" Theodosia asked doubtfully.

"Yes! Yes! Open the latch! Hurry, Theodosia!"

The moment the old woman opened the door, Tasha burst into the house and hurried to her room.

"Are you all right?" Theodosia called as she ran after her. "Gospodin Zarevsky said you would be staying with Father Iosaf until he returns."

"Well, he was quite wrong," Tasha said, as she pulled on fresh undergarments and selected a green broadcloth dress from her armoire. "In fact, I do not even intend to remain in Petropavlovsk."

"How can you say that?" Theodosia gasped. "Surely you do not intend to disobey your husband? That would be a grievous sin, and God would surely punish you for it."

"God's punishment can be no worse than what I will suffer if I remain here, with or without Yuri Zarevsky. Save your breath, Theodosia. You cannot dissuade me and I haven't time for your arguments."

She grabbed a portmanteau and began piling in dresses, undergarments, and toilet articles. "A ship is in the harbor. I intend to board it before dawn. You may accompany me or stay here, as you wish. But I cannot stay in Petropavlovsk another day."

Theodosia wrung her hands in dismay. "But why must you flee at night?" she whined. "You haven't committed a crime, have you? You didn't," she stopped and crossed herself fervently, "you didn't kill Father Iosaf or something?" Again she crossed herself, alarmed by the very seriousness of her question.

"No," Tasha replied grimly. "I did not kill him, though the thought is sorely tempting." She snapped the case shut and looked around wildly for anything else to take. Staring at Theodosia, who was still in her nightgown, she demanded, "Do you intend to stay here, then?"

The maid shrank back, frightened at the determination she saw in Tasha's eyes. "No, mistress, I'll come with you. In your state, there's no telling what you might do. I promised Gospodin Lisovsky back in Novoarkhangelsk that I would look after you, and I could never forgive myself if some evil befell you. But I must confess I cannot understand your actions at all." With a loud sigh, she scurried away to dress.

While she waited for Theodosia, Tasha paced nervously in the parlor. What if someone had seen her running in the streets? Or if someone saw them on the way to the ship? Would she be followed? Could she trust the ship's crew to deliver her safely to another port? Where would the ship be bound? Would she be put ashore in some strange land, unable to fend for herself?

Assailed by doubts and fears, she was momentarily tempted to unpack her small store of belongings and call out to Theodosia to go back to bed and forget she had ever mentioned leaving. But when she considered the certain anguish life in Petropavlovsk would bring, the uncertainties of her chosen future seemed infinitely more appealing. When Theodosia entered the parlor, fully dressed and carrying her own small satchel, Tasha took a deep breath, picked up the portmanteau, and quickly led the servant out into the darkness.

On the street, Tasha could not resist running, fearful of being seen. Theodosia panted as she struggled to keep up with her mistress. When they reached the shore, Tasha realized the ship was anchored some distance out in the bay.

Glancing around frantically, Tasha caught sight of a wooden boat beached nearby. She supposed it belonged to one of the local Cossacks, who fished for herring and king crab in the bay. She ran over to the boat, threw her portmanteau inside, and began to push the small vessel into the water.

"Mistress," Theodosia panted, hurrying to her side, "you cannot mean to steal this boat."

"No, I don't mean to steal it. I simply wish to borrow it so that we can get to the ship," Tasha panted as she strained to free the boat. "And if you intend to accompany me, I suggest that you help me."

Sighing, Theodosia tossed her satchel into the boat and joined her mistress in the struggle. When at last the boat was afloat, Tasha helped Theodosia into it, then scrambled in after her. Taking pity on her tired, breathless servant, Tasha struggled with both of the oars herself. She took several strokes before she managed to coordinate the oars correctly, but eventually she was pulling on a smooth, steady course toward the ship. The distance was greater than it had seemed from the shore, and her arms and shoulders ached by the time she had rowed the boat close to the hull of the ship.

Pausing to catch her breath, Tasha gasped as the lighthouse beam swept over the bow of the ship, briefly illuminating the name painted on its side. The ship's name was *Svoboda*, the Russian word for freedom.

Tasha's head reeled as she recalled in vivid detail her time aboard the American ship *Freedom*. Thinking of Jared's caress, so tender yet so fiery, she wondered if it was even worthwhile to flee. She could spend her life trying to elude men like Yuri Zarevsky or Father Iosaf, men who wanted her only as an ornament or as an instrument by which to slake their lusts, but she could never again know the unbounded joy she had found so briefly in Jared's arms.

Without him, without even the hope of seeing him again, life in Petropavlovsk had been worse than unhappy: it had been hollow and meaningless. Could she ever hope for a time and a place when that hollowness would disappear? Overcome by despondency, Tasha felt all determination drain from her body. She slumped forward in the small boat, oblivious to the watchman peering down from the deck of the *Svoboda*. At the same time, she felt a wrenching cramp in her abdomen.

"Who goes there?" the sailor on watch demanded gruffly.

Theodosia, having recovered her breath and strength during the ride, crawled to Tasha's side and shook her gently. When Tasha did not respond to her touch, she called up to the sailor in alarm, "I think my mistress has fainted! I must have help at once!"

Chapter Twenty-four

1866

Tasha awoke to find herself in a spacious bed, swathed in a warm comforter. A gentle rocking motion told her she was aboard a ship, and the luxurious style of the cabin made her assume she was in the captain's quarters. She sat up and smiled uncertainly as the door opened and a gray-haired man with a bushy moustache entered.

"I trust you are feeling better," he said crisply.

"Yes," she answered weakly. "I'm sorry if I caused you any trouble."

He shrugged. "No trouble. But it is beyond me what a young woman like yourself was doing bobbing around in the bay alone at this time of night."

"But I wasn't alone!" Tasha cried, suddenly afraid

that something had happened to Theodosia. "My maid was with me."

The man snorted. "That old babushka? I hardly think she could be of much help to you. When my men brought you aboard, she was practically hysterical, carrying on about how she had allowed something to happen to you. I finally ordered her up on deck, so she would not disturb you with her rantings."

Tasha smiled affectionately. "Dear Theodosia," she murmured, "always so concerned about me." She looked up at the man and spoke in a stronger voice. "Am I to assume you are the captain of this vessel, and this is your cabin?"

"Both assumptions are correct. I am Admiral Evgeny Shermitov of his Imperial Majesty's Navy. And who, may I ask, are you?"

"I am Madame Natalya Zarevskaya."

"I see," his brows shot up in question. "Tell me, Madame Zarevskaya, where is your husband that he allows you to wander so late at night?"

"My husband, Lieutenant Zarevsky of the Imperial Navy, has been summoned to St. Petersburg on business. He left this morning on the *Constantine*."

Admiral Shermitov nodded gravely. "A pity that he was forced to leave behind so young and foolish a wife. Your fainting was a clear case of overexertion. A young woman in your delicate condition had no business rowing a boat so far. You were fortunate the *Svoboda* was here to rescue you. Unfortunately, the child was not so lucky."

"The child?" Tasha shook her head in confusion. "I don't understand."

"The ship's physician tells me you lost the child you were carrying. He said you are strong and should recover with rest, but, there is some chance your child-bearing facility may have been impaired for the future."

In her panic to escape Petropavlovsk, Tasha had forgotten about the child growing within her. The news of its death was numbing, but she felt strangely unconcerned. She would have loved any child she might bear, but she had never wanted to have Yuri's baby. And the thought that she might not be able to conceive again had little effect on her. She would have wanted only Jared's child, and she knew that could never be.

Admiral Shermitov, expecting her to act more alarmed, eyed her curiously, then shrugged. "Rest here for the remainder of the night. I'll send your maid to you. Early tomorrow some of my men will return you to the town. We've only this one night to spend here before we depart for Novoarkhangelsk."

He was gone before Tasha could protest that she did not want to go back to Petropavlovsk. She lay back against the pillows, trying to devise some new plan. Despite the weakness and soreness she felt from the miscarriage, she resolved anew that she would not return to the town—there could be no rest for her there. The fact that the ship was bound for Novoarkhangelsk helped to strengthen her determination. She could see her father again! Life could be just as it had been those first months, before she married Yuri!

By the time Theodosia entered, carrying their luggage, Tasha had gotten out of bed and was anxiously pacing the cabin, trying to recall what she knew of a ship's layout. There had to be some place to hide! She would not allow the admiral to put them ashore. Below-decks, perhaps. She had never been in a ship's hold, but she imagined it must be filled with things she could hide behind.

"Theodosia," she whispered, as the old woman closed the cabin door behind her, "where is the admiral now?"

Theodosia shrugged. "I don't know. He told me to come down and see to your needs, then he wandered away on the deck. Rather a gruff fellow. I don't think he's very pleased to have us—"

Tasha cut her short. "Is there anyone in the passage-way now?"

"No one that I noticed."

"Good. Follow me." Tasha cracked open the door, quickly scanned the passageway, and ran lightly down it until she found the hatch covering the ladder below. Grunting with exertion, she pulled open the hatch and peered into the darkness of the hold.

It was impossible to see beyond the first two steps of the ladder, and the place smelled dank and musty. But they would not have to stay there more than a day or so, just long enough for the *Svoboda* to be on its way to Novoarkhangelsk. If the ship was sailing under a strict naval schedule and she and Theodosia were eventually discovered, Admiral Shermitov could not risk delaying the voyage by returning them to Petropavlovsk. No doubt he would be angry, but once they reached Novoarkhangelsk her father could smooth over his ruffled feelings.

"Climb down," Tasha told Theodosia firmly. "I'll follow you and close the hatch."

Theodosia stared at her in disbelief. "Are you mad, gospoja? It's darker than night down there and in all likelihood the place is swarming with vermin."

Tasha stamped her foot. "Don't try my patience, Theodosia. You chose to come with me, and I expect you to obey me without question."

The servant sniffled in a hurt manner. "I was only thinking of you, Gospoja Zarevskaya. In your weak-ened condition, it would not do for you to get a chill."

"And it would do even less for me to be returned to Petropavlovsk as Admiral Shermitov intends. I can rest perfectly well in the hold. Now, will you ac-company me below or not?"

Shaking her head disapprovingly, Theodosia never-theless haltingly climbed down the ladder. Tasha fol-lowed, pulling the hatch shut just as she heard the thud of feet descending the ladder from the deck. She froze on the ladder as she heard the person walking directly above her, then relaxed as the footsteps receded. Feeling her way in the dark, she continued to the bottom of the hold, where she grasped Theodosia's trembling hand.

"We must be very quiet," she whispered in the servant's ear. "We cannot risk being discovered. Hold my hand and follow me. I'll try to find a suitable hiding place."

Moving cautiously, lest she trip over something and give their presence away, Tasha felt her way around a cluster of barrels. Once her foot touched something soft and furry, and she quaked as a series of alarmed squeaks filled the air.

Behind her, Theodosia drew in her breath sharply. "Is there no other place we can hide?" the servant whined.

"Shh!" Tasha hissed. "The rats make enough noise without your adding to it." She felt Theodosia shiver as she mentioned rats, but she pushed forward resolutely.

Beside the bulkhead she found a small space, almost completely surrounded by barrels. Pulling Theodosia into the enclosed area, she crouched down and whispered. "You'd best try to sleep a bit. We'll be here several hours."

"I'm sure I cannot sleep," Theodosia replied tremulously. "How can I sleep with rats about?"

"They fear us more than we need fear them," Tasha whispered with more assurance than she felt. "At any rate, they won't bother us if we don't disturb them. Come now, Theo," she coaxed, putting a comforting arm around the woman's shoulder, "rest a bit, won't you?"

Sighing, Theodosia huddled close to her mistress. Their furry neighbors in the hold fell silent, and eventually, her fears lulled by the sound of the waves lapping against the hull, she, too, fell asleep.

Tasha, however, remained awake. Staring into the blackness of the hold, listening to the occasional sound of a sailor lumbering down the passageway above her, her thoughts turned, irresistibly, to Jared. For months she had fought every impulse to think of him. Filling her life with the trivia of Petropavlovsk society, she had tried to ignore the hurt burning in her heart. She had tried to blame her unhappiness on her hatred for Yuri, refusing to admit that even a more considerate man could not have soothed the ache that pervaded her being.

Now, waiting anxiously for the ship to depart, she realized there was only one other person in the world for whom she cared with any intensity. There was only one other person who might bring at least some measure of peace to her life. Her heart swelled with gladness at the thought that she was going home to her father. She never should have left Novoarkhangelsk, she told herself.

The warmth of father love could not bring her the deep satisfaction of the passion she had shared with Jared. Nothing could ever fill that void. But her father's love was all she had now, she felt she must treasure it above all else.

She was still awake when she heard someone wrench open the hatch, and she blinked painfully as lantern light spilled into the hold. "It's a waste of time looking down here," declared a man's deep voice. "From the looks of her, she was a lady, and no lady would willingly put herself into a pit like this."

"I'd have to agree with you, Fyodor," came a slurred reply. "But the admiral said to search everywhere. Can't imagine how a couple of women could disappear right on board the ship."

Roused by the noise and light, Theodosia raised her head. "What—" she began sleepily, before Tasha clapped a hand over her mouth.

On the ladder, the two sailors stopped. "I thought I heard something," said the deep-voiced one.

Tasha froze, sure they were about to be discovered.

"What?" laughed his companion, "are the ship's rats talking to each other now? Just because we've got an admiral running this ship, don't think our rats are any smarter than any others!" The man guffawed at his own cleverness.

"No, I'm serious. I could swear I heard a woman's voice."

"Ah, you've just been without a woman too long, and now you're imagining things. I told you you should have come ashore with me tonight. Now, that Varvara I met at the captain's house tonight—" he paused and whistled under his breath, "I tell you, Fyodor, she had breasts as big and soft as a pair of down pillows. Slipped out with me right under her husband's nose, she did."

The one called Fyodor sighed. "You can tell me about your exploits later. Let's just look for the women now." The lantern's light swept dangerously close to the massed barrels behind which Tasha and Theodosia hid, and both women shrank lower down. Half-heartedly, the men moved a few of the barrels, disturbing a family of rats in the process.

"Let's go," urged the man with the slurred speech. "I spent the night with an angel, and there's no way I want to spend the morning with a bunch of filthy rats."

"All right," the other agreed, "if a hardy sailor like you is put off by this hellhole, I don't suppose a lady could stay here. My guess is if they haven't found her by now, the admiral will just give up. He won't want to miss the sailing time. Who knows, maybe she decided to swim back. If she was fool enough to row all the way out here, there's no telling what she might do."

They clambered back up the ladder, and closed the hatch. With the hold in darkness once more, Theodosia settled down again and was soon breathing peacefully in sleep. Tasha, too, succumbed to relief and exhaustion, drifting into sleep as the *Svoboda* glided toward the entrance to Avacha Bay.

When she awoke the first time, Tasha had no idea how long she had been asleep. The sound of waves slapping against the hull made her assume they were in the open water. But she could not guess how long they had been underway, or how far they were from Petropavlovsk. Since Theodosia was still sleeping soundly beside her, she decided to sleep a while longer, too. The longer they waited to reveal themselves, the farther they would be from Petropavlovsk, and the less inclined Admiral Shermitov would be to turn around. Tasha maneuvered herself into a more comfortable position and fell asleep again. There would be plenty of time later to decide when and how to reveal their presence.

But Tasha was not to decide the moment of their discovery. The next time she awoke, it was to the sound of frenzied, uncontrollable coughing. She reached out and felt Theodosia, leaning forward miserably as her body was wracked by the coughing. Before she could think of what to do, she heard the noise of the hatch opening again.

In a moment, a man had descended into the hold. Guided by the sound of Theodosia's coughing, a sound that seemed to reverberate through every barrel in the hold, the man strode toward them swiftly. Pushing the barrels out of his path, he held his lantern aloft and stared exultantly at Tasha and Theodosia.

"Aha," he exclaimed. "So we did not leave you in Petropavlovsk after all. But who would have imagined a fine lady like you would be hiding among the rats?" He pushed the lantern closer to Tasha, ignoring Theodosia's obvious distress. "By God, you're better looking than Varvara!"

Tasha cringed as his hand stroked her tangled hair, and she realized from his voice that he had been one of the sailors who searched the hold before they departed, the one whose speech had been slurred by drink.

"Don't touch me, you dirty drunkard!" she snapped.

He laughed, and impudently tweaked at the bodice of her dress. "Why not? You and I could do much to make each other more comfortable on this voyage. I could see that you have food and drink, and whatever else you might require, while you could attend to some of my needs. Yes," he appraised her thoughtfully, "you would do very nicely."

"You presume too much," Tasha said icily. "I am a married woman, and not to be trifled with."

He shrugged. "Married or not, it makes no difference to me. I see no husband hanging 'round your neck to dispute my claim. And that old woman," he cast a disdainful look at Theodosia, who had collapsed from her prolonged coughing spell, "hardly seems fit to defend your honor. If you're thinking about fighting me, I would remind you that it is a crime to stow away on a vessel of the Czar. I could easily inform Admiral Shermitov of your presence."

"Who is below?" a gruff voice interrupted them from the hatch. Quickly the intruder snuffed out his lantern and froze in the darkness.

"I say, who is it?" the voice demanded, giving Tasha the opportunity to recognize it as Admiral Shermitov's.

Deciding it was preferable to suffer the admiral's wrath rather than what the brute threatened, she called out loudly, "It is Natasha Zarevskaya, sir!"

"What?" the admiral thundered. "Come over into the light where I can see you, girl!"

Obediently, Tasha felt her way toward the hatch and climbed the first steps of the ladder. The man who had discovered them meanwhile slid away to a hiding place of his own. Feeling stiff and uncomfortable, Tasha looked up into the admiral's scowling face.

"Confound it, it is you!" the admiral fumed. "After my crew searched the whole ship and assured me there was no sign of you, I assumed you had found your own way back to Petropavlovsk. What in God's name are you doing down in the hold?"

"Hiding," she replied simply. "I did not want to be returned to Petropavlovsk. I want to go to Novoarkhangelsk."

"So you stowed away, eh? If that was the case, why

did you leave the hatch open? Did you want to be discovered?"

She hesitated, debating whether to announce the sailor's presence. He had not had time to do her any real harm, so it seemed pointless to expose him to possible punishment just for his intentions. "Someone was down here a while ago, sir," she said. "He left the hatch open when he left. But I did intend to present myself to you eventually, as soon as we were far enough away from Petropavlovsk."

"I see," the admiral nodded. "Very noble of you, though it still does not change the fact that you are a stowaway. Is your maidservant there with you?"

Suddenly, Tasha remembered the cause of their discovery. "Yes, sir, she's here, but I'm afraid she's taken ill. She's developed a terrible cough. Do you think the doctor who tended me could see her?"

Nodding grimly, the admiral turned and called to a passing sailor. "There's an old woman in the hold who's fallen sick. See that she's taken to my cabin and summon Doctor Zagoskin."

He turned back to Tasha, addressing her in the formal French. "You, Madame Zarevskaya, may accompany me to my cabin immediately. It seems we have a great deal to discuss."

In his cabin, while two sailors carried in Theodosia, the admiral confronted Tasha. He was livid with rage.

"Now, madame," he exploded, "suppose you try to explain to me just why you decided to stow away on board this ship!"

"I already told you," Tasha said, struggling to remain cool under his angry glare, "I wish to go to Novoarkhangelsk."

"That is hardly a fitting reason for stowing away on one of the Czar's ships. May I remind you, madame, that this is a naval vessel, on a naval mission to the colony. You have no place aboard this ship. Even if this were a passenger vessel, you would hardly be allowed aboard without prior payment for your passage. You are quite right in assuming it is too late now to return you to Petropavlovsk. But I wonder if you are prepared to pay for yourself and your servant?" He raised his brows questioningly, waiting for her answer.

Tasha swallowed hard. In her haste to escape from the town, she had not thought to search the house for any rubles Yuri might have left behind. It had not even occurred to her that she would have to pay for their passage, since she had not handled any of the details of her two previous crossings. "I'm sorry," she began, "I didn't think—"

"Of course you didn't think!" the admiral snapped. "You seem to have given very little thought to this entire escapade. You ought to be whipped for your foolishness! But I'll leave that to your husband. No doubt he'll find a way to discipline you—after you've taken any punishment meted out by Czar Aleksandr's police."

"Police," she repeated weakly.

"Of course. You don't think we can allow your actions to go unreported, do you? My dear young lady, you are guilty of thievery. If you had claimed to have fallen asleep, or gotten lost while exploring the ship, I could have found a way to pardon you. But as you brazenly admit you intended to stow away, you leave me little choice. Were I not such a gentleman, I would throw you back into the hold for the rest of the trip!" He turned abruptly and went to his cabin door. "The whole situation disgusts me!"

"Please wait," Tasha gasped, causing him to stop with his hand on the door handle. Faced with being turned over to the police, she suddenly decided to tell him the reason for her flight. It could not hurt, and perhaps her story could move him to more merciful treatment. "I did not want to return to Petropavlovsk because I feared what might happen to me there," she began.

He turned and considered her coldly. "I hope you do not mean to tell me you were fleeing after committing a crime?"

"No sir, nothing of the sort." She hesitated, suddenly unsure of herself. Was it too much to hope he might believe her story that the priest—the spiritual shepherd of the community—had attacked her?

"Well, then?" Admiral Shermitov prodded irritably. "If you've something to say, out with it! I've a ship to run, I can't wait all day for your lame excuses."

There was no recourse but to tell the story. She took a deep breath and plunged ahead. "When my husband was summoned to St. Petersburg, he left me in the care of Petropavlovsk's priest, Father Iosaf. Petropavlovsk is still a rather crude town, and my husband feared for my safety if he were to leave me alone there with Theodosia." She knew that the reason she gave was not entirely true, but it seemed pointless to detail their marital discord.

Her voice became strained and nervous as she continued. "I stayed at Father Iosaf's house, with him and his housekeeper, for one day and part of that night. That night, the same night I rowed out to the *Svoboda*, I retired to the father's guest chamber. When the house was quiet and I thought everyone was asleep, Father Iosaf crept into my chamber. He tried—" she choked on the words— "he tried to rape me!" Humiliated by the revelation, and upset at having to think again about the incident, Tasha hid her face in her hands and sobbed.

"Can it be true?" the admiral breathed. "Is there no chance you could have been mistaken about his intentions?"

Tasha shook her head violently. "I wish I were wrong, but there was no question. He was naked, I—" her voice was drowned by her sobs.

Admiral Shermitov, outraged by her statements, walked to Tasha and patted her back uneasily. "You should have told me at once. Such an incident must be reported to the proper authorities. The man should be defrocked."

Tasha stared up at him. "You do believe me, then?"

The admiral nodded, and she continued in a stronger voice. "I was afraid to tell anyone, afraid they would not believe my word against a priest's, especially since he was of the Black order, pledged to celibacy."

"Unfortunately," the admiral sighed, "reports of debauchery among our clergy have become all too frequent. Your story is shocking, but I fear it is most believable."

He paused to look at her compassionately. "Was there no one in Petropavlovsk to whom you could have reported the incident?"

"I don't know. I didn't think about it at the time. I was frightened, and I just wanted to get away."

Admiral Shermitov nodded sympathetically. "That is understandable. But what will you do in Novoarkhangelsk?"

"My father lives there. Mikhail Lisovsky. It would be best for me to stay with him until my husband returns from St. Petersburg."

"Then you are indeed fortunate that the *Svoboda* is bound for Novoarkhangelsk. In light of your revelation, you can rest assured I will not turn you over to the police. But I must urge you to have your father pursue the matter of the priest with the church authorities. The man should not be allowed to remain in his position! Now then, for the remainder of the voyage, you may consider this your cabin. I will seek shelter elsewhere and see that no one disturbs you."

"You are too generous, admiral. Surely we could be quartered somewhere less elegant. But I've only just remembered, my portmanteau is still in the hold. It contains an emerald pendant, a gift from my father, which could pay for our passage."

Admiral Shermitov smiled. "Under the circumstances, it would be most ungallant of me to take something you received from your father. I am quite sure Czar Aleksandr would not object to allowing you free passage. Now, if you will excuse me, madame—"

A clearing throat interrupted him, and he turned to face Doctor Zagoskin. In the intensity of their discussion, both Tasha and the admiral had forgotten about Theodosia's condition. Now Tasha ran to the bed to embrace her maid. The old woman's eyes told her she had heard everything, and at last comprehended Tasha's anxiety to flee Petropavlovsk.

"Will she be all right?" Tasha asked the doctor fretfully.

He nodded. "She'll live, though a few more days down there might have been the end of her. As it is, she's suffering from acute congestion and should be confined to bed for the rest of the trip." He frowned at Tasha accusingly. "If you care for her at all, you'll see that she gets better treatment in the future. The constitution of a woman her age is not so strong as that of a young woman like you."

"I was rather selfish," Tasha admitted, lowering her eyes shamefacedly to the floor.

"Well, with rest, she will recover. I'll look in on her periodically."

Nodding to the women, both Admiral Shermitov and Doctor Zagoskin left the cabin.

Thankful for the admiral's kind treatment, Tasha remained in the cabin, nursing Theodosia, for most of the remaining days of the voyage. She ventured out only when Admiral Shermitov himself called to escort her on deck.

Standing at the rail, watching the Aleutian Islands slide by, shrouded by fog, as always, Tasha could not help but remember her first voyage to Novoarkhangelsk. Still only eighteen, already she had made the crossing—one that most Russians wouldn't make even once in an entire lifetime—three times. And in the years marked by those three crossings, she had lived more fully and suffered more deeply than she would have imagined possible.

She had known the tenderness of a first infatuation, the soaring passion of unleashed love, and the bitter disappointment of a loveless marriage. She had tasted the rewards of true love and nurtured the ecstatic hope of a love-filled future, only to see her hopes and memories splintered and obliterated like a frail ship on a stormy sea. Now she was going home; yes, in her heart, Novoarkhangelsk had become her home. Birchwood and Moscow were part of an earlier, separate life. Kamchatka was part of yet another life, one which had no place in her heart or in her memories.

They reached Novoarkhangelsk the morning of the sixteenth day out of Petropavlovsk. Rounding Mount Edgecumbe, Tasha felt a thrill of joy as she sighted the ravens gathering on the spire of St. Mikhail's, welcoming the *Svoboda,* just as she had seen them welcome every other ship that sailed into the harbor during the months she lived in the city.

Stronger from her days of rest, Theodosia stood beside her mistress, her eyes moist with tears as she viewed her homeland again.

The moment the ship docked, before Admiral Shermitov could offer any assistance, Tasha scampered down the gangplank and ran up the Governor's Walk in the direction of her father's street. Recognizing her, people on the street called greetings, but she only waved and ran on. Behind her, Theodosia struggled with their suitcases, finally giving up trying to keep pace with her mistress.

Tasha arrived at her father's house breathless, her hair streaming down her back in a wild, disheveled mane, her skirt splattered from running through puddles on the street. She pounded furiously on the door until Xenia came to open it, then tore past the astonished housekeeper to the breakfast room, where she expected to greet her father. Not finding him there, she ran to his study, but it, too, was empty. On her way to the stairway, she collided with Xenia, who clucked her tongue and held her firmly at arm's length.

"Have you no greeting for me?" the housekeeper chided.

"Of course." Tasha gave her an affectionate peck on the cheek. "But where is my father?"

"Gospodin Lisovsky is not at home. He's gone to San Francisco."

"San Francisco!" Tasha was crestfallen. It had never occurred to her that her father might be away. "When did he leave?"

Xenia shrugged. "This morning. He was to sail on a ship named *Strelka*."

Tasha closed her eyes and pictured the docks again. There had been another ship there, but in her hurry to disembark she had not given it much notice. Perhaps it was the *Strelka*, still preparing for departure. "If the *Strelka* has not yet sailed, I am going with him!" she declared, rushing back to the door.

"But where have you come from? Where is your husband?" Xenia called plaintively after her as she ran down the front stairs.

"Theodosia can explain everything when she arrives," Tasha replied over her shoulder.

Rounding the corner to the Governor's Walk, Tasha almost collided with Theodosia. She stopped long enough to grab her portmanteau from the servant and instructed her to continue home where she could rest.

"But where are you going?" Theodosia asked as Tasha began running again toward the docks.

"To San Francisco, if I'm not too late!"

Dumbfounded, Theodosia stared after her, then plodded on toward the Lisovsky house.

Tasha reached the docks just as two sailors were preparing to pull up the gangplank on the ship docked beside the *Svoboda*. "Stop!" she screamed, rushing on to the plank and then up to the ship. As one of the sailors helped her aboard, she asked breathlessly, "Is this the *Strelka*?"

"Yes," he nodded. "But I thought all our passengers had already boarded."

"Well, you've gained another passenger," she said, then noticed his dubious frown and quickly added, "Don't worry, I'll pay for my passage."

"But the cabins are all full," he mumbled. "I'm not sure the captain will approve of your being on board."

Tasha was not listening. Scanning the crowd of passengers ranged along the rail, she finally located a familiar tall form. Her heart leapt. "Papa!" she screeched, rushing forward to fling herself into his arms.

After the first shock, Mikhail held her tightly, then stepped back, his blue eyes moist as he looked her over. "My Tasha," he exclaimed happily, "always appearing when I least expect you! What a joy it is to see you again! But what are you doing here, aboard the *Strelka?*"

She grinned mischievously, "Why, going to San Francisco with you, of course."

Mikhail glanced around in confusion. "Is Yuri here?"

She shook her head and he studied her seriously, a worried look springing to his eyes. "I hope nothing is amiss between the two of you?"

She had intended to immediately declare to her father that she would never return to her husband, but she could not bear to mar their reunion. "No, papa," she said quietly. "Nothing is wrong. Yuri was simply called to St. Petersburg on short notice and I was unable to accompany him. In his absence, I decided to return to Novoarkhangelsk for a visit. I must confess I had grown quite homesick, and I missed you almost more than I could bear."

He squeezed her hand, and his eyes sparkled with affection. "You seem to know exactly what words will please my heart. Have you purchased passage?"

"No. By the time I went to the house and Xenia told me you had left, there was no time."

"Well, never mind, I'll take care of it. You can share my quarters since I've reserved a suite."

"Thank you, papa. I can't tell you how glad I am to be with you."

"Yes," he smiled, "I can see that you will take the drudgery out of this business trip."

Chapter Twenty-five

1866

During the voyage, Tasha enjoyed her father's never-ending indulgences and the heady freedom of being away from Yuri Zarevsky. The only thing that marred her happiness was Mikhail's insistence that she return to Kamchatka to wait for her husband as soon as the trip to San Francisco was completed.

"But Yuri might be a year in traveling to St. Petersburg and back," she protested.

"Or he could return in a much shorter time," Mikhail pointed out. "Travel is faster these days, and he may have to hurry to a new assignment. In any case, you should be there when he returns or sends for you. I love having you with me, but your first duty is to your husband."

Tasha sighed, but did not protest more. The trip south was so peaceful and beautiful, and her father's joy in her company so great that she could not bear to spoil things. Several times she considered detailing to her father just how cruel a husband Yuri had proven himself to be. If he knew the circumstances, she was sure Mikhail would forbid her to return to her husband. But she was equally certain that the information would hurt him deeply, and she thought there was no harm in putting that off.

In the end, of course, she would have to tell her father everything. Even her wish not to hurt him could not force Tasha to continue her mockery of a marriage to Yuri. But it would be best to have such a talk in the warm surroundings of his home in Novoarkhangelsk. Yuri was far away en route to St. Petersburg. The trip to San Francisco would be smoother and happier if she simply avoided talking about him for its duration.

Without Theodosia to help her, Tasha found she had little patience for arranging her hair. Most days, she brushed it to a sheen, then tied it back with a ribbon. She enjoyed the feel of the sea breezes ruffling through it as it hung loosely around her shoulders and face, and the admiring glances of some of the other passengers told her the style was most becoming.

One day as she stood alone by the rail, gazing out to sea, her hair blowing wild, she heard a voice at her side.

"It is hard to guess which view is more enticing," said the mellow voice, "the one you see, or the one I see."

She turned to look at a chestnut-haired man wearing a stylish woolen frock coat and green silk waistcoat. He was of medium build, and she supposed he was about forty years old. He studied her with amused eyes.

"Do you realize what an enchanting picture you make?" he asked.

"I realize when I am being flattered," Tasha replied coolly.

His eyes took on a wounded look. "Ah, but I speak only the truth. It is refreshing to view a woman so sure of her own innate beauty that she does not depend on powders and rouges and ringlets to catch a man's eye. But tell me, where is the man whom I usually see accompanying you?"

She shrugged. "He had business to attend to in the cabin."

"How fortunate for me. I have been watching you for days, and have wondered when I might have the opportunity to speak with you privately. I assume the man I've seen you with is your—how shall I put it—protector?"

"Monsieur!" Tasha shot him a reproachful glare, then turned to gaze at the sea again. "You assume incorrectly. The man is my father, Mikhail Lisovsky of the Russian-American Company."

302

"Ah, I humbly beg your pardon, Mademoiselle Lisovskaya."

"Madame Zarevskaya," she corrected curtly.

"Then you are married! But I have not seen a husband in your attendance. Are you widowed so young, perhaps?"

"My husband, I assure you, is very much alive. He is simply engaged in business elsewhere and I, meanwhile, am staying with my father." She tossed her head haughtily. "But you presume too much on my good nature, sir. You have elicited from me the most personal information when we have not even been properly introduced."

"Allow me to remedy the situation." He bowed stiffly. "I am Pyotr Maksimovich Stanovsky, emissary of his imperial majesty, Czar Aleksandr II, on official business from Russian America to the United States of America."

Tasha eyed him critically. "From Russian America, you say? Strange that I never met you in my months in Novoarkhangelsk. I attended most of the balls at Baranov Castle, and I am sure Prince Maksutov would have invited anyone so important as an emissary of the Czar." Her voice had a touch of sarcasm, as she was certain she had caught him in a lie.

"Perhaps I should say I am from St. Petersburg. I've only toured the colony in the last months, and even then I spent most of my time in the farthest outposts, passing very few days in your charming city."

"Oh." She turned away, not wishing to appear too interested in his affairs. Still, it intrigued her to think he was the Czar's emissary, and since he had been bold enough to question her, she felt he should not escape having to answer a few questions in return.

"Tell me," Tasha asked, "what is the nature of your business that it involves both the colony and the United States?"

"That," he replied, "is a matter of strictest confidence. I can only say that from San Francisco I will continue, by steamer, to New York City on the Atlantic coast. Might I inquire where you are bound?"

"To San Francisco. Papa has business there concerning trade with the American Russian Commercial Company. We have shipped them ice for several years, but just last year they expressed interest in the Russian-American Company's fur trade."

"I see." He moved his hand along the rail until it touched hers. "I'd hoped you might be going further. The voyage around Cape Horn will be long and boring without the company of an attractive woman."

Tasha moved her hand away. "Surely there will be women on the steamer you board in San Francisco."

"Perhaps," he shrugged, "but none are likely to be as beautiful and intriguing as you." Impulsively his fingers caught one of her whirling tresses, brushing her cheek as they did so. "You would not, perhaps, consider accompanying me?"

"Monsieur!" Tasha stood back abruptly. "Have you forgotten so soon that I am a married woman?"

"No. But it is not unusual for a married woman to enjoy a brief interlude with another man. In St. Petersburg, all the women of means take lovers."

"Then find yourself a St. Petersburg woman!" she snapped. "I am not one." She turned to leave, adding, "Since you persist in bothering me, I am forced to go below."

Reaching out, Stanovsky caught her arm and bent to brush her hand with a light kiss. "I must apologize. I did not mean to offend you, madame. But if one does not ask, one can never hope to receive. And even an emissary of the Czar sometimes suffers from loneliness. Perhaps I may have the pleasure of seeing you again before we go our separate ways in San Francisco." Lightly dropping her hand, he turned and walked away.

To her surprise, Tasha no longer felt angry. The sincerity of the man's tone softened her feelings toward him, and she suddenly felt that she would not be at all opposed to seeing him again. Shaking her head in bewilderment at her own change of heart, she went back to the rail and studied the blue expanse of the Pacific Ocean.

During the remaining days of the trip, Pyotr Stanovsky joined Tasha and her father often on the deck, in the ship's dining room, and once, for a private dinner in the Lisovsky suite. He was charming, intelligent, and witty. He never alluded to his first meeting with Tasha, and she found that she completely enjoyed his company.

Steaming through the golden gate and into San Francisco Bay, Tasha was reminded of her first view of the Aleutians. The area was veiled in fog so heavy that just standing on deck her hair and clothing became damp. She went below to change dresses, and by the time she returned to the rail, the *Strelka* had docked and was busily unloading passengers and cargo. Taking her arm, her father led her off the ship to the street, where he hired a carriage to take them into the city.

The carriage took them to an establishment called the Emerald Necklace, where Mikhail explained they would be staying during their visit in San Francisco. The main floor consisted of a restaurant, a saloon, and a gambling hall, while the upper story contained several hotel rooms. Leading her quickly up the stairs to their rooms, Mikhail cautioned his daughter to stay away from the saloon and gambling hall.

"There are boorish men and loose women in there," he said, pulling her away as she stood on tiptoe to see over the swinging double doors. "Nothing to interest a well-bred woman like you, but plenty of trouble if you venture inside. San Francisco is too far from this country's government, and it's still full of lawless men. Some of them drink themselves to insensibility, and tempers run high over card games. It's best that you steer clear of the whole lot."

Tasha shuddered. "You needn't worry, papa. I've no intention of consorting with such a crowd."

"Of course not," he nodded. "I simply meant to warn you, lest your curiosity tempt you to observe them more closely." He stopped before the room he had reserved for her. "I'll call for you at seven for dinner. In the meantime, get some rest and enjoy the feel of solid ground beneath your feet. You've been on one ship or another for the better part of a month now."

Tasha laughed and let herself into the small room. It was sparsely furnished with a bed, a nightstand, a washstand with ewer and basin, and a small dresser with a cloudy mirror. She unpacked the few belongings from her portmanteau and fell across the bed to sleep without the rocking motion of a ship for the first time in weeks. Closing her eyes, she tensed as she realized she was in Jared's homeland. She might be far from the place called New Bedford, where he had lived, but it was part of the same nation, and probably as close as she would ever come to the area where he had been born and grew up. If he had lived, they could have honeymooned in San Francisco, perhaps in this very hotel and room. She dozed off dreaming about that lost possibility. So vivid were her dreams that she awoke groping for Jared's warm body. But there was no one to return her embrace. Slowly she recalled where she was, and with whom, and tried to fight the emptiness that started to envelop her.

After a relaxing bath in a metal tub filled by a girl who worked at the hotel, Tasha dressed carefully, trying to distract her thoughts from the haunting vision of Jared. In an attempt to seem festive, she donned a yellow taffeta gown with a deep decolletage and a ruffled train. Then, in tribute to the occasion, she put on the emerald necklace her father had given her. She spent a few minutes arranging her hair into a halo of ringlets held just above her temples by a satin ribbon the same color as her dress. She finished dressing just as someone knocked on the door.

As she opened the door, Mikhail sucked in his breath in approval. "You are indeed a vision of loveliness." Then, a little sadly, "You've grown up since you first arrived on my doorstep in Novoarkhangelsk."

"Oh no, papa," she laughed nervously. "I will always be your little girl!"

He smiled affectionately. "At times I wish that were true. There's no question I shall miss your company when you go back to your husband. But, I have you now for a little while." He offered his arm. "Shall we see what fare the dining room has to offer?"

To Tasha's delight, as they entered the velvet-draped dining room, they saw Pyotr Stanovsky sitting alone at a corner table. Immediately sighting them, Stanovsky rose and beckoned to them to join him, gallantly holding a chair for Tasha. Tonight, Tasha thought, she would especially welcome the diversion of his conversation.

"What a pleasant surprise," Stanovsky exclaimed. "I had no idea you would be staying at this establishment." He smiled approvingly. "May I say, Madame Zarevskaya, that you are looking especially exquisite tonight."

She murmured a demure "thank you" as he turned to her father. "It is beyond me, Mikhail Pavlovich, how you ever could have allowed her to marry and move away. I'm afraid if I were her father, I would have been too jealous to allow her out of my house."

Mikhail smiled and shrugged. "Well, it is hard to face, but all parents must allow their children to grow up at last. Tasha was very fortunate. She made a fine marriage."

"Let us hope so. It would be a pity to think of her being wasted on a man who did not appreciate her. But no doubt you are anxious to order dinner. I'm told the lobster is superb. I myself was just about to order when you arrived."

They dined on lobster tails and champagne in celebration of being in San Francisco. Stanovsky explained that the *Aleksandr II*, the Russian steamer he was to take to New York, would not be departing until the day after tomorrow, so he had arranged for a room at the Emerald Necklace for two days. "I was at first anxious to be off," he said, "but now I count myself fortunate to be able to share your company for a few days more."

His conversation throughout dinner was as animated and witty as always, and Mikhail seemed to enjoy his presence. Tasha, however, could not overcome her gloomy mood; images of Jared continued to beckon to her over and over, until she felt consumed by an almost unbearable longing for him.

By the time dessert was served, a throbbing headache plagued her. "I beg your pardon, papa, Monsieur Stanovsky," she whispered, rising from the table, "but I feel as if my head is about to split. It must be all the excitement of arriving in San Francisco. I hope you will excuse me. I simply must lie down."

Both men rose with worried expressions. "You must allow me to accompany you to your room," said Stanovsky, gently taking her arm.

"No, no," she shook him off roughly, then, seeing his eyes cloud over with distress, she quickly explained. "I couldn't think of taking you from your meal. I insist that you stay here. What harm can possibly come to me simply climbing the stairs to my room?"

Mikhail settled himself in his chair and nodded to Stanovsky to do the same. "Very well, dear, I'll look in on you later."

The words were barely out of his mouth when Tasha turned and fled from the room, almost running in her anxiety to escape. As she reached the stairs, the sounds of a heated argument drifted through the double doors of the saloon. She started up the stairs, but froze on the third step as the words being spoken penetrated her fog of despondency.

"I tell you, man," a voice declared belligerently, "I was aboard the *Shenandoah!* Fact is, I personally put the torch to half a dozen whalers!"

Cautiously, Tasha crept back down the stairs. She stood outside the swinging doors, straining to hear every word.

"What kind of fool do you take me for?" another voice contested. "If you were part of that crew, how'd you escape hanging? Everyone knows the United States Navy stalked the seas for that bastard of a cruiser for months afterward. Half of the stalker ships sailed right out of this harbor. The *Shenandoah* had no business torching the whaling fleet. The war was over."

"Sure," responded the first voice, "and as soon as Captain Waddell found that out he sailed under cover straight for England, where the Confederacy had bought her in the first place. We all jumped ship and scattered. Being an adventuresome soul myself, I decided to come back to the States and try my luck in the West."

"I still don't believe you," the other man argued. "If you were really on board the *Shenandoah,* just name me one ship you burned."

"Fair enough." The man paused dramatically. Outside the saloon doors, Tasha held her breath, waiting, somehow knowing the ship he would name. The silence seemed interminable, and she felt droplets of perspiration on her forehead.

"The *Freedom,*" the man declared at last. "Now there was a spunky little whaler—"

Before he could finish the sentence, Tasha burst through the swinging doors and flung herself at the man, raking her fingernails across his face. "Murderer!" she shrieked.

"Hey, somebody get this little hellcat off me," he shouted, raising his arms to fend her off. "No need to be so pushy, honey. I got plenty of time and energy for all the tumblin' and tusslin' you want."

Held off by another man's iron grip, Tasha squirmed and kicked, glaring at the man from the *Shenandoah.* Her eyes blazed with fury. "Murderer!" she repeated.

The man dabbed at the reddening scratches on his face. "Now hold on there, honey, that's a mighty strong name to be calling a man!"

"You murdered my fiancé!"

The man laughed and took a swallow of whiskey from a glass the bartender set before him. " 'Taint likely I even knew your fiancé. And I never murdered no man."

"Liar!" she spat, still struggling in the other man's grasp. "I just heard you bragging about it. You said you burned the *Freedom*, and he was on board the *Freedom*."

"Whoa, there, honey," the man held up his hands, obviously amused by her logic. "Just because I burned the ship don't mean I murdered him. I mean, I doubt that any judge would accept that as convincing evidence."

"Then what happened to him?" Tasha demanded.

The man shrugged. "He probably got put aboard a deputized ship to get taken to a prisoner-of-war camp in the Confederacy."

"Don't lie to me!" she snapped. "I know the war was over by then, and I don't believe there were any prisoner camps then."

"Right you are. So my guess is he eventually got released."

Tasha stared at him openmouthed, wanting desperately to believe Jared could be alive, but afraid of being deceived. Finally, she shook her head emphatically. "I don't believe you," she said. "If Jared had been released, he would have come for me by now."

"Well, that's between you and him. I'm just telling you what probably happened. You can't blame me if you picked a fickle fiancé!"

The crowd that had gathered around them laughed loudly at this last remark. Suddenly Tasha felt as if everyone in the saloon was closing in on her. Her eyes moved from face to face, and they all seemed to be laughing, taunting her to accept the fact that Jared had deserted her. She felt her face burning and she squirmed vainly in the grip of the man who held her.

"Let me go!" she screamed. "I want to go to my room!"

Obligingly, the man turned her toward the doors, releasing her as he shoved her through. "Don't go, honey," the man from the *Shenandoah* called, "if this Jared don't want you no more, I'll take you. At least I'll be glad to bed you!" he added with a loud guffaw. His comrades laughed heartily.

Upset and humiliated, her eyes brimming with tears, Tasha stumbled up to her room. She threw herself across the bed, sobbing and wondering whether to believe the man's story. Wasn't it possible he had never been on the *Shenandoah,* and knew nothing about the fate of the crews of the whalers? Couldn't he have learned the *Freedom's* name from newspaper accounts of the attacks?

Still, what if he had been aboard the *Shenandoah* and spoke from personal knowledge? That could mean Jared was alive! The joy she felt at the thought was quickly replaced by confusion and anger as she remembered the taunting faces in the saloon. If he had survived, why had he never come for her, or at least contacted her? Had he found another woman when he last visited New Bedford? Or had he simply used her—as her father originally believed—playing on her vulnerability and never intending to marry her?

But he had seemed sincere and she had believed him, going so far as to plan her whole future around his promises.

The idea that he might have deceived her made her livid with rage and she flushed with shame at her own gullibility. She had grieved for him, thinking him dead, when all the time he may have been alive and enjoying himself in some eastern city, with not a thought for her. While one part of her rejoiced in the hope that he had survived, the rest of her cursed him for using her so callously.

Now fully enraged, she felt Jared was to blame for everything that had happened to her since she met

311

him. If he had not taken her, awakening her dormant passions, she would never have fallen so hopelessly in love with him. Had he not returned to Novoarkhangelsk with his fiery touch and promises of marriage, she might never have admitted her love for him—and she would never have despairingly agreed to wed Yuri Zarevsky when she heard the *Freedom* was lost. She would never have gone to Kamchatka, never have encountered the evil Father Iosaf. He had ruined her life, without so much as an apology.

Well, if he was alive, he could be damned! She would not allow him to haunt her any longer—he had destroyed enough of her life. Still, she could not resist wanting to know for certain whether he had survived. She had to admit she was curious (no, not *jealous*) about who might be enjoying his caresses now. Perhaps no one, she thought, feeling strangely relieved by the possibility. Hadn't he once told her he was married to the sea, and had no room in his life for other women? It would not hurt so much to lose him to a force as overpowering as the sea. At the moment, the way she was feeling now, it would hurt even less to know he really was dead, just as she had thought for more than a year. At least then she could feel that he had not betrayed her.

If only there was some way to be sure, some way to resolve the war of opposing emotions raging inside her!

A gentle knock at the door interrupted her brooding. "Are you all right, Tasha?" her father's voice called.

"Yes, papa," she replied, trying to sound as if she had been asleep, "I'm in bed for the night."

"Well," he called, "then you needn't bother to get up. I'll simply go on to my own room. Have a pleasant, restful night, my dear. Monsieur Stanovsky said to bid you goodnight as well."

"Thank you, papa. I'm sure I shall feel much better tomorrow. Goodnight."

She listened to his footsteps continuing down the

hall, then got up and removed her gown and undergarments. In the dark, she groped for a sheer lawn nightdress and dressing gown. Slipping both garments on, she lay down again, waiting for the hotel to become quiet.

It was well after midnight when Tasha tiptoed to her door. Opening it a crack, she glanced cautiously up and down the empty hall. In the course of their dinner conversation, Stanovsky had mentioned the number of his hotel room. Now she stole quietly toward that room.

A muffled, sleepy voice answered her knock. "Who is it?"

"Tasha Zarevskaya," she whispered. "Will you let me in? I'd like a word with you."

"Of course! One moment." His voice registered surprise. She could hear him fumbling to light a lamp, then moving around the room a bit more. Her heart pounded as she worried that someone might enter the hall and mistake her for a prostitute. Perhaps she should not have come. Perhaps her action had been too hasty. She was about to turn and flee when Stanovsky opened the door and, smiling, drew her into his room.

His dressing gown was open at the neck, revealing a mat of brown chest hair. Tasha realized instantly that the dressing gown was all he wore. The thought that he hadn't even a nightshirt beneath it added to her discomfort.

"Well," he said patiently, taking her two icy hands into his warm grasp, "what is it you wish to speak to me about? It must be very urgent that you would get out of bed and seek me out at this hour."

"I wish to accompany you to New York," she blurted.

His eyes widened in shock and Tasha felt herself blushing. "That is, if you still desire my company," she stammered. "Perhaps your invitation was not meant to be taken seriously. Or perhaps you have already found another companion."

He took a step nearer her, holding her eyes locked in his gaze. "The invitation was meant to be taken quite seriously, Tasha," he said, using her pet name for the first time. "And I am more than pleased to have you accept. But are you sure?"

She nodded, biting her lower lip nervously. "Quite sure. But I have no funds with which to pay my passage. And I can't ask my father. He insists that I return to Kamchatka as soon as his business here is completed, so I know that he would never approve of my running off to New York. I dare not even tell him my plans before—"

Stanovsky lay a finger across her lips, gently cutting her off. "Say no more. All will be taken care of, I promise you. Can you be ready tomorrow night at eleven?" When she nodded, he continued. "Good. We will board the *Aleksandr II* at that time, as it is scheduled for an early morning sailing. By the time your father discovers your absence, we will be far from San Francisco."

Tasha smiled weakly and turned toward the door. "I'd best return to my own room now. Thank you, Monsieur Stanovsky."

Stanovsky caught her shoulder, turning her gently toward him. "I think that Pyotr Maksimovich would be more appropriate now. And thank you, Tasha. Your decision makes me very happy."

Chapter Twenty-six

1866

Riding beside Pyotr Stanovsky toward the harbor where the *Aleksandr II* was docked, Tasha still wondered if she was doing the right thing. Had she been too impulsive in grasping this chance to journey east? Would she regret her hastiness if she discovered Jared to be alive and happy?

She was sure of one thing: her father would be terribly hurt and disappointed when he read the note she had left him. Not wanting to disappear without leaving him any explanation, she had spent most of the day trying to compose a suitable note. Finally, she had settled on a brief message, which revealed to her father the outcome of her marriage for the first time:

Dearest Papa,
I know I cannot expect you to understand, or condone what I am doing, but I have departed for New York with Monsieur Stanovsky. When he invited me, I was so overwhelmed with excitement about the chance to see a great American city that I could not refuse. I had not wanted to tell you, but my marriage to Yuri has been heartbreaking. Perhaps I am as much to blame as he, but I simply could not bear the thought of returning to Kamchatka and beginning that misery once again. Maybe after I return to Novo-arkhangelsk, which I intend to do one day, he and I can make a new start. Please forgive me for going against your wishes, and please believe that I do love you.

Your always loving daughter,
Tasha

It was deceitful, she knew, to imply that she hoped for a reconciliation with Yuri. And not to mention Jared, the real reason for her departure.

In truth, she hoped never to see Yuri Zarevsky again, but there was no point in going into that now. Perhaps the note would at least prevent her father from feeling too bitter toward her. If she could keep open the lines of paternal love, she felt certain she could explain everything more fully the next time she saw him.

"You're very quiet, Tasha," Stanovsky smiled as he helped her aboard the *Aleksandr II.* "I hope you are

315

not regretting your decision to accompany me. If that's the case, there is still time to change your mind. I will, however regretfully, accompany you back to the Emerald Necklace, and no one would be the wiser."

"No," she shook her head emphatically, "I was just thinking of the extent of my travels. In just a few months' time, I shall have traveled halfway around the world."

"Quite an accomplishment for one so young," he agreed. "And I'll wager you've left a string of broken hearts in every town you've visited."

"Flattery again, Monsieur Stanovsky?" she laughed flirtatiously.

He returned her laugh, his green eyes sparkling. "As I've told you before, I speak only the truth. But, please call me Pyotr Maksimovich. Your formality makes me feel far too old."

"As you wish, Pyotr Maksimovich."

Taking her hand, he pulled her toward the companionway. "It's late. Let me show you to our suite. I hope you will find it to your liking."

The suite was undeniably exquisite. Stanovsky opened the door to a sitting room plushly decorated in green and gold velvet. A vase brimming with yellow roses stood on a small table next to the green velvet settee. At Tasha's exclamation of delight, he explained, "I thought they were a perfect match for the lovely gown you wore to dinner last night."

On the table at the other end of the settee stood a polished silver samovar and a set of crystal tea glasses in silver filigree holders. Two massive gold velvet chairs completed the room's furnishings, and a full length mirror in an elaborately carved, gilded frame covered one whole wall.

"It's lovely!" Tasha exclaimed. "I never dreamed such a cabin could exist." An image of the tiny stateroom she had shared with Jared flashed through her mind, and she grimaced slightly.

Unaware of her change of expression, Stanovsky led her toward another door. "This is only the beginning," he said, pulling her into a small dressing room with mirrors and dressing tables on two facing walls.

"Over here," he pulled her into another small room, "is a room expressly for bathing." It contained a large porcelain tub, a neat stack of velvety bath towels, and an assortment of scented soaps, oils, and other bath accessories arranged on a polished brass cabinet on the wall.

"Finally," he slid his arm around her waist and approached another door, "we have the bedroom." He flung open the door with a flourish.

A large, high, brass bed, covered by a floor-length green velvet coverlet, dominated the room. A small writing table and chair stood in one corner, and a high chest of drawers stood against another wall. But it was not the room's furnishings that caught Tasha's attention—it was the article spread carefully across the bed.

Stanovsky pulled her into the room, watching her uneasily. "Aren't you pleased?" he asked. "I know it cannot match your beauty, but I thought on our first night together it might bring you some pleasure."

Tasha gulped, still staring at the garment gracing the bed. It was a nightgown made entirely of frothy white lace. The neckline formed a deep V, almost to the waist, where the gown was tied with two thin satin ribbons, its only closure. Below the ribbons, it fell open again, so that if she were to walk in it, her legs, in addition to a good deal more, would be fully exposed. The sleeves were full, flowing, and wrist-length. Tasha reached out to finger the lace, as if hoping the garment would disappear at her touch. All day she had ignored the implications of her decision to travel with Pyotr Stanovsky. Now she felt unable to face them.

Turning her troubled eyes to his, she murmured, "I can't, I can't—" she broke off, unable to continue.

A veil fell over Stanovsky's green eyes. "But I assumed we had an understanding," he whispered. "When you agreed to come with me, I assumed you meant—"

"I know!" she sobbed. "I know what you thought. But I can't. I'm sorry, I just can't!"

Pressing his lips tightly together, Stanovsky wheeled and left the room. A moment later, she heard the door to the passageway slam as he left the suite.

Sinking down on the bed, Tasha wondered what to do. She could leave and return to her father, but then she might never get to the Eastern United States and find the answer to the question that was plaguing her. No, she decided firmly, she would not leave. She would stay, but she would act exactly as she pleased. She had suffered enough at the hands of men who used her only for their own benefit.

Hours passed before she heard Stanovsky return. He did not come to the bedroom, and she did not invite him to join her. By the time she awoke in the morning, he had already left the suite.

Standing in the sitting room, she stared out the porthole at the blue Pacific. She had no idea what time it was or how long ago they had left San Francisco. She felt terribly hungry, and wondered if she would have to go out in search of food or if Pyotr Maksimovich would bring her something. Since she had refused to satisfy his appetite, would he in turn refuse to satisfy hers?

Thinking about the night before, Tasha suddenly felt guilty. She knew he must have spent an uncomfortable night on the cramped settee, while she slept soundly in the huge bed. He had never deceived her about wanting a lover to share his trip. He had made his desire clear from their first meeting. In fact, it would seem that she had deceived him.

She had never actually promised herself to him, but she had allowed him to believe she would share his bed. Any other man, faced with such deceit, would have taken her by force, demanding his due. Yet he had respected her wishes, leaving her without so much as stealing a kiss.

No matter how she tried to rationalize her position, Tasha could not drive the guilt from her heart. She had made a bargain with Stanovsky. How long could she refuse to fulfill it? Was it fair for her to make him suffer because of her bitterness toward other men?

Stanovsky seemed to be the only man who had honestly offered her something in return for her favors. Her husband wanted her only as an ornament and a tool to greater power, taking what he could, without regard for her feelings or desires. If what the man in the saloon said was true, Jared had used her too, playing on her innocence and then casting her aside. But Pyotr Maksimovich Stanovsky offered her kindness, gentleness, comfort, and companionship on a voyage to freedom in a new land. He did not try to bind her to him with false claims of love. He asked only that she open herself to him. In view of what she had given other men, for much less in return, was it so much for him to ask?

Sighing, Tasha turned from the porthole and went back to the bedroom. She straightened the bed linen and pulled up the spread, then sat for a long time on the edge of the bed, vigorously brushing her hair until it shone like a length of satin. Slowly she rose and picked up the nightgown of frothy lace.

When Stanovsky returned to the suite in mid-morning, Tasha was sitting in one of the gold velvet armchairs. The gown he had bought for her was draped discreetly over her body, and she sat stiffly, trying to prevent it falling open to reveal her nakedness.

At the sight of her pink and ivory flesh peeking through the lace, Stanovsky froze, the color draining from his face. "Must you torment me?" he asked hoarsely.

In reply, Tasha rose gracefully, holding her arms wide in welcome as she walked slowly toward him. Her breasts swelled and strained against the lace until the hard, pink buds forced their way through the openwork. As she walked, loose panels of the gown strayed open to reveal her smooth, shapely legs and a glimpse of the dark triangle he so longed to touch.

Needing no further invitation, Stanovsky closed the door and ran to envelop her in an embrace. Strong hands, hot with desire, pressed against her spine, drawing the full length of her body against his. His fingers traced the contour of her throat, then dropped to massage the hollow between her breasts. Gently, he tipped back her head and covered her mouth with his, kissing her at first tenderly, then more insistently, as she parted her lips and welcomed his fiery tongue.

"Oh, my sweet Tasha," he whispered. "Can it be true that you have decided to share yourself with me? Will you let me take you now, without protest, and without regret?"

"Yes, Pyotr Maksimovich," she breathed, surprised at the passion she felt. "Oh yes, yes!"

Trembling with excitement, he lifted her in his arms and strode quickly through the dressing room and bathroom into the bedroom. Laying her gently on the bed, he stepped back for a moment to study the tempting vision before him. Her flesh and gown were a striking contrast to the dark green spread, making her appear all the more pure and fresh.

She lay still on the bed, watching as he quickly removed his clothing. His body was not as lean as Yuri's or Jared's, but his flesh was still firm and taut. As his trousers dropped to the floor she could see his desire reflected in his growing manhood.

Sitting on the edge of the bed, he untied the ribbons at her waist and carefully peeled back the gown to reveal her body. She closed her eyes as his lips touched her breasts, then slid lower, planting fiery kisses along her belly. He picked up his head and moved his lips to her knee, beginning a line of kisses that edged up along her inner thigh, stopping just before he reached her innermost sanctuary. He

320

seemed to know exactly how to arouse a woman, moving slowly, in no hurry to release his own building passion. With a moan of pleasure, Tasha surrendered to his touch.

She had gone too many months without the tender touch of a man. Yuri had never made any pretense of tenderness, and it had been more than two years since her last ecstatic union with Jared. Now Pyotr Maksimovich was awakening a deep hunger in her. By the time he entered her she was more than ready, lifting her hips to meet him, then falling back in satisfaction as he filled her. He moved slowly at first, allowing her to adjust to his tempo and rhythm. Gradually the intensity of his movements built, and she strained against him, moving as one with him.

Sliding his arms beneath her back and buttocks, he rolled onto his side, bringing her with him. She squirmed and pressed closer to him, all else forgotten as she tried to make him fill every crevice within her. Clutching her to him, he rolled again and Tasha gasped as she found herself on top of him, while he lay flat on his back beneath her. She froze, unsure of what to do, until she heard his encouraging whisper.

"Relax, little Tasha. Relax and move as you feel. Do what you wish to bring yourself the same pleasure you are bringing me."

He pressed his hands into the soft flesh of her buttocks, holding her hips firmly against his as she began to rock over him. She lifted her chest, brushing her nipples against his chest as she moved. Without warning, a new flood of fire surged through her body. Her moans of pleasure filled the room. Pyotr groaned passionately, as she stopped to savor the feeling, squeezing, pulsing, as she collapsed against him. He waited a moment, letting her enjoy the fading glow, then began moving rapidly beneath her, thrusting and straining until they both felt their passions explode in a blazing moment of joy.

They lay silently, waiting for their breathing to return to normal. At last he rolled to his side, gently moving away from her to stare into her eyes. "Why did you change your mind?" he asked tenderly.

"About sailing with you, or about this?"

"Both." His fingers massaged the soft tip of her earlobe.

She lowered her eyes, unwilling to meet his gaze. "Papa would have insisted I go back to Kamchatka after his business in San Francisco was completed—back to a husband I despise." She hesitated, quickly deciding she would not tell him about her desire to find out about Jared. That was too personal to share, even with a man with whom she had just made love. "As to the other," she shrugged, "I felt we had a bargain and I could not cheat you."

"Oh." Pyotr smiled wryly. "I had hoped at least one of your reasons might be a desire to share the trip with me. But you have been honest, and I am grateful for that."

Tasha flushed, ashamed at having hurt him. "But of course you are part of the reason, Pyotr Maksimovich! If I did not find you intelligent, and witty, and—attractive, I would never have decided to come. I could have found any number of other ways to avoid returning to Kamchatka, no matter what my father might have said."

He cupped one of her breasts, then slid his hand slowly down her side, causing gooseflesh to erupt all over her. "And do you regret having kept the bargain? If you do, I will not hold you to it. If you wish, you may share all other aspects of this trip and all the comforts of my suite, but you need not share my bed."

Smiling, she kissed his cheek. "I don't regret having made the bargain, and I would be most disappointed if you chose not to hold me to it. You are a divine lover, Pyotr Maksimovich, and I shall not allow you to cheat me of even one moment of your attention." She giggled self-consciously. "It seems I have become just like the St. Petersburg women you told me about —the married women who take lovers."

"Not just like them, Tasha," Stanovsky replied as he returned her kiss. "I speak from long experience, and I find you are much more beautiful and far more satisfying."

Late that night, after a champagne dinner and another passionate interlude, Tasha lay awake beside Pyotr Maksimovich. For the first time in months, she felt a sort of contentment and security. At that moment, she thought she would gladly consent to spend the rest of her life with Pyotr Maksimovich Stanovsky, traveling openly as his mistress and flaunting the rules of hypocritical society. Yet, at the same time, she realized she would not be overly upset if he wanted to part with her when they reached New York.

Though his lovemaking left her breathless and tingling, it did not leave her with the same intense satisfaction she had experienced both times with Jared. She was sure she did not love Pyotr Maksimovich Stanovsky. In fact, she doubted she could ever love another man as she had loved Jared Northrup. Perhaps that was just as well. Not loving anyone would be a way to protect herself against the hurt that still plagued her whenever she thought of Jared.

Tasha and Pyotr remained lovers for the rest of the trip, never allowing a day or night to pass without indulging their sensual appetites. Though he often praised her beauty and her ability to bring him pleasure, Pyotr Maksimovich never spoke to her of love, and Tasha was relieved to be able to skirt the subject. She found joy and solace in his caresses, but afterwards, always suffered a painful sense of emptiness.

When alone together, and in the presence of others aboard the ship, Stanovsky treated Tasha with the utmost respect and courtesy, never flaunting her as a prize as some men might have done. She felt relaxed with him at all times, and, if not happy, at least content. Being with Pyotr Maksimovich Stanovsky was a vast improvement over the life she had endured with Yuri Zarevsky, and for the moment Tasha felt she could not ask for more.

Except for some severe weather and adverse winds the ship encountered as they rounded Cape Horn, the trip was a smooth one. They arrived in New York City in late fall, and Tasha felt as if she was in a new world.

She could not guess what ghosts would continue to haunt her from the world she thought she had left behind.

Chapter Twenty-seven

1866

To Tasha, whose knowledge of large cities was limited to her brief stay in Moscow before she first departed for Novoarkhangelsk, New York seemed a wonderland of massive buildings and spacious thoroughfares. Pyotr made arrangements for rooms in the American Hotel at Broadway and Barclay streets. Their suite was comfortable and well-equipped. She spent many afternoons walking on Fifth Avenue, the most fashionable promenade in the city. The avenue was lined with grand mansions in the European style, and the brick roadway teemed with horse-drawn buses, broughams, and an assortment of private carriages and merchants' wagons from early morning until after midnight. The whole area radiated wealth and excitement, and under Pyotr Maksimovich's protection, Tasha was exhilarated to be part of it.

Most of the time, Pyotr left her at the hotel, explaining that he had business to look after for Czar Aleksandr. Though Tasha made a show of pouting, and begged to accompany him, he steadfastly refused, saying that matters of business and politics would only bore her. When she tried, at intimate moments, to induce him to discuss those matters, he remained close-mouthed, stating crisply that the Czar's affairs were not fit for idle gossip at ladies' tea parties. Eventually, Tasha resigned herself to spending the days without him and remaining ignorant of his work.

Always generous, Pyotr left her a large sum of money each day, instructing her to hire a carriage, explore the city, and purchase whatever caught her fancy while he was away.

On one of her first outings, she discovered Lord & Taylor's expansive department store at Broadway and Grand streets. Awed that any shop could offer such a wide selection of goods, she spent hours exploring its aisles. On later excursions, she discovered Arnold Constable's and R. H. Macy's and spent equally long periods examining their attractive wares, especially their ready-to-wear women's clothing.

Her own clothing, which had seemed satisfactory enough in Novoarkhangelsk and Kamchatka, now struck her as hopelessly outdated. Within a few days, she had purchased several fashionable gowns featuring full skirts, fitted waists, and elegant trains. To complete her ensembles, she acquired corsets, stiff crinolines to give her skirts the required hoop shape, and ankle-high bootikins, which had replaced the flat-heeled slipper as fashionable footwear. Finding that her hooped skirts would not accommodate a conventional coat, she then purchased a casque-style cape, which fell loosely from a fitted shoulder yoke.

Pyotr Maksimovich accepted Tasha's purchases in good humor. She had many opportunities to wear her new finery, since the Russian emissary and his lady-friend were immediately swept up in New York's social whirl. Rumors that both Stanovsky and his dark-haired mistress were of imperial blood made them among the most sought-after guests in society, and they were invited to operas and symphonic concerts, dramatic and musical recitals, and countless private parties.

Often, during her free afternoons, Tasha thought about running away to New Bedford, or trying in some way to learn about Jared. But, each time, fear of what she might discover would make her postpone the project. There was a serenity to her life with Pyotr Stanovsky which she was reluctant to disturb.

Occasionally she wondered about what would happen when Stanovsky's business in New York was completed. Would he feel that his bargain with her had been fully met, or would he want her to continue traveling with him when he returned to St. Petersburg? Tasha felt she could accept either decision. It would be pleasant to stay with Pyotr Stanovsky, but it would not be a shattering experience to part from him.

What she could not accept was the possibility of meeting her husband again. If she traveled to St. Petersburg with Stanovsky, there was a chance Yuri might still be there, and he would be sure to make a scene about his marital rights, both on legal and religious grounds. Even if he had left the capital, friends of his at the Russian-American Company who noticed her liaison with Stanovsky might send Yuri word of her presence. And there was always the possibility that Yuri was, even now, traveling to the United States on official business. After all, if Pyotr Maksimovich had been sent to New York on business concerning the company, Yuri could well be, too.

Tasha felt she could face Yuri without fear, if she had to, but she simply preferred never to see him again. Compared to the gaiety she was experiencing in New York, her months with him seemed like part of a distant, unpleasant world. Most days, she managed to bury those sordid memories amid the glitter of New York's social whirl.

At one party, Tasha captured the attention of everyone when she arrived wearing a gown with an ivory satin skirt and a flowing train of ice-blue brocade. The same brocade formed an off-the-shoulder bodice draped low to reveal the tops of her breasts.

As the center of attention of every man—young and old—at the soireé, Tasha enjoyed the evening in a blur of laughter and champagne. But the party lost some of its appeal when she danced with a tall, serious young man wearing gold-rimmed spectacles. "Tell me," her partner asked, "what is your opinion of the proposed sale of your American colony to the United States?"

"I beg your pardon?" Tasha gasped, not sure she had heard him correctly.

The young man blinked. "Surely you've heard? The news has been reported in all the papers. It seems the Czar is anxious to be rid of the property, and he thinks the United States would be foolish enough to buy it."

"Oh, but I'm sure you're mistaken, sir. I know for a fact that the Russian-American Company, the organization that manages the colony, only this year was promised a renewal of their charter for a term of twenty years." In the back of her mind, she wondered uneasily, hadn't she once overheard her father heatedly discussing with his friend, Semyon, the fact that the renewal was four years late—four long years during which the Council of State debated the fate of the colony?

"Well," her partner shrugged, "I suppose it's pointless to worry about it. There is little likelihood that it will come about. The only man in the United States who seems to favor the purchase is Secretary of State Seward, and he hasn't the power to swing the Senate to his way of thinking. I simply wondered how a Russian viewed the proposal."

"I think," she said quickly, "that it is a shocking idea, and the rumor hasn't a grain of truth to it. Czar Aleksandr would no more think of selling Russian America than he would think of selling Moscow or St. Petersburg! Novoarkhangelsk is a thriving community, and the colony is filled with natives who have been baptized into Orthodoxy. It would be an absolute sin to sell them to another country."

She was convinced the reports were wrong, yet it troubled her to learn that a sale was being discussed. She couldn't concentrate on anything else the young man had to say while they finished the dance, and was impatient for the music to stop so she could seek out Pyotr Maksimovich. As an emissary of the Czar, he could put her mind at rest on this point.

Spying Pyotr standing on the other side of the room, deep in discussion with a portly, conservatively-dressed gentleman, Tasha pushed her way toward him, shaking her head to decline several invitations to dance.

When she reached his side, she clutched his arm and blurted, "Pyotr Maksimovich, I must talk with you immediately."

He smiled and his eyes sparkled in amusement. "Is your problem so urgent that it cannot wait until we are alone?"

"Yes, it is. If you cannot attend to me now, I shan't be able to enjoy myself another moment."

His brows shot up questioningly. "And what is it you would like to discuss?"

"Why do the New York newspapers report the possibility of the Empire selling Russian America to the United States?"

The man to whom Pyotr had been speaking shifted uneasily, while Pyotr Maksimovich cleared his throat. "I was not aware you had been reading the newspapers, Tasha." He grinned facetiously at the man beside him. "Ah, what havoc results when a woman can read not only her own language, but three or four others as well."

"Pyotr!" she snapped. "You are making light of my question!"

"So I am," he continued to smile. "Forgive me, Tasha. I had forgotten for the moment that, unlike other women I have known, you are not to be taken lightly."

He paused and cleared his throat. "The explanation is really very simple. More than a decade ago, when the Empire was battling England in the Crimean War, there was some concern over the safety of the colony. English ships had ventured as far as Petropavlovsk, and everyone knew it was only a short hop across the North Pacific to our colony in America. Novoarkhangelsk hadn't sufficient troops to protect the colony against British attack, and the empire couldn't spare any military forces.

"Some parties feared the English might attempt to take over the colony. So, to thwart a British attack, a false bill of sale was drawn up, deeding Russian America to the American-Russian Commercial Company, the company your father does business with in San Francisco. You see, if England thought the United States owned our property, it would presumably reduce the threat of attack."

"The whole scheme sounds preposterous," Tasha breathed.

Pyotr nodded. "As it happened, the British never threatened Novoarkhangelsk or any of the colony's other outposts, and all of the machinations turned out to be unnecessary. Still, the scheme gave rise to the rumor, advanced especially by certain senators from California, that we were willing to sell the colony."

"But if, as you say, all this happened more than a decade ago, why do the rumors still persist?"

He shrugged. "Apparently the American press does not give up a good story so easily. Now that the war between the states is over, they must find something else to fill their pages. Don't be surprised if you read my name in some of these stories. No doubt some of these journalists wouldn't hesitate to use my presence in New York to lend credence to their rumors."

"But they would be lying if they involved you in their stories, wouldn't they, Pyotr Maksimovich? You could stop them from publishing such lies."

He smiled at her indulgently. "My dear, innocent Tasha, newspapers in America are notorious for publishing untruths. They have no Czar's police, as our periodicals do, to insure that they print only the truth. Consequently, an intelligent person believes very little of what the local papers publish."

"I see." Tasha sighed with relief. "I didn't believe the reports myself, but I wanted your assurance that they weren't true. Thank you, Pyotr Maksimovich."

Later that night, before they drifted into sleep, Tasha whispered, "Pyotr Maksimovich, do you think Czar Aleksandr will sell the colony?"

He sighed, "What do you think, Tasha?"

"I don't think so. He has agreed to renew the charter, and I'm sure he would not deceive his subjects on the matter."

"Then it appears you have all the answer you need."

"Yes, I suppose so. It's a relief to know there is no truth to the rumors. Papa has given so much of his life to Novoarkhangelsk; he would be completely crushed if the Czar surrendered the colony to another country." In the dark, she rolled toward Stanovsky and kissed his cheek. "Thank you for enduring my questioning, dear Pyotr Maksimovich. Goodnight."

If Tasha had any further doubts about the sale of Russian America, they were buried beneath the news she received a few evenings later at a Christmas ball.

She was dancing a waltz with a young man named Philip Vanderman, who had a smile wide enough to split his face. "It's times like these," he said, dipping violently to the pulse of the music, "that make me glad I gave up whaling and returned to New York society."

"You were a whaleman?" Tasha tried to sound nonchalant, despite the way her heart jumped at his words.

"Yes, ma'am," he grinned. "My father was so mad when I ran off to New Bedford, I thought he would disown me. Said a young man of my standing had no business signing on as a forecastle hand, that I should have stayed home in the family banking business.

But it was something I just had to get out of my system."

Tasha smiled understandingly. "If you'll forgive me, I think you look a good deal more like a whaleman than a banker."

"That I do," he laughed, "but don't let my father hear you say so. He expects me to become president of his bank some day."

"Well, I suppose a banker's life does have a bit more future than a whaleman's. Still, your voyages must have been exciting."

"I only had one voyage, ma'am, but you're right about the excitement. We had plenty of that. You're also right about there not being much future in it. That voyage, and my whaling career, came to a sudden end."

"Oh." With an uneasy premonition of what was coming, Tasha tried to sound unconcerned, "why was that?"

His smile faded as he said grimly, "We were sunk by the Confederate raider *Shenandoah* in the Bering Straits."

Tasha felt her knees weaken, fearing she was about to receive confirmation of the news given to her by the man in San Francisco. "How fortunate that you survived!" she forced out the words.

"Yes, ma'am. But, so far as I know, every man on the ship survived, except Captain Dawson. I hear some of the other crews weren't so lucky. A score of their men drowned in the icy waters."

Tasha shivered. "Tell me," she struggled to keep her voice even, "what was the name of your ship?"

"The *Freedom*. She was the most beautiful vessel you ever saw. When all her sails were filled with wind—" He stopped suddenly, studying her ashen face in alarm. "Are you all right, ma'am?"

She gulped and nodded. She knew this much: it could not hurt her any more to press for further details.

"Was there," she began weakly, her voice shaking,

then cleared her throat and started again, "was there a man named Jared Northrup aboard your vessel?"

"Mr. Northrup? Sure, he was the second mate. Being only a forecastle hand, I didn't get to know him too well. I mean, he kept to himself mostly; wasn't one to shoot the breeze with the crew. But he seemed like a fine enough officer." The young man's eyes narrowed as he stared at Tasha. "How is it *you* know him, ma'am?"

Feeling her cheeks color beneath his stare, she said quickly, "I didn't say that I knew him."

Her partner cocked his head quizzically and she hurried to explain. "One of my maids is from Siberia. She lived in Okhotsk for a number of years, and the *Freedom* put in there one summer. It seems she met Mr. Northrup then, and ever since she's fancied herself in love with him. I wouldn't have remembered the name if she hadn't repeated it so often."

"I see," there was a note of skepticism in Philip's voice. Then his eyes brightened. "It seems I do remember some talk among the seasoned crew, those who had sailed aboard the *Freedom* in previous voyages, about Mr. Northrup being in love with a Russian girl. Damned if I can remember the details, though."

Tasha felt her heart lurch as she struggled to maintain a cool tone. "You whalemen must enjoy many passing love affairs in the course of your travels."

Philip shrugged noncommittally. "It occurs to me, if your maid is in New York with you, I'd be glad to take her up to New Bedford to visit Mr. Northrup."

Tasha paled. So he was alive! Of course, he must be if Philip spoke of visiting him. And so near, too! She felt Philip staring at her curiously, waiting for some response to his suggestion, so she spoke quickly, hoping to sound convincing. "Unfortunately, I had to leave my maid in St. Petersburg. Pyotr Maksimovich objected to my dragging around a retinue of servants. But," she could not resist asking the next question, though she almost was afraid to hear Philip's response, "do you really suppose Mr. Northrup is in New Bedford?"

"I think so, though I wouldn't want to lay hard cash on it. We were separated from the ship's officers after the *Freedom* went down. I guess the rebs didn't want to risk having the officers organize us against them. They didn't even put us on the same ship when they sent us to the prison camps. But just a few months ago, I did hear that everyone except the captain got back safe and sound, so I would guess Mr. Northrup would be in New Bedford. Unless, of course, he's shipped out on another whaler."

Philip hesitated, studying Tasha's strained expression. "You weren't thinking of perhaps going to see him on your maid's behalf?"

She laughed nervously. "Heavens, no! My servant's love affairs are no concern of mine." The news was beginning to numb her now, swirling wildly in her mind so that it was an effort to concentrate on Philip's conversation.

"Ah, well," he smiled dejectedly, "I was hoping I might offer myself as an escort. It would be pleasant to have your company away from the watchful eyes of Mr. Stanovsky."

"Monsieur!" she laughed coquettishly. "What do you mean to imply?"

"Only that you are a very intriguing woman," he assured her quickly. "And I should like to know you better. Perhaps sometime I might take you riding in Central Park. It was completed only a few years ago, and the landscaping is quite exquisite."

"Perhaps," she agreed absently, preoccupied with thoughts about Jared.

A short time later, pleading a severe headache, Tasha convinced Pyotr to accompany her to their hotel. He ordered a bath for her and sat on the edge of the bed, watching as she lay back in the hot, sudsy water.

"I'm so sorry to see you under the weather, Tasha,"

he said with evident concern. "You seemed so radiant at the beginning of the evening."

"I know," she mumbled. "I don't really know what came over me."

He crossed the room and knelt beside the tub. Taking the washcloth from her, he soaped it and began gently to wash her breasts. She lay still as he washed her whole body, allowing his fingers to linger wherever they chose. Then he rinsed her with pitchers of warm water.

"Come," he murmured, lifting her lightly from the water, "I know how to make you forget your pain."

He carried her, dripping, to the bed and lay her on top of the covers. Leaning over her, he licked the droplets of water from her breasts while his fingers loosened his clothing. He slid his legs between hers and began to lower his body over hers. Suddenly, Jared's face, etched in total detail, flashed through Tasha's mind.

Shaking her head emphatically, she pushed her palms against Pyotr's lowering chest. "No, Pyotr Maksimovich! Please, not tonight! I can't!"

He frowned. "Do I fail to excite you any more, Tasha? Did someone else at the ball tonight catch your fancy?"

She turned her head away, and a tear dropped onto the pillow. "No, no, Pyotr Maksimovich. It's not another man. It's just that my head plagues me so terribly I would not be able to enjoy and return your caress. Please don't ask me to make love now."

He pulled away from her, rolled off the bed, and straightened his clothes. "Then perhaps you had best try to sleep."

"Yes, I think I shall." She slid beneath the covers. "But it's foolish for you to be penned up here, with nothing to do but watch me sleep. Why don't you return to the ball and try to enjoy yourself?"

"I suppose I could." He looked at her guiltily. "Are you certain you would not mind?"

"Of course not, there's absolutely nothing you can

334

do for me. I'd be relieved to know I did not completely spoil your evening."

"Well, then I think I will return for a bit." He bent
to kiss her forehead, tucking the covers close around
her shoulders. "Sleep well, dearest. I hope you feel
much better on the morrow."

He closed the door, leaving Tasha alone with her
thoughts. She might have doubted the man in San
Francisco, but Philip Vanderman had offered conclusive evidence that Jared Northrup was alive—not only
alive, but probably in New Bedford at that very moment! In her mind, she pictured the map of the
United States she had once found in her father's
study, trying to estimate the distance between New
York and New Bedford. It couldn't be more than a
few hundred miles. Compared to all the distances she
had covered in the last four years, Jared was hardly
more than a stone's throw away.

Impulsively, she thought she might after all go riding with Mr. Vanderman. She could tell him everything, and beg him to take her to New Bedford. Or,
he could simply advise her on the best route and
means of travel, and she could go there alone. Pyotr
Maksimovich might be a bit upset, but then their arrangement was mutually understood to be only temporary. He would have little trouble finding another
mistress, perhaps even from among the countless
young American women who were so impressed with
his romantic Russian background. She would be reunited with Jared! Her whole being burned with
the joyous prospect.

Almost immediately, the flames died, as she considered that a year and a half had passed since the
Freedom sank, and Jared had not so much as contacted her. She would look like a fool rushing to him
in his home town if he did not really care for her.

But, part of her mind protested, he did care for
her. Hadn't James Sanders told her so in Novoarkhangelsk? Or had Sanders merely been trying to comfort a grief-stricken girl? Still, if Jared loved her, why

335

hadn't he come for her? Why had he allowed her to think him dead?

No, she decided firmly, no matter how much she ached to go to him, she would not bare her heart for more hurt. She would not go to New Bedford. If Jared wanted her, he could come for her. If only she could be sure he knew she was in New York!

Suddenly, Tasha was glad she had introduced herself to everyone in New York as Tasha Lisovskaya. At first her purpose had simply been to avoid using her husband's surname—a name she despised. Now she searched for a way to have the name Tasha Lisovskaya communicated to New Bedford, where at least one man, if indeed he was there, would be sure to recognize it.

She was still awake when Pyotr Maksimovich returned. "Tasha," he whispered, "are you awake?"

"Yes, Pyotr Maksimovich."

"And how is your headache?"

"Much better, thank you."

"Good." He chuckled. "You may have been forced to leave the ball early, but you were the toast of everyone who saw you. No doubt your name will crown all the society columns in tomorrow's newspapers."

She became attentive, as an idea began to take shape in her mind. "Pyotr Maksimovich, do you suppose New York's newspapers are read in the town of New Bedford?"

"Quite possibly. New York being the metropolis it is, I've no doubt its papers enjoy circulation in a rather widespread area. Why the interest in New Bedford?"

"Just idle curiosity. Something someone said to me at the ball tonight." She snuggled into her pillow, a contented smile spreading across her face. It seemed her name might travel to New Bedford quite easily after all.

Chapter Twenty-eight

1866-1867

Bubbling over with enthusiasm, Tasha attended every Christmas and New Year's ball to which they were invited. She amazed Pyotr Maksimovich with her tirelessness, dancing until dawn, always insisting that they be among the last guests to leave. By day, with Pyotr's permission, she often went riding or strolling in Central Park with Philip Vanderman or another of her host of admirers.

Before long, all of New York seemed to be talking about the vivacious Russian beauty who had taken the city by storm. Her name appeared almost daily in the society columns, which reported who she had been seen with, and where, and what she had been wearing. On a few occasions, sketches of her, resplendent in her tiny-waisted, hoop-skirted gowns, illustrated the articles.

Watching the stack of news clippings grow, Tasha sighed in satisfaction. Jared Northrup surely at some time would see one or more of the articles. And if they did not induce him to come to New York to find her, at least they might convince him that she was happy and well-adjusted without him. He would never feel the satisfaction of knowing the agony he had caused her!

Early in March, when Tasha had begun to give up hope of Jared ever coming for her, Pyotr Maksimovich returned to the hotel one afternoon waving a cable from St. Petersburg.

"Well, my young femme fatale," he grinned, "in ten days you should have another city, the capital of the United States in the palm of your hand. We leave for Washington, D.C. within the week."

Tasha stared open-mouthed. Washington, D.C.! Would Jared, assuming he ever came to New York, know enough to follow her there? Perhaps she should go to New Bedford after all. No, her pride stubbornly protested, she would stay with Pyotr Maksimovich. If Jared Northrup wanted her, he would take the trouble to find out where she had gone.

"Doesn't the prospect please you?" Pyotr Maksimovich asked.

"Of course," she smiled weakly. "It's just that I've done so much traveling these last years that I've grown a bit weary of it. But it will be great fun to see the capital of the United States."

"That's my spirited Tasha," Pyotr said, affectionately kissing her cheek. "I shall be proud to present you to Washington society."

"Why are we going there? Certainly not just to dazzle society."

He laughed, then shrugged, feigning innocence. "I can only say that Czar Aleksandr orders it. Baron Edouard de Stoeckl is returning to the capital as Russia's foreign minister, and he shall be needing my assistance. I can assure you the social whirl will be quite exciting. Baron Stoeckl is terribly popular among Washington's elite, especially since he chose to wed an American, Eliza Howard of Springfield, Massachusetts. No doubt they shall be hosting many elegant affairs."

"Good," Tasha answered absently, unable to keep from wondering how close Springfield was to New Bedford.

Five days later, Tasha and Pyotr boarded a train for Washington, D.C. To her relief, a brief article appeared in that morning's edition of the *New York Herald*, lamenting the departure of "the darling of society, Tasha Lisovskaya, and the dashing Russian emissary, Pyotr Stanovsky." Perhaps, Tasha thought, the item would be the last indication of her whereabouts to reach Jared—if indeed he cared.

338

Her first glimpse of Washington was unimpressive. It was raining when they got off the train, and the streets were a mass of mud. Tasha turned up her nose as she felt the muck oozing around her bootikins. The place seemed a poor excuse for the capital of a great nation.

As their carriage rumbled along toward the Hotel Oxford on 14th Street at New York Avenue, she allowed herself to revise her opinion somewhat. The Capitol and the Executive Mansion were prodigious structures, worthy of a European capital, and the malls and public parks showed evidence of elaborate planning. Still, tucked between Maryland and Virginia, Washington seemed to lack the cosmopolitan flavor she had grown accustomed to in New York.

Despite her initial disappointment, Tasha found it exciting to be in the capital of a large nation. How ironic, she thought, that she should visit the capital of the United States before she had so much as glimpsed St. Petersburg. She quickly discovered the social affairs hosted by Baron Stoeckl and his wife were every bit as exciting as Pyotr Maksimovich had predicted, being crowded with dignitaries from Russia, the United States, and the foreign legations of several other nations.

The baron himself, though nearly sixty years old, was still sprightly and handsome, and presided over his parties with great aplomb. No one seemed to know when or how he had acquired the title of baron, since his ancestry was Italian and Austrian, but no one begrudged him the title. Educated, though not born, in Russia, he had served two Czars in the United States for over twenty-five years, and was equally popular with Americans and foreigners. His wife was a good deal younger than he, and was regarded as an ideal hostess.

On March 29, Tasha and Pyotr were invited to an especially elegant reception at the Stoeckls' mansion in Georgetown. In honor of the coming spring, Tasha dressed carefully in a pale pink brocade gown with a décolléte bodice and a satin train of a deeper shade of pink. Around her neck she wore a string of pearls, which Pyotr had presented to her especially for the occasion. She spent more than an hour arranging her hair in elaborate layers of ringlets through which she wove another string of pearls. As a final touch, she added some bloom to her cheeks from a pot of rouge.

"Well," Pyotr sighed, his eyes twinkling as he adjusted his waistcoat and black evening coat, "I can see I shall have to claim the first few dances or I shall never be able to fight my way through all your admirers this evening."

"Ha!" Tasha sniffed in mock anger, "you never seem to have time for me at the Stoeckls' gatherings. You are always off in a corner conferring with some dignitary. And you never even tell me what it is that occupies you so thoroughly."

"Business, my dear. Simply business. But tonight, I promise you, will be different. You look too delectable to be left to the wiles of the other men."

Laughing, Tasha stood on tiptoe to kiss his nose, then pulled away. "Come along, flattering sir, we haven't time to dally. I intend to wring every possible drop of enjoyment from this evening."

"Very well," he grumbled good naturedly. "Since we must go, we had best be on our way." Taking her arm, he led her down the hotel's sweeping staircase to the carriage he had hired for the evening.

During the ride to Georgetown, Tasha thought of the decision she had come to that day. It was apparent to her now that she and Jared Northrup were not destined to share a life together. He had not come for her in Novoarkhangelsk. There had been no word from him while she was in New York, and none while in Washington. Perhaps her scheme had been foolish. He may never have seen the articles about her in the New York papers. But the fact remained that he had not kept his promise to return to Novoarkhangelsk for her. She had to assume that he had never meant to keep it.

Lying in her bath that afternoon, anticipating the evening's party, she had determined to bury her memories of Jared forever.

In celebration of the new, free Tasha Lisovskaya, she intended to let herself go completely that night. She would dance with whomever asked her, flirt outrageously, and if she drank a bit too much champagne, who would reprimand her?

As for the future, she would remain with Pyotr Maksimovich as long as it was comfortable to do so. If their feelings for each other changed, she would find someone or something else to occupy her. But she would not simply fill time until Jared found her again. Her life was her own, and she would do what she wished with it.

The foyer and drawing room of the Stoeckl mansion were crowded with elegantly attired people when they arrived. In deference to Russian custom, long tables of zakooska and vodka had been set up in the drawing room, reminding Tasha of the entertainments at Baranov Castle. In a madcap spirit she audaciously downed several small glasses of vodka along with tidbits of herring and cheese, causing several of the American women to widen their eyes in disapproval.

Smiling sweetly, she nodded to them and explained, "It's a Russian custom, you know. You should try it— it puts fire in the blood. Isn't that right, Pyotr Maksimovich?"

He nodded, then pulled her aside and whispered. "Tasha, perhaps you would do better to confine yourself to brandy or champagne. It may be a very long evening."

"Nonsense, Pyotr Maksimovich!" She tossed her head and turned back to the tables. "I am a Russian and I can handle a Russian drink!"

"Well, perhaps," he said diplomatically, then cocked

341

his head. "I hear music coming from the salon, and I believe you promised me the first dance." Weaving skillfully through the crowd, he led her away from the tables and onto the dance floor.

They had danced only a few moments when Baron Stoeckl himself tapped Stanovsky on the shoulder. Pulling the couple to the side of the dance floor, the baron apologized discreetly to Tasha, then turned to Stanovsky.

"I'm afraid business must intrude once again, Pyotr Maksimovich. A courier just arrived with a cable from the Czar. We are directed to go to Mr. Seward and proceed immediately with the plan."

"Then Czar Aleksandr sends his approval?" Pyotr asked excitedly.

Stoeckl nodded. "Under the circumstances, I think it would be wise to approach Seward immediately—this very evening."

"Agreed." Pyotr Maksimovich turned to the mystified Tasha and said apologetically, "Little did I suppose anything so momentous would intercede when I promised to spend the evening by your side. I trust you will forgive me, sweet Tasha."

She sighed. "What is it that calls you away tonight?" she pouted, trying to recall where she had heard the name Seward before.

Pyotr Maksimovich smiled. "In a few days you shall know everything. Be patient, Tasha. If I haven't returned by one in the morning, and I suspect I may not, go to the carriage and instruct the driver to take you back to the Oxford. In the meantime, try to enjoy yourself." Gently kissing her cheek, he turned and followed Stoeckl from the salon.

Scarcely had Stanovsky disappeared within the crowd when Tasha found herself swept into the arms of a young man who identified himself as a member of the French ministry in the United States. Determined to have a good time, she stared boldly and flirtatiously into his eyes until he blushed and lowered his gaze. His lowered eyes fell on her barely concealed bosom, and he quickly averted his eyes to a point across the room.

Tasha giggled. "Monsieur seems very shy tonight. I had always supposed Frenchmen to be self-possessed."

Suddenly, a large, tanned hand clapped down on the Frenchman's shoulder as a familiar voice, recognizable even after three years said, "Perhaps madame desires the company of one who is more of a man." Stunned and embarrassed, the young Frenchman stepped aside, surrendering the open-mouthed Tasha into the arms of Jared Northrup.

She had never imagined how he might look dressed for society. His black tails and maroon waistcoat were impeccable, contrasting breathtakingly with his straw blond hair. But though his clothes were elegant, his tanned face and weathered hands still spoke of hard labor in the outdoors. Looking into his blue, unreadable eyes, Tasha swallowed hard.

"Have you no greeting for me, Tasha?" he asked, breaking into a grin.

After the anguish she had suffered—first thinking him dead, then that he had deserted her—it galled her to see him looking so jaunty. "What are you doing here?" she whispered, her shaking voice betraying her emotions.

Jared frowned. "Not quite the greeting I expected, but a fair enough question, I suppose—though it seems to be one I might ask you as well." He paused to study her sophisticated make-up and the daring cut of her dress. "You seem to have changed considerably since our last meeting. I am not sure I like what I see."

She squared her shoulders, trying to still her trembling nerves. "Whether or not you approve is no concern to me!"

He cocked an eyebrow. "But I see your quick temper has not changed. Does my opinion now mean so little to you, when once you vowed to marry me?"

"You have said it, sir!" she replied curtly, surprising herself with the calm iciness of her tone. "Once we pledged ourselves to each other, but that was in a different lifetime, was it not?"

"Was it?" His eyes clouded for a moment, then became hard, sapphires glittering in his bronzed face. "And what if I were to say I have come to claim my bride?"

Tasha tossed her head defiantly, ignoring the pounding of her heart. "I would say that I am not a piece of property to be claimed by any man!"

Jared's hand tightened against her spine. "What then? Have you become a whore to be claimed by *many* men?"

She tried to pull away from him, only to feel his grip tighten. "Let go," she hissed through clenched teeth. "I will not dance with you and bear your insults any longer."

"So be it." He led her toward a side wall, holding her casually but firmly around the waist. "We need not dance if you don't wish to, but you *will* listen to me. I believe we have a great deal to discuss," he paused as his eyes roamed the crowded salon, "away from the watchful eyes and eager ears of the other guests."

"That's impossible," she laughed nervously. "I intend to enjoy the Stoeckls' hospitality for the rest of the evening. Perhaps we could make an appointment for some afternoon later this week."

He had made her wait and wonder for so long! Now she would make him do the same. Besides, she would be better equipped to deal with him after she had had time to think. She was afraid to be alone with him now, afraid her icy reserve would crumble and she would welcome him too readily, only to be abandoned again.

"No," he whispered, his voice steely with controlled anger. "We talk tonight, or I go back to New Bedford on the morning train."

Tasha gulped. After all the months of waiting and longing, could she really send him away without giving him a chance to explain?

344

"All right," she answered at length. "We can go to my hotel." Immediately, she wondered why she was offering him the intimacy of her private room. Couldn't they talk just as well in the carriage? Or did she really want something more?

"I'll order a carriage," Jared said.

"No, Pyotr Mak—" she stopped herself, not wishing to complicate matters by bringing in her relationship with Stanovsky. "That is, I have a carriage waiting."

"Very well," he nodded curtly, "then let us be on our way."

They were silent as the carriage jolted over the streets. Tasha fidgeted nervously, afraid she was wrong to take him to the hotel. What if Pyotr Maksimovich returned while they were there? Surely he would think it improper for her to entertain another man in the room they shared, no matter how innocent the purpose. He might think she had only used him as a traveling ticket to the major cities of the United States. In the end, she could lose not only Jared, but Pyotr Maksimovich as well.

The carriage stopped in front of the Hotel Oxford and Jared jumped out, turning to help Tasha to the street. Trying to ignore the electricity she felt as their hands touched, she pushed her doubts and fears to the back of her mind. She led him through the hotel lobby, up the stairs, and into her room.

Standing with his back against the closed door, Jared let his eyes scrutinize her as she moved across the room. "Despite the painted face," he said quietly, "you do look very beautiful this evening. I suppose I am just too jealous to want to share your magnificence with other men."

Unable to respond, she stared out the window, her back to him. Finally, when the silence in the room became too oppressive to bear, she spoke in a crisp, controlled voice. "What do you want, Jared? Why have you come after all these months?"

In reply, he strode across the room, grasped her shoulders, and spun her around to face him. "I want *you*, Tasha!" His eyes, now glowing with passion, penetrated hers. One finger traced the line of her collarbone, then slid down to the cleavage revealed by her gown. A hand inched beneath her dress and nestled into the hollow between her breasts.

"No, Jared!" she pulled away abruptly.

"Why?" he thundered, maintaining so fierce a hold on her bodice that she feared he might rip it. "Are these work-worn hands not good enough for the mysterious Russian princess? Am I too low-brow for you, now that you have tasted the rewards of socializing with bankers and businessmen and politicians?"

"Don't be unfair!" she protested. "I never—"

Her response was cut short as he pulled her to him and bent over her. At the touch of his lips, her resolutions melted as the memory of their full-blown passion raged through her. All thought of Pyotr Stanovsky, all anger over the long months she had mourned and waited, vanished in a second. Her lips parted hungrily, accepting his, and when she felt his fingers loosening first her gown, then her corset, she could not protest. Instead, her own hands worked feverishly to free herself of the bulky crinolines that kept her from pressing as close to him as she wanted. When gown, corset, and crinolines finally fell to the floor in a heap, he lifted her as though out from a cocoon, running his hands over her warm, tantalizing flesh.

Lowering his head, he caressed her nipples with his tongue, coaxing them to form taut, tingling peaks. Overcome with desire, she unabashedly unbuttoned his coat, waistcoat, and shirt, then deftly undid the fastenings of his trousers. The trousers dropped and he shrugged himself out of his other clothes, revealing a tanned torso and the light brown fur of his chest. Luxuriating in the feel of his flesh, Tasha pressed closer to him, catching his mouth with hers and darting her tongue nimbly between his teeth. Groaning with pleasure, he moved his hands down to grasp her buttocks, then gently lifted her and held her directly over his swelling shaft.

Tasha moaned as he entered her velvety recess. Squirming as he filled her, she wrapped her arms and legs around him and clung to his strong body. Holding her to prevent any separation of their bodies, he tenderly carried her toward the high, brass bed. Still joined, they fell upon the mattress, writhing in mutual ecstasy as they rediscovered the secrets of each other's body.

"Tasha, my love," he murmured, "say that you are still mine! Say that we shall still be wed!"

"Oh, yes Jared!" she cried. "Yes! Yes! I love you. I have always loved you. Even when I tried, I found it impossible to stop." She could speak no more as their mutual thrustings became ever more rapid and ungovernable.

After the swooning pleasure of the crisis, she continued to hold him within her until she felt him growing again with insistent desire. Sighing rapturously, she responded with enthusiasm as again they traveled together to the heights of voluptuous love.

Chapter Twenty-nine

1867

It was after midnight, and still they lay entwined, each unwilling to break the spell of love that enveloped them. Snuggling against Jared, Tasha ran her fingers through the light fur on Jared's chest. Sighing, she forced herself to ask the question that had plagued her most, though she feared it might shatter all the dreams his touch had reawakened.

"Jared?"

"What is it, love?"

"Why did you stay away from me so long?"

He sighed. "I thought I explained that in the letter I sent you in New Archangel."

Tasha tensed. "I never received any letter from you. When was it sent?"

"The moment I got back to New Bedford. Around Christmas of 1865, I guess. I wanted to send you a telegram, but the fellow at the telegraph office told me Russian America had no telegraph service. Fact is, an American firm is up there right now, trying to establish one. But you say you never got my letter?"

"No." She stifled the desire to tell him that in early 1866, when the letter would have arrived in Novo-arkhangelsk, she was in Kamchatka, married to an-other man. There would be time enough to discuss her marriage—and arrange a divorce—later. "All I knew was that the *Freedom* had been sunk by the *Shenandoah*. From all reports, I assumed you were," she stopped, embarrassed to say it, "—dead."

"Oh, my God!" Jared exclaimed. "That explains it! When you didn't respond to my letter, I imagined you no longer cared, or that your father had con-vinced you to look more favorably on someone else. Even so, I was determined to go to New Archangel and find out for myself as soon as I could earn enough money for passage."

"Wait!" Tasha interrupted. "I'm so confused. Could you start at the beginning? What happened to you after the *Freedom* was burned?"

"The entire crew was taken prisoner. As a peace-able whaler, we were in no position to defend our-selves against a raider with cannon and steam power. Most of the men were put aboard another ship, but the ship's officers were thrown into the *Shenandoah*'s hold, along with some officers they'd picked up from other whalers they'd burned. When they finished all the raids, they set us ashore on Tristan da Cunha Island, before sailing off to England to save their own hides."

"Where is this Tristan da Cunha?" Tasha asked.

"In the South Atlantic. Nearer to Africa than to

348

South America." Jared shuddered at the memory. "A more godforsaken place I've never seen! We were there for two months before a United States ship discovered us and took us back to New Bedford. By that time, six of our group, including Captain Dawson, had died."

"Oh!" Tasha gasped, remembering that Philip Vanderman had mentioned the captain had not survived. "And how did you fare during the captivity?"

"Not very well," Jared replied grimly. "Most everyone developed some sickness or other during our time in the *Shenandoah's* stinking hold. They fed us barely enough to keep us alive while we were on board, and never allowed us time for exercise. On Tristan da Cunha, we had to fend for ourselves, and none of us was fit to do much. Even after we were rescued, a long time passed before we were fully recovered. That winter in New Bedford, I didn't have the strength to hold a decent, paying job. I could barely scrape together enough money to stay alive, and there was no surplus to put aside for passage to New Archangel."

"But what about your lay from the *Freedom?*"

"I was carrying it with me all along for the time when I planned to jump ship, so it went down with the *Freedom.* Since the *Freedom* did not return, there were no profits from the final voyage, and no one collected a lay from that trip."

"And had you no family to care for you or offer you assistance?"

He shook his head. "Both my parents had died during my absence and most of their possessions had been sold to pay their medical and burial expenses.

"I've a sister, Clarissa, whom I told you about at our first meeting, but she had married at the end of the war and moved West with her new husband. They had a baby coming then, so I could hardly ask them for funds. Anyway, by the spring I was well enough to get a job in the shipyards, and I've been there ever since. For a time, I thought about shipping out again on a whaler and jumping ship for New Archangel, but there were damn few whalers left to go out after the *Shenandoah*'s raids. Besides, I wanted to take no more chances with the hazards of whaling. I figured the safest way to reach you would be as a steamer passenger."

"Then how did you end up in Washington, and at the Stoeckl home, of all places?"

"A couple of weeks ago I decided I had enough money to make the trip. I'd heard that the Russian steamer *Aleksandr II* was docked in New York, and would be leaving soon for New Archangel. I purchased some new clothes, packed my bags, and went to New York. I'd already purchased passage on the ship and was wandering along Fifth Avenue, enjoying the view, when I ran into Philip Vanderman."

"The banker?" Tasha gulped as she remembered how the red-haired young man had confirmed her suspicions that Jared was alive.

"Yes, the banker—but formerly a forecastle hand on the *Freedom*. I have to admit I wouldn't have recognized him if he hadn't hailed me first. He said it was a real coincidence to meet me since only a few months ago a woman had been asking him about me. I could hardly believe my ears when he told me the woman's name was Tasha Lisovskaya, and that she claimed I'd had an affair with one of her maids! I couldn't understand why you had lied about us, or why you had not come to me in New Bedford."

"I—I was afraid you didn't want me!" she stammered. "When Philip told me you were alive, I was so hurt and angry that you had not come to me as promised. I thought you had found someone else, and I didn't want to be hurt again."

He kissed her forehead, twirling his fingers through her hair. "Believe me, Tasha, there was no one else. Even if I wanted someone else, there was no time. I was working night and day for the chance to be reunited with you."

He fell silent. Tasha tensed apprehensively.

"But I wondered," he said wearily, "if you had not found someone else. Philip took me to his office that day. He had a stack of articles about you he had clipped from the New York newspapers. It was obvious he was a little bit in love with you. From the few clippings I could bear to read, it seemed there were others as well—the elite of New York society. At first I could not believe it was you, but then I saw the sketches and there was no doubt left in my mind."

"Please, Jared," she cut in quickly, "you must understand! It was all very innocent. I went riding with Philip and a few others, dancing sometimes, and strolling, but there was never anything more. I never allowed any of them to kiss me, and there certainly was never anything more intimate between us. In fact," she paused, embarrassed by the admission she was about to make, "had I not learned you were alive, I would never have made myself so visible. You see, I was afraid to come to you, but I hoped you would read about me in the newspapers and would come to New York to fetch me."

Jared laughed sharply. "I had no time for reading society pages. By the time I finished my work each day, I could barely drag myself to bed."

Again he was silent, then he sighed and said quietly, "All right, I believe all you've told me just now. But what about this Pyotr Stanovsky?"

She caught her breath, hesitating. How much did Jared know without asking? "He is an emissary of the Czar. I met him on the way to San Francisco with my father. Since we parted from my father in San Francisco, he has been my—traveling companion."

"And your lover?" The words sounded hollow.

"What makes you ask that?" her voice trembled.

"I can read between the lines, Tasha. A woman does not travel halfway around the world with a man unless there is more than friendship between them."

She sighed heavily. "How can I make you understand? Put yourself in my place, Jared. When I met Pyotr Maksimovich, I thought you were dead. I had

351

no reason to continue living myself. I needed solace."

"And Stanovsky gave you what you needed? Was he a replacement for me, Tasha?" There was an edge of bitterness in Jared's tone.

"No, of course not! You misunderstand, Jared. He was—very kind to me. But he could do nothing to heal the hollowness I felt without you."

"Do you love him?" The bluntness of his question startled her, but she did not have to think before replying.

"No. And I do not think he loves me. We are fond of one another. As I said, he has been very kind. But you are the only person I love, Jared, or ever shall love."

He pulled her close to him, lightly stroking her back. "That's all I wanted to hear. How I feared on the train ride from New York that you wouldn't be able to say that; that I would never have the joy of holding you again."

She snuggled against him. "You still haven't told me how you came to be at the Stoeckls' reception."

"Philip told me that you had gone to Washington, in the company of Stanovsky. At first, I was tempted to return to New Bedford and try to forget about you. But, knowing you were so close, I just had to seek you out. My sister had attended school with the younger sister of Eliza Howard. In fact, she spent several holidays at the Howard home in Springfield, and often spoke about Eliza and her handsome husband, the Russian minister, Baron Stoeckl. Remembering all this on the train, I decided to seek out the Stoeckls, hoping they might be able to give me some clue to your whereabouts.

"I arrived this afternoon and took the horse-drawn streetcar directly to their mansion in Georgetown. Eliza received me very graciously, and when I asked about you, she said you would be attending a reception at their mansion this evening. She immediately invited me to attend as well, and, in fact, extended me the courtesy of one of their guest rooms, saying it was unthinkable that I should have to travel back into the city, and then retrace my path to their home in the evening."

"Then you are actually staying with the Stoeckls?"

"Exactly. But you have yet to tell me your story. How did you end up in New York, and now in Washington?"

She rolled away from him, careful to hold her voice steady. "There is little to tell. Certainly nothing so sensational as being sunk and captured by a Confederate raider! Between us, I think we've enough sunken ships for several lifetimes!" She laughed nervously, trying to decide how to begin her story.

"I first learned of the *Shenandoah*'s raids when a whaler called the *Arctic Princess* docked in Novoarkhangelsk."

"The *Arctic Princess*," Jared repeated. "I believe we had a gam with her shortly before the raid."

"You did," she replied. "A mate named James Sanders was kind enough to talk with me. He told me the *Freedom* had been burned and it was believed there were no survivors. He also said some very comforting things about you and how you had told him about me, but I was crushed, thinking you were dead."

She paused, then, quickly deciding to postpone any mention of her marriage, continued. "Last summer, papa went to San Francisco to conduct some business with the American-Russian Commercial Company. Having nothing better to do, I joined him on the trip. On the ship to San Francisco, we met Pyotr Stanovsky, who introduced himself as an emissary of Czar Aleksandr. He asked me to accompany him to New York, where he was bound on the Czar's business.

"I had been so unhappy since hearing of your presumed death, I decided to accept his invitation, simply as a diversion. We spent several months in New York, and only this month traveled to Washington.

353

"After Philip told me you were alive, I did toy with the idea of traveling to New Bedford, but I guess I was too proud." Perhaps, she thought ruefully, if Yuri had not so embittered me, I might have behaved differently.

Jared chuckled. "It's a good thing my pride is not quite so strong as yours! I imagine your presence has been a great asset to Stanovsky's work."

"Not at all. In fact, he refuses to discuss his work with me. He says the Czar's business must be conducted in the strictest confidence."

"Then you know nothing of why he is in Washington?" Jared sounded incredulous.

"Nothing. Why, do you?"

Jared cleared his throat and looked serious. "Yes, I believe I do. But, under the circumstances, I hesitate to reveal the matter to you."

"You've aroused my curiosity, Jared, so you must come out with it! Whatever it is cannot be so bad. I can't believe Pyotr Maksimovich would be involved in anything sinister—though your tone seems to suggest he is."

"You may alter that opinion when you hear what I have to say. I believe Stanovsky is here to aid Baron Stoeckl in negotiating the sale of Russian America to the United States."

Tasha sat upright, clapping her hands to her head. "No, that's impossible! I don't believe it! Pyotr Maksimovich himself assured me that—" She broke off, thinking of her conversation with Stanovsky in New York several months earlier. He had not exactly assured her of anything in so many words; rather, he had let her believe what she wished, without giving her a precise answer. But it was unthinkable to imagine he would have deceived her!

Sensing her turmoil, Jared sat up behind her. Sliding his arms over her shoulders, he pulled her back against the comforting warmth of his chest. She leaned against him silently for several minutes before turning her head toward him.

354

"What evidence do you have of this matter?" she asked quietly.

"I overheard some conversations today between the baron and some of his aides. He said he was awaiting final clearance from the Czar—that he expected a cable any day. Then, tonight, I was coming downstairs when a courier, in fact, arrived. I surmised from the baron's subsequent excitement that it was the message for which he had been waiting. Did he and Stanovsky say where they were going?"

"Yes, to see a Mr. Seward." Suddenly, she remembered where she had heard the name before. Her young dance partner in New York had referred to a diplomat named Seward as the only man in the United States who seemed to favor the purchase.

"That pretty well confirms what I've been saying," Jared said. "William Seward would be the man to see about drawing up the treaty of purchase."

"So you think the sale will really be made?"

"I've no doubt but that they're drawing up the treaty right now."

"In the middle of the night? Wouldn't they wait until morning to pursue such an important step?"

"Not if they are as anxious as my observations led me to believe. In fact, we passed the Department of State on our way here from the Stoeckls' and the place was ablaze with lights—rather odd at this hour of night, unless official business is being conducted."

"Then we must go there at once!" Tasha exclaimed. "Perhaps we can still stop them from signing."

Jared laughed. "Do you really think an emotional woman and an ex-whaleman from New Bedford can alter a course set by emperors and politicians? Be sensible, Tasha. There's nothing either of us can do at this point."

"I can't believe Czar Aleksandr would do this to his subjects," she exclaimed. "Everyone in Russian America believes the colony has his continuing support. Only a few years ago, Prince Maksutov assured us we would continue to prosper for many years. Oh, how could Pyotr Maksimovich have deceived me so! I swear, if I had guessed his purpose, I would have found a way to murder him!"

She rose from the bed and began to pace the floor, oblivious to her nakedness. "I don't understand, Jared. How can they secretly sign a treaty when so many people on both sides oppose it? I thought the United States was a democracy. If the citizens disapprove of the purchase, can one man's signature on the treaty make it valid?"

Sliding out of bed, he stopped her pacing by taking her in his arms. "The signing won't be the end of it," he soothed. "The United States Senate must approve the treaty before it is accepted, and the House of Representatives must vote to provide the funds for the purchase. Despite all the secret negotiations, Russia may retain the colony in the end."

"No!" she sobbed. "If the Czar is determined to sell, he will find another buyer."

"Then let us hope the United States Congress approves the purchase. Tasha, if you love the land so much, it will not matter which nation governs it. After our wedding, you will be as much an American citizen as I am, and we will be free to live in any United States possession we care to. We can still return to New Archangel, if that is what you want."

She shook her head helplessly. "It's not myself I'm concerned about, Jared, it's papa. He's given the ablest years of his life to the colony, and I've no doubt he expected to grow old there. The news will crush him. His work is all he has. If what you say is true, I must get back to him at once to comfort him and help him through this difficult time."

"Don't fret, my love," Jared tenderly kissed her neck. "I will take you home to him. If we leave immediately, we might still make the sailing of the *Aleksandr II*. Pack your things now and we'll be on our way."

She hesitated, pulling away from him and walking to the window. Staring into the deserted street, she whispered, "I can't leave yet, Jared. I don't know if you can understand, but I must stay and speak to Pyotr Maksimovich one more time. In my heart and in my mind, I know that you would not lie to me about his helping to sell Russian America. Yet, I cannot fully accept his deception. I must hear it from his own lips, and have the opportunity to tell him what I think of his deeds."

Turning back to Jared, she asked, "Can you understand how I feel?"

He shrugged. "Not really. But then, I have not just learned that my home was being sold without my consent. I suppose you must feel a bit as I did, watching the *Freedom* go down in flames. I'll wait with you then, and help you face Stanovsky."

"No!" She shook her head adamantly. "Having you here would becloud the issue. He would think I was disturbed about a man, instead of about the colony. I must talk to him alone. But you needn't worry —no matter what he says, when our conversation is done, I will leave with you. I never want to be separated from you again, Jared."

"Nor I from you, Tasha my love." He crossed the room, folded her in his arms, and gave her a lingering kiss. Reluctantly pulling away, he looked down on her. "I'll go and collect my things from the Stoeckl mansion. From there, I'll go directly to the train station. Can you meet me there?"

Tasha nodded. "I'll hire a carriage if necessary, but I shan't have much to carry. Only, I hardly know when to say I'll arrive. It's already early morning, and I've no idea when Pyotr Maksimovich will return."

"Don't worry, whatever the hour, I will be waiting."

Lightly kissing her again, he turned and walked toward the door. Halfway across the room, he turned and asked, "You're sure you will be all right? I mean, Stanovsky won't become violent or behave badly when you confront him with the evidence, or when you tell him you're leaving?"

"No. I'm sure we've nothing to worry about. He

won't try to stop me. And even if he tried, he couldn't. I will meet you at the train station without fail." She smiled reassuringly as he opened the door and stepped into the hallway.

Returning her smile, Jared called, "Hurry, my love. I've already suffered enough separations to last me a lifetime."

Chapter Thirty

1867

Alone in the room, Tasha paced nervously. Jared had been gone more than four hours, and still there was no sign of Pyotr Maksimovich. As each minute passed, she became more and more anxious to put the confrontation behind her. It seemed unthinkable that Czar Aleksandr would sell the land she and more than a thousand other Russians had come to love. And, try as she might, it was impossible for her to accept Pyotr Maksimovich's role in the wretched scheme. After visiting the colony and seeing how happy the people were . . . how hard they worked; after sharing so much time with her father . . . after living with her . . . how could he conspire to rob them of their home? Was it possible that all the time they were in New York together, he had actually been working toward that sale, while allowing her to think that the talk of selling the colony was only idle rumor?

No! No! she told herself over and over again. Pyotr Maksimovich was too thoughtful, too considerate, to have been party to such deception. But surely Jared had no reason to lie to her. He had no reason to turn her against Pyotr Maksimovich after she had already assured him he was the only love in her life.

Besides, all the evidence confirmed Jared's report. Why had Pyotr Maksimovich steadfastly refused to discuss his work with her? Where was he that he had been kept occupied the entire night? Would less momentous dealings have torn him and Baron Stoeckl away from the reception?

With a sinking heart, she remembered a conversation with Eliza Stoeckl soon after meeting her. Eliza had said that only the previous fall her husband had been appointed to a prestigious position at the Hague. They had returned to Europe, and been there several months, when the Czar personally requested that Baron Stoeckl sail back to the United States. Surely nothing but the most pressing business—such as the sale of Russian America—could have precipitated such a request.

Finally, she worried about whether the news of the sale would reach her father before she could reach him, and whether Pyotr Maksimovich's role in the negotiations would be publicized. Would her father suppose that she had known of Pyotr's involvement all along; perhaps even think she had aided him? The fear that her father might think she betrayed him sickened Tasha, making her all the more angry with Pyotr Maksimovich.

Taking an old portmanteau, the one she had carried from Kamchatka, from the wardrobe, Tasha began to stuff her belongings inside. One by one, she took out the dresses she had bought in New York and lay them across the bed.

Suddenly the idea of wearing anything purchased with Pyotr Maksimovich's money, the Czar's money, nauseated her. With one excessive movement, she swept all of the dresses onto the floor. Crinolines, corsets, and other undergarments followed, along with the cape she had purchased to wear over her finery.

Taking grim pleasure in trampling on the costly clothes, Tasha took out the few gowns, nightclothes, and undergarments she had brought with her from Kamchatka. They would serve well enough for her travels with Jared, and her reunion with her father.

No doubt both men, though for different reasons, would prefer not to see her dressed in clothes that reminded them of the Czar's emissary.

She was about to add Pyotr's pearls and a few other pieces of jewelry to the pile of discards, when she had second thoughts, and tucked them into her portmanteau instead. She could sell them to pay her way home and buy whatever else they might need; from what Jared had said, he had barely enough money to pay his own passage.

Jared! Just thinking of him again, knowing he was completely hers, warmed every inch of her. Thinking of their relaxed intimacy, she wondered how she could ever have doubted his love. Knowing how he had struggled faithfully toward their reunion, she felt ashamed of the outrage she had felt when she learned he was alive. If only his letter could have reached her! Of course, by then she had already married Yuri Zarevsky. Still, she wondered why the letter had never been delivered to her. Could someone have intentionally intercepted it?

Her wonderings were cut short as the door opened and Pyotr Maksimovich Stanovsky, looking tired but pleased with himself, entered the room. Tasha stared at him, her eyes smoldering with anger as his eyes surveyed the room, widening in surprise as they took in the disarray.

"Has there been an intruder?" he asked, striding to her side and placing his hands lightly on her shoulders. He gazed at her in concern. "Are you hurt, Tasha?"

"Yes," she whispered bitterly, "I have been robbed and I am hurt! I and hundreds of others who trusted Czar Aleksandr and those who do his bidding!"

His green eyes looked away. "You speak in riddles, Tasha. I'm too tired this morning to try to understand."

He started to move away, but she caught his hands and held them before her. Her voice shook as she stared at them in contempt. "What, is there no blood?

Or did you wash your hands after receiving the blood money?"

Pyotr Maksimovich snatched his hands away. "I don't know what you're talking about, Tasha! You'll have to speak more clearly if you expect me to understand."

"All right!" her voice rose shrilly. "Is this clear enough for you—you've sold us, haven't you? You've sold Russian America to the United States!"

Embarrassed, he clapped a hand over her mouth. "Tasha, I beg you, control yourself! You'll be waking everyone in the hotel. No one has been sold! You sound as if the Czar considered his citizens his slaves, allowing them to change hands without so much as asking their consent. I repeat, no one has been sold."

She wrenched her face away from his hand. "Pyotr, I am in no mood to argue semantics. Do you deny the colony has been sold?"

"Well," he shifted uncomfortably, "the sale is far from complete. In this country such an act requires the approval of—"

"But," she cut him off abruptly, "there was a treaty signed during the night, was there not?"

"What makes you think so?"

"That hardly matters. Just answer me, Pyotr Maksimovich!"

He sat down wearily on the edge of the bed. "Yes, Baron Stoeckl and William Seward signed the treaty at 4 A.M."

Tasha's voice softened and her eyes filled with hurt as he confirmed her worst fears. "Why did you lie to me, Pyotr Maksimovich? When I talked to you in New York, you insisted there was no thought of a sale."

"I did not lie to you, Tasha!" His own voice sounded hurt. "Everything I told you in New York was true. I allowed you to draw your own conclusions."

"But you did not tell me all of the truth! You can't deny that you kept the most important facts from me! That you deceived me!"

Pyotr Maksimovich shrugged. "Perhaps I did deceive you. But I valued your company, and I knew how the whole situation would upset you. After our discussion in New York, I guarded the secret more closely than ever, fearing you would leave me."

"But didn't it occur to you that I would have to find out in the end?"

"I tried to put off thinking about that. At any rate, until tonight there was still some doubt as to whether the Czar would go ahead with the plan, and also whether the United States could be persuaded to agree."

"And now there are no more doubts?"

"Very few," he said quietly. "The baron and I have been authorized to spend several tens of thousands of dollars to insure the treaty's acceptance by Congress. I am already in touch with several newspaper publishers, both here and in New York. In return for substantial payment, they will campaign for approval. In addition, I understand an influential Congressman, Mr. Walker, is in need of funds and might be induced to support the sale."

Tasha listened, aghast. "You mean you would resort to bribery, to force something that neither the Russian nor American people want?"

"I do as I am ordered," he said defensively. "It is my duty to the Czar." Clutching her hand, he looked up to her with pleading eyes. "You mustn't think too harshly of me or Baron Stoeckl, Tasha. We are merely pawns in the hands of Czar Aleksandr."

"But why is he so anxious to be rid of the colony?"

"Czar Aleksandr himself did not feel particularly strongly about the matter. It was his brother, Grand Duke Constantine, who convinced him the colony was a millstone around the neck of an otherwise healthy empire."

"That is preposterous! What logic could Constantine have used to convince the Czar?"

Pyotr Maksimovich sighed. "The reasons were many, and I am too tired to enumerate them, but

362

briefly, the colony was not providing enough income. Russian America is too far away to be governed and defended efficiently. It seems wiser to limit the Empire to Europe and Asia. Besides, at the rate the United States has been expanding, it is evident they will soon govern all of North America. Surely even you can see it would be better for the Czar to sell the colony and receive something in return, than be forced to surrender it and lose the friendship of a rising world power."

"I can see nothing of the sort!" Tasha snapped. "The only fact evident to me is that you and the others involved in this plot have become so enamored of your own fine logic that not one of you has bothered to consider the feelings of the people most affected by the sale. Tell me honestly, has anyone so much as mentioned the people who live in Russian America?"

"Yes, indeed. In fact, one of Grand Duke Constantine's strongest points was that the company has used and mistreated the Aleuts and the Indians in a way ill-befitting a Christian nation."

"That's a lie!" she fumed. "The company has given them most of what they own. It has established strict conservation policies so the Aleuts can make a living from fur-trapping for many years to come. It has all but eradicated disease in the islands—with the exception of syphilis, which was spread by the Americans—and it brought them the true light of Orthodoxy. Does the Czar intend to abandon all those souls who depend on Russian benevolence?"

"Tasha, Tasha," Pyotr said soothingly, "you mustn't be so emotional. Perhaps Constantine's judgments are not all correct, but I suspect your heart is too much a part of the colony to allow your mind to see things clearly. No one is being abandoned. The Americans will take care of the natives."

"And who will take care of the Russians? What is to become of people like my father?"

"As a good Russian citizen, he will of course be welcomed back to the Empire."

"But what if he doesn't want to go back to the Empire? His home is there in Russian America! Why should he be uprooted at this time of his life?"

Turning away, Pyotr Maksimovich began to undress. He dropped his coat and waistcoat on the bed, then bent to pull off his shoes. "I can see that this conversation is at an impasse. You will not relent, and I cannot. There is little more I can say by way of explanation, so I think I shall just go to bed. After you've had time to think, perhaps you will be able to accept the inevitable."

Removing his shirt, he pulled back the covers on the bed, the bed where she had lain with Jared only hours before, and stretched out. Patting the mattress beside him, he smiled weakly. "Will you join me and help me find the sanctity of sleep?"

"No," she replied crisply. "I shan't join you, now or ever again. If you can sleep with the fate of Russian America on your conscience, you are not half the man I thought you to be!"

"Tasha, please," he closed his eyes tightly, as if hoping to close out her accusations. "I'm too weary for further argument."

"You needn't worry that I shall plague you any longer!" She picked up her portmanteau and started for the door. "As for myself, I pray to God I shall never have to see you again! Goodbye, Pyotr Maksimovich!"

His eyes flew open as her words penetrated. "Tasha, wait!" He looked lamely at the heaps of clothing scattered pell-mell around the room. "Won't you even take a moment to pack your gowns?"

"Give them to the next woman who is fool enough to become your mistress!"

"No. If you must go, I insist you take your clothing. I couldn't bear to see another woman wearing them." He hesitated as he rose from the bed and took a step toward her. "Still, I wish you would reconsider. By now, you know I am not one to beg, but I admit I shall be very unhappy without you."

His eyes clouded over and for a moment, Tasha wavered. After all the months they had shared together, she could take leave of Pyotr Maksimovich a bit more kindly. Then she thought again of her father and all the others in Novoarkhangelsk, who had been betrayed during the night, and the bitterness returned.

"Even if you did beg, I wouldn't stay!" she said, opening the door with a determined toss of her head. "As for the dresses, you can sell them. Perhaps you will find you need more money for your filthy bribes!" She slammed the door behind her and ran breathlessly to the stairway.

It was less than an hour since dawn, and, fortunately, the hotel lobby was still deserted. Stepping out into the street, Tasha decided to walk the three blocks to Pennsylvania Avenue, where she could catch a streetcar to the train station. The streets were still uncrowded, and it felt good to inhale the crisp spring air. Looking around her, Tasha again saw Washington as a dirty, unpleasant city. She was glad to be leaving this place, where a people and their homeland could be bargained for as easily as for a sack of grain.

Despite the early hour, the train station was milling with people. Standing on tiptoe, Tasha craned her neck in search of Jared. Feeling someone try to grab her portmanteau from her, she jerked it back and held it more tightly, still scanning the crowd for some sight of Jared's blond head.

"Pardon me, ma'am," a familiar voice chuckled. "I only thought a pretty lady like you shouldn't have to carry her own bag."

She spun around to meet Jared's laughing blue eyes. Oblivious to onlookers, she dropped the portmanteau and threw her arms around him. "Oh, Jared! You startled me," she laughed self-consciously as she buried her face against his neck. "I was afraid I wouldn't be able to find you."

"And I was beginning to think you'd never get here." He gently untwined her arms from him and bent to pick up her bag, carrying his own portmanteau in his other hand. "Come on, we'll have plenty of time for hugging and kissing later. The train to New York leaves in ten minutes. It's already in the station."

"Do you have tickets?" she asked, quick-stepping to keep pace with his long stride.

He nodded and steered her toward the waiting train.

They had hardly settled themselves in the dusty coach car when the train began to jostle its way out of the station. Jared slid his arm around her and smiled as she dropped her head against his shoulder.

"Glad to be going home?" he whispered.

Tasha nodded, tears of joy filling her eyes. "To be going home with you, Jared."

Nestled against him, fatigue overcame her and she closed her eyes, lulled by the rhythmic clacking of the train and the reassuring beat of Jared's heart beneath her ear.

For the moment, she could close out thoughts of other people and forget about the implications of the sale of Russian America. She had been reunited with Jared, and as long as he was with her, no matter where that might be she would always feel at home.

PART FOUR
1867

Chapter Thirty-one
1867

Tasha and Jared reached New York late in the evening. They rushed directly to the South Street docks, hoping to board the *Aleksandr II*, but they were crushed to learn it had left early that very morning. To Jared's inquiries, the harbormaster replied that he knew of no other ship scheduled to leave for Russian America within the month.

"You might try booking passage to San Francisco and see what you can find from there," the man suggested. "I believe the *Mary Elizabeth* will be shipping out for Frisco in about two weeks."

Tasha shook her head emphatically. "We can't wait that long. With the travel time added on, it might then be almost three months before we'd reach Novoarkhangelsk. By that time, Papa would be sure to have heard the news already. Isn't there any better way, Jared?"

"Nothing better that I know of. We could go transcontinental, but it would be more dangerous and probably take even longer. The railroad's not nearly completed, so we'd have to go through some pretty rough, hostile country by coach or horseback. I think we'd be better off waiting for a ship."

"Say," the harbormaster cut in, "did you ever think of going to Panama?"

"Then what?" Tasha asked hopefully.

"Take a train across the isthmus and catch a ship

367

north. Could save you a heap of time if you make good connections."

"What do you think, Jared?" her voice took on a pleading tone.

"I don't know." He looked at the harbormaster. "Is there a ship leaving for Panama soon?"

"Yes sir, the *Tropical Queen,* right over there." The man pointed to a steamer docked a short distance away. "Leaves day after tomorrow."

"And you're sure it's a safe route?"

"Absolutely. Take you about eight days to get down to Colon, and from there you can take a train right across to Panama City."

"All right." Jared shrugged dubiously. "Thanks for the information. I'll check with the *Tropical Queen* about passage in the morning. Good night."

He led Tasha away, hailed a carriage, and directed the driver to Broadway near Wall Street, where the City Hotel stood.

The hotel desk clerk, a pale, spindly man wearing rimless spectacles, studied them carefully as they approached the desk. His expression grew puzzled as Jared asked for a room for Mister and Mrs. Jared Northrup, but he silently handed Jared a key and directed him to sign the register. Jared and Tasha were about to go up to their room, when a light of recognition spread over the clerk's face.

"I knew you looked familiar," he exclaimed, staring at Tasha, "and now I remember where I've seen you before. You're the Russian girl, Tasha Lis—something like that, aren't you?"

Tasha stared at him, sure she had never met him. "I—"

"Of course you are!" the man continued excitedly. "Your picture was plastered all over the New York newspapers up until a few weeks ago. But I thought you were traveling with a Russian gentleman."

"The lady is my wife," Jared cut in coldly. "If you wish to address her at all, you will call her Mrs. Northrup, is that clear?"

368

Shrinking back from Jared's towering form, the man nodded. "Yes, sir, as you wish." But he could not resist letting his eyes sweep to Tasha's left hand, bereft of the usual wedding band. He smiled knowingly, "Good night, Mrs. Northrup."

With a dark scowl, Jared turned away from the man and led Tasha upstairs to the room. Shaking his head, he closed the door. "I'm sorry to have put you through that scene. Perhaps I should have booked separate rooms."

"Nonsense," Tasha began gaily, "Pyotr Maksimovich always—" she stopped, embarrassed at her carelessness. "I mean, I'm accustomed to the snide looks and low manners of hotel clerks. And I would be most uncomfortable to stay in a room without you. Besides, it hardly matters what anyone says, since we'll be leaving New York in a few days."

"I suppose you're right, but it hurts me to see you treated like some common woman off the streets. It makes me all the more anxious to marry you."

Turning her head away, Tasha frowned. She would have to tell him about her marriage to Yuri Zarevsky soon—but not tonight. Not on their first night alone together. "You mustn't worry too much about it, Jared," she murmured, unfastening her bodice and moving toward him with outstretched arms. "In our hearts, we both know we belong to one another. That is marriage enough for the present."

Smiling seductively, she looped her arms around his neck and pulled herself against him. Before he could say anything else, she had caught his mouth with hers, and in a very short time, both of their bodies were begging for release.

Later, as Jared slept calmly beside her, Tasha lay awake, wondering when to tell him about Yuri. She felt guilty keeping the fact from him, but it was too soon to risk the happiness they had rediscovered with one another. She knew he had been hurt by her affair with Stanovsky, and even by her innocent flirtations with the young men of New York. Though he had readily forgiven her those indiscretions, she feared that news of her marriage might be too much for him to bear.

She needed a few days to cement their relationship and heal his wounds. Then she would explain everything to him, calmly and gently, assuring him that she intended to divorce Yuri the moment they reached Novoarkhangelsk. Surely, Jared would be able to understand, and he would forgive her.

Jared rose early the next morning, slipping out of bed and dressing quietly while Tasha slept. Watching her breathing calmly, her dark lashes contrasting against her ivory cheeks, her black hair a gossamer veil spread across the pillow, he smiled happily. Now he could forget all the hardships he had suffered for the chance of finding her again. He could forgive her the impulsive decision to travel with Stanovsky. It had, after all, brought them together two months sooner than if he had had to travel all the way to New Archangel.

Seeing her in the Stoeckls' salon, in her high-fashion gown and painted face, he had worried that she was not the same Tasha with whom he had fallen in love. She had been haughty, aloof, even bitter at first. But the girl now before him had the same innocent beauty he had so loved from the time he first carried her aboard the *Freedom*. Of course, she had grown up in the years since their first meeting—and she had suffered all the pain and disillusionment that were part of growing up. But, she had remained the same warm, honest, receptive person he had been dreaming of for the past three years.

He walked to the window and moved aside the curtain to look out on Broadway. The city was awakening, and carriages and wagons were beginning to clog the cobbled street. The sun bounced off the spire of nearby Trinity Church, promising a warm spring day.

Behind him, Tasha stirred in bed. "Jared," she said sleepily, "are you going out already?"

"Soon, love," he replied, turning to smile at her. "I thought I'd get our ship reservations made early, so we can have the rest of the day to relax."

"Oh, then I'd better get up and get ready. You should have awakened me." She sat up and stretched.

"I wanted to let you sleep. Stay in bed and rest another hour or so. I can book our passage myself, and then come back for you."

She considered the proposition a moment before flopping down against the pillows. "Well, I am rather tired. Are you sure you wouldn't mind? Wait, I almost forgot. There's a pearl necklace in my bag you can sell to pay for my passage."

"All right." He turned back to the window, staring at Trinity's spire while an idea formed in his mind. "You should sleep late," he murmured, "for today shall be your wedding day."

Tasha felt her throat constrict painfully. He couldn't mean it!

What on earth would she do? Silence hung heavily in the room, until Jared asked in a concerned voice, "Tasha, did you hear me?"

"Yes." She could choke out no more than that word.

Slowly he turned to face her, frowning in consternation. "But the idea doesn't please you?"

"I—" she groped helplessly for words. "It's so sudden, Jared. I wonder if there's time."

"Of course there's time. After I book passage, we've the whole day with nothing else to do. And the night to celebrate."

"But it's too soon," she whispered lamely. "It would be better to wait."

"Good lord, girl, we've waited three years! How much more time has to pass?" He stopped and cocked his head questioningly. "Surely, you're not still worried about getting your father's consent. I doubt that he gave it when you ran off with Stanovsky. But if that's what's troubling you, I'm willing to wager he'd prefer we travel together as husband and wife than as lover and mistress."

371

Tasha turned her face away, unable to meet his eyes. "No," she said thickly, "that's not it."

"You do still want to marry me, don't you?"

"More than anything in the world! But—I can't, just yet."

"Why?" He sat down on the edge of the bed and, taking her chin in his hand, gently turned her face toward him. "Is it because you fear you might be carrying Stanovsky's child?"

She was silent, dropping her lids over her eyes rather than face his searching gaze.

"Tasha, if that's it, I swear it doesn't matter! I'll gladly raise the child as my own, just knowing it is yours."

Still she remained silent, unable to speak, as a hot tear coursed down her cheek. She felt Jared's finger gently brush the tear away.

"Tasha," his voice was strained, "tell me, is my guess right or wrong?"

She shook her head.

"Then tell me why we can't be married now. You must admit, I have a right to know."

With an effort, she forced herself to meet his gaze.

In the dark depths of her eyes he read confusion and love and earnest pleading, and then, at last, with shocked horror he read the truth.

"Oh, no!" he breathed, dropping his hand from her chin and standing up abruptly. "It can't be! You couldn't have! Why, Tasha?" Feeling a stabbing pain in his chest, he turned away from her.

"I thought you were dead," she whispered. Somehow, with him standing before her, the reason seemed lame and unworthy.

"You thought I was dead!" his voice rose and he whirled to face her again, his hurt giving way to anger. "You thought I was dead! My God, woman, is that to be your excuse for every sin you've committed since I left you in New Archangel?"

"I was numb," she sobbed, tears streaming freely down her face. "I didn't know what I was doing! My

372

father favored the man and with you gone I knew I could not please myself, so I thought at least to please papa."

Jared struggled to bring his voice under control. "When were you wed?"

"Late June of 1865."

He threw up his hands in disgust. "The embers of the *Freedom* had scarcely cooled and already you were rushing to the altar with another man! You expect me to believe in your love for me?"

"Yes!" she cried. "If I didn't love you so much I wouldn't have been so distraught—I would never otherwise have agreed to marry Yuri."

"I suppose next you'll be telling me you already have a child or two!"

With a wrench, she recalled her first night aboard the *Svoboda*, when she had lost Yuri's child. "No," she said quietly, "we have no children."

"And where is this husband of yours now? Can I expect him to materialize at any moment?"

Tasha shrugged. "When last I saw him he was bound for St. Petersburg. By now he may be back in Petropavlovsk, where we lived, or the company may have transferred him elsewhere."

"You seem very little concerned about him."

"I am not at all concerned. I despise the man! I hope never to see him again!"

Jared went to the window and stared out silently for several minutes. When he finally spoke, his voice was strained and he did not turn to face her. "Why did you keep this from me, Tasha? Why didn't you tell me in Washington?"

"I was afraid you would be hurt and angry, just as you are now. I was afraid you would leave me without giving me a chance to explain."

"What is there to explain? You are married to another man! Do you expect me to stay with you as your lover while your life belongs to someone else? I don't want that kind of arrangement, Tasha! If that's what I wanted, I could have remained a whaleman and had a different woman at every port. But for three years I've dreamed of having you as my wife! How could you rob me of that dream?"

"I haven't robbed you of anything, Jared! You shall have me as your wife, if you will only be patient. I intend to divorce Yuri Zarevsky as soon as I return to Novoarkhangelsk."

"So you offer me yourself as another man's cast-off, is that it? Well, I'm not sure I want to accept you under those conditions!"

Ignoring her renewed sobs, he strode to the door, slamming it as he stomped into the hall.

For an hour after Jared left, Tasha tried to convince herself that he would be back after his resentment and hurt had worn away. He had planned to go to the South Street docks before their discussion began; no doubt he was there now, booking passage for both of them. In his hurry to leave, he had forgotten to take her pearls, but since he would have to pay the *Tropical Queen* for passage only as far as Panama, he probably had enough cash of his own.

Perhaps she could run down to the docks to look for him, to reassure him of her love. No, it would be better to remain at the hotel and wait. Besides, he needed time to think things out. Eventually, he would come back to the hotel. After all, he'd left all his belongings there.

To keep from becoming morbid, she occupied herself with trivial activities, washing herself at the nightstand, carefully dressing in a blue and white gingham dress, and brushing out her hair. Hesitant to go to the dining room, for fear of missing Jared, she ignored her growing hunger.

The morning stretched into afternoon and still Jared did not return. When the sun began to fade from the sky, Tasha worried that he did not intend to come back for her at all. She might sit up all night waiting while he wandered around the city, or made his way

374

back to New Bedford. If he was angry enough, he probably wouldn't bother returning for his clothes. Even while she fretted, the *Tropical Queen* might be preparing to sail without her; she could miss her trip to her father and lose her beloved all in the same day.

No, Tasha decided firmly, jumping from the bed where she had been sitting in dejection. If it was within her power, she would neither miss the sailing nor lose Jared. She had waited long enough. Now she would go out and find him.

Hurriedly she threw her belongings into her portmanteau and repacked the few pieces of Jared's clothing he had strewn around the room into his portmanteau. Clutching her cloak around her, she picked up both bags and raced out of the hotel.

Twilight enveloped the city, making Tasha feel vulnerable to the criminals she imagined lurked in the streets, searching for unescorted women. Quickly she hailed a carriage and directed it to the South Street docks. Not knowing where else to begin her search, she hoped that someone aboard the *Tropical Queen* might be able to tell her if Jared had been there. When they reached the docks, she called to the driver to stop, and got out of the carriage.

The dock area was crowded with cargo waiting to be loaded, and passengers preparing to board for the ship's early morning sailing. Tasha pushed her way through the people and onto the ship, where she asked to see the purser. One of the crew led her to a small, cluttered office where a middle-aged man sat hunched over a stack of documents.

The man frowned as he saw Tasha approach. "Well, what is it?" he demanded brusquely, instantly turning his attention to his papers again.

"I was wondering, sir," Tasha began hesitantly, "if a man came today to book passage for Mr. and Mrs. Jared Northrup."

"And who might you be, that I should give you such information?"

"Mrs. Northrup," Tasha said quickly.

"Hmph," the purser snorted. "Do you mean to tell me you don't know whether or not your husband booked passage?"

"I—that is we—we were separated in the crowds during the day. It's our first visit to New York, you see. After wandering around all day looking for my husband, I thought I'd best check the ships."

The purser snorted again and eyed her dubiously. "Very well," he sighed and turned to his list of passengers. "Northrup, you say?" He ran his finger down the list. "Yep, here it is. Northrup, Jared." He scowled at the list before looking back at Tasha. "You sure he didn't try to lose you on purpose? There's no missus listed here. Fact is, he's assigned to share a third class cabin with three other men."

Tasha's head swam. It didn't make sense. If Jared wanted to leave her for good, he wouldn't ship out to Panama! Surely he would go somewhere else, where she would be less likely to find him.

"Sorry to disappoint you," the purser said sharply. "Now, if you don't mind, I've got work to attend to."

Backing toward the door, Tasha had a sudden idea and blurted, "Could you see if you've a reservation for Tasha Lisovskaya?"

The purser shook his head irritably. "Look, lady, I make it a point not to get involved in family squabbles. If you want to check up on your husband's mistress, you'll have to find some other way of doing it."

"Mistress, you say? *I* am Tasha Lisovskaya."

"I thought you told me you were Mrs. Jared Northrup."

"I am. I mean, I thought—" she flushed under the purser's scrutiny. "Could you just check, please?"

With an exasperated sigh, he turned again to the passenger list. "Nope. No Tasha Lisovskaya." His voice took on a taunting edge. "You got any more names you want me to check before I call someone to escort you off this ship?"

Her mind raced. Jared had only heard the name

once, but it was worth a try. "Yes, thank you. Perhaps Tasha Zarevskaya," she whispered timidly.

"Zarevskaya." He flipped to the back of the passenger list and his finger stopped as he looked up in surprise. "Yeah, I've got a Tasha Zarevskaya. A private cabin in first class. Now I suppose you're going to tell me your name is Zarevskaya, too."

Tasha nodded.

The purser's eyes narrowed. "How many names have you got, anyway? Are you some kind of, er— wrongdoer, that you have all these aliases?"

She laughed nervously. "No, sir. I'm Russian. You know, we Russians have so many names even we have trouble keeping them straight."

"Is that so?" He stared at her doubtfully. "Well, you'd think at least your husband could get your name right."

"Well," she explained, "we're newlyweds. He really hasn't had time to think much about my name."

"Newlyweds, eh? So new that you have to sleep in separate cabins?"

Tasha felt her cheeks grow hot as she flushed. "Well, we had a bit of a tiff today." Suddenly she stopped herself, squared her shoulders, and glared at him angrily. "Really, sir," she snapped, "I hardly think that our personal affairs are any concern of yours!"

"You're quite right." The purser turned back to his bills of lading. "The passage is paid for, so I really don't care who you are or what your relationship with Northrup is. My assistant can show you to your cabin."

Inside her cabin, Tasha sank down on the bed, wondering what to do next. The situation baffled her. If Jared intended to travel with her, why had he reserved separate cabins, in separate classes? Why had he given her married name? Why hadn't he come back to the hotel to get her? Should she go back out in search of him now, or should she wait for him to return to the ship?

An insistent pounding on her cabin door answered her last question. Tasha opened the door to see Jared,

377

his hair and clothes rumpled, his eyes bloodshot, and a streak of blood running from his nose to his chin. He stared at her a moment as if she were a ghost.

"What the devil are you doing here?" he finally barked.

"I might ask you the same question!" She could smell the rum on his breath, and noted that he swayed unsteadily in the doorway.

"You were supposed to wait for me at the hotel!" he said accusingly.

Tasha arched her brows. "And you were supposed to return for me immediately after making our reservations."

"Well," he shrugged, "I was waylaid."

"By several bottles of rum, from the smell of you. What is all this nonsense about separate cabins and making my reservation in the name Zarevskaya?"

"It's your name, isn't it?" He looked at her peevishly, making it apparent the rum had not managed to drown his anger.

"The courts might say it is my name, but I would not agree. I can't understand why you are bothering to take the trip at all if you don't intend to share my accommodations."

"I said I would take you to New Archangel and I'm a man of my word—even if other people can hardly wait to break the promises they make!" He glared at her meaningfully. "I've also got enough respect for the institution of marriage not to carry on with another man's wife! You can rest assured I won't be touching you again!"

Tasha felt her heart lurch. "Jared," she said quietly, "I've already explained everything to you. In my heart, I do not consider Yuri Zarevsky my husband, and I intend to make our divorce a fact as soon as I reach Novoarkhangelsk."

"But it's not a fact now!" he whispered bitterly. "The only fact is that you married someone else while I was imprisoned in the *Shenandoah*'s stinking hold."

Throwing up her hands in despair, Tasha turned

away from him. "It's impossible to talk with you in your present condition! Your portmanteau is over by the bed. Take it down to your own cabin and sleep off your drunkenness."

Jared swayed as he advanced into the cabin, attempting to focus on the portmanteau on the floor by the bed. He didn't notice Tasha's bag, which she had dropped midway between the door and the bed upon entering the cabin. His left foot caught on the corner of the bag, and he staggered, then fell forward. The mattress in front of him cushioned his head and broke the fall, but he was already unconscious before his body hit the floor.

Tasha stifled a scream, fearing he was injured. She rushed to his side and straightened him out on the cabin floor. Finding no lumps or fresh wounds on his head or body, she surmised that his unconsciousness was more the result of overindulgence in rum than the impact of his fall.

She closed and bolted the cabin door, then, humming to herself, washed away the dried blood that streaked Jared's face. Carefully, she peeled off his clothes, and covered him with one of the blankets from the bed.

Tasha smiled to herself as she prepared for bed. If Jared spent the night in her cabin, she would still have tomorrow to try to convince him anew of her true feelings. And this time, she felt sure she would succeed.

Chapter Thirty-two

1867

Jared awoke with a pounding headache and a sense of disorientation. He squeezed his eyes tightly shut, trying to block out the sunshine streaming in through the porthole. From her watchful perch on the bed,

Tasha noticed his first signs of wakefulness. Silently, she knelt down on the floor beside him and began stroking his forehead with her cool fingers.

His face relaxed, and he sighed contentedly under her soothing touch. Smiling to herself, Tasha slid one leg over his waist and, pushing the blanket aside, sat lightly on his stomach. He winced slightly as he felt her bare skin against his, but he did not push her away. Her fingers moved to his chest, massaging his firm muscles. Jared moaned appreciatively, still keeping his eyes closed against the light.

She felt his rising desire as she lay forward and pressed her breasts against his chest. Her lips found his and his mouth opened to welcome her. While nibbling teasingly at his tongue, her hand caressed and squeezed his shaft of desire. Her legs pressed tightly around his waist as she felt her own passion becoming stronger.

Jared's arms encircled her, stroking her back as she slid her body over his. She lifted herself above him, poised in readiness, before her fingers guided him into her warm, moist channel. He exhaled ecstatically as he felt her weight come down on him. For a moment she lay perfectly still atop him. Then she began to move up and down on him with a smooth, rocking rhythm that made everything pale beside the urgency of the moment.

His groans of pleasure blended with her whimpered moans as together they stretched toward the peak of ecstasy. Her movements accelerated and he found himself moving with her, first rocking, then bucking with the intensity of his desire. She inserted her hands underneath his buttocks, holding him more tightly to her, until neither knew where one body ended and the other began. A shudder possessed their bodies, building and growing, until they reached the final mutual eruption, then releasing them to drift slowly downward through a cloud of sweet euphoria.

Moments later, his calm, even breathing told Tasha

he had fallen asleep. She lay still, her head on his chest, listening to the steady thump of his heart. Tensing her muscles to rise, she felt his hands slide suddenly over her back, holding her down. He opened one eye, and his lips tightened in a thin smile.

"Don't think you can get away so easily, wench."

Unsure how to interpret his words, Tasha laughed nervously. "I'm sorry. I thought you were asleep."

"Not asleep. Just thinking." His hands still held her to him.

"Oh." The timidness of her voice surprised her. "Might I ask what you have been thinking about?"

"You might," he replied lightly. "And I might be enticed to tell you. But not just now."

He rolled her onto her back, following her body closely with his own. Moving slowly and tenderly, he returned to her a hundred times over the pleasure she had just given him. Afterwards, when they both panted in delicious exhaustion, he lifted his weight off to lay alongside her, sliding his arm beneath her back to pull her close to him.

"Mmmm," he murmured, "that is a marvelous cure for a hangover."

She traced her fingertips over his light chest fur, now damp with perspiration. "Now will you tell me what you were thinking of?"

"Is it not obvious, Tasha? Do you still need the words?"

"The words would be a reassuring addition to what I think I already know."

Jared stroked wisps of dark hair away from her cheeks, surprised to find tears gliding silently along her cheekbones. He raised his head up to kiss each of her eyes, lingering above her to gaze into their depths as he spoke. "Then you shall have the words, Tasha. I love you. I have already been forced to wait far too long to claim you for my wife, but if I must now wait a little longer, so be it."

Tasha hugged him, snuggling against his chest. "I

love you too, Jared. Only you. The wait will not be long, I promise. And I will do everything possible to make you feel it was worth the wait."

In the silence that followed, she felt closer to him than ever before, and she knew there was one thing more she had to confide in him. "Jared," she whispered, stroking the taut muscles of his stomach, "there's something else I must tell you."

He groaned teasingly. "Not another husband in your past, I hope?"

"No. But something serious. Something that may change your mind about wanting to marry me." She hesitated, then plunged ahead, "I can't promise you children."

"Tasha, no woman can promise her husband children. It's something that either happens or does not."

"But I have more reason than most to worry about not being able to bear children. I—I lost Yuri's child when I left Kamchatka, and the ship's doctor said my childbearing facilities may have been impaired."

Jared sighed, then said lightly, "Ship's doctors are notorious for knowing little about their work. Why, I remember a rather attractive doctor aboard the *Freedom* who once disinfected my wound with rum!"

She smiled, remembering that night aboard the *Freedom*, the night they had first made love, but her smile quickly faded. "Be serious, Jared!"

"I am, love. I'm sorry for the suffering you must have borne, losing the child, but you mustn't worry too much about the future. If we are destined to have children, we will have them. If not—we will always have each other. My only worry is how you can be so sure of getting a divorce. Won't this Zarevsky object?"

"I suppose he will. But I think that Bishop Petr in Novoarkhangelsk will agree that I have good reason to request the dissolution of our marriage."

Jared's voice became gruff. "Did your husband mistreat you? If he did, I'll tear him to shreds with my bare hands!"

382

Tasha smiled to herself, thinking how pleasant it would be to see Yuri punished by Jared, but she forced herself to respond in an even voice, "Let us simply say Yuri and I did not get along. I suppose a large share of the blame belongs to me. I never should have married him, feeling as I did. But let us talk no more about that. Only tell me, have you forgiven me now for marrying?"

He sighed. "What is there to forgive? At first I could not understand. I was hurt, thinking you had given another man the vows and devotion you should have reserved for me. But how can I blame you when you suffered with the certainty that I was dead and endured the pain of a loveless marriage?

"Now I see that you married out of youthful foolishness and grief, not out of any infidelity to me. I can't doubt your love when you sacrificed your pride to come to this ship, let me sleep off my drunkenness on your cabin floor, and greeted me this morning like a loving angel of mercy and forgiveness."

Impishly, she touched his nose. "To say nothing of washing away the evidence of yesterday's tussles. How did you get the nosebleed?"

Jared smiled sheepishly. "The clerk at the City Hotel."

Tasha giggled, remembering the frail, bespectacled little man. "The clerk bested you? You must have been even more intoxicated than I imagined!"

"I didn't say he bested me!" Jared growled in mock annoyance, swatting her rump playfully. "I imagine that today he is sporting two black eyes as evidence of our encounter. But that's none of my concern. The man brought it on himself."

"And just how did he do that?"

"When I came back to the hotel to get you, I couldn't find you anywhere. Out of frustration, I asked the clerk if he had seen my wife. He replied that he had seen you leave a quarter of an hour earlier, carrying your bags. He then went on to imply that

383

you had no doubt gone to meet someone who was more of a gentleman. Obviously the fellow wanted a fight, so I felt forced to oblige him."

"Well," Tasha tried to control the laughter in her voice, "I hope you didn't overly impair the poor fellow."

"Just enough so he'll think twice before casting any more slurs on paying customers and their ladies."

Jared rose and squinted out the porthole. "It must be close to noon, and I'm starving." He turned and grinned at Tasha wickedly. "You seem to have overworked me for one morning. Will you allow me to escort you to the dining room for lunch, madam?"

"I will," she laughed, "if you will be so kind as to put on some clothing before we go. I'll not stand for having half the women on this ship panting after you!"

"Half?" He shot her a wounded look. "I would have thought all! But I will agree to get dressed if you will do the same." He pulled her to her feet and glanced around the cabin. "Where is that portmanteau, anyway? I believe before I fell into your clutches I was about to carry it to my own cabin."

"This is your cabin, Jared," Tasha said firmly.

He smiled broadly. "I wanted only to hear you say so, my love."

The next seven days whizzed by in a flurry of joyful incidents piled one on top of the other. Jared, unaccustomed to the idle luxury of being a ship's passenger, at first felt awkward not having any duties in connection with the sailing of the ship. But Tasha provided him with physical activity of a more fulfilling kind and their days aboard the *Tropical Queen* brought them both great satisfaction.

By the time they reached Colon, on the Atlantic Ocean side of the isthmus of Panama, they were completely at ease with one another. The rocky moments during the first days of their reunion had sharpened their sensitivity, allowing them to read each other's emotions more clearly than ever before. The trip was like a honeymoon, marred only by the fact they were not yet married.

At Colon, they boarded a train and traveled through lush green jungles to Panama City on the Pacific Ocean side of the isthmus. The day they arrived in Panama City, they were fortunate enough to find another American steamer, the *Adventurer*, bound for San Francisco. They booked passage and boarded immediately, departing the following morning. Thirteen days later, after a brief stop in Acapulco, the *Adventurer* steamed into San Francisco Bay.

They had to wait almost a week in San Francisco before a ship put in that would be continuing on to Novoarkhangelsk. San Francisco was already buzzing with the news, received by telegraph, that Russian America had been sold to the United States. The United States Senate had ratified the treaty on April 9. Now all that remained was for the House of Representatives to authorize payment of the seven million dollars.

While she traveled, immersed in the joy of being with Jared, Tasha had thought very little about the real reason for the trip—to inform and console her father. Now she worried again that the news would reach him before she did. She was grateful that Novoarkhangelsk had no telegraph service to speed the woeful tidings to him, but she still feared some American steamer might bypass San Francisco and reach Novoarkhangelsk before she could.

She also worried about another problem. Not only would her father have to adjust to the news about the colony, but he would have to accept her plan to divorce Yuri and wed Jared. Would he support her decision? It was one thing for him to have consented to their marriage two years ago, but it was quite another matter to seek his indulgence after she had wed someone else. She would marry Jared no matter what the obstacles, but she desperately wanted her father's approval.

Every hotel in San Francisco seemed to be crowded with adventurers anxious to go north to explore the United States' latest acquisition. Some, who had participated in California's gold rush almost twenty years earlier, were spurred by rumors of untouched goldfields in the unknown northlands. Others simply sought adventure and the chance to establish a homestead in a nearly uninhabited area. A few wanted only to examine what the Russians had accomplished in the icelands they jokingly called "Walrussia."

When the *Strelka*, the same ship Tasha had once sailed on with her father, steamed into San Francisco before continuing north to Novoarkhangelsk, Tasha and Jared had to compete with hundreds of others for a place on board.

The competition was quickly eliminated. The *Strelka*'s captain, having just received news of the sale, refused to allow any Americans to board his ship. A Creole, born and raised on Kodiak Island, he was convinced that the United States had somehow tricked the Czar into selling the colony, and he had no intention of transporting any deceitful Americans there. He quickly agreed to take Tasha, especially when he remembered she was Mikhail Lisovsky's daughter and had traveled on the *Strelka* before. But he was adamant in refusing to carry Jared.

"The American can find his own way!" he spat. "If Americans want to come to Russian America, let them swim there—and I hope they all drown on the way!"

"But you don't understand," Tasha cried. "You have to let Jared come along! He's brought me all the way from New York!"

The captain shrugged. "Well, maybe you needed him until now—to protect you from the other American barbarians. But aboard my ship you need no scummy American to look after you! I will personally guarantee your safety. All the men aboard my ship are gentlemen."

"They are no more gentlemen than Jared!" she

snapped. "He is my fiancé. If he does not travel on this ship, then neither do I."

"Fiancé, you say?" The captain's eyes squinted suspiciously. "I find that difficult to believe. The last time you traveled on the *Strelka* you were a married woman. Your husband was, I believe, in St. Petersburg. Of course, your private affairs are none of my business, but I will tell you this much—you will not force me to carry a citizen of the United States! And if you insist on traveling with this man, it will not be on this vessel! Good day, Madame!" He wheeled sharply and stalked away.

Tasha turned to Jared in despair. "What are we to do?"

He put his arm around her and gently led her off the *Strelka*. "We will go back to the hotel and get your portmanteau. Then I will bring you back here and you will board the *Strelka* for New Archangel."

She stopped suddenly, refusing to walk any further. "But that is out of the question. You heard what the captain said. He will not carry you. And I refuse to travel without you."

"Even if I think you should?"

She shook her head doggedly. "No! Three years without you was far too much. I could not endure another day of separation, much less the weeks we would be apart if I leave you behind."

Jared grasped her by the shoulders, his tone gentle but firm. "You can endure another separation, Tasha. I don't expect you to like the prospect, but I expect you to accept what must be done and do it. If we love each other as much as we say—and I know in my heart we do—a few weeks' separation cannot harm us. If you cannot trust me to follow you, then our bonds are weaker than I thought."

"Of course I trust you, Jared. But fate has already treated us so cruelly that I wonder if I dare to hope for another reunion."

"You mustn't think that way. I'll admit that fate has

387

dealt us some heavy blows, but in the end it brought us together again. And I am sure this separation will only be temporary."

"Perhaps we could wait a few more days. Another ship bound for Novoarkhangelsk may arrive, one that is willing to carry Americans."

Jared shook his head. "If that happens, I will be on that ship. But you must go on the *Strelka*, Tasha." Gently he pulled her further toward the hotel. "Think about it, Tasha. Your whole reason for making this trip was so that you could reach your father before the news of the sale. If New Archangel has not already received news of the treaty, the *Strelka* will surely carry it. How much better it would be for your father to hear the story from you, and to be reassured that you had no part in the dealings, than to hear it from someone else and wonder, even for a day, if you were involved. Think how hard it was for you to accept the sale, and then think how much more difficult it will be for a man who has lived there for almost twenty years."

"I know you are right," she whispered, "but I can't bear to think of going on without you."

"I'll follow as soon as possible," Jared soothed. "With all the people clamoring to see the new territory, it can't be long before another ship will be available. Besides, it might be better for you to reach New Archangel a few days before me."

"What do you mean?"

He smiled. "It will be difficult enough for your father to learn of the sale without having an American who intends to become his son-in-law thrust on him at the same time. Together with the first news, he may feel toward Americans very much like the *Strelka*'s captain."

Tasha nodded grimly. "I had worried some about his acceptance of you."

Still sensing her reluctance to leave, Jared continued his argument. "For one so young, you have survived more than your share of trouble and grief.

388

But your suffering has made you strong. Surely you are strong enough to face a few days without me, if it means securing for your father the comfort he needs. After all, we will have the rest of our lives to share."

Smiling weakly, Tasha gave him a loving look. "Of course you are right, and I won't disappoint you by pleading further weakness. I'll sail on the *Strelka*, Jared, but I won't live again until you join me in Novoarkhangelsk."

Early the next morning, the *Strelka* slipped out of San Francisco Bay and steamed north towards Novoarkhangelsk. Tasha stood silently at the rail, watching and waving till Jared was obscured by the fog rolling in from the narrow channel of water known as the Golden Gate. The fog seemed to blanket the ship with droplets of water, blending with the tears that streamed down Tasha's cheeks.

Chapter Thirty-three

1867

The green spire of St. Mikhail's, surrounded by circling ravens, greeted Tasha as the *Strelka* steamed into Novoarkhangelsk's harbor. For the first time in the two and one-half weeks since she had left Jared, she felt a surge of joy, knowing she was almost home and would soon be embracing her father.

She was the first person down the gangplank after the ship anchored, and immediately ran toward the Lisovsky house. Xenia, looking as old and stern as ever, opened the door to her furious pounding, stumbling back in shock when she saw who was there.

"God preserve us, child!" Xenia exclaimed, quickly crossing herself. "I had my doubts that we'd ever be seeing you in this house again. When your father returned from San Francisco without you and we learned where you'd gone, well—" she cut herself off abruptly, crossing herself fervently again.

"How is papa, Xenia?" Tasha asked breathlessly. "Is he home today?"

The old woman nodded. "He's home. In his study. Seems to spend most of his time there since—but, you'll see for yourself."

Dropping her portmanteau, Tasha hurried to the study door. She inched open the door, stifling a gasp as she caught a glimpse of her father. His once-fair hair had become almost completely white, and his face was deeply lined. He had aged more than she had thought humanly possible in the months since they had parted. He was seated at his desk, hunched over his books, unaware that she watched him. Knocking timidly, Tasha cleared her throat and took a step into the room.

"What is it, Xenia?" Mikhail asked in a tired voice, not bothering to look up.

"It's not Xenia," she said quietly, unable to control the quiver in her voice.

Mikhail's head jerked up. He stared at her for a long moment, his blue eyes clouding with unreadable emotion. "So you've come back," he said in a hollow, strained voice.

Tasha nodded uneasily, advancing another few steps into the room. "Are you not happy to see me, papa?"

He stared at her another moment before scraping back his desk chair and moving slowly around the heavy cedar desk. As he moved, his eyes never left hers, as if he feared she might disappear if he so much as blinked. He stopped in front of the desk, shaking his head hopelessly before throwing his arms wide. "Of course I'm glad to see you, Tasha! What a poor father I would be if I refused to welcome home my prodigal daughter!"

Sobbing, she rushed into his arms, tasting his tears as she kissed his cheeks. She squeezed him, glad for the comfort of his firm, broad chest. "Oh, papa!" she sobbed, "I'm so sorry for all the hurt I've caused you!"

Mikhail sighed. "At first when I read your note, I could not believe it. I was sure you had been kidnapped and your abductors had forced you to write it. Later I reconciled myself to the fact that you had gone with Stanovsky, and I asked myself over and over again, why? Why did you, Tasha?"

She pulled away from him a bit and shrugged. "There were many reasons, some of which I could not even admit to myself at the time. But I can try to explain it all to you later, papa. For now, it just feels so wonderful to be home!"

He smiled, then hugged her again. "You can't feel any better about being here than I do, having you home. But come, sit down and tell me about your travels."

He led her to a small leather-upholstered couch. "Is Stanovsky with you? What made you decide to return?"

Gulping, Tasha realized that he knew nothing yet of the colony's sale to the United States. But with the docking of the *Strelka*, the news was sure to spread through the town rapidly. If she waited even an hour, one of his friends might come to tell him. She pictured Jared nodding to her encouragingly as his words flashed through her mind, "How much better it would be for your father to hear the story from you—."

"No," she said slowly, "Stanovsky is still in Washington. I came alone. I came back to see you, papa. There's some important news I learned in Washington, and I knew immediately I had to hurry to your side."

Cocking an eyebrow inquisitively, Mikhail asked, "And what news is that? Whatever it is, I must be grateful for it, since it brought you home to me."

Tasha sighed deeply, as the task suddenly seemed even more difficult than she had imagined. "It's not pleasant news, papa. But I wanted you to hear it from my own lips and know that, whatever Pyotr

Stanovsky's role in the negotiations, I knew absolutely nothing about it until the end—when it was already too late."

Her father frowned, waiting for further explanation.

Hesitantly, Tasha took his hand, staring into his compassionate blue eyes, and wondering how she could bear the hurt her words would bring him. Taking a deep breath, she began. "I left Washington on the morning of March 30, after I learned that on that very morning, at four o'clock, the minister of the Russian Empire and the Secretary of State of the United States had signed—"

A disturbance in the hallway outside the study door suddenly drowned her words. Xenia's voice rose shrilly, "I tell you, Gospodin Lisovsky should not be disturbed right now! Tasha has just come home! He needs time alone with her!"

"Out of my way, woman!" a man's voice barked. "Mikhail can talk to his daughter later. I bring urgent news. Mikhail Pavlovich!" Mikhail's and Tasha's eyes swung to the study door as Semyon Sukenak pushed his way into the room. Tasha instantly realized the news he bore, but before she had time to gather her wits and stop him, the blunt, uncushioned fact poured from his lips.

"Have you heard, Mikhail Pavlovich? The Czar has sold the colony!"

Tasha cringed as she watched her father pale as if his friend had just dealt him a death blow. Slowly he moistened his lips and choked out, "Where did you hear such lies, Semyon Borisovich?"

"Not lies, Mikhail!" the man exclaimed. "Truth. The *Strelka* docked this morning with the news."

Grasping Tasha's hand, Mikhail shook his head stubbornly. "No! I won't believe it! It must be nothing more than a sailor's fantasy, invented to pass the time on a long voyage. My Tasha just arrived this morning herself. If the colony had been sold, surely she would have—" His voice trailed off as the words of her hesitant preamble came back to him. Turning tear-glazed eyes to Tasha, he begged, "Tell me, is this the news you were about to give me?"

Slowly, Tasha shook her head. "I'm sorry, papa. I wish," she paused to swallow the sobs rising in her throat, "I wish I could say nay, but the news is true. Russian America has been sold to the United States of America!"

"Are you sure, Tasha? Is there no way you might be mistaken?"

"I'm not mistaken, papa. Pyotr Stanovsky was there when the treaty was signed. Czar Aleksandr sent him to America expressly to facilitate arrangements for the sale. But I knew nothing about it until the treaty had been signed. He always insisted the Czar's business was to be kept secret, and I was too naive to pry. I must tell you, I was as shocked as you to learn of the sale. After the first shock wore off, my first thought was to hurry back to you."

Her father continued to shake his head in disbelief. "It is just too incredible to imagine the Czar would sell the colony. All my life Czar Aleksandr, and his father, Czar Nikolai before him, fought to expand the reaches of the Empire, and to defend those areas already claimed. Why would the Czar suddenly sell us when we are not even threatened with war?"

"Stanovsky told me there were many reasons," Tasha said softly, "though none of them made any sense to me. He said the colony was not profitable enough, that it was too far from St. Petersburg, that Russia's destiny was in Asia, while the United States' was in North America—"

Her words scarcely penetrated Mikhail's fog of grief. "But to sell us like a piece of cloth, or a battered samovar! It makes no sense! A colony is people —people who have given their hearts and souls and life's blood to its survival! What is to become of us? Would Czar Aleksandr, the Czar-Liberator, the emperor who granted freedom to the serfs, sell us and all we hold dear like so many sacks of grain?"

"If it is any comfort," Tasha soothed, "Stanovsky says the Czar was not at all anxious for the transaction. It was his brother, Grand Duke Constantine, who insisted on it."

"Ah, we should have suspected Constantine!" Semyon spat. "He was the one who convinced the Czar not to renew the company's contract when it expired the last time, in '62!"

"But I thought those problems were resolved last year, when the Council of State promised us another contract," Mikhail said.

"We all thought that!" Semyon replied bitterly. "But did you ever hear any news of a contract actually being signed? Of course not!" he added indignantly. "And even if it had been signed, what is a contract in the eyes of the Czar? Nothing more than a scrap of paper, easily torn up or burned!"

"Semyon Borisovich!" Mikhail cut in sharply. "I will not have you talk so of our sovereign in my house, before my daughter!"

"And why not?" Semyon flared. "What has Czar Aleksandr ever done for you? If you had stayed in St. Petersburg, you would still be working in a furrier's shop, making a decent living, but denied the respect of nobility and royalty. Here, thanks to your own efforts, you have risen to the highest ranks of society. Are you willing to go back to Russia now and sacrifice all you have labored for these many years?"

Mikhail sighed wearily. "I don't know. I have always considered Novoarkhangelsk a part of Russia— an extension of the homeland. To learn so suddenly that that is no longer the case leaves me feeling unsure of myself."

He rose and addressed his friend apologetically. "Semyon Borisovich, I beg your indulgence, but I'm afraid I would be a very poor host for the next several hours. I badly need some time to think."

"I understand." His friend embraced him and turned to the door. "I am sorry to have been the bearer of such ill tidings."

Tasha rose as well and hugged her father tightly. "Oh, papa," she sobbed, "I wish there were something I could say or do to change the news."

"But there is not," he said heavily. "At least I have my daughter again. Thank you for coming home, Tasha. We'll talk later."

Blinking rapidly to stop the tears that threatened to overrun his cheeks, Mikhail fled from the study and hurried up the stairs.

Mikhail did not join Tasha for dinner or supper. He stayed in his room the entire day, refusing to eat, or speak with Tasha or any of the servants.

Heartsick over her inability to comfort her father, and consumed by loneliness for Jared, Tasha wandered from room to room, trying to divert her thoughts from the sorrowing man upstairs. In the drawing room, she stopped before the piano, wondering how long it had been since the instrument had been played. She sat down on the bench and began to play, from memory, Mikhail Glinka's *Kamarinskaya*, a symphony celebrating spirited Russian dances.

"Bravo!" Enthusiastic clapping interrupted her as she began the third movement. Tasha turned her head to see her father enter the room, smiling broadly. "My dearest Tasha, you always did know how to dispel my worst moods with your wonderful music." He sat down beside her on the bench. "Please, play some more. The music is a soothing balm for my heart and mind."

Gladly, she obliged him, stopping only when her fingers, unaccustomed to playing, could no longer find the right keys.

"Thank you, child," he smiled and kissed her forehead. "How fortunate I am to have you here when I most need you. You know, I don't believe this piano has been played since you left for Kamchatka with Yuri." He stopped abruptly, realizing he had inadvertently touched on a subject that demanded further discussion.

At the mention of her husband's name, Tasha cringed and her father stared at her intently, trying to gauge the misery she had hinted at in the note she left in San Francisco. The silence in the room became overwhelming, and when Mikhail spoke again his voice had lost the contentment of a moment before.

"Forgive me, Tasha, but in my own grief and shock and disillusionment today, I neglected to give you the news about your husband."

"That is quite understandable, papa." Her voice was flat and unemotional.

"No. It is really inexcusable." He paused, clearing his throat uneasily. "I hardly know how to tell you this. From the note you left me, I know your marriage was not perfect. Still, you did mention your hopes of reconciliation, and I suppose you could not have lived with a man for almost a year without feeling some affection for him—" His voice trailed away.

"Papa," Tasha interrupted impatiently, "what are you trying to tell me? Have you heard from Yuri? Does he want to divorce me for deserting him?" She tried to suppress the hopefulness in her voice.

He shook his head wearily, taking her hand in his. "No, I haven't heard from him, Tasha. And you won't be hearing from him either." He sighed. "I suppose there is no easy way to tell you. Yuri Zarevsky is dead."

Her heart jumped, and she stifled a sob of relief. Forcing a note of concern into her voice, she asked, "What happened? When?"

"On his way to St. Petersburg, barely a month after he left you in Kamchatka, he contracted a fever while sailing through the tropics and died just three days later."

"And how did the news reach you?"

Mikhail got up from the piano bench and walked to a window, staring out at the terrace. "It is a long story, child. After I got back from San Francisco I was so sick at heart, knowing you had gone and knowing

396

how unhappy you were in your marriage. I wanted to help, and I feared there could be no chance of reconciliation if Yuri returned to Petropavlovsk and found you gone without his permission. I spoke to Bishop Petr, and he suggested I write to the priest in Petropavlovsk, Father Iosaf."

Tasha flinched, but forced her voice to remain steady. "And what did you write to the priest?" She could not bring herself to say his name.

Her father cleared his throat nervously. "I'm afraid I lied a bit. I told him you had become so homesick you had come to stay with me in your husband's absence, and that Yuri could come for you here or write and tell me where to send you to meet him. You see, I hoped that by the time he returned from St. Petersburg you would have returned to Novo-arkhangelsk, and I could talk some sense into you—somehow convince you of your duty to your husband."

"And the priest informed you that Yuri had died?"

"Yes. He wrote back that word of your husband's untimely death had reached Petropavlovsk. He also suggested that you might wish to return to take care of the possessions you left in the house you shared with Yuri, and assured me he would personally see to your welfare while you were in Petropavlovsk."

"I'm sure he would," Tasha muttered.

"There was more to his letter, Tasha. Words that confused and upset me. Father Iosaf claimed you were wanton, undisciplined, and not a God-fearing person. He strongly advised that you be put in his care so he could send you to a nunnery until you learned to mend your ways. Reflecting on the way you had fled from your husband and run off with another man, I was forced to wonder if there was any truth to his assessment."

He turned his wounded eyes to her. "What in the name of all that is holy has happened to you, Tasha?"

"I'll tell you what has happened to me!" she cried, slamming her hands down on the piano keys, making the room ring with a discordant clangor. "I married a man for the wrong reason—out of grief instead of love—and I endured all the insults he could heap on me. Then, when he left me in the care of Father Iosaf, the good priest tried to rape me. Because I resisted him and fled to Novoarkhangelsk, it appears he has even tried to turn my father against me. I'm not an evil person, papa! I know I should not have gone off with Pyotr Stanovsky, but I could not bear the thought of you sending me back to Petropavlovsk."

Having listened openmouthed to her outpourings, Mikhail rushed across the room to his daughter's side. He held her head against his chest. Gently stroking her hair, he murmured, "Tasha, Tasha, why did you not confide in me sooner? Do you think I would have sent you back if I had known how much you suffered?"

She sniffled. "I think you would have tried to do what was right, and you would have said it was wrong to leave my husband."

"But I never would have sent you back to the clutches of Father Iosaf. I must speak to Bishop Petr about the man immediately. It is unthinkable for a lecher to be masquerading as a priest!" He paused, then asked softly, "Was life with Yuri Zarevsky so bad, Tasha?"

Tasha hesitated before raising her head and looking earnestly into her father's eyes. "There were times when I thought I could not bear another day with him, and others when he surprised me with his lack of hostility, but never was there any hint of love between us."

She shook her head helplessly at the hurt and unhappiness in her father's eyes. "I know I never loved him, papa, and I'm afraid he never loved me either. Oh, he wanted me—he made that clear from the beginning. He wanted to possess my body, and my soul, and my mind. He wanted to use me in bed and to use my beauty and intelligence to further his career. He wanted to prove that he could tame me. And he wanted other men to envy his possession of me. I think he married me just so no one else could have me."

Huddling closer, she whispered, "I do not rejoice in his death, papa. I would not wish death for anyone. But I cannot honestly say I grieve for him. It is a relief to know I will never see him again." With a sigh, she lowered her eyes. "Perhaps if I had not loved Jared so much I might have had a better marriage with Yuri."

Mikhail stiffened at her final words. "Oh God," he mumbled feebly. "I tried so hard to do what was right for you, and now it seems I may have robbed you of all future happiness."

"What are you talking about, papa?" She stared at him in perplexity.

He gulped. "There was a letter. From the United States. It came the winter after your marriage, and it was addressed to you. You were already settled in Petropavlovsk with Yuri, and I was so afraid it might disturb you. In fact, I feared you might break your sacred marriage vows if you learned your Jared was alive. So I—burned the letter—," his voice trailed away in a whisper.

"What!" For a moment, Tasha's eyes flared up with anger. "You burned Jared's letter to me?" Remembering how she had agonized, first thinking Jared dead, then thinking him alive but uncaring, she was tempted to berate her father and blame him for all her unhappiness. But as her eyes met his, she swallowed her anger.

"Please, Tasha," he pleaded, "try to understand. I had no idea how unhappy you were with Yuri, but I did know that if you learned the American was alive, you would be tormented by thoughts that you should have waited for him. I thought if I sent you the letter, it would destroy whatever peace and security you might have found in Petropavlovsk. So I did what I thought was best. I destroyed it."

Fearing he was about to cry as he realized his contribution to her unhappiness, Tasha squeezed his hand and smiled reassuringly. "It's all right, papa. I know you acted out of love for me. And in the end everything worked out for the best. You see, Jared finally found me in Washington."

"He did?" Mikhail's eyes glowed with happiness for her, but the glow quickly faded to a look of confusion. "But where is he now? Did you decide you were not right for one another after all?"

"No, no," she laughed merrily. "We have decided God never made two people more right for one another." Patting the spot beside her on the piano bench, she invited her father to sit down as she began the whole story of Jared's capture, rescue, his lonely suffering, and their eventual reunion in Washington, D.C.

She told of the conversation she had overheard in the San Francisco saloon, her decision to travel with Stanovsky, Philip Vanderman's revelation to her in New York, and how her own stubborn pride had almost kept them apart. Finally, her cheeks flushed with the memory of her time with Jared, she explained how he had taken her away from Washington, accompanied her by ship and train to San Francisco, and insisted that she continue on without him when the *Strelka*'s captain had refused to carry him.

Mikhail nodded thoughtfully. "It's plain he must be an exceptional young man to put my feelings before his own desire to have you near. Were I in his position, I doubt that I would have had the strength to let you out of my sight after so long a separation."

"Oh, he is exceptional," Tasha beamed. "But you will see for yourself. I never would have left him had he not promised to follow as soon as possible. Perhaps he will even be here tomorrow! At any rate, I'm certain we won't have to wait more than a few weeks. Oh, I'm so anxious for you to know him as I do!"

Hugging her, Mikhail mumbled, "So it seems you have come back to me only briefly, until another man comes to claim you from my arms."

400

"But not from your heart, papa," Tasha whispered gently. "No matter where we go, part of me will always stay with you, and I will always carry part of you with me."

"I know," he said, gently kissing her cheek. "And you must not worry about me. I was just being selfish for a moment, wanting to keep you with me forever. But, as you say, I will always have a part of you. During the months you were gone with Stanovsky, I was afraid I had lost you forever. I worried that you cared nothing for how I felt. Now I understand, and I feel I have found you again."

He paused reflectively, then tipped her chin up to gaze into her eyes. "Except for those brief moments with your mother, I have lived without the happiness true love can bring. You have found the one man who can give you that kind of happiness. Cherish him, Tasha. And return to him all the joy he gives to you."

"I will, papa. Thank you for understanding." She threw her arms around his neck, burying her face in his chest to hide the tears glistening on her cheeks. "Papa," she asked quietly, "what *will* you do when the colony changes hands and the Americans come to claim their property?"

She felt his chest heave as he sighed. "I don't know, child. I've thought about it all day, and still I cannot say. For now, I suppose I will wait. Wait and see what compensation Czar Aleksandr offers us, and what terms the Americans will propose."

Novoarkhangelsk did not have to wait long for the official announcement. Less than a week after the *Strelka* docked, Prince Maksutov stood on the steps of Baranov Castle, addressing the solemn-faced Russians and Creoles who had gathered to hear the news. It was clear the announcement pained him, since he had personally assured the citizens, less than three years earlier, that they could look forward to a prosperous future in Russian America. His wife, Maria, stood beside him, her young face swollen by days of weeping.

"My fellow citizens," the prince began, in a loud, wavering voice, "it is my unfortunate duty to inform you that the colony of Russian America has been sold to the United States of America. Although the Czar has not yet received the purchase price of seven million, two hundred thousand American dollars, the Americans will take over the colony in October of this year."

"October!" many voices in the crowd rumbled. "Can't they give us more time? What will become of us?"

Holding up his hands, the prince calmed the crowd and continued. "All Russian military personnel will return to Russia immediately after the ceremony of transfer. My wife and I will remain here with our children until the end of the year. Then we, too, will return to Russia. The rest of you have two options. You may return to the motherland, with free transport provided anytime within the next three years, or you may remain here and become United States citizens, entitled to all the rights and privileges accorded to all citizens of that country. The United States will extend citizenship to any who wish to apply, with the exception of the Kolosh and the other Indian tribes. Word of the sale and its provisions will be sent by dispatch to the other settlements of the colony.

"Let me assure you this announcement shocks and pains me as much as it does all of you." Taking his wife's arm, Prince Maksutov turned and, with stooped shoulders, led her into the castle.

Though rumors of the sale had pervaded the city for days, the official announcement left the crowd stunned. Gradually, the prince's words became clear to them. "Three years!" People turned to one another excitedly. "We need not give up our homes! We have three years to decide!" A relieved buzz spread through the crowd. "It cannot hurt to wait and see what kind

402

of life the Americans offer. We can always leave later."

At the edge of the crowd, Tasha turned to her father. "Do you hear, papa? You can stay if you wish! You can stay in your beautiful home, close to all the people and things you hold dear!"

Sadly, Mikhail shook his head. "I can stay if I become a United States citizen. But I am a Russian citizen, Tasha. I cannot change that, no matter what others may think. I will stay until your Jared comes, and until you are married and safely settled here, or I have seen the two of you off to another home. Beyond that, I cannot stay. My heart is Russian, and I must go home."

Chapter Thirty-four

1867

All that summer, Americans poured into Novoarkhangelsk. They came by the shipload—some to settle in the city itself, some to explore the farther reaches of the territory.

The American settlers got along well with their Russian and Creole neighbors. Soon they were establishing stores and saloons and other businesses. Except for the incessant rain, they seemed pleased with the area and enjoyed the abundance of game, salmon, and other fish.

Every time a new ship arrived, Tasha ran expectantly to the docks, scanning the crowds for Jared. Some days she sat by the harbor until it was nearly dark; then she would return home, alone and disappointed.

"He'll come, Tasha," her father would console her at supper each night. "Just give him time. No doubt it is very difficult to book passage from San Francisco right now. In a few weeks, when the frenzy has diminished, he'll be here. He'd be a fool to let you escape from him again, and from what you've told me about him, the man is no fool."

But he did not come. The months dragged on—July, August, September—and the flood of incoming settlers subsided, but Jared Northrup was not among the late stragglers into Novoarkhangelsk.

A variety of worries began to plague Tasha. Perhaps he had been hurt, trampled in the stampede of people rushing to get aboard a ship. Or, perhaps his ship had met with an accident. In her worst moments, she thought he might have changed his mind and decided she was not worthy of his devotion. Given time to think, he may have become disgusted with the fact she had married Yuri Zarevsky and had taken Pyotr Stanovsky for her lover. He may have gone home to New Bedford. What then?

No, she told herself stubbornly, over and over again. They had come too far together and he had pledged his love too sincerely for her to entertain such thoughts. She had let her mind's foolish fabrications keep them apart before, but she would not let it destroy her confidence now. Nevertheless, where was he? She cursed the fact that Novoarkhangelsk—or Sitka, as the new settlers had begun to call it—had no telegraph. If only she could contact him! She thought of going to San Francisco to search for him, but feared he would arrive the moment she left. And so, she continued to wait.

Early in October, a ship called the *John L. Stevens*, accompanied by two gunboats, anchored offshore. Word quickly spread that the ship had come from San Francisco and had brought two hundred fifty American troops to administer the take-over of the colony. Tasha paced near the docks, wondering if Jared was aboard. The Russian officials refused to let anyone from the *Stevens* ashore until the official American and Russian commissioners arrived for the ceremony of transfer.

For ten days, the *John L. Stevens* remained off-shore. Finally, on October 18, the U.S.S. *Ossipee* steamed into the harbor, carrying Captain Aleksei Peshchurov, the Russian commissioner, and Brigadier-General Lovell Rousseau, the American commissioner.

To alleviate the tense atmosphere that by this time gripped the city, the commissioners consented to hold the ceremony of transfer at three o'clock that very afternoon. The troops would disembark from the *John L. Stevens*, and the city would finally get its first taste of American rule.

By the time Tasha and her father arrived at the parade grounds in front of Baranov Castle, the area was crowded with spectators. Prince Maksutov and his wife stood at the edge of the crowd, but very few other Russians were present to see the Russian flag lowered for the last time, to be replaced by the American stars and stripes. Mikhail Lisovsky himself had not intended to witness the ceremony, but, at the last moment, decided to accompany Tasha and observe Novoarkhangelsk's final moments as a Russian city.

With a roll of drums, ninety Russian sailors and double that number soldiers, who comprised the Novoarkhangelsk garrison, marched up the hill from the barracks and crossed the parade ground. At the command of Captain Peshchurov, they came to attention before the ninety-foot-high flagstaff, and, to a man, raised their eyes to the gently waving flag of the Russian Empire.

The troops from the *John L. Stevens*, commanded by Major-General Jefferson C. Davis, were next to march onto the parade ground. Brigadier-General Rousseau and the commanders of the two American gunboats followed. Tasha scanned the crowd in vain for some sign of Jared.

When all were assembled, the first ceremonial cannon blast erupted from the Baranov Castle artillery. The guns of the U.S.S. *Ossipee* answered the castle cannon. A uniformed American soldier stepped up to the flagstaff and started to haul down the Russian flag.

The flag descended slowly as the alternating cannon blasts continued. When it was only a few feet from the top of the flagstaff, a brisk gust of wind snapped the flag to attention. It hung over the assembly for a moment, hovering like a last blessing, then the wind gusted again and the flag whipped tightly around the flagstaff ropes. The soldiers on the ground rattled the ropes in an effort to unfurl the banner, but it only seemed to become more entangled. So positioned, it hung over the square, neither raised nor lowered, a seeming rebuke to the two governments which had resolved to remove it.

The few Russians in the crowd began to murmur among themselves. It must be a sign that Russia's destiny remained in America. The Americans laughed nervously, some of them calling advice to the soldier struggling at the flagstaff. Major-General Davis stepped forward, angrily ordered the youth away from the flagpole, and gave instructions for some members of his company to rig a bosun's chair. A quarter of an hour later, a soldier was seated in the device, advancing toward the flag, an unsheathed knife in his hand.

The cannon salute had ceased, and an ominous quiet hung over the crowd as the soldier hacked away at the Russian flag. Grasping it firmly he pulled it free, then hurled it to the ground, watching as it fluttered over the polished bayonets of the regiment to land on the muddy parade ground.

Overwrought by the tension of the last months, Princess Maksutova crumpled in a faint. Tasha buried her head in her father's chest, sobbing uncontrollably at the callousness of the incident. As a loud cheer swept the audience, she looked up to see the American flag waving smartly at the top of the flagstaff. To her surprise, on the dais constructed especially for the occasion, Brigadier-General Rousseau was motioning to the crowd to be quiet, as if he sympathized

406

with the feelings of the few Russians who were present.

Whatever solemn mood of ceremony had existed at the beginning of the proceedings had been completely destroyed. The commissioners gave terse speeches, reiterating the offer of United States citizenship or free passage back to Russia, and the transfer was completed. Novoarkhangelsk was to be called *Sitka*, and Russian America, formerly a colony of the Russian Empire, would be called *Alaska*, deriving from an Aleut word meaning "continent."

The crowd was beginning to disperse when Major-General Davis pushed aside the commissioners and bellowed, in a harsh, uncompromising voice, "As of this moment, by the authority granted me by the United States government, I assume command of this territory. Maksutov, you will make room for my wife and myself in your castle immediately. My troops are to be quartered in the barracks without delay —they have been cooped up on the *Stevens* too long. Make no mistake about it, until further notice, this territory is to be governed under the authority of the United States Department of War, and I am the commander!"

"See here, Davis," Brigadier-General Rousseau interrupted, "there's no need to be harsh. These people are civilians. They need time to adjust to a new government. You'd be more effective if you went a bit easier on them."

"Don't tell me how to execute my command!" Davis retorted. "I outrank you and I know what needs to be done. You have your orders and I have mine. I suggest you tend to your own business, Brigadier-General Rousseau." Turning stiffly, he disappeared into the castle.

Sick at heart, Tasha held onto her father's arm as they walked slowly back to his house. Around her, she overheard snatches of conversation. "Perhaps we should not wait to see any more of the American rule. Hasn't the Major-General made it quite clear how life

407

here will be? What is this talk of government by the War Department? Wasn't this to be a peaceful exchange of property? Perhaps it would be best to seek passage on the next transport back to the motherland, after all."

Mikhail Lisovsky said nothing during the walk home. Sighing wearily, he kissed Tasha's forehead as they entered the foyer, then trudged upstairs, calling to Xenia that he had no appetite for supper.

The commissioners stayed a week, using the time to inventory the properties belonging specifically to the United States, those belonging to Russia, and to private individuals. When they announced their imminent departure on the U.S.S. *Ossipee*, Tasha considered asking them to take her with them. Brigadier-General Rousseau seemed of a sympathetic nature, and surely the Russian commissioner, Captain Peshchurov, could find a place for her on the ship.

But she had a new concern that prevented her from leaving Sitka, no matter how desperate she was to find Jared. Her father had fallen ill soon after the ceremony of transfer. Telling herself she could not leave him, that Jared would surely think less of her if she did, Tasha put all thought of departure from her mind. Once her father recovered, she could think of going to find Jared, if he had not turned up by then.

The Russian doctor, who was himself preparing to return to Russia, diagnosed her father's ailment as a severe case of grippe, which might easily be precipitated, due to Mikhail's depression and refusal to eat, into pneumonia and possibly other serious complications.

"You must cheer him up and see that he takes nourishment to build up his strength," the doctor warned, "else he will not recover. And, as soon as he is well, I strongly advise taking him back to Russia. Your father will never be at peace here, seeing what the Americans are doing to the city he helped build."

Tasha nodded blankly, knowing the doctor was

right. With each passing day, Sitka became more unbearable. The first wave of American settlers had been
friendly, hardworking individuals, who had given the
Russians rosy expectations of what would ensue under
American rule. In addition to other businesses, they
had founded a newspaper titled the *Sitka Times*, and
elected a mayor who was a friendly, decent sort.

But the soldiers were another matter entirely. They
swaggered along Sitka's streets, behaving as if they
personally owned the city; their behavior was coarse
and brutal, and verged on lawlessness. Within weeks
after their arrival, they had set up a distillery to
produce whiskey from molasses. The majority of them
were drunk most of the time. For amusement, they
encouraged the Kolosh to join them in drinking, then
they would entice them into drunken brawls. On at
least two occasions, the soldiers created major dis-
turbances which ended in the shooting of several
Kolosh men.

They turned the main floor of Baranov Castle into
an officer's club, destroying most of the historic furnishings during their drinking parties. Even St. Mikhail's Cathedral did not escape the looting that
swept the city. And Major-General Davis did little to
discipline the men. Sometimes he was seen taking
part in their raucous activities.

Tasha kept the worst of the news from her father,
taking care to present a cheerful smile whenever she
visited his bedside. She played the piano for several
hours each afternoon, in the hope that the notes
drifting upstairs would ease his melancholy. Besides,
the music helped to keep her from constantly fretting
about Jared.

All through November, while Americans continued
to arrive, shiploads of Russians, disgusted with American rule, departed for the Empire. The city was con-
gested with the Russians and Creoles—and their
belongings—who came from all areas of the former
colony, to await the promised free transport. Those
who stayed behind prayed for a swift end to military

rule, hopeful that life under a civilian American government would not be so bad. But the United States House of Representatives had not yet approved the purchase price, and conditions continued to worsen in Sitka.

By late November, another two hundred fifty American troops were added to the Sitka garrison. Rumors spread of soldiers breaking into Russian homes at night and forcing the women to satisfy their desires, then looting the homes. Even the American settlers began to complain about the soldiers' lawlessness, but their elected mayor was no more than a figurehead, powerless in the face of the military machine that occupied the territory.

When the citizens approached Major-General Davis, he laughed in their faces, pointing out a law passed in 1807, forgotten until now, prohibiting settlement on any land acquired by treaty unless Congress specifically provided for such settlement. The settlers, Davis patronizingly explained, had no legal right to be in the territory, and his troops could forcibly remove them if he so ordered. Disgusted with his irresponsible attitude, many Americans packed their belongings and returned to the United States.

More and more Russians, grumbling that the promises of citizenship and the property deeds issued by the commissioners were meaningless, also made preparations to leave.

By early December, Mikhail had recovered sufficiently to be up and about, and he too began to think wistfully of returning to Russia. In the face of the havoc that now gripped the city, the motherland beckoned temptingly, throwing into shadow the reasons he had left it twenty years earlier. But he worried about Tasha, still waiting impatiently for her Jared. He knew she would not consent to sail with him for Russia, so it seemed he could only continue to wait with her.

Sensing her father's anxiety to escape the nightmare that Sitka had become, and certain that leaving was imperative to his health, Tasha broached the subject at dinner one day. "I understand Prince Maksutov and his family will be leaving on December 31st."

"Yes," Mikhail nodded. "I spoke with him today. He has sold whatever he could of the company's property to California businessmen, hoping they will use it for the future good of those who remain behind. He seems a bit melancholy, leaving a place to which he has given so much, but no doubt it will be a great burden lifted from his heart."

"Why don't you go with him, papa?" she asked quietly.

Mikhail shook his head slowly. "I cannot do that. What sort of father would I be to leave you here alone among the ruffians who have taken over this town? No, I will stay until your man comes to claim you. After that, I can consider leaving with a clear conscience."

"But it seems such a shame to miss the sailing," Tasha protested. "There may not be another ship leaving for Russia for months."

"So?" he shrugged. "I can wait."

Swiftly an idea took shape in Tasha's mind. "But that would be such a waste!" she cried. "I forgot to tell you sooner," she lied, "but while you were ill, I received a letter from Jared. He said he had encountered some difficulties in California, but that they are now resolved, and he has booked passage on a ship that will arrive here no later than the first of the year."

"Is that true?" her father regarded her dubiously. "I cannot imagine why you did not tell me sooner."

"Yes! Yes!" She hoped her smile looked radiant enough to convince him. "You were so ill when the letter arrived, I could not think of bothering you with my personal affairs. But it would be such a shame for you to miss the sailing by a day and then be left waiting for months afterward."

"I suppose that is true. But, truly, I had hoped to stay long enough to see the two of you wed. After all,

411

I only met the young man for a few minutes more than four years ago."

"Are you thinking that you might withdraw your approval of the match?" Tasha smiled cajolingly.

"Of course not." Her father patted her hand. "Just knowing he makes you happy is reason enough to give the two of you my blessing."

"Then you must make me happy and sail with the Maksutovs. You know, papa, Jared and I cannot be married in Sitka, anyway."

He frowned. "Why is that?"

"I read something in the *Sitka Times*, explaining that so long as Alaska remains a customs district, under the jurisdiction of the War Department, no one is legally entitled to marry, settle, or even be buried here. They call it the 'era of no government'."

"That," Mikhail sighed, "is certainly an apt description. But I don't know, Tasha. I hesitate to leave here, even for one night. I don't trust Davis's soldiers."

"Don't be so protective, papa. I've traveled three quarters of the way around the world, and I can take good care of myself. Didn't I come from Kamchatka with only Theodosia to accompany me? Besides, what can happen to me in one night? Jared will arrive before the soldiers even know you are gone."

"Still," he shook his head, "I worry about leaving you alone."

"Come now, papa," she entreated, "Jared and I will be anxious to be off to California, or someplace else where we can be legally married. But if you are still here, we will feel obliged to wait with you until the next free transport can take you to Russia. You wouldn't want us to have to wait, after all the years we've already waited, would you? Or perhaps," she grinned wickedly, "you would prefer to have us live in sin?"

Mikhail threw up his hands in defeat. "All right. If you are so determined to be rid of me, it seems there is nothing I can do but agree to go. I will see about the arrangements tomorrow."

Tasha looked pleased. "Good. I'm sure you will see it is for the best. We will get word to you after our marriage, and, in time, surely we can come to visit you."

Feeling a wave of relief, she rose from the table and went to her room. With the burden of her father's future removed from her mind, she would be able to concentrate on finding Jared.

Somehow she would find a way to return to California, and she would not rest until she was reunited with her beloved, never again to be separated from him.

Christmas was a bittersweet time in the Lisovsky household. Mikhail looked forward to leaving Sitka, but still felt a twinge of guilt over deserting his daughter. Tasha, anxious to see the ship sail so she could begin her quest for Jared, felt sad that she had deceived her father. Though both tried to maintain an air of joviality, they realized in their hearts that this might be the last of all too few holidays they had shared.

The *Dvorets*, the steamer on which Mikhail was to sail, was scheduled to depart in midmorning on the last day of the year. Tasha accompanied her father to the docks, where she kissed Xenia goodbye, and warmly embraced the other servants who had elected to travel with Mikhail to Russia.

Only Theodosia chose to remain in Alaska. "I am a Creole," the old woman said, "I have Russian blood in me, but I am not Russian. Russia is not my homeland, and I'm too old to settle among people who do not welcome those of mixed blood. I will stay here, and after Tasha leaves, I will go back to my relatives on Chichagof Island."

While Xenia and the other servants went aboard, father and daughter stood on the quay, searching for the words to convey what they felt in their hearts. Sleet was falling, coating the city with a thin layer of slush. Tasha thought of the day more than two years

413

ago when they had shared the final moments before her departure for Kamchatka. How much her life had changed since then! She had left that day with no hopes or expectations for the future, and now, having seen hope renewed, she clung to the last fragment of it still glowing in her heart.

"Well," Mikhail looked down on her, clearing his throat uneasily, "perhaps I had better board. You will get sick standing out here in the wetness so long."

Tasha smiled weakly. "I'm all right, papa. But it wouldn't do for you to get chilled just after you have regained your strength."

"No, I suppose not." She saw tears in his eyes as he clasped her to him. "Oh Tasha, I've had you for so little time, yet it seems I am forever saying goodbye to you. Forgive me for acting like a silly old man, but I cannot help but feel our parting is forev—"

"Don't, papa," she cut him off quickly, swallowing the lump in her throat. "Don't say it and try not even to feel it. It's just a goodbye like any other," she insisted, though she, too, felt it was not.

In reply, Mikhail squeezed her tightly and she felt his tears against her cheek. "I'll go then. Take care of yourself. And Tasha, thank you." He started to turn away so she would not see his tears.

"Papa?" she clutched his arm, holding him back. "Thank *you*—for answering that first letter from Prince Demidov. For having me come to you. If you had not welcomed me, I would never have known a true father's love, and I would never have known the joy of loving a father."

Smiling, he turned and kissed her again. "Dearest Tasha, those words are the most cherished gift anyone could give me." Before more tears could betray him, he fled up the gangplank to the *Dvorets*.

The docks were crowded with Russians and Creoles, begging to be allowed passage on the steamer. Many had made the decision to leave at the last moment and the captain hadn't the heart to turn them away. Loading the extra passengers and their belongings delayed the departure for hours and all the while, Tasha stood in the sleet, afraid her father might come on deck for a final glimpse of her. But Mikhail could not bear the pain of looking again at the city he loved and the daughter he was leaving behind, so he remained in his cabin and attempted to get settled.

Finally, in the late afternoon, the last passenger boarded and the *Dvorets* slipped away from the docks. Tasha ran to the edge of the pier, watching until the ship disappeared behind the bulge of Mount Edgecumbe. Though heartsick at knowing her father was gone, she was now at least free to pursue her own future. She felt confident that she would find Jared and that, maybe before her twentieth birthday, she would become his wife.

Chapter Thirty-five

1867

Darkness was threatening as Tasha hurried from the harbor. She knew it wasn't safe to be out after dark, but she had one more important errand to perform before returning home.

In the months since the American occupation began, she had become acquainted with a few of the Kolosh people, and had found them not at all as frightening as she had once supposed. Now she turned toward their village, clasping some jewelry within her reticule as she hurried toward the shack of a Kolosh known in the city only as Tom.

During the weeks since her father had agreed to sail on the *Dvorets,* she had thought over her course of action many times. With the arrival of winter, it seemed unlikely that any passenger ships would be coming from the United States. There might be a few troop transports during the winter, but, having seen how the soldiers behaved in Sitka, Tasha had no desire to travel on the same ship with any of them. If she could get to British territory, further south on the coast of North America, perhaps she could find a ship bound for San Francisco. She knew the brisk fur trade kept the shipping there busy all winter. Tom, with his sturdy skin bidarka, could ferry her to one of the British islands, if she could convince him to do so.

Tom, wrapped in the traditional blue blanket of the Kolosh, was coming out of his shack just as Tasha reached it. He would have passed her by in his hurry had she not grabbed his arm.

"Please, Tom, I must talk with you."

"No time now, Gospoja Tasha," he mumbled, "must hurry to barracks. Soldiers are giving out free liquor to celebrate the new year. Must get there before all given away."

Tasha grimaced. If Tom downed several bottles of the soldiers' cheap whiskey, he would be of no use for several days. Desperately, she dug into her reticule, withdrawing a sapphire and diamond bracelet and a pair of matching earrings, the last pieces of jewelry left from the gifts she had received from Pyotr Stanovsky. Tom's eyes widened appreciatively as the gems glittered in the shadows. He reached out a finger to touch the jewelry.

"For me?" he breathed.

Tasha nodded encouragingly. "Perhaps, if we can make a bargain."

"What kind of bargain?"

She took a deep breath and tried to sound nonchalant. "I want you to take me to the Queen Charlotte Islands."

The Indian blinked and shook his head in disbelief. "Not possible. Too far."

Tasha clucked her tongue disapprovingly. "Tom, I thought you were the bravest and strongest of the Kolosh. How can you say it's too far?"

He shrugged in embarrassment. "Not too far for

me. But too far for you. Woman not strong enough for long journey."

"That is where you are wrong," she said steadily. "I intend to go, whether you take me or not. Will you sell me a bidarka for the price of these earrings?"

"No."

Tasha dropped the jewelry back into the reticule. "Then I shall have to seek the aid of someone else. Is Misha at home?" Without waiting for an answer, she took a few steps toward a neighboring shack.

"Wait!" Tom's voice stopped her. He walked around to face her. "I will take you. But jewelry you showed me is not enough for such a long journey. I must have more payment."

She gulped. "I have nothing else."

"No more jewels?"

"No." Tasha shook her head, then remembered the emerald necklace her father had given her. Could she give up that one keepsake she had guarded through all her travels? Of course she could. Her memories of Mikhail were stronger than gold and jewels. "Yes," she blurted, "there is something else. A very precious necklace—and perhaps a bit of money." She could give him some of the money her father had left, as long as she put enough aside to pay her own passage from the islands to San Francisco and to transport Theodosia to her relatives.

Tom shook his head. "No money. White man's money is useless. Jewels are better. You give me jewels and I will take you. When you want to go?"

"Tomorrow morning," she said firmly.

Tom sighed. "So soon? Can you not wait a few days?"

"Tomorrow, or I will find someone else to take my jewels!" Tasha hoped her voice did not betray her uneasiness. If Tom would not take her, it was unlikely that any of his neighbors would. She took out the bracelet again to help convince him.

He fingered it appraisingly before grunting in

417

agreement. "Tomorrow. Eight o'clock. Now you leave bracelet with me. Bring earrings and necklace tomorrow."

"No. I will give you the jewelry tomorrow when we start the journey."

Tom turned aside, speaking in a hurt voice. "You ask me to take you on long journey, but you not trust me to keep bargain."

Tasha hesitated; he was right, of course. She was afraid his liking for alcohol would tempt him to trade the bracelet to the soldiers for a supply of liquor. If he did, he would be in no condition to paddle a bidarka in the morning. Still, if she did not show some token of trust, he might even now change his mind about taking her.

"All right," she sighed, reluctantly handing over the bracelet. "But you won't drink tonight, will you Tom?"

"You trust Tom," he said proudly. "Meet me tomorrow."

There was nothing to do but hope he would keep the bargain. Trying to still her troubled thoughts, Tasha hurried out of the village, through the gates into the city, past the barracks already ringing with raucous, drunken laughter, and, finally, into her father's house. She called for Theodosia as she entered, but received no answer. Assuming the woman was visiting a neighbor, she went upstairs, where, emotionally and physically exhausted, she threw herself across her bed. Later, she thought, she would tell Theodosia of her plans and pack what little there would be room for in the bidarka. But, for the moment, she craved only the solace of sleep.

Tasha had no idea how long she had slept when the sound of tramping feet in the second floor hallway awakened her. She lay motionless, still groggy, wondering if she could be imagining the sounds. Suddenly, the bedroom door flew open and three uniformed soldiers stood framed in the doorway. She screamed hysterically, and they laughed until her screams subsided.

In a panic, Tasha jumped off the bed on the side away from the door, putting the huge four-poster between herself and the soldiers. "What do you want?" she demanded in English.

They advanced slowly into the room, stumbling and grinning lewdly. "Well, I'll be," one of them, a chunky, short man with sandy hair said, "this one speaks English. I think she's gonna give us a real happy new year!"

"What do you want?" she repeated harshly.

"Come on, honey," the tall, brawny one guffawed, "you know what we want! And I'll bet you want the same thing, if you'll only admit it."

"I don't know what you're talking about!" she screamed. "But you'd better get out of here before my husband finds you in my bedroom!"

"And where might this brave husband of yours be?" asked the third man.

"He—" she faltered, already knowing they saw through her bluff. "He stepped out. But he'll be back any second."

"And I suppose you think he's a match for the three of us?" the brawny one smirked, obviously enjoying the game.

"Yes! He and his rifle are!"

"I see." He leaned across the bed, just missing grabbing her as she stepped back.

"She's lying," the chunky one squealed impatiently. "I don't think she has a husband. Norton and I saw her standing around on the docks all day, just waiting for someone to pick her up. Then around twilight, I saw her coming from the injun village."

"You mean she's so desperate she'd settle for one of those savages?" the black-haired one asked.

The chunky one laughed cruelly. "She's so desperate she'd *pay* a savage. Look what one of them gave me for an extra bottle of whiskey!"

419

Tasha groaned inwardly as he pulled her bracelet from his pocket and held it aloft. Clearly, Tom had not been able to resist the temptation offered at the barracks.

"Ain't they pretty jewels?" the man laughed.

"She's the only jewel I'm interested in," the brawny one said.

Tasha backed away, her eyes desperately roaming the room for some weapon with which to fight off the intruders. "There is no question in my mind," she said icily, "about who the savages in Sitka are!"

"Oh ho!" the brawny one laughed cynically, "so you're a philosopher, too! I'll bet someone wasted a fine education on you. What a pity. A woman with a body like yours is only meant for one thing."

"Oh really?" she smiled sweetly, playing for time. "Then I suppose I could not interest you gentlemen in a piano recital. I'm told I'm quite accomplished in the field of music." Behind her she could feel the dressing table. Reaching slowly behind her back, she located a hand mirror and a heavy silver hairbrush. If she could just divert their attention long enough. "Or perhaps," she continued, smiling innocently, "we could go downstairs and I could cook you a fine meal. Have you ever had a Russian New Year's feast?"

"Honey," the brawny one laughed, "you're enough New Year's feast for all of us!"

All three doubled over in laughter at their own wit and her apparent naivete. Seizing the opportunity, Tasha hurled the mirror and the hairbrush at their heads and raced for the door. The hairbrush hit the black-haired one squarely on the bridge of his nose, stunning him. Miraculously, the mirror smacked into the tall soldier's jaw, shattering on impact and peppering his face with tiny slivers of glass.

She had reached the hall when she heard their anguished cries and curses. Suddenly, the chunky one, the only one of the three to escape injury, realized she had slipped out of the room. With an infuriated howl, he dashed for the door and with a flying leap, lunged for her just as she neared the staircase. He landed hard on the hallway floor. Determined not to let her escape, his hand reached out just in time to grab her ankle.

Screaming, Tasha vainly kicked out her leg, trying to free her foot from his iron grip. His other hand slapped over the first, and with a wrenching twist, he brought her to the floor.

"I've got her! I've got her!" he yelled to his companions as he crawled forward to cover her body with his. Furiously, Tasha flailed and kicked and scratched, trying to repulse him.

"Damn you!" he muttered through clenched teeth, "stop fighting, woman!"

"Out of the way, Charley." She recognized the tall soldier's voice. "We'll get her."

The man named Charley rolled away, and before Tasha could escape, a voluminous mound of cloth enveloped her. It took her a moment as she kicked and squirmed, attempting to cast it off, before she realized it was the comforter from her bed.

She could hear muffled laughter as she struggled in the cloth cocoon. The more she moved, the more hopelessly entangled she became. She felt herself losing all sense of reason, all notion of exactly where she was. All she knew was that she had to find a way to get away from the three fiends laughing above her.

With a sudden lurch, she felt herself hurtling through space, rolling downward in a series of painful bumps. "Better grab her before she hits bottom!" a man's voice yelled.

The next moments were a confusing melee of sounds and sensations. She felt herself being lifted, still enshrouded in the comforter . . . a familiar, worried woman's voice calling her name . . . a man harshly bidding the woman to be quiet . . . the sound of an open palm slapping against a cheek, followed by anguished sobs and pleading . . . motion . . . the chill, damp feeling of outdoors . . . then a mixture of men's voices . . . snatches of conversation about the officers'

club, about burning something . . . the crackle of
flames . . . again, agonized woman's screams . . . and
finally, the blessed blackness of unconsciousness.

Tasha's eyes focused slowly as she awoke and found
herself on a red velvet couch. In the dim candlelight,
she recognized the drawing room of Baranov Castle.
But something about it was not right. The velvet
draperies were torn and drooping, and several of the
mirrors were cracked or shattered.

Gradually, she remembered. The castle was no
longer the governor's mansion, but the officers' club.
The Russian governor no longer lived here, and she—
she covered her face and sobbed aloud as she recol-
lected the assault made on her. She could recall fighting
at the house, being trapped beneath the comforter,
falling down the stairs, hearing Theodosia's screams,
and being carried outside. But what had happened
afterwards? Had all three of her attackers defiled her
and then left her there?

She heard a chuckle and the tall, brawny soldier
moved into view. "Quite an exciting evening so far,
don't you think?" he taunted.

She glared at him, feeling too weak to fly off the
couch and pummel him, though she desperately wanted to. "Haven't you had enough amusement for
one evening?" she asked bitterly.

"Not nearly enough," he smiled cynically. "In fact,
the main course is yet to come. I thought I would
wait until you were conscious so you could share the
fun."

"And your companions?"

He shrugged. "They got tired of waiting for you to
come around, so they went off to have a few drinks.
They'll be back later. If not, they can enjoy you some
other time. You'll be living here from now on, you
know."

Tasha sat up with a determined toss of her head.
"I think not!"

"If I were you," he chuckled, "I wouldn't be so

hasty in rejecting the offer of shelter. Your house seems to have met with an unfortunate accident!"

Then she remembered the talk of fire and the sound of crackling flames. "You burned my father's house!" she screamed accusingly.

"Oh, is it your father's now? Have you forgotten that earlier you claimed to have shared it with a husband?"

His smug smile infuriated her. "What did you do with Theodosia?" she demanded.

"The old hag?" He shrugged nonchalantly. "If you mean, did she burn up with the house, not unless she was stupid enough to run back in there herself. We didn't tie her up and throw her into the flames or anything. Despite what you might think, we're not cruel fellows."

"How nice to hear that!" she said sarcastically, forcing herself unsteadily to her feet. "Thank you for your hospitality, but if you'll excuse me, I really must be on my way."

"Sit down!" he growled. "You and I are not finished yet." As she opened her mouth, he clapped a hand over it. "I'll warn you once. You can scream if you want, but it won't make things any easier for you. In fact, it'll just bring in the other men to watch, and lend a hand, and demand their share." Smiling, he removed his hand. "Of course, that's entirely up to you. Perhaps you would enjoy performing for an audience. Either way, I get what I want, and I don't mind sharing after I've had my fill."

Stifling a scream, Tasha lunged for the drawing room door. His arm shot out mechanically, grabbing her by the wrist and squeezing it unmercifully as he dragged her back toward the couch.

"Haven't you had the fight knocked out of you yet?" he muttered.

In answer, Tasha squirmed violently, gritting her teeth as she sought to ignore the pain in her wrist. She tried to kick him, but his long arm enabled him to jump out of her range while still maintaining a firm hold on her. His other hand flew to her bodice, and with a sharp rip, he split her dress to the waist. He hesitated a moment, transfixed by the sight of her heaving breasts, then he continued ripping at and pulling off her skirt and petticoats. Shreds of material were hanging from her shoulders, until he ripped even them away. His arm swept around her shoulders and slammed her body into his as he bent over to impart a slobbering kiss.

"Leave me alone!" she hissed through clenched teeth, refusing to allow his tongue into her mouth. "Leave me alone or I swear I'll kill you!"

"I doubt that," he chuckled, moving his lips to her throat. "I'll leave you alone—later."

Lifting her from the floor, he flung her onto the couch, loosening his trousers as he sprawled over her. She tried to jerk her leg up as his body covered hers, but his hand locked over her knee, forcing it down. "Easy now, baby," he murmured, "you wouldn't want to incapacitate me before we got started, would you?" Chuckling, his hands wandered over her body, fondling and squeezing her flesh while she lay helplessly trapped beneath him.

Dimly, Tasha thought she heard the drawing room door open. She closed her eyes, her face burning with shame, as she wondered who had come to witness her humiliation. A moment passed, and her attacker, consumed by lust, gave no indication that he had heard the noise.

When no raucous laughter or crude statements from onlookers filled the room, Tasha assumed she had imagined the noise, and again concentrated all her strength on holding her thighs together as she felt him probing for an entrance.

"If you value your life, you will release the lady immediately!"

The familiar timbre of the voice exploded into Tasha's consciousness. She must be imagining it! Surely desperation and fear were playing tricks with her mind! Yet, her attacker had frozen over her. Fearing her hopes would be dispelled, Tasha slowly opened her eyes. She blinked, then blinked again as her heart pounded exuberantly. It was her own, dear Jared! He had a beard now, a wild, golden mane tinged with red. But the eyes were the same, and the nose, the strong shoulders, and the well-muscled body. He was really there! His voice was not a creation of her wild imagination; nor his form an image conjured up by her hysterical dread.

His lips set in a grimly determined line, Jared stood behind the couch. His linsey-woolsey shirt was open at the neck, and she could see the sweat beading his chest as he held a pistol to her assailant's head.

The soldier tried to remain cool, but the quiver in his voice betrayed his anxiety. "What does it matter to you, man, if I enjoy a bit of sport with some Russian whore?"

"Not some Russian whore!" Jared corrected menacingly. "You dirty scoundrel, this is my wife!"

"Your wife?" the man chuckled nervously. "You expect me to believe that? She's already told too many stories about husbands and fathers who don't materialize. Now you expect me to believe you're her husband. What would an American want with a Russian wife, anyway? Why don't you go find an American woman to protect?"

Calmly, Jared cocked the pistol. "You're trying my patience and insulting my wife," he said quietly. "Now, remove yourself from the lady, or I will be forced to blow you off."

"I wouldn't advise that," the soldier replied, suddenly confident. "If you care for this woman at all, you'd better wait outside until I've finished with her. I could move just a fraction of an inch, even while you pulled the trigger, and the bullet intended for me might easily go astray. But then," his voice turned nasty, "there are plenty of other women in Sitka."

The last word was hardly out of his mouth when Jared dropped the pistol and vaulted over the back of the couch, tearing the soldier off Tasha and tumbling with him to the floor. The commotion knocked

Tasha to the floor as well, stunning her momentarily.

Dazed, she stared at the two fiercely interlocked bodies. The soldier outweighed Jared by at least fifty pounds, but he was not in the best condition due to the slothful lifestyle of the soldiers in Alaska, plus the fact he had been drinking. Jared, on the other hand, was all firm muscle. Tasha felt sure he could overwhelm the marauder. Still, she groped instinctively for the abandoned pistol.

Holding her breath, she watched as Jared forced the soldier almost onto his back. Grunting like an enraged animal, the soldier rolled to his side and edged his body over Jared's, flattening him beneath his superior weight. The cords in Jared's neck bulged as, gritting his teeth, he tried to summon enough strength to throw the man off. Sweat poured from his brow and matted his hair and beard.

The cold weight of the gun in her hands prodded Tasha to action. She could not watch helplessly as this martial beast robbed her of her beloved. Shaking mightily, she raised the weapon and pointed it at the soldier's back. She had never fired a gun, and was not even sure how to take aim. But at that moment, she was sure of only one thing. She wanted to kill this man who had humiliated her and was now threatening Jared's life. She crawled closer, trying to steady the pistol.

Her movements caught Jared's eye and he shouted, "Tasha, no!"

That cry was enough to divert the soldier's attention. He loosened his grip on Jared as he whirled toward Tasha, grabbing for the gun.

At the sound of Jared's voice, Tasha froze, her finger glued to the trigger as she stared at him in confusion. Why wouldn't he let her end the battle? The soldier lunged for the barrel of the gun in an attempt to wrest it from her hand. In that instant, the pistol went off and Tasha watched in horror as a red splotch spread across his shoulder. The man crumpled, cursing under his breath as he clutched the wound.

Jared scrambled to his feet. Scooping Tasha into his arms, he strode to a window and ripped a faded velvet drape from its rod. Swiftly, he wrapped her in the drapery, muffling her sobs against his chest. He started toward the drawing room door, but reconsidered when he heard the excited voices of soldiers, obviously drawn by the sound of the shot, approaching in the hallway. Throwing open the casement window, he tossed Tasha onto the ground, then quickly leaped after her.

As she hit the hard ground, Tasha began to recover her wits. Struggling to her feet, she wrapped the drapery tightly around her and pushed Jared away as he bent to lift her again.

"I can run," she whispered urgently. "It will be faster this way. Follow me."

He hurried after her as she streaked down the deserted boardwalk. Jared took her hand, pulling her to her feet as she stumbled. The shouts from Baranov Castle were obliterated by the wind rushing in their ears.

Determined to outrun the wind, the shouts, and the unhappiness of the past, Tasha suddenly felt exultant. They were together again and nothing else mattered —this time she was sure nothing would ever separate them again.

1868

The bells in St. Mikhail's Cathedral chimed one o'clock as the first hour of the New Year passed. Tasha snuggled drowsily against Jared's shoulder.

They were safe for the time being, having taken refuge in Bishop Petr's house, which had been vacated only a week earlier when the bishop was ordered south to oversee the Orthodox diocese which had its seat in San Francisco. Only moments after they arrived at the house, Theodosia appeared and threw herself into Tasha's arms, sobbing with joy to find her mistress alive and unharmed. The old woman quickly realized Tasha's and Jared's need to be alone and had excused herself to another room, where she immediately fell into peaceful sleep.

Having overcome the first hysterics of escape, and having exhausted themselves with the sweetest intimacy of reunion, Tasha and Jared curled up together for the inevitable questions and explanations.

"It's strange," she began, "I told Papa you would be here by the first of the year—and here you are. How did you find me, Jared?"

Slowly he wound a strand of her hair around his finger, bringing it to his lips for a light kiss before answering. "I arrived this evening and ran all the way to your home. I could see the flames before I even reached the corner of your street, but I refused to believe the fire could be coming from your house. Even when I stood before it and felt the heat, I couldn't believe my eyes. Theodosia was wandering in the street. Of course I had never met her, so I thought she was just some wailing old woman—until she grabbed me and screamed your name over and over.

"I tried to get her to tell me more but—she could

not speak English, and you know I speak no Russian. Assuming you were trapped inside, I tried to shake her off, but she would not let go of me. She kept babbling and pointing toward the end of the street. Finally, I realized you were not in the burning house, but you were in some kind of danger somewhere else.

"While I was relieved to know you weren't in that inferno—I doubted I could have saved you, since the second floor came crashing down while I stood there —I still figured something terrible was happening, because Theodosia was half out of her mind.

"She practically dragged me to Baranov Castle, and stood outside pointing at the door and babbling something that included 'Tasha' and 'Offeetserov'."

"I wonder how she knew to trust you?" Tasha mused.

"Perhaps she saw me with you that day more than three years ago when I visited your father's and proposed to you," he suggested. "Or," he chuckled, "maybe she just surmised I was the man you have been waiting for for so long. You have been waiting for me, haven't you?"

"What do you think? Of course I've been waiting! And Theodosia did know that much. But finish the story. What happened when you got to the castle?"

"I went to the door, which was unlocked; so I let myself in. There was a good deal of noise coming from the rooms toward the back, and I thought if I just burst into the middle of some rowdy party I might get both of us killed. So I decided I'd better proceed through the house slowly, and give myself time to think. Fortunately for both of us, the first door I opened led to the drawing room." He paused and expelled a long sigh. "You know the rest."

"All too well," she whispered. "I was sorry to have you see me that way. But, oh dear God, I was so glad to see you!"

He slapped her rump playfully. "For a moment

430

there, I wondered about that. Why did you try to kill me?"

"What?" Her voice was shocked. "I didn't—"

"Did anyone ever instruct you in the use of a pistol?"

"No."

"Well," he laughed lightly, "you made that quite obvious. If I hadn't yelled, your soldier friend might be holding you now, instead of me!"

Tasha stiffened. "He isn't my friend! The fact is, I don't even know his name."

"Shush," Jared soothed, gently stroking her back, "I'm only teasing you. And everything turned out for the best anyway. Do you want to tell me how you came to be there?"

"I think you could probably guess."

"He took you from your house?"

She nodded. "He and two others. I fought, but they overcame me."

"And did they set the fire themselves?"

"I'm sure of it. They had me rolled up in a comforter, so I couldn't see, but I heard the crackle of the flames. I passed out after that."

"Why do you suppose they burned it?"

"Purely for spite. And to add some more excitement to their evening. It isn't the first thing they've burned. Several barns have gone up in flames."

Jared hesitated uneasily, unsure how to phrase his next question. "There wasn't—was anyone else in the house?"

"Happily, papa sailed for Russia only this afternoon, taking all the servants but Theodosia with him."

"And your—husband."

Tasha brightened. "I have no husband. I am a widow."

He sucked in his breath. "Not by your own hand, I hope?"

"No. I hated Yuri, but I never would have killed him. I wouldn't want to begin our marriage with

431

blood on my conscience. He died of a fever in the tropics. I never saw him again after he left Kamchatka. By the time I met you in Washington, he had been dead several months."

Jared laughed shortly. "And so we could have married in New York after all! Well, it doesn't matter now. You can be sure that after these last months apart I will never let you out of my sight again."

"And you can be sure I will not let you." Playfully, she nibbled his ear. "But what *did* keep you away so long?"

"A woman." He chuckled.

"Don't bait me, Jared! If you're trying to test my trust, I'll have you know I won't believe such nonsense! Now tell me truthfully, what kept you from me?"

"I am being truthful, Tasha, my love. It was a woman."

"Ohh!" A slight note of irritation crept into her voice as she turned away from him abruptly. "You are as infuriating as ever. It's beyond me how I ever thought I could spend the rest of my life with someone like you!"

Laughing, he pulled her back to him. "Well, it's too late now to reconsider. I intend to hold you to your promise. In all seriousness, Tasha, it was a woman who caused my delay. The day after you sailed, I was on my way to the harbor to check about passage when some woman accosted me and claimed I murdered her husband."

"Did you?"

"Of course not! I've never murdered anyone in my life, and I'd never seen the woman before or met anyone who looked like her husband. At any rate, she had brought some of the sheriff's men along and they promptly threw me in jail."

"But how could they do that?" Tasha demanded indignantly.

"I asked the same question, and they told me just to relax, that everything would come out in the trial. Everything did come out, but almost too late to save me.

"It was the last day of the trial, and all the evidence pointed to a man who looked like me. All my protests were unavailing, and I was beginning to fear they'd hang me and I wouldn't even be able to get word to you. All the time I was in jail, I couldn't get anyone to deliver a letter to one of the ships bound for Alaska.

"But I swear, what happened on the last day was like a miracle. Do you remember the purser on the *Tropical Queen*, the ship we took to Panama?"

"It's not likely I'd forget that pompous idiot!"

"Your opinion of him might change when you learn how he saved my life."

"*He* saved your life?" Her voice was unbelieving.

"So it seems. The trial was the talk of San Francisco. According to local gossip, everyone was anxious to see me swing. The man who had been murdered was a local dignitary and everyone wanted to see his death avenged."

"But how was the purser involved?" Tasha interrupted impatiently.

"I'm getting to that now. The *Tropical Queen* arrived in San Francisco the day before my trial ended, and the purser heard about the case at his hotel. Apparently, he recognized my name—primarily because of the long discussion you had with him before we sailed from New York. At any rate, he came forth with records from the *Tropical Queen* proving I arrived in Colon on the very day of the murder, so the jury had no choice but to acquit me."

"Did they ever find the real murderer?"

"At that point, I could hardly have cared less. I'd already wasted too many months sitting in jail or in a courtroom, and I was beginning to imagine I had really lost you this time. It was impossible to find a ship with space for a single passenger, and the thought of staying in San Francisco any longer didn't much appeal to me—first, because I was afraid I might never get passage, and secondly because life was just too precious. Some of those folks were so hot for a hanging I was afraid they'd string me up no matter what the courts said.

"So, in the interests of preserving my skin and my sanity, I started north by an overland route. It wasn't an easy trip through Oregon and the Washington Territory, and by the time I'd made it to British Columbia I was beginning to wonder if I wasn't a damned fool. But every time I got sick of traveling, I just thought of you waiting here, and my body seemed to find all the strength it needed. I made the last leg of the trip by bidarka from the Queen Charlotte Islands."

Tasha giggled.

Startled, Jared asked, "Do you find my sufferings so comical?"

"Not at all," she soothed. "I was simply thinking that I intended to leave for those same islands tomorrow, to take a ship to California so I could search for you."

"Oh, Tasha!" he kissed her tenderly. "That's a terrible trip to make alone—it's more than two hundred miles through icy waters."

"I hadn't intended to go alone, though it seems in the end I might have been forced to. The Kolosh who was to take me apparently got drunk last night."

"Well, I love you more than ever for thinking of making the trip, but I'm glad you didn't go." He groaned. "I don't know if I could have borne the frustration of arriving here only to find you gone."

"Let's not even think about it. We're here now and all is well."

"Well enough for the present," Jared sighed. "But in the morning I am going directly to the commander of this garrison and demand an apology for the way you were treated, as well as restitution for your house and property."

Tasha tensed. "Don't, Jared!" she pleaded.

"Yes, I must! It's unthinkable to remain silent about

434

something like this! Those soldiers must be sternly reprimanded!"

"But they won't be," she sighed wearily, "no matter what you might say. Jared, you don't understand because you haven't lived here these last months. You can't imagine what a hellish place this city has become. Major-General Davis would laugh at your complaint. And the two of us can't fight a garrison of five hundred, no matter how right we are."

"Then what would you have me do?" he asked quietly.

"Just take me away! This is no longer the Novo-arkhangelsk I loved! I'll gladly go anywhere, so long as we are together."

He sat up slowly, considering her words. "Would Theodosia go with us?"

"No. She insists Alaska is her home and she will die in the territory. She has some relatives on one of the other islands and she's talked several times of going to live with them after I left."

"All right," he stood and walked to his bag, which Theodosia had salvaged while he was rescuing Tasha. "How soon do you want to leave?"

"As soon as we are able."

He nodded. "Good." He rummaged in his bag until he found a shirt and trousers. Tossing them to her, he quipped, "Oversized, I'm afraid, but if I remember correctly, I once shared my bunk on the *Freedom* with a girl who looked rather stunning in men's clothing. Get dressed, my love. It's a mighty long way to Oregon, and the sooner we leave the better."

Tasha gasped. "Do you mean to leave tonight?"

"Why not? It's a new year. Why begin it in a dying city? My bidarka is still on the beach, and the moon is full enough to provide the light we need." He opened his arms to her invitingly. "Shall we begin our new life?"

Tasha ran to him, suddenly feeling refreshed and drained of all the fatigue she had felt only an hour earlier. She threw her arms around his neck, thrilling at the feel of his firm, smooth muscles as she pressed her body against his.

"I think," she whispered contentedly, "that it has just begun."

ABOUT THE AUTHOR

LYNN LOWERY is a student of Russian history and culture, so that nineteenth-century Russia was a logical choice for her first romantic historical novel, *Sweet Rush of Passion*. With her husband, she has written several juvenile books. Ms. Lowery lives in Evanston, Illinois.

A Special Preview of
the exciting opening pages of the
first novel in the new "Wagons West" series
from the producer of the "Kent Family Chronicles"

INDEPENDENCE!
By Dana Fuller Ross

The enthralling saga of the turbulent lives
of the daring men and women who joined
one of the first wagon trains thundering West.

I

"I disagree with you, Mr. President," Sam Brentwood said. "I think you're dead wrong."

Andrew Jackson averted his face so his visitor wouldn't see his grin, and stared out of the window at the thick coating of white snow on the neat lawn. Winter had come early to Washington City, his last full winter in the White House. He reflected that, in the more than seven and a half years he had spent as President of the United States, few people had dared oppose him to his face. Sam Brentwood, of course, was afraid of no one and always spoke his mind.

Composing himself, Jackson turned back to the man he had summoned from the distant frontier town of Independence, Missouri, and studied him in the unexpectedly strong sunlight that had streamed into the President's office in the wake of the snowstorm. Sam wore well, in spite of the wrinkles at the corners of his eyes and a skin that, after years in the Rocky Mountains, resembled old leather. Sam had to be close to forty now, the President thought, remembering him as a seventeen-year-old scout back in the winter of 1814–15, when he had contributed so much to Jackson's celebrated victory against the British at the Battle of New Orleans. Sam hadn't gained an ounce in all those years. His life as a hunter, trapper and guide kept him fit.

"You're taking a short-sighted view, lad," Jackson said, speaking in the gentle tones he reserved for old and trusted friends.

"The hell you say, sir!" Sam was still vehement. "When I pulled into Independence with the season's load of furs from the mountains and found your letter asking me to come here in a hurry, I dropped everything. If I'd known you were aiming to destroy the West I'd have taken my time."

Jackson couldn't keep a straight face any longer, and laughed heartily.

There was no malice in Sam's return smile, but he shook his head. "I'm damned if I'm joking, Mr. President. You can go for days at a time in the Great Plains without seeing another soul. Just like you can spend weeks alone in the Rockies. And you're asking me to fill up the West with settlers."

"Not exactly. I'm trying to organize my last major campaign before Martin Van Buren takes over this job of mine in March. If I can get the financial backing of men who have a vested interest in the West—and I believe I can—I'm asking you to lead a covered wagon train out to the Oregon country on the Pacific. Or at least to take it as far as you can, and get somebody else as wagonmaster for the rest of the trip."

"You know how the Indians are going to react when they see hundreds of strangers coming into their territory in wagons?" Sam said.

Andrew Jackson nodded. "I reckon. At least some of them will be unhappy until they find out we mean them no harm. That's why I need a man with your experience in charge, Sam. You served with me against the Choctaw in Tennessee and the Seminole in Florida when they were ornery, and you helped work out the treaties that were as fair to them as they were to us. So you understand Indians."

"Maybe so, Mr. President." Sam Brentwood could be stubborn when he made up his mind. "But I hate to see the West get filled up with people."

"So do I," Jackson replied quietly. "But there's no choice. Immigrants are still coming here from the Old World faster than the cities and towns of the East can absorb them. We're the only viable democracy in the world, and there's only one way we can expand—by moving people westward."

Sam sighed, realizing that, like the president, he had to accept the inevitability of national growth. "I suppose so," he said grudgingly.

"There's still more behind all this," the President said, "and I'll thank you to regard it as highly confidential."

His tone as well as his words caused the lean visitor to sit upright. "Yes, sir!" he said.

"The claim of the United States to the Oregon Territory is unclear and muddled." Jackson spoke soberly now, his eyes clouded. "Great Britain has a claim every bit as valid as ours. So has Imperial Russia. They were the first nation to occupy Oregon, but they pulled out when we and the British began to contest it. Pulled out a little too fast and too easily to suit me."

"What you're saying, Mr. President, is that this country is in a battle with two of the world's most powerful nations."

"It could be three of them if Spain should decide to press her claims. But London and St. Petersburg are worrying me, not Madrid. We've fought the British twice in the past sixty years, and we could whip the Redcoats again. However, wars are a luxury a young nation really can't afford. The British have the world's strongest navy, plenty of manpower and all the money they need. The Russians aren't as well off, but they're still rich and strong. We need everything. Manpower. Factories. More agricultural products. Meat on our young bones."

Sam nodded, seeing the problem for the first time from a new perspective.

"Every American," Jackson said, "automatically expects us to stretch from the Atlantic to the Pacific."

"Well, sure." Sam himself thought in no other terms.

"If the British or the Russians can establish a solid foothold first," the president declared, "that's the end of America's dreams. The British can start moving from west to east, using Canada as a base for their operations. They can take the Rocky Mountains. They can even move into the Great Plains, and we'll have another major war on our hands if we want that land. We could be pushed all the way back to the Mississippi River."

Sam was starting to forget his objections to the settlement of the West.

"We have one natural advantage over London and St. Petersburg. We're closer. By thousands of miles." Jackson was emphatic. "It will be difficult for the British to occupy the Pacific Northwest, and even harder for the Russians. I'm not saying we can just walk in. But we can send our people as settlers, first by the hundreds and then by the thousands. Once they've established homesteads and built towns and roads, British and Russian claims won't amount to a pot of burned beans. If America really intends to fulfill her destiny and become a great nation, our citizens have got to go into Oregon. There's no two ways about it."

A handful of mountain men might prefer isolation, Sam realized, but the needs of the country as a whole were paramount.

"Much as we need settlers in Oregon," the president continued, "we're not asking them for favors. I'm told that not even Tennessee and Kentucky have land that rich, forests as full of game or rivers as crammed with fish."

"So I hear, sir."

The president stared at his visitor in ill-concealed dismay. "You just hear, Sam? You don't actually know Oregon?"

"No, sir. I've done no traveling the other side of the continental divide. But I won't let you down, Mr. President."

"That's good to hear. How well do you know the town of Independence?"

"There isn't all that much to know, sir. It has a general store and a couple of taverns."

"That's going to change. The settlers bound for Oregon will need a supply base, and we aim to build up Independence. Would you be willing to act as wagonmaster to the first train as far as Independence, and then stay there to organize a depot for later trains?"

"I'll do anything you want, Mr. President."

"Thank you. Now, once I find a guide who'll take the first band of settlers from Independence to the Pacific, I'll be ready to start talking to the financiers."

"I have your man," Sam Brentwood said.

Jackson leaned forward in his chair.

"Mike Holt is my friend. Out in the Rockies he's known as 'Whip' because he can do things with a bullwhip as a weapon that you wouldn't believe. He's still in his twenties, at least ten years younger than I am, but he's been a hunter and trapper for a long time. He knows the Great Plains and the Rockies as well as I do, and he's friendlier with the Indian tribes out there. And he's gone through the Oregon territory at least twice."

"Do you suppose he'd be willing to replace you at Independence?"

"I think he'd do it for me. And I know he'd ride a log down the Colorado River rapids if you asked him to do it. You're his idol."

"That's comforting to hear, even if I question his judgment," Jackson said. "Where can he be reached?"

"If he hasn't already brought his furs down from the mountains to Independence, he'll be arriving there mighty soon. Just looking out these windows tells you the whole country is going to have an early winter, and Whip Holt is no more inclined to freeze to death up in the mountains than I am."

"Send for him, Sam. Tell him I want to see him, and the Government will pay his expenses. But put no details in writing. We can't take any chances if we hope to beat the British and the Russians to the punch."

Sam nodded.

Suddenly the President of the United States sighed. "I'll tell you another secret, Sam," he said, looking forlorn. "When I leave office in another three months I'll go back to my property outside Nashville and rusticate. Meanwhile you'll be on the road with a wagon train, you and this fellow Whip Holt, if he works out as you think he will. You'll be having all the fun. And between us, Sam, I envy the living daylights out of you!"

"I'm not a vixen, I'm not a witch and I'm not an overbearing woman!" Claudia Humphries spoke quietly, as befitted a New England lady of the 1830s, but her voice carried far beyond the confines of the Long Island farmhouse kitchen. "I'm a former schoolteacher, I have the misfortune to be a widow, and I refuse to be buried in a premature grave beside my husband or to let other people manage my life for me! And that's final."

As she marched up and down her brother-in-law's kitchen, her kohl-rimmed green eyes alight and her shoulder-length blonde hair tousled, not even her voluminous silk dress and petticoats could totally conceal the lithe figure of a twenty-seven-year-old woman in radiant good health. She not only meant every word, but seemed to be speaking the truth.

Claudia's relatives realized that she was extraordinary, just as her friends and neighbors in New Haven claimed. There was no one else in the world quite like her. Daughter of a widower, she had reared herself and her little sister Cathy before making the mistake of marrying a man who not only had her father's servile temperament, but also suffered from an appetite for liquor.

In Claudia's opinion there were no contradictions in her nature. Intelligent, hard-driving and sensible, she had been horrified when her late husband accused her, in a drunken stupor, of wanting to be the man of the family. Untrue! She was a woman, first, last and always, and proud of it. Since that day, she'd gone out of her way to emphasize her femininity, using cosmetics liberally and wearing clothes that most New England ladies considered much too revealing. Claudia's reaction to their criticism was characteristically blunt. If her detractors had her charms they wouldn't hide them!

On a deeper level, she considered herself self-sufficient. Having managed Papa's affairs for a long time, she had taken charge of her husband's business when he himself proved incompetent. It was Claudia's private conviction, zealously guarded, that men were little better than bumblers, inferior beings all.

Occasionally she revealed her innermost attitudes without realizing it. A New Haven physician, who had known her for a long time, tried to put it in a nutshell: "What Claudia needs is a man who can handle her. But I doubt if the good Lord ever created a man that strong, that wise and that patient."

Certainly her relatives couldn't restrain her. Her younger sister, Cathy van Ayl, who was twenty-one and resembled her, was the mistress of her own home, at least theoretically, but she knew better than to reply. Long familiar with Claudia's temper, she could only shudder.

Claudia pointed a slender finger at her middle-aged brother-in-law, Otto van Ayl. "You're neither my father nor my husband, so I won't permit you to dictate what I do."

Otto sighed. Married to Cathy for four years, trying in vain to earn a decent profit from his farm near Montauk Point on the eastern tip of Long Island, he had enough trouble trying to handle a spirited wife young enough to be his daughter. Attempting to control Cathy's fiery, sophisticated sister also, was way beyond his capacity.

"You can sell this place and take Cathy anywhere you please. Kansas City, the Ohio Valley, even the wilds of Illinois for all I care. But I'm not going with you!"

Otto rubbed a hand across his balding head. He'd never known anyone like her. "I didn't ask Gil Humphries to make me the executor of his will or to put me in charge of his wife's business, and for the past couple of years, ever since he died so suddenly, I've been sorry he did. But the law is the law and I have no choice."

"Indeed you do," Claudia was swift to respond. "You can sell your farm, if that's what you want, and go west. Settle there, if that's your fancy. But allow me to manage my own property. My house in New Haven is snug, my woolen mill earns me enough to pay my bills, and I'm content."

Otto refrained from pouring himself a drink of brandywine from the decanter on the shelf, and helped himself instead to more tea. "You're intelligent," he said, "for a woman. You must have the brains to understand that the law won't let you keep either the mill or the house under your own control. They've got to be supervised for you by a trustee who's a man."

Claudia glared at him.

"I wonder what Mrs. Thomas Jefferson thought when her husband neglected to write that all women are created equal too." Claudia began to pace again, her hips swaying slightly, neither knowing nor caring that she was the epitome of outraged femininity. "Be sensible, Otto. You know very well that for all practical purposes I've been in charge of the mill and the house. I was doing that long before Gil died."

Otto disliked being crossed. "You're the one who's got to be sensible," he said. "Suppose Cathy and I find us a new property a thousand miles from here. No court of law is going to believe I could keep an eye on what you're doing, not from that distance. And the judge would be right. If our system is wrong, change the system." He added, dryly. "But till you do, women aren't allowed to direct their own business affairs, and that's that!"

Otto smiled with a satisfied air. How smug he looks, thought Cathy, like always when he made a conclusive point. That was one of the problems of being married to Otto van Ayl: he was so seldom wrong. All the same, he didn't seem much like a husband; he reminded her of Papa, whose friend he had been. She couldn't feel close to him. They hadn't been intimate since their wedding night, which had been a disaster for both of them. She knew such thoughts were disloyal, however, so she put them out of her mind. In the present instance she happened to agree with him, although she wouldn't dare admit such a thing to Claudia. There was no telling what her sister might do if she really lost her temper.

Claudia was fighting for self-control and gradually winning the battle. She poured herself a cup of tea and sipped it before she spoke again. "Rather than go off into some godforsaken wilderness," she said, "I'd prefer to marry again. There must be some man I could make an arrangement with."

Cathy was so shocked she couldn't remain silent. "Claudia! You wouldn't marry a fortune-hunter."

Her sister's shapely shoulders rose and fell. "I'm not likely to tempt a fortune-hunter. I'm hardly all that rich."

"She isn't marrying anybody," Otto said. "Because she'd need my permission as the head of the family, and I'm not going to give it. Claudia, you're forcing me to act like the villain in that foolish play we saw in New York last month. And I don't like it."

"Well, Otto," Claudia said, "you're trying to force me to leave my home for a wretched life in the wilderness, and I don't like it either," Claudia said, glaring at him defiantly. "I'm aware of your predicament here, Otto, and I sympathize with it. I know the soil on your farm is poor, and salt air isn't good for your crops. You want to sell out and buy a big piece of land where the soil is rich. More power to you—and to Cathy. But it isn't fair to insist that I join you."

INDEPENDENCE!

"I'd be much happier without your nagging, I'm sure," Otto told her. "But I've got to earn my fee as your husband's executor."

Cathy dared to intervene again. "How do you know you wouldn't like it out west, Claudia? You've never been there."

"It's different for you, dear," Claudia replied with asperity. "You were young when you and Otto got married, and you've lived on this isolated farm ever since. But I'm accustomed to the finer things of life, and a little comfort. I enjoy the lectures at Yale College and the theater in New York. I certainly don't look forward to the prospect of hunting for elk or moose—or whatever wild beasts there may be in the Ohio Valley."

Otto chuckled. "You'll have to go out to the real wilderness, all the way to the Rocky Mountains, before you'll find elk and moose."

Claudia tried to cover up her ignorance. "You know very well what I mean. It's become the fashion to be uncouth these past seven and a half years, thanks, no doubt, to President Jackson. But, I can tell you, Andrew Jackson isn't my version of the ideal President, and I'll be very pleased when Martin Van Buren takes office. He's a gentleman."

"God help this country," Otto said, "if women are ever given the right to vote."

Cathy had to laugh. Claudia smiled, too, but her green eyes were cold as the winter waters of the Atlantic.

"Mock me if it gives you pleasure," Claudia said, "but I make you a solemn promise. If you force me to pull up my roots and make a ridiculous journey to some place where no one else lives, if you insist that I live in a cabin like those of the poor Scottish immigrants in Tennessee, if I'm forced to eat wild onions and tough boar meat—well, Otto dear, I won't be alone in my misery."

Free, Rich
LAND!
in the
Oregon Country
New Homesteads for all!

The arthritic pains in Sam Brentwood's hip were intense as he limped to a table in a dark corner of the New York waterfront tavern, but he ignored them. A man learned to live with pain, and at the age of thirty-nine Sam was no stranger to discomfort. With his graying hair and lined face, he looked much older than his years. The bullet wound he had suffered at New Orleans had contributed to that, and so had the scars he still bore after his torture by the Kiowa tribe.

At first glance Sam looked like a city dweller, in his dark broadcloth suit, half-boots and white shirt and stock. But his hands were those of a man who had known hard physical labor. His skin was that of a man who had lived most of his life out of doors and, most of all, his eyes told their own story. Clear and gray, they were the eyes of a fighter, a man who had tasted life to the full, a man of many experiences who had been forced by necessity to pass judgment on his fellow humans in order to survive.

So a stranger who studied him would take him for a frontier dweller, not realizing that he had been born in this part of the country. But his past was very private. Not even his few close friends knew all of it.

Just before the beginning of the nineteenth century, when he had been a small boy, his mother had deserted his father and run away with another man, never again to be seen by her husband or son. So Pa had taken Sam out west, and he had grown to manhood in the wilds near the Mississippi River.

Only since he had come east at President Jackson's request had Sam thought about those days, buried in his memory almost four decades in the past. After all, he had been standing on his own self-reliant feet for a long time. But, he realized, many of his attitudes grew out of those dark days of early childhood.

For example, he hated "ladies," particularly those who put on airs and wore fancy clothes. He found them no better than the whores who, from time to time, took care of his physical needs. On the other hand, he went out of his way to be polite to ordinary women, particularly cooks, chambermaids and others who had to earn their living. Not that he would ever marry one. No woman would ever hurt him the way his Pa had been hurt. Actually, just being in the East now made Sam uneasy, although he could face an entire herd of stampeding buffalo without flinching.

The Eastern Seaboard was too civilized now, boasting theaters and inns, elegant dining places and shops that might rival the best that London and Paris could offer. But Sam made no apology for the curved, bone-handled knife he carried in his belt. He was one of Andy Jackson's cubs, a veteran of more battles than he cared to remember, and New York footpads who regarded him as an easy mark because of his limp hastily changed their minds when they drew closer to him.

The barmaid took it for granted that he wanted whiskey, and stayed out of his reach because she assumed he would try to paw her. Sam surprised her on both counts, treating her with elaborate courtesy as he ordered a small mug of non-alcoholic ginger beer. When he smiled his thanks he looked far younger than his years.

Everyone in this rough establishment—sailors and dock workers alike—gaped at the younger man still in his twenties who arrived to join Sam Brentwood. The heavily tanned Mike Holt was almost painfully thin and towered above everyone else in the tavern. He wore his usual soiled buckskins, disdaining the clothes that New Yorkers regarded as proper, and when he removed his broadbrimmed hat he revealed a shock of pale, blonde hair. What caused the most stir, however, was the coiled bullwhip looped casually around his belt. It seemed a natural part of him, like the moccasins that were molded to his feet.

Holt slid into a chair opposite Sam, moving with

effortless ease. Then he lived up to the barmaid's expectations by slapping her lightly across the buttocks as he ordered a glass of whiskey.

"You're late, Whip," Sam Brentwood said.

Whip Holt had the grace to flush beneath his tan. "I can find my way through a blizzard in the Rockies," he said, "but I get lost in this town. I'm blamed if I know why I had to come here in the first place."

Sam sipped his ginger beer. "You can head west again in a few weeks," he said with a grin, then sobered. "Andy Jackson wanted you to join me for a spell at the start of this expedition, and when General Jackson gives an order it's got to be obeyed."

Whip was well aware of his friend's opinion of the great Andrew Jackson, and wanted no dispute. Sam was the one man he knew who could beat him in a fist-fight, wrestling match or free-for-all.

The barmaid saved him the need for a reply by bringing his drink and favoring him with the broad smile that most women bestowed on him, sooner or later. Whip raised his glass to his companion, then downed its contents in a gulp.

"You and Jed Smith got me into this fix," he said, "but I reserve the right to quit after I see how you make out between here and Independence."

"I can't say I look forward to acting as a nursemaid to misfits, dirt farmers and God only knows what else we'll dredge up on this trip. I wasn't cut out for the life of a nanny. But I reckon the settlement of the Oregon country will be worth a few headaches."

Whip brooded in silence. "It's the most beautiful land there is. Mountains of fir and spruce and pine. Wild onions and berries waiting to be picked. So many salmon in the Columbia River you can almost scoop them out with your bare hands. There's no call there for dirt farmers, or for towns that will be big and ugly as this one is, either. Oregon ought to be left the way it is."

"That's not what Andy Jackson wants," Sam said, and so the issue was settled. "We'll find us an inn where we can stay overnight, and tomorrow we'll go out to Long Island and start to work. There's a farmer out there by the name of Van Ayl—the first to answer

Mr. Astor's advertisement. We'll show him how to fix up a covered wagon nice and cozy. And soon as he's ready we'll start our caravan on its way."

Whip sighed. "I wish I was hunting elk in the Ute Mountains."

"You'll be back there soon enough—which is more than I'll ever do again with my ailing hip."

Whip was abashed. "Sorry, Sam. I didn't mean to—"

"No harm done, boy. Even a stupid old stallion knows when his time to turn out to pasture has come. I told Andy Jackson that this is my last job before I find me a quiet place to live out my days." Sam reached into a fat purse he'd been given earlier in the day at John Jacob Astor's office, selected a gold coin and placed it on the table.

He and Whip were unaccustomed to city ways, and neither realized, as they waited for their change, the stir that the purse and gold coin created. Significant looks were exchanged, silent signals were given and when the pair left the tavern and moved out into the alleyway beyond, they were followed by a half-dozen burly men who quickly surrounded them.

The leader planted himself in front of Sam, blocking his path. "I'll take that purse you're carrying," he said. "Hand it over, or you'll limp on both legs."

Sam's response was rapid and violent. His fist lashed out with great force, smashing the robber full in the face, and the man went down.

Another man drew a pistol from beneath his cloak. Before he could use it, however, Sam was wielding his knife with unerring expertise, slashing his assailant across the hand.

The man howled in agony and dropped his pistol.

In the meantime Mike Holt demonstrated how he had earned his nickname. He uncoiled his bullwhip quickly. It cracked only once—and a third robber screamed in pain. On the second crack, another man dropped his pistol and ran, a red welt forming across his face.

The remaining two men beat a hasty retreat down the alley.

The entire encounter had lasted barely thirty seconds.

INDEPENDENCE!

Sliding his knife into its sheath, Sam calmly nudged the body of the unconscious gang leader with his toe. "Reckon we ought to find us an inn in a better neighborhood for the night," he said, hobbling along at Whip Holt's side. "I'm a mite tired out this evening, and I don't want my sleep disturbed by rowdies."

Claudia, Cathy and Otto—along with other pioneers—join the wagon train headed by Sam and Mike. This is their story, a stirring saga of triumph and tragedy, of love and loss, of adventure and romance.

The complete Bantam Book will be available Feb. 1, 1979, wherever paperbacks are sold. Also look to the future for further books in this Wagons West series—NEBRASKA and OREGON—coming later in 1979.

RELAX!
SIT DOWN
and Catch Up On Your Reading!

☐	11877	**HOLOCAUST** by Gerald Green	$2.25
☐	11260	**THE CHANCELLOR MANUSCRIPT** by Robert Ludlum	$2.25
☐	10077	**TRINITY** by Leon Uris	$2.75
☐	2300	**THE MONEYCHANGERS** by Arthur Hailey	$1.95
☐	12550	**THE MEDITERRANEAN CAPER** by Clive Cussler	$2.25
☐	11469	**AN EXCHANGE OF EAGLES** by Owen Sela	$2.25
☐	2600	**RAGTIME** by E. L. Doctorow	$2.25
☐	11428	**FAIRYTALES** by Cynthia Freeman	$2.25
☐	11966	**THE ODESSA FILE** by Frederick Forsyth	$2.25
☐	11557	**BLOOD RED ROSES** by Elizabeth B. Coker	$2.25
☐	11708	**JAWS 2** by Hank Searls	$2.25
☐	12490	**TINKER, TAILOR, SOLDIER, SPY** by John Le Carre	$2.50
☐	11929	**THE DOGS OF WAR** by Frederick Forsyth	$2.25
☐	10526	**INDIA ALLEN** by Elizabeth B. Coker	$1.95
☐	12489	**THE HARRAD EXPERIMENT** by Robert Rimmer	$2.25
☐	11767	**IMPERIAL 109** by Richard Doyle	$2.50
☐	10500	**DOLORES** by Jacqueline Susann	$1.95
☐	11601	**THE LOVE MACHINE** by Jacqueline Susann	$2.25
☐	11886	**PROFESSOR OF DESIRE** by Philip Roth	$2.50
☐	10857	**THE DAY OF THE JACKAL** by Frederick Forsyth	$1.95
☐	11952	**DRAGONARD** by Rupert Gilchrist	$1.95
☐	11331	**THE HAIGERLOCH PROJECT** by Ib Melchior	$2.25
☐	11330	**THE BEGGARS ARE COMING** by Mary Loos	$1.95

Buy them at your local bookstore or use this handy coupon for ordering:

Bantam Books, Inc., Dept. FBB, 414 East Golf Road, Des Plaines, Ill. 60016

Please send me the books I have checked above. I am enclosing $_____ (please add 75¢ to cover postage and handling). Send check or money order —no cash or C.O.D.'s please.

Mr/Mrs/Miss_____

Address_____

City_____State/Zip_____

FBB—11/78

Please allow four weeks for delivery. This offer expires 5/79.

DON'T MISS
THESE CURRENT
Bantam Bestsellers

☐	11708	**JAWS 2** Hank Searls	$2.25
☐	11150	**THE BOOK OF LISTS** Wallechinsky & Wallace	$2.50
☐	11001	**DR. ATKINS DIET REVOLUTION**	$2.25
☐	11161	**CHANGING** Liv Ullmann	$2.25
☐	10116	**EVEN COWGIRLS GET THE BLUES** Tom Robbins	$2.25
☐	10077	**TRINITY** Leon Uris	$2.75
☐	12250	**ALL CREATURES GREAT AND SMALL** James Herriot	$2.50
☐	12256	**ALL THINGS BRIGHT AND BEAUTIFUL** James Herriot	$2.50
☐	11770	**ONCE IS NOT ENOUGH** Jacqueline Susann	$2.25
☐	11470	**DELTA OF VENUS** Anais Nin	$2.50
☐	10150	**FUTURE SHOCK** Alvin Toffler	$2.25
☐	12196	**PASSAGES** Gail Sheehy	$2.75
☐	11255	**THE GUINNESS BOOK OF WORLD RECORDS** 16th Ed. The McWhirters	$2.25
☐	12220	**LIFE AFTER LIFE** Raymond Moody, Jr.	$2.25
☐	11917	**LINDA GOODMAN'S SUN SIGNS**	$2.50
☐	10310	**ZEN AND THE ART OF MOTORCYCLE MAINTENANCE** Pirsig	$2.50
☐	10888	**RAISE THE TITANIC!** Clive Cussler	$2.25
☐	11267	**AQUARIUS MISSION** Martin Caidin	$2.25
☐	11897	**FLESH AND BLOOD** Pete Hamill	$2.50

Buy them at your local bookstore or use this handy coupon for ordering:

Bantam Books, Inc., Dept. FB, 414 East Golf Road, Des Plaines, Ill. 60016

Please send me the books I have checked above. I am enclosing $_____
(please add 75¢ to cover postage and handling). Send check or money order
—no cash or C.O.D.'s please.

Mr/Mrs/Miss_____

Address_____

City_____State/Zip_____

FB—11/78

Please allow four weeks for delivery. This offer expires 5/79.

Bantam Book Catalog

Here's your up-to-the-minute listing of over 1,400 titles by your favorite authors.

This illustrated, large format catalog gives a description of each title. For your convenience, it is divided into categories in fiction and non-fiction—gothics, science fiction, westerns, mysteries, cookbooks, mysticism and occult, biographies, history, family living, health, psychology, art.

So don't delay—take advantage of this special opportunity to increase your reading pleasure.

Just send us your name and address and 50¢ (to help defray postage and handling costs).